Hammer of Amahté

Book I of the Triumvirate Trilogy

Hammer of Amahté
Book I of the Triumvirate Trilogy

By Brad Anderson

ISBN 978-1-105-49219-8

To Alok Gupta

You had so much more yet to give this world.

And of course, Ed, Hilda & Joelle, the rocks of my life.

Prologue

My brother Calvus is dead. I am now my parents' only child. He died during the assault on Larna a week ago. Some bastard of a lieutenant just finished giving me the whole Fates-damned I-regret-to-inform-you speech. Slag him. Slag them all.

I can't take this anymore. I know if one of those Fates-blasted officers reads this journal they'll charge me with treason for putting what we're all thinking down into words, but I can't stand this. I don't get it! I never got it! Why are we doing this, why do we want to hurt each other? We are our only companions. There are no others that do, or will know what it is to be human. Yet all we do is rage at each other. Hating the Other we're trapped with, we look for something more, something better than who we are—God, king, country, science. And at the end of our search, all we find is some poor bastard, just as sad and scared as we are.

Sometimes I wonder if the reason the Progenitors back on Earth created the seedships and then made damn sure we'd never find the path back was out of hope that with a new start we'd free ourselves from the cycles of hatred that no doubt bound them. If that's so, then we've failed their dream.

I remember the day of the Summer Madness when the Triumvirate War started. Can you believe it? Slag, I was just a kid, not even in school, and didn't have a clue what was going on. But I knew it was big, I knew the people yelling and screaming in the streets were happy about something. Fates, I remember Calvus, who's a little older than me, climbed a tree in front of our house and hung a flag from one of the highest branches. Mom and Dad never took it down. When I last saw it, must be two years ago now, it was tattered, filthy, and old.

And now, I'm a soldier fighting the same Fates-damned war that's been the backdrop of my whole piss-stained life—the same war that's taken Calvus and destroyed my family. Will Mom have any tears left for me when my number's up?

Now that I'm in it, now that I'm fighting, the war makes even less sense to me than it ever did. Yeah, I know what we were taught. The Nephretians attacked us 'cause it's what their god Amahté demands before he'll reveal the path back to Earth—the fact they figured we assassinated one of their prelates was just a pretense to start a war their gods ordained. And when it finally came to light that it was actually Alathia and not Kalbarai who assassinated Prelate Mnoti, we had no choice but to fight Alathia, too. I know these things, these ... reasons. But can such simple facts truly explain, truly justify the mobilization of entire civilizations for total war? No.

We wanted to fight. The facts were excuses so we didn't have to feel like monsters as we marched off to kill each other. Isn't it true with all war? Each of us—Kalbarai, Nephreti and Alathia—we were rising powers, cocky and full of ourselves, certain of our place as rulers of all. Yeah, we sought war like mad dogs after a bitch in heat to prove ourselves and to secure our place on top where no one could harm us.

And now look at us. We teeter on the brink of collapse. Worlds have burned and a generation of young men and women are dead. Where once armadas spanning star systems clashed, battle is now limited to piss-ass little skirmishes. Soldiers who once rained fire and hate down on their enemies find themselves quelling rebellions amongst their own starving people. Whatever order still remains struggles to stay intact as flames lick at its foundations. If we are fighting for something other than our own ruin, damned if I know what it is.

I pray to the Fates this war ends soon and we can stop dying. I pray my brother died for something more meaningful than power-politics. And if the Fates don't grant my prayers, then slag 'em for the bastards they are.

From the journal of Ensign Gnaeus Sallustius Nerva, dated Kalestary 11th, 9832
—Retrieved from the Kalbarian Military Archives

Part I

"There are many tribes of humanity, and each tribe has its own faiths, its own culture, its own sense of morality. But it was not always so. On Earth, humanity spoke with one voice and knew one truth. To punish us for our sins, Amahté, god of creation, not only separated us by space after exiling us—he also separated us through different beliefs, confounding our sense of reality, which keeps us apart even after we have found one another.

"I understand there are other cultures, other concepts of righteousness. But these other ways are wrong. The universe is what it is—there can only be one truth, and Amahté has shown me what that truth is."

—Prophet Djal Anemro, Nephretian Holy Writ, Credenda of the Prophets, Chapter 8

Chapter 1

"By the nine heavens, I can't stand this place," Marco da Riva cursed to himself in frustration as he pulled his foot out from a rivulet of filth that oozed from the grate of an overwhelmed sewage system. He moved to the side of the street, leaned against a graffiti-covered wall of one of the dilapidated warehouses, and began trying to scrap off the semi-solid muck that clung to his boot.

The sun blasted down on the city of Firentz on the planet of Deurgal. Once the epicenter of an ancient trading empire, Firentz's golden days were behind it—far behind it.

For centuries, it had suffered unremitting decline as the ebb and flow of trade drifted to other realms of the galaxy, marginalizing the city. Once, in antiquity, it wielded wealth like a sword to shape the fate of the planet. Now the city of Firentz was known for two things—filth and violence. To the newcomer, the stench of the city seems to crawl into the back of one's nose where it curls up into an acrid, lingering ball of stink.

Organized leadership dissolved long ago into glorified street warfare. Today, a handful of nobles—who, in truth, are little more than gangsters—claw for power against one another.

From the surrounding plains, the buildings of the city seem large and magnificent. Elegant arches and towering spires attest to the skill of architects from long ago. Closer inspection, however, reveals faded colors and neglect. Shattered windows, like yawning mouths, stare onto impossibly narrow streets that twist and lurch across the city like a drunkard staggering in the dark.

Marco had found a hand-sized plastic wrapper littered nearby and was using it to try and wipe the muck off his boot. The street was busy and filled with dockworkers sauntering into the city to spend their pay on games of chance, whores, and drink. Shipping trucks rumbled by without care for the pedestrians who had to leap out of their way. Of all the dank holes Marco had visited in his life, he hated none more than Firentz. Yet, once a month for the past year, business compelled him to make the trip.

Almost two years ago, Deurgal had joined the Alathian Alliance. This treaty was far from equitable for Deurgal, and very few willingly embraced their new rulers. Consequently, Alathia's grasp on the planet was weak. The city of Firentz was a source of constant defiance to Alathian rule.

One of the city's warlords, Hormoz Kasra, contracted with Marco to smuggle in supplies and weapons in his bid to usurp the planet's new rulers. It was not honorable work, and undermining the Alathian blockade was dangerous. But, Marco was not in a position to turn down contracts.

As he gave up trying to clean his boot, a gaunt and scarred dog loped out of a nearby alley and stopped in front of Marco, smelling his foot with great interest. "You're looking hungry, puppy," he said as he leaned over to scratch the hound's head. "You'll have to keep looking though. I'm as hungry as you look." Marco cut a lean figure, though he had known better times in his youth. The dog went on its way across the bustling street into another alley. Leaning against the wall, he closed his eyes and remembered a time when as a child on his home planet of Verna he would play with his own dog, Lupo, chasing one another between shelves stacked heavy with sacks of coffee and spices in his family's trading warehouse.

However, that was a long time ago.

Cursing the heat, Marco rubbed his partial beard. Once he had collected payment from Hormaz's contact he could get away from the stench of the city for another month until his next shipment was due. He lifted the hood on his dust colored cloak to shield him from the sun as he stepped out once more into the foot-traffic bustling along the street.

* * *

Aria looked out on the street from a dark corner of her room. The room had been her home since last night. She had been fleeing the enforcers of a drug den from which she had stolen a handful of ration chips. She barely evaded her pursuers by slipping into this apartment. She had found a couple of squatters sleeping in the fetid quarters, but that was of little concern. Their bodies now littered the alley behind the building where the dogs could fight for their remains.

Aria was a true child of Firentz. Her mother was a gunrunner for the Ardeshir cartel, but was strangled to death when Aria was young. Her father was an addict who died in a selrenthium den. Although only in her late teens, the crucible of Firentz had hardened Aria into a merciless predator.

Across the street, she saw a man lift a dust colored hood over his head and walk away. She caught a glimpse of his rough shaven face. She suspected many women would consider him handsome. Aria, however, did not consider people on the merits of their attractiveness. She only judged them on whether they were hunters or the hunted.

The man moved like a foreigner. This close to the port he was likely an off-worlder. Perhaps a trader, she thought, flush with SpeCred. And if he didn't have and SpeCred, then perhaps he'd have goods she could acquire and sell. Within moments, she was following the stranger along the arabesque streets of Firentz.

* * *

"Wait, who's that?" Symeon asked.

Hovering kilometers above Firentz in a surveillance pod, Captain Ariadne Maleina studied the monitor over Symeon's shoulder. "He's picked up a tail," she said.

For months, the Alathian blockade had been leaking weapons and supplies to rebels on Deurgal. Ariadne's team had worked day and night for weeks locating the source of the leaks. Already her team had caught three smugglers and neutralized the factions they supplied. The city of Firentz, chaotic by nature, was becoming a hotbed of rebellion. Cutting off the supply line to the rebels here would bring more than one fraction to heel.

They received a breakthrough in their investigation earlier today when an informant at the docks noted an anomaly in the landing schedule pertaining to a freighter that had recently arrived. A ground team was already poised to seize the ship as well as its pilot—one Marco da Riva, whom Ariadne was presently tracking from the surveillance pod—once he met his Firentzian contact.

Ariadne did not know who Marco's tail was, but knew that no one must interfere with their target until he had made contact with his employer in Firentz. She pressed the communication link attached to her collar, "Sergeant."

"Yes, Captain," a voice responded into a subdermal responder deep in her ear.

"Marco's acquired a tail," Ariadne said. "Take your team and follow the tail. Protect Marco—I want him alive for questioning."

On the streets of Firentz below, a group of figures detached themselves from the shadows of the alleyway and began following Aria at a discreet distance.

* * *

Marco cursed under his breath. He knew someone had been following him for several blocks now. He had tried to lose his pursuer by taking several quick turns down the labyrinthine streets of Firentz. Without warning, the crowds he had been wading through dissipated and he now found himself in an empty street.

If the person following him meant him harm, this was their opportunity. In a single, fluid motion, Marco turned to face his follower with blaster in hand. He had a heartbeat to look at the face of his pursuer. She was a child, barely sixteen, he reckoned. Despite her youth, Marco was chilled by her dark, soulless eyes and gaunt face etched with hunger. She, too, had a blaster in hand trained on Marco.

Her chest exploded.

Marco stood stunned as she collapsed at his feet, his mind momentarily frozen as he tried to make sense of what was happening. He hadn't fired, and there was no sound of gunshots. He felt a warm wetness on his face. He touched it with an uncertain hand and looked at his fingers. It was blood—her blood.

He saw the movement of shadows up the street, and understanding quickly dawned—Alathians.

He had faced Alathian soldiers before. They had raised subterfuge to the level of an art long ago. Their weapons were soundless and gave off no flare when fired. Wounds simply seemed to open up on their enemies.

Whoever the girl was, whoever those shadows were, Alathians were nearby. Instinctively, Marco dove through a nearby ground floor window, glass shattering and raining down as he hit the floor and rolled into a crouch. The room he found himself in was dark and empty. He had to move before the Alathians could close their trap. But move where?

* * *

Ariadne observed events from the surveillance pod. Marco had entered a building and a squad of her soldiers was closing in.

The voice of the sergeant spoke calmly over the comm link. "Team Fox, setup position to the rear of the building. Team Wolf, ready a drone to pursue the target."

Ariadne monitored the teams positioning themselves. "Use non-lethal force; the target is required for interrogation," she said over the comm link.

An explosion belched forth from the building Marco had entered. She could see the figures of her soldiers thrown to the ground by the shock waves that kicked up clouds of dust.

"Sergeant, report." Ariadne said into the comm link. Silence. "Sergeant, report!"

"Aw, by Sor T'van's lies, it was a thumper. All teams, defensive perimeter. Does anyone have eyes on the target?" the sergeant's voice finally spoke over the comm link. A string of negative replies followed his question.

A thumper, Ariadne thought to herself. That's a rare weapon these days, though considering Marco was smuggling munitions into the city, she supposed she shouldn't be surprised that he had a few tricks. The thumper created a shock wave that, though not terribly destructive, handily stunned soldiers and knocked small drones out of commission.

"Team Wolf, enter the building. Find him," the sergeant's voice said over the comm link.

Ariadne had spent her career playing life and death games of subterfuge, and her instincts were telling her Marco had somehow escaped under cover of the thumper. After several tense minutes, her suspicions were confirmed. "Team Wolf reporting. Target is not in the building."

"Sergeant, tear the street apart. Find him," she said, struggling to keep her voice sounding cool and detached.

Chapter 2

"For Fate's sake, get over top of her!" Captain Lucia Salonious Taura, commander of the K.S. Novafire, shouted loud enough to be heard over the sounds of explosions rippling through her ship. "Ascend ten degrees one-quarter speed, bearing twenty degrees starboard." Her stomach churned as her ship spiraled hundreds of kilometers above the single remaining Nephretian battleship, the null-graviton drive allowing the massive bulk of the ship to maneuver seemingly in defiance of the standard laws of physics.

The Kalbarian battleship, the K.S. Novafire, sliced through space. Whereas in most cultures menace and intimidation were crude and brutish tools, Kalbarai had raised these qualities to art and the K.S. Novafire was a testament to this. The battleship took the shape of two massive castles—one rising from the equator while the other proudly jutted below like a reflection in calm waters. Artisans had covered each panel of the craft with vibrant engravings depicting animals fighting and armies battling. The violent past of Kalbarai—both mythical and historical—was recorded in carven allegory. Statues of birds of prey that adorned the towers of the ship stared hungrily into the void. Sculptures of giant wolf-like beasts proudly guarded niches along the equator between the two halves of the ship.

The dull thud of cannons reverberated through the Novafire as it sent a continual barrage of RAC missiles soaring across the gulf of space separating the two adversaries. The glittering mass of tiny explosions several kilometers away from the Nephretian ship indicated the robotic missiles hadn't yet managed to breech the Nephretian's flak firewall. However, the current barrage of RACs was already re-configuring to optimize their tactics in order to punch through the flak and strike at the vessel beyond.

"Slag!" Commander Vetus Servius, Taura's second in command cursed. "Their flak firewalls're getting smarter. The RACs should've been boring through their blast shields by now."

"Just shut up and get on the forward battery crew to get our own flak firewall back up," the captain ordered. "We can't afford to take another hit like the last one."

Captain Taura was short, as many Kalbarians were. Her body was broad, but not overly massive, although life in the military had kept her physique at a peak of physical conditioning. Her hair was dark, and she kept it in a braid so intricate it was the marvel of her officer's mess.

Like most of her countrymen, Taura was augmented with technological accoutrements that were the pride of artisans throughout Kalbarai. So efficient were they at synthesizing a synergy between flesh and machine that the process had become a high art where the design of one's machine body became a form of expression and pride.

Taura's eyes had no visible pupil or iris. They were elegant, pale blue orbs marbled with milky white and capable of a vast array of visual modalities. The flare adjusters automatically dampen the effects of over-stimulation as areas of her bridge disintegrated in blinding flashes of fire. Her right arm conformed to the dimensions of her flesh-arm, and moved just as smoothly. However, it was the color of black obsidian with a beautifully intricate inlay of delicate molten red metal. Within her head, invisible to the naked eye, communication linkups with her ship were maintained. Critical problems the ship incurred were instantly relayed to her consciousness, and the position of her vessel in relation to all other objects nearby was visualized within her optic centers.

Her mind was abuzz with incoming damage reports. She felt physically ill as she scanned the casualty reports.

The void of space quenched the sounds of battle raging before the backdrop of stars. On the bridge of the K.S. Novafire, however, the squeal of rending metal was deafening and the heat of flame unbearable. Men, women, and small spider-like drones rushed to extinguish fires, clear out wreckage, and drag the wounded or dead out of the way.

There had been two Nephretian vessels to the Kalbarian's one at the start of the skirmish—Kalbarai almost always found itself outnumbered. The Nephretians fashioned their battleships after the mythical phoenix, a holy emblem of their nation's faith, with wings outstretched into space and claws grasping forward, clutching for their prey. Like dragons, the two had circled the massive Kalbarian battleship. But despite Kalbarai's smaller population, few cultures could match their martial prowess and tenacity. Though the K.S. Novafire had taken considerable damage, it had managed to destroy one of the ships, the glowing embers of its wounds fading as its carcass spun off into the void. The Novafire now engaged the last ship of its enemy, one-on-one.

The crew of the single remaining Nephretian ship fought with wild abandon as only true fanatics can, every death a gift to their god Amahté. The Nephretians believed that the path to humanity's birthplace, Earth had been lost and humans scattered over the galaxy for their sins. It was, of course, a mandate of their religion to reunite the human race in order to find the route to the fabled homeland. The fact that few, if any, societies wanted to be united with the Nephretians was irrelevant, and nothing more than a sign of ignorance they would soon correct.

The front monitor of the Novafire showed a wave of flashes from the Nephretian's front cannon bank as a new barrage of missiles were launched. At the same time, thousands of tiny, glittering orbs streamed from the Novafire to a point several kilometers away. These orbs were flak—tiny mines programmed to intercept incoming weapon's fire or ships. Several tense heartbeats passed as the first wave of Nephretian missiles collided with the flak firewall. Standard Nephretian missiles were not designed to re-configure and adapt to the tactics of the flak firewall as the Kalbarian RAC missiles were, but rather relied on overwhelming the Kalbarian defense with sheer numbers. Even though the Kalbarian's flak firewall was shifting to adjust to the Nephretian attack pattern, it was being overrun.

"Fates damn it, the firewall's not going to hold," Taura said. Before she had finished the sentence a dozen missiles broke through the flak and bore down on the Novafire. The null-bosonic field surrounding the battleship deactivated nine of the incoming missiles, but the final three managed to project a protective force field of their own. As the three missiles approached, she closed her eyes and images of the wreckage of humanity they would surely cause on her ship played themselves out in her mind. She was so tired of watching her soldiers die.

Taura's ship rocked violently as the missiles struck. The captain was thrown from the bridge and landed roughly on the command deck below, the sound of crackling electronics unnoticed as the breath was slammed out of her. Before she could suck air back into her lungs, Commander Servius helped her up, shielding himself from a shower of sparks with his free hand.

"Communications picking up a foreign signal," Lieutenant Kaeso yelled.

"Classification?" Taura asked, regaining her breath.

"Unknown."

"What do you mean 'unknown?' Lieutenant, identify that signal—I don't want anyone surprising us. Helm, descend one-hundred-fifty kilometers, fire all top-side weapons!" Again, the stomach wrenching movement of the ship, the dull thud of cannons, more flares along the enemy ship's flak firewall, the quiet backdrop of space behind it. With a jolt, the K.S. Novafire came to a stop.

She could see in her mind's electronic eye that the Nephretians had swooped down with them, closing the gap between the two battleships to less than a hundred kilometers and were maneuvering their cannons towards the engines of her ship.

"Initiate Gaian Alpha 5 maneuver," the captain ordered.

The enemy launched another barrage at Taura's vessel, but her flak firewall took the brunt of the attack as the K.S. Novafire began rotating, lending the engines the maximum protection while exposing its underbelly bristling with cannons. With a brilliant flash, those cannons fired a massive barrage of RAC missiles. The Kalbarian's RAC missiles were much smarter and faster than the Nephretian defenses, and this combined with the sheer mass of the attack devastated the enemy's flak firewall. The underside of the Nephretian vessel was engulfed in explosions of venting gasses quickly extinguished by the emptiness of space as several dozen missiles struck.

With deftness and speed aided by the null-graviton drivers, Taura's ship rotated around the enemy sending a deadly rain of

RAC missiles down upon them. The enemy desperately attempted to maneuver out of the path of destruction.

Then, with a hail of tiny explosions occurring deep within Taura's own ship, her engines failed and the K.S. Novafire drifted into space, carried by the momentum of its last move.

"Engines down in the enemy craft, Captain," a voice spoke over the command room. "She's dead in space."

"As are we, Captain," Commander Servius whispered quietly to Taura. The high-g move used to position her ship to fire had overloaded the damaged circuitry of their engines the readouts in her inner eye were informing her.

"Lieutenant Kaeso."

"Aye, Captain," the communications officer replied.

"Hail their ship and demand their surrender."

"Yes, Captain," Lieutenant Kaeso replied. A moment later, he continued, "Uh, Captain, you remember that unknown communications signal we picked up in the battle?"

"Yeah—did you identify its source?"

"Yes, Captain. You'd better have a look at this."

Taura limped over to the communications center and stared at the read-out.

"Fates!" she said once she had finished reading.

"What is it?" Commander Servius asked. He looked at the monitor over Taura's shoulder. The commander was short and stocky with a closely shaved head. On the side and back of his scalp, integrated circuits the color of quicksilver inlaid with black pearl crossed each other in the shape of Celtic knots. His left hand and forearm were the color of mercury.

"Damn," Servius said, "it's a bloody—"

"Shut it!" Taura interrupted. "Both of you. No one breathes a word of this, is that understood?"

Both soldiers acknowledged the order. Servius muttered, half to himself, "If the Nephretian Council of Prelates learns of this, it'd raise one hell of a damn slag storm."

"I know," the captain said. "Lieutenant Kaeso, jam any transmission the Nephretians try to make. Do whatever you have to, but don't let them send a message of any sort. Then, encrypt the contents of the signal we intercepted with an alpha level security code and transmit it to Rear Admiral Canus. And Kaeso, Servius," she added, with a dark glare, "this is classified. You whisper a word of this to anyone, you'll spend your dying days digging in the mines of Marlax, understand?"

"Yes, captain," both her officers briskly replied.

"Nerva!" the Captain shouted to another officer.

"Aye."

"Ready the gun crews to blast them into slag on my command."

Before the soldier could reply, the Nephretian ship still visible in the front monitor erupted in a massive explosion. Debris rained into the Novafire, sending the lame Kalbarian ship spinning wildly for several moments before its inertia dampeners could right itself.

"Commander, what happened?" Taura asked after she regained her footing.

"Looks like they scuttled their ship."

"Captain," Lieutenant Kaeso called, "they punched a signal through our interference."

Taura turned a smoldering glare at the young lieutenant. "I thought I told you to jam their communications. I don't have to tell you what will happen if the Nephretians catch wind of the signal you just identified."

"They diverted all their power to push the signal through. Their explosion drained power away from our jammers to the inertia dampeners."

"Damn the Fates! Damn the Fates!" the captain said. Captain Taura looked at her second officer. "Commander Servius, see the crew gets the Novafire up and running. The Claw Cluster is our nearest port. I want to be there in a day, tops."

"Aye, captain."

The captain's gaze drifted across her tattered bridge and she struggled to bury the feelings of guilt and failure, those mad furies that plagued her whenever she saw soldiers under her command maimed and wounded. The Nephretians had most certainly intercepted the same mysterious signal during the battle. True to their fanatical nature, they had sacrificed all to send a message home telling their people what they had heard. And once they heard, the Triumvirate War was going to take a dark turn.

* * *

Several days had passed since Marco's narrow escape from the Alathians. Unfortunately, part of his escape had driven him into the crumbling sewers of Firentz for the better part of an afternoon. Marco had never imagined anything so revolting in his entire life. He had continued retching long after he left the sewers, and still the stench lingered in his nostrils despite vigorous and numerous washing.

Marco had stolen a small passenger ship and hacked its transponder to hide it from Alathian surveillance. He was now two star systems away from Deurgal. He had just finished yet another shower that he hoped would remove the smell of the Deurgalian sewers from him. Clad only in a towel, his wavy brown hair, still wet, hung down to his shoulders. His green eyes stared at his reflection in a mirror as he finished trimming his unkempt stubble into a thin beard.

His personal communications link beeped from the next room. Leaving his grooming, he moved quickly into the adjoining room and answered the call. Donato's face appeared on his monitor. Marco had met Donato several years after his family's trading business had been wiped out and they had worked closely together for a while. Donato had not done any work in the field for some time, but had excellent connections. It was he who lined up most of the contracts Marco took these days.

"Bit of trouble in Firentz, I hear," Donato said with a smile ruined by a set of crooked teeth.

Marco returned the smile. "A bit. I'm afraid Alathia is bringing Deurgal's cause to an end."

Marco tried not to let bitterness enter his voice. He never let politics come in the way of a good contract, but he had no love for any of the powers that made up the Triumvirate. He relished those jobs that allowed him the opportunity to undermine their dominance, although in truth, he had worked for each power as much as he had worked against them. One had to eat, after all.

"That's a pity. A good bit of SpeCred, that contract," Donato said. "I suppose you'll be looking for work, then."

Marco raised an eyebrow. "You got something for me, Donato?"

A big smile spread across Donato's face. "Do I have something for you? Marco, have I ever let you starve?"

"Donato, we both know it's my commissions that put food in your belly."

Donato chuckled. "Well then, I am going to eat well tonight. Seems the Kalbarians need a freelance expert in exotic computer salvage operations. I haven't seen a computer system you can't crack, so I figured I'd give you dibs on the contract."

"Kalbarians," Marco repeated. Although he didn't like any of the Triumvirate, Kalbarians were the easiest to work with. Alathians were snakes and Nephretians repugnant in their self-righteousness, he had found. Kalbarians were brutes, but very straightforward in their dealings.

"They're paying big money for this Marco," Donato said.

"Big money?"

"Ten thousand SpeCred just to meet with them."

Marco was impressed. Ten thousand SpeCreds was almost enough for a down payment on a freighter to replace the one he lost on Deurgal. And that was just for showing up to meet with them.

He rubbed his newly trimmed beard. "What do they mean by 'exotic computer salvage?'"

"Dunno. Make sure you ask 'em when you meet. So, are you in or what?"

"I'm in. Where and when will I be meeting with them?" Marco asked.

"They want you at the Claw Cluster in two days. You'll rendezvous with the K.S. Novafire where you will meet with Captain Lucia Taura. She'll fill you in on the details."

"Thanks, Donato."

"Watch your back, Marco." Donato's image flickered off.

Taura. Marco rolled the name around in his mind. He hoped two days was enough to wash the smell of sewage from him. He absent-mindedly scratched at one of many rashes that had recently started to cover his body.

Chapter 3

Taura stared at the repair logs streaming in front of her on a monitor in her makeshift office in the Claw Cluster shipyards. She had her artificial hand, flawless in design, black as night with fiery red inlay, nervously bunched into a fist. The Novafire had been under repairs for three weeks since its battle with the Nephretians. Three weeks since they intercepted a mysterious communications signal. Three weeks since the Nephretians intercepted that same signal and sacrificed themselves in order to send a message, telling their home world of what they had stumbled upon.

The Novafire was alone in this sector of space—the nearest military vessel was weeks away. Taura couldn't believe how thinly spread the Kalbarian lines were stretched. They even had to hire a contractor to investigate the source of the signal.

The captain called up the file they had on the proposed contractor—a Mr. Marco da Riva—and reviewed it once more. "Contractor," Taura scoffed to herself. He was a smuggler for hire. If the communication signal they received was true, then this discovery, if Kalbarai could claim it for itself, would end the war and assure victory. For the first time since she donned the captain's uniform, she could actually send her crew home safe and alive. She had almost given up hope that such a dream was possible.

Yet, one of the mission-critical resources required to make it happen was a scoundrel whose loyalty was for hire. The war had taken so much from Kalbarai, Taura mused darkly.

Yet this was the way of it.

She continued reviewing the growing list of repair logs as she waited for Mr. da Riva to arrive.

* * *

Marco arrived at the Claw Cluster, named after a belt of asteroids orbiting a distant sun. The system was under Kalbarian control, but apart from the sun, asteroids, mining colonies, and a space dock, there was nothing.

The dock's computers were guiding Marco's ship into the port, leaving him with nothing to do but stare out the view port. A pair of Kalbarian robotic fighters, each one shaped like a red talon with black inlay, was accompanying his vessel.

The spaceport was shaped like a grasping hand, dwarfing the numerous tankers drifting nearby. The auto-guidance systems were bringing his ship alongside a battleship, presumably the K.S. Novafire. The ship was seriously scarred—a wonder in fact that it was space-worthy enough to sit in a dock without falling apart. Damage notwithstanding, like all Kalbarian warships it was a vision of menace.

Kalbarian history, Marco recalled, had been far from gentle, and they had been taught the art of battle through thousands of years of succession wars to establish a planetary government. It wasn't until almost a thousand years ago when they first met the Alathian Alliance, a power strong enough to stand against the Kalbarian's grasp, and, indeed, impose a significant threat of their own that the succession wars had brutally ended.

Since that time, the Kalbarians had been taught the art of battle through a centuries old on-again-off-again war against the Alathians, followed soon after by the Nephretians. They were a people who had not had a generation of peace since the first children of the seedships took their first steps upon their new world.

Once Marco's ship landed by an airlock, he walked down to the docking bay pathways. A single Kalbarian soldier greeted Marco as he left his ship.

Although quite short, the Kalbarian was a fortress of a man. He seemed to have muscles upon muscles and was nearly as wide as he was tall. He had obviously had muscle and bone implants and Marco, never actually having seen an individual with such dramatic augmentations in person, was dumbstruck. As if that were not enough, the implants had a design embedded in them that raised ridges along the skin of the man's arms and up past his sleeves. The highly detailed design formed the flowing image of intertwined roses and slender dragons.

The soldier spoke with a strong voice. "I'm Lieutenant-Commander Quintilus Victor. Follow me." The soldier turned to go, but Marco lagged behind, still stunned by the man's appearance. The soldier, seeing Marco's rapt attention smiled and flexed his bicep. This action caused it to bulge to horrifically unnatural proportions—to the point that Marco was certain it would rip through the skin. The embedded designs in his biceps glowed an unearthly red and writhed as if alive.

Victor said, "Just you be remembering this if you ever think to mess with ol' Vic. Now, will you be coming or did you fly all this way to gawk?"

Marco tore his eyes from the soldier's still bulging bicep and noticed for the first time his face. He was older than Marco expected, with tousled gray hair and deep creases lining his face. His eyes, pale blue, had yellow cross hairs embedded in the pupil. Although not apparent to Marco the cross hairs in the soldier's eyes were connected to a synthetic neural network that coordinated the direction he was pointing a weapon in his hand with what he was looking at.

Marco regained his composure enough to reply, "By all means, Lieutenant-Commander, after you."

Victor, moving with the slow persistence of a tank, led Marco from his ship down an array of corridors into a spartan office. An attractive woman greeted him and dismissed the lieutenant-commander. Her eyes were solid blue marbled with creamy white. She extended her hand, which he took and shook, as was the custom. He noticed it was black as obsidian and inlaid with an intricate red pattern. Despite its appearance, it felt pliable, although slightly cooler than normal body temperature. That arm probably had enough firepower to blast him through the containment walls and into outer space, Marco mused.

"I'm Captain Lucia Salonious Taura," the woman said.

In addition to gaining all the scientific knowledge possessed by the Progenitors, one of the advantages of civilizations spawned from the seedships was a universal language—the Seedtongue. Although each seedship colony had evolved their own language as they developed independently, Seedtongue was used extensively in the arts of politics, trade, and science. Most learned people studied enough of the Seedtongue to communicate at a rudimentary level at the very least.

With a scowl, the captain continued, "What's that smell?"

Marco groaned inwardly and suppressed an urge to scratch one of his lingering rashes he had acquired during his travels through the sewers of Firentz on the planet of Deurgal. "It's Deurgalian cologne," he replied as he smiled. "It's strong and is reputed to drive their women crazy."

"It doesn't drive me crazy. I'll ask that you not wear it again," she said sitting down. She motioned for him to do likewise in a chair opposite her desk as she leaned back in her seat, crossing her legs. "You're Marco da Riva?"

"I am."

"Your work in the Regalian system suggested you for this mission. Like that job, this is a salvage operation. The risks cannot be determined at this time, but you will be compensated any damages." Taura folded her hands, pressed her first fingers together as a steeple and rested her chin on them. An eyebrow rose, and she continued, "As well, you'll be paid a hundred-thousand SpeCred, half now, and the rest upon completion. You interested?"

"Can you tell me anything else about the job?" Marco asked.

"Not if you don't accept it."

One-hundred-thousand SpeCred would buy Marco a new freighter. It was good money. Nonetheless, he replied, "I'm sure the Kalbarian government would have no qualms about paying one-hundred-fifteen-thousand for a mission as important as this one seems to be—especially as you're expecting me to go in blind."

The captain's eyebrow slowly lowered. "Kalbarians don't barter. This mission is worth one-hundred-thousand SpeCred to our government. Our offer stands."

Kalbarian's were, if nothing else, straightforward. They seldom bartered, but it had been worth a shot. The money was good, and Marco did not have any other work lined up. Moreover, if the Alathians were still stalking him after his escape from Deurgal, a Kalbarian battle ship was about the safest place to be. He replied with a charming smile, "Then I accept."

A smile spread across Taura's face. Marco was startled at the pleasant effect it had. "Good," she continued. "A ship of interest to Kalbarai has gone down on a planet in the K5SR star system." The rather prosaic name indicated an as of yet uncharted system. She continued, "We received the distress call three weeks ago. Since then, a probe has been sent after it, but it too has been lost on the planet. Long-range scans of the planet show no signs of a technological civilization, so the disappearance of both the ship and probe remain a mystery."

She uncrossed her legs, and then re-crossed them in the opposite direction. "It is highly important that the presumed wreckage and the information it holds be reclaimed by Kalbarai with all due haste. Nephretian activity has been noted in this sector."

"I suppose it's the Nephretians who've graced your ship with blaster fire then," Marco said. The captain smiled in reply. "What do you need me for?" Marco asked.

"We need someone capable of hacking into … unusual computer systems. The K.S. Novafire is a battleship and is not equipped for the job at hand. It would take altogether too much time for one of our other ships with the appropriate expertise to travel here—too much time has been lost already. So, we're contracting out this mission."

Marco replied, "Fair enough. When do we leave?"

"The Novafire will be space worthy in fourteen hours. We leave then."

Apparently, Kalbarians were rather flexible with their definition of "space worthy," Marco noted ruefully.

"One more thing," the captain said, "any unauthorized signals or transmissions sent from you or your ship will result in your immediate death. You will have a locked communication link with the Novafire, and any deviation will be viewed as an act of hostility. My ship may no longer look pretty, Mr. da Riva, but I assure you, every one of her weapons works fine."

"Please," he smiled politely, "call me Marco."

* * *

Lord Suten Hamu of the Firstborn, the Fist of the High Prelate, one of the most powerful individuals in the Holy Nephretian Empire— second only to the High Prelate himself—stood in luxurious quarters on his personal battle cruiser, the Reclaimer. Through his window he gazed at a verdant planet looming below that circled the previously uncharted K5SR star.

He had never known excitement such as this before.

As all Nephretians, Lord Hamu, or simply The Fist, as the masses called him, was tall and slender, and bore a regal air about him. The skin of his people was brownish red to protect themselves from their fiery sun and a dark nictitating membrane covered their eyes that they could open and close at will, same as their eyelids.

As always, he wore his ceremonial uniform, consisting of loose fitting black pants and a buttonless black jacket with a white crest on the torso in the shape of a shield. The Holy Crest of the phoenix rising from the fire, symbolizing humanity rising above its sins, was emblazoned in blood red upon that shield. His hair, blonde, was thin and grown past his shoulders. His eyes, blue and intense, were sheltered under arched eyebrows.

Running his fingers gently across his lips, the Fist was savoring a glass of kholarian wine. In the background, the lilting melodies of Tameri's Ninth Concerto played, one of Hamu's favorite pieces of music even though Tameri, the master composer, had been dead for centuries now. The mood was shattered as the chimes for his door sounded. The Fist knew it was Commodore Hetshepsu Kahotep, Lord Hamu's personal attaché.

"Enter," he said.

"My superior," Hetshepsu said as he kneeled before The Fist. He wore the officer's uniform of the Nephretian navy, highly polished boots of black, loose brown pants, a dark red shirt with a black phoenix rising upon a white shield. His hair was gray as steel and combed straight back, reaching the nape of his neck. His eyes were green and hard.

"Rise, Commodore. Your report?"

"Lord Hamu," the commodore said while rising, "our ground scouts have reported the presence of a new seedship civilization."

"A civilization?" An eyebrow arched inquisitively, his eyes gaining a fiery intensity. "The Reclaimer's scanners showed no signs of a civilization as we approached."

"Yes, my lord," he continued, "nonetheless, a civilization is reported, and they've defeated our scouting parties."

"Is this incompetence?" the Fist asked. "Any civilization not showing up on our sensors should be brutish tribesmen—barely more than animals. Yet you tell me they defeated our soldiers."

"Yes, my lord," the commodore bravely ventured. "But they are not primitive tribesmen. Based on the reports of our surviving ground forces, their technology is highly sophisticated, though ... unlike anything we've encountered."

Hetshepsu braced himself for the unpredictable reaction of his master.

The Fist's lips stretched into a broad smile. "Today is a great day, Commodore," he said turning back to his window, "for not only do we take our first footsteps down a holy path, but we have also been graced with a new people to bring into our fold." With voice turning to steel he continued, "Prepare my landing craft. I wish to meet this new civilization."

Chapter 4

The flight from the Claw Cluster to their final destination in the K5SR star system took two days at hyper-light, enabled by travelling through the Q-wave slipstream. The trip had been uneventful to the point of boring. Marco's ship was anchored to the Novafire, and the captain had confined Marco to guest quarters for security reasons. Marco did not seem to mind and spent his time reading and immersed in vids.

The K.S. Novafire was now in orbit above the planet that was the source of the unknown communications signal intercepted by Taura's ship during their battle with the Nephretians a little over three weeks prior. The planet was deep green and blue with thick cloud cover. Teeming with life, it seemed a vibrant world untouched by human hands, for the scanners detected no signs of any technologically advanced civilization.

Marco and Taura were currently on a landing craft smashing through the atmosphere with several soldiers and officers including the Novafire's communications officer, Lieutenant Procyon Gallus Kaeso, chief weapons officer, Lieutenant-Commander Quintilus Victor, the muscle-bound officer Marco had first encountered at the Claw Cluster, Lieutenant-Doctor Gaia Murena, the chief medical officer and a handful of troops. Presently, Lieutenant Kaeso was piloting the landing craft.

Taura was loath to leave her ship with repairs ongoing. But, she had her orders from Rear Admiral Canus himself to oversee this mission personally. Of all the members of her crew, only Taura, Kaeso and her second in command, Servius, were fully aware of the operation they were now undertaking. The truth would be revealed to the rest of her crew soon enough, but by then their objective would be safe under Kalbarian protection.

Everyone on the lander was quietly checking their equipment or lost in thought with the exception of Marco, who was playing on his data pad a holographic game ancient beyond years—chess—a game that Taura herself was quite accomplished at. Although apparently a proficient player, the captain noticed Marco presently seemed to be losing. She felt a pang of guilt looking at him, for she knew he would have to be detained at the end of this operation until the full ramifications of their mission had been achieved. Unfortunately, Mr. da Riva was a pawn in a greater game of powers. But, if using Marco was what was required to end the war and send her soldiers home, then so be it.

Taura watched Marco take his opponent's bishop by sacrificing a knight. His queen-side rook was now in danger, but he had opened the board for an attack with his remaining bishop and queen. He played an aggressive, perhaps reckless game, she thought.

The landing craft's approach vector brought it to an altitude that skimmed the trees of the forest below, leaving a trail of whipping branches and whirling leaves in its wake. Excitement surged in Taura's chest as they skimmed along the treetops of this lush rain forest planet. Five more minutes and they would be at their destination.

It was that moment when, without warning, Taura was slammed into the restraints securing her to her chair. The landing craft flipped violently bow over stern. Each passenger was pushed into their restraining harness by the g-forces exerting themselves as the ship tumbled while anything not battened down swirled and crashed throughout the cabin. Curses and yells filled the air as warning lights flashed and the engines squealed trying to right the craft.

"Prepare for impact!" Kaeso managed to yell at the same instant the lander crashed into the woods. The trees were solid and large. The momentum of the ship caused it to whip and flip about as it slammed through the thick canopy of the forest. For several moments, their world was one of massive bumps and wild twists. With a bone-jarring thud the landing craft hit the ground and the ride came to a definitive stop.

"Nice landing, Kaeso," Marco said with his head clasped in hands.

"Lieutenant, report!" the captain ordered.

Pulling his head up, Kaeso groaned. "Some kind of … net shot from the forest, snagged the nose of our craft, Captain."

The lander should have shredded through any net made of natural materials without a bump, Taura thought. "Victor."

"Aye, Captain," the lieutenant-commander replied.

"Get your men and set up a defensive perimeter around our craft."

Lieutenant-Commander Victor rose from his seat, muscles rippling along his unnaturally massive chest. "All right lads, time to earn yer pay. Everyone, link up!"

Kalbarian infantry units used internal communications gear implanted into the base of their skull to organize maneuvers and the phrase "link up" meant the soldiers were electronically connecting to their implants to create an integrated command nexus. The visual inputs of soldiers in the field were transmitted to the commanding officer's internal receiver where it was formed into a 3D representation of the terrain, with allied soldiers marked in one color, and observed enemy positions in another. The commander could silently deploy his forces as he saw fit through the communications network and the unit could coordinate their activities to an unnatural level.

The result was what the Kalbarians referred to as the phalanx—a unit of soldiers acting as one. When battling the phalanx, an enemy was not fighting a group of individuals, but rather one organism with multiple weapons, multiple eyes and an unnerving ability to quickly adapt to the rapid changes of the battlefield. Few sights were as fearful to behold.

"Lock and load your RACs!" Victor barked. At the command, the soldiers slammed massive magazines into their weapons that were attached directly into their arms.

Marco whistled, impressed. "Are those the new K-96 heavy RAC rifles?"

Victor looked back at the smuggler. "You know your weapons, don't you?"

"Come on, you'd have to be living in a swamp not to know of the K-96. State of the art, direct bio-insertion and neuronal firing control. Versatile, packing an energy blaster and rapid-fire projectile cannon spraying miniature RACs gods know how fast."

"You sound like you're making a sales pitch," Victor said with a scowl. "Now shut up and let me work, unless you want to meet the business-end of a RAC."

The Robotic Auto-reConfiguring Projectile or RAC technology was the weapon of choice in the Kalbarian arsenal. These were more akin to miniature robots than bullets. As they cut through the air at super-sonic speeds, they continually relayed information to one another. When one RAC hit a target it relayed tactical details back to the remaining RACs. Information such as whether the target had been killed, or if the RAC had hit an obstacle such as a null-bosonic force field or body armor. Within picoseconds, the remaining incoming RACs would adjust, changing course to hit another target, emitting null-bosonic fields of their own to cancel out the defender's force field, or reconfiguring to maximizing the chances of penetrating the specific type of armor protecting the target.

"Time to bust outta here, dogs!" Victor yelled.

As one, the troops stood facing the exit hatch. The door was bent out of shape from the crash and was jammed. The two nearest soldiers beat on the door with massive kicks that rocked the fallen craft. After three bone-jarring barrages, the hatch flung open and a wave of hot, humid air heavy with the smell of peat belched into the cabin. With the silent intensity of panthers, the phalanx was out in the surrounding rain forest in a heartbeat. Quintilus Victor silently commanded the troops from the hatch of the landing craft through their neural net with his weapon at the ready and body taunt.

Kaeso remained in the cockpit, a small side arm drawn, eyes scanning through the front window for an enemy. He was not as powerful and ominous as his compatriots tended to be. Kaeso was young—in his early twenties—but carried himself with a serious austerity uncommon for his youth. His hair was jet black and close-cropped and his eyes dark brown. Also, unlike his fellow Kalbarians, he was not highly augmented other than a number of cable ports in the base of his skull that allowed him to hook up to his ship's computers.

Taura and Marco remained tensely quiet in the center of the craft with Dr. Murena behind them.

"Report, Victor," the captain ordered.

"Nothing but damn forest, Captain," Victor replied in his gravelly voice. "The men can barely move through it ... slag! Bassus was ambushed! He's down!" Outside the landing craft, the dense woods erupted in gunfire. In the blink of an eye Marco was crouching behind a seat in the craft, pistol in hand, Dr. Murena behind him. Although short, Victor's berth was massive, and he blocked the entire door with his body as he scanned the dense foliage beyond. Taura stood in the middle of the cabin, fists on her hips. "By Fangere's teeth," she swore.

"Galeo's down!" Victor said. He continued giving Taura periodic reports. "I'm ordering the troops to close their perimeter to the ship ... No one's seen an enemy yet ... Visual distortion in IR ...Yeah, that distortion is the confirmed target ... We got about twenty-five targets. They're damn tough to see, even in IR. With the blasted heat of the rain forest, everything's hot."

Whereas at the start of battle, the Kalbarians' weapons barrage had been constant as they laid down a stream of suppressing fire, now that an enemy had been identified the shooting was much more focused, punctured with staccato of explosions.

"Laenas is injured," Victor continued his report, receiving real-time updates of his men through the neural net. "Iulla and Drusus are down ... Targets spotted in the trees ... Looks like forty hostiles now ... I'm ordering the trees cut down with energy blasters—let's see how the sneaky bastards like that." The gunfire was now punctuated with the searing sound of blasters, followed by the crashing of trees and screams of men.

"Oh, they didn't like that," Victor said with a chuckle. "All hostiles withdrawing under cover fire, Captain."

Two soldiers were dragging Laenas, the wounded Kalbarian, back to the landing craft. Once there, Victor manhandled Laenas with one hand, passing him to Marco who staggered under the soldier's weight. Laenas was a young man in his early twenties. His face was pale and he was semi-conscious. His left shoulder had a thumb-sized hole in it out of which blood flowed. Marco and Dr. Murena dragged him back from the door where she set about him immediately.

"Have the men cut down and clear the forest around the landing craft," Taura ordered. "I want a defensive perimeter we can easily patrol."

"Aye, Captain," Victor replied. There was more blaster fire and the sound of falling trees outside as the command was silently communicated through the neural net. "Captain?"

"Yes, Lieutenant-Commander?"

"Fullo heard the enemy ordering their troops to retreat. It didn't sound Alathian or Nephretian. We could be dealing with a new seedship colony."

Marco said, "With no observable signs of a technological civilization, their seedship must have shut down early. They should be quite primitive, one would expect, which is hard to reconcile with the fight they seemed to stage against Kalbarian troops."

Victor replied, "Aye, the smuggler's right. Their tactics were pretty sophisticated, and they fired on us with some nasty weapons capable of punching through our armor. Plus, they possess a damn good camouflaging technology. We could hardly see the Fates-blasted bastards."

Taura cursed under her breath.

"Captain Taura," interrupted Dr. Murena. She had several pieces of equipment over the wounds of the now sedated injured soldier with wires hooked into inputs within her own arm. Her fingers flashed over buttons on the console revealed in an inner compartment within her forearm. She continued, "Laenas has some kind of viral infection centered around his wound. The projectile itself appears to have fragmented into the surrounding tissue, and I believe the fragments are the epicenters of the infection."

"Will the virus contaminate us?" the captain asked, taking an unconscious step back.

"I don't believe so, Captain. The infection seems to be spread intercellularly. I've never imagined anything this virulent—the disease appears to simply devastate tissue," the doctor exclaimed. "Sweet Fates, the infection has doubled the radius of his wound. If the disease continues at this rate, his left lung will be infected in about two minutes, the aorta and larynx in about five. The virus isn't tissue specific—it lyses any cell in its path."

"Cauterize the wound. Burn the infected tissue," Marco suggested, frantically wiping Laenas' blood off his hands on his shirt and pants.

"It's too late; the virus has spread to the bloodstream," the doctor replied with a tinge of anxiety. "I'm seeing red blood cell lysis and the vascular structure is being damaged. He's hemorrhaging from his brachiocephalic artery. I'm attempting antiviral protocols." The doctor continued administering to her patient for several tense moments. "Negative so far, the infection has reached his lungs." Laenas' breathing became labored and several more moments passed as Dr. Murena frantically treated her patient. "His venous system has carried the virus to his heart—damage to the internal cardiac structure observed. Fates be damned, he's having a heart attack!" Lights flashed and alarms beeped on the doctor's equipment as she frantically tended to Laenas.

"The heart's nerve plexus has been digested; he's going into complete cardiac arrest." She struggled with the patient for several moments. "Fates! That's strange."

Taura, looking from Laenas to Gaia asked, "Damn it, doctor, spit it out. What is it?"

"All viral activity has stopped," she replied, not taking her attention off her work. "It all stopped, as if on cue. His injury's about five times its original size!" There was a monotonous drone from one of the machines. "There is nothing I can do—his heart and lungs are partially digested." She closed Laenas' now lifeless eyes.

Marco shook his head. "Dust and ashes, doctor, I got his blood on my hands. Should I be worried?" he asked, showing his stained hands, shaking a little bit.

She looked at his hands closely. Marco could see a flicker behind her eyes as she examined Marco using the different imaging tools implanted in her eyes. "You seem to be fine. The tissue damage from the initial wound seems to be important in initiating the attack."

Marco sat back, visibly relieved. Speaking more to himself, he commented, "The bullet enters and fragments. If that doesn't kill you, the virus increases the damage five-fold in minutes, increasing your chances of sustaining a critical hit. It's an old idea, but a rather phenomenal way of implementing it. Add to it the chance of the virus spreading to some vital organ through the blood stream, and we have ourselves one very potent weapon. Even a simple wound can be deadly."

Dr. Murena added, "The fact the virus shuts off after several minutes seems rather remarkable as well. Probably to prevent any rampaging plagues that could affect their side eventually. I'd be surprised if such a convenient weapon evolved naturally. I doubt these are grunting primitives we are dealing with."

Taura turned to her lieutenant-commander. "Victor, update the troops on our enemy and their weapons. Have them dig a defensive perimeter and use the fallen trees to build fortifications."

"Aye, Captain."

Taura turned to her communications officer. "Lieutenant Kaeso, you and Mr. da Riva take Laenas' body out of the craft. After a perimeter's been cleared, we'll make a pyre and cremate the fallen tonight."

"Yes, Captain," the lieutenant replied with a salute.

"Please," Marco interjected, "call me Marco."

Ignoring Marco, Taura turned to Lieutenant-Commander Victor. "I'll contact the Novafire. We'll have more troops down here raising slag with us before the hour's out."

* * *

Kilometers above the atmosphere of the planet, the K.S. Novafire shuddered as a continuous barrage of cannon fire from two Nephretian battleships overwhelmed the defending flak firewall and slammed into the Kalbarian ship.

"Pavo!" Commander Servius yelled over the sound of groaning metal. "Have you locked into da Riva's ship yet?"

"No, Commander. His security's—interesting."

Two Nephretian ships slipped out of the Q-wave slipstream moments ago and ambushed the Kalbarians. They were not interested in prisoners.

Commander Servius had ordered the Novafire to keep one of the Nephretian ships between the Novafire and the second enemy vessel at all times, effectively limiting the number of attackers to one. They only achieved a moderate amount of success with this task. The result, however, was a deadly ballet as the ships swung around one another, only to stumble from brilliant explosions when missiles managed to pierce a ship's defense and land a blow.

"Fates damn it," the Commander said, pointing at a mass of tangled robot parts and twisted metal, "will someone clear that mess away from the engineering station!" Orders and reports were being yelled, and crew members were sent sprawling as the Novafire took yet another hit.

"Where's our flak firewall?" Servius demanded. "Officer Nerva, get the damn firewall back up! We're getting torn to slag!"

The sound of their weapons, and the explosions caused by the enemy's blows were a constant roar.

"Lanata," the commander barked to the officer manning the helm, "divert power from communications to the null-graviton drivers. We've got to get our maneuverability up."

"Aye, Commander. But our drivers were still a mess when we left port. I don't know how much more they'll take before stalling out," Lanata said.

"We'll find out when they stall, then!"

More damage reports were streaming into the commander's consciousness through his neural net with the ship. The blast shield—a nano-homogenized synth-titanium belt armor surrounding a missile bulkhead made of high tensile silksteel—was a patchwork when leaving port, and the two Nephretian ships had been tearing through it. Several decks had been depressurized from blasts. All the Novafire's weapons, however, were fully functional, and Servius was using every single one of them to hammer back at the Nephretians.

The far Nephretian ship suddenly rose over top of the near one and both launched a barrage of hammerhead missiles. Hammerhead technology sought to mimic the Kalbarian RAC, but was much slower at reconfiguring to adapt to the evolving conditions of the battlefield. Energy beams cut into the Novafire's blast shield like a welder's torch, cutting ribbons out of it before the Kalbarian battleship's null-bosonic field could be tuned to cancel out the energy stream. The nascent flak firewall that was just assembling several kilometers away from the Novafire managed to destroy most, but not all, incoming hammerhead missiles with brilliant, silent flashes of light. The impact of the remaining inbound missiles tore away the front, starboard quarter of the blast shield and sent the Novafire spinning wildly out of control for several moments until the inertia dampeners could correct the spin.

Through the computer inputs in his brain, Commander Servius immediately knew those hits had resulted in the depressurization of fifteen percent of the ship. The loss of life from that would be staggering. As well, the starboard engines were off-line. The Novafire could travel in circles, but little else.

"Oh that is it!" Servius said, slamming his human fist into the palm of his metal hand. "Nerva, prepare to enact firing sequence Lucia-alpha on my mark."

"Yes, Commander," replied Officer Nerva who was manning the weapon's console.

Servius rubbed his bald head with his flesh hand, fingers running over the intricate Celtic knots of the circuits that crossed the sides and back of his head. He looked at Officer Nerva. Fates, he was only a boy, Servius cursed to himself, probably shy of his twentieth year. Looking across the bridge, the entire crew looked like they belonged in a high school, not the bridge of a ship that was being torn apart thousands of kilometers above a planet no one had ever heard of. When did the Kalbarian army start recruiting boys and girls, Servius wondered. He knew the answer, though. Decades of war had left only the old or young. Men of Servius's age were rare.

Firing sequence Lucia was a last gasp. Once enacted, the Novafire would fire all weapons at the enemy targets at once, but this was only a distraction. Hidden within the cluster of weapon's fire directed at the enemy were twelve RAC missiles that would take alternate paths down to a target on the planet surface. That target was the objective of the mission to this planet—if the Kalbarians could not have the prize they were here for, no one would. The Novafire would then do whatever was necessary to detain the enemy from following the planet-bound RACs.

"Commander," Officer Pavo said looking up from the communications console, "I've broken da Riva's security code. I'm in his system."

An ember of hope flickered in Servius' chest. "Pavo, feed the co-ordinates from the helm for target beta to his navigation computers and initiate his engines at maximum acceleration." Turning to his weapons officer Servius ordered, "Nerva, cancel firing sequence Lucia and enact firing sequence Nova at target alpha."

To maximize maneuverability of the K.S. Novafire, Servius had cut Marco's ship loose to drift at the start of the battle. "Do you think his ship is big enough to destroy the Nephretian battleship? It's just a small freight ship." Pavo asked. The commander heard the worry in the young officer's voice.

"I'll be happy if it manages to tear another hole in the blast shield and depressurize a couple more decks," the commander replied. "Target beta's in pretty bad shape, so that just may be enough to knock it out of the game."

Marco's ship streaked across the front monitor towards one of the Nephretian ships. The silent eruption from the battleship was magnificent as Marco's vessel slammed into it, tearing a hole in its flank. Lights flickered off throughout the first Nephretian vessel as it suffered massive depressurization from the collision. Spinning chunks of debris from the impact rammed into the side of the second vessel moments before the Novafire sent an overwhelming barrage of RAC missile fire into it. The force of the resulting explosions sent the second Nephretian ship spiraling far above the Novafire, oxygen venting through terrible gashes in her hull. Miraculously, though, she was not destroyed, and she returned fire.

Strategy had, for the most part, left the game as the two crippled ships exchanged barrages. Bombs from the Nephretian rained down upon the Novafire, overwhelming the tired remnants of the Kalbarian's depleted flak firewall and erupting in tiny flares of light along the fortress of a ship. However, in this type of fight, the Novafire had the advantage of superior firepower and shielding. In moments, the mid third of the Nephretian's underside was shredded in a series of eruptions. Servius followed with a string of RAC missiles directed at the yawning holes in the enemy's hull, though it wasn't necessary. The Nephretian ship was completely dead in space, but the startling explosion disintegrating her was a nice touch.

"Target alpha neutralized," Officer Nerva reported.

"What's the status of target beta?" Servius asked.

Nerva checked his monitors for some moments, "Massive depressurization has crippled her. She's dead in space."

The data flowing into Servius's mind informed him that the Novafire was barely sustaining life support. The starboard engines were severely damaged, requiring a great deal of time to completely repair with the facilities offered in the emptiness of space, and the port engines were only running at thirty-four percent efficiency. The computer systems throughout the majority of the ship, including the hanger bay, were melted and fused trash as a result of the Nephretian's last barrage. Servius did not even want to think about the casualties sustained. They were also in a decaying orbit around the planet—in a week they would smash into the surface. It would be a tough stretch, but if the Novafire remained unmolested, her crew could probably repair the engines enough before the week ended to push them away from the surface. It would take several days to make the hangars operational, too.

Turning to the communications officer, Servius ordered, "Pavo, inform Captain Taura of our situation. Until we get the hangar doors online, she'll be trapped on the surface and we won't be able to help her." Then, he added as an afterthought, "Oh, and have her inform Mr. da Riva that his ship's been destroyed."

Chapter 5

The mood in the camp was somber. Marco stood at the edge of camp staring into the dense foliage. The sun had barely begun to rise after a sleepless night and mist filled the gray dawn. His jaw was sore from being clenched throughout the evening as he fumed that the ship he had recently stolen in his escape from Deurgal had been destroyed in the space battle between the Kalbarians and Nephretians high above the planet's atmosphere.

The humidity was immense, stifling any chance of comfort. Since crashing on this planet, not a moment had passed when Marco was not saturated with his own sweat. He took a moment to wipe the beads of perspiration from his forehead with his sleeve. The sun's presence was felt more than observed as the towering foliage blocked all but the slenderest of rays from the forest floor. The world they walked in was one of perpetual twilight, filled with a palpable heat and omnipresent mist.

The forest never slept. All through the night, strange cries of beasts crashing through the growth kept the entire camp tense. Now, as the sun rose, new creatures cried out to greet the day and forage for breakfast. Marco's breakfast had consisted of Kalbarian army rations, which required little foraging to obtain, but necessitated large quantities of liquids to effectively wash the taste from his mouth.

As he stared out in the woods, Marco's thoughts turned back to the day everything he loved in life died. He was in his teens when it happened. He closed his eyes and remembered the house he had grown up in on Verna—a tall, stately structure built right on the space docks. Other trading houses lined the docks with narrow walkways winding their way through them. The exotic scent of spices and fabrics, mixed with the sweat of the dock hands still filled his nose when he reflected on the only home he had known.

His father was a shrewd man, quick to spot an opportunity. Although charming and boisterous, he was a ruthless negotiator. His mother was introspective by nature. She taught computer science at a local university and was, interestingly enough, a chess grand master on Verna. As it happened, Marco was playing chess with her the day his family died and he still wore tied around his neck a rook he had taken from the board they had been playing on. He was of an age when he would rather not spend time with his parents, but his mother was quite adamant about playing one game of chess with him a day. "Focuses the mind," she would say. Indeed, it was she who designed the chess program Marco still played on his data pad computer.

On that day, a squad of Alathian warships ambushed a Nephretian armada as they were docking on Verna for supplies. Marco did not know which side won the battle. All he knew was that vessels damaged in the battle crashed down onto his city in a rain of fire. His home was destroyed in the blast of one of those crashing ships.

But Marco lived. He lived to see his mother crushed by collapsing ceilings and walls as the house crashed down around them. He lived to see his father's charred corpse on the docks in front of their warehouse.

Since that day, Marco had known no home except refugee camps, the inside of freighters and trader's pubs in the ports he frequented. He had never returned to Verna, though it still existed. Alathia had claimed control of it for a while before Kalbarai shattered the Alathian fleet posted there. Currently, Kalbarai nominally ruled the planet, though it hadn't the resources to exert any real power over the beleaguered world.

Taura approached Marco as he stared out into the woods. She stood for a moment, awkwardly, then, hands on hips, spoke, "You make a wonderful target, standing alone at the edge of our camp."

"I have complete faith in the protection your troops afford me, Captain," Marco replied, retreating from his reverie.

"Nonetheless, you are no use to us dead."

"Your tenderness is touching," Marco said, turning to face Taura. She wore a sly smile that told him she was joking. Marco found Kalbarian humor to be in poor taste. He noted that she, too, was soaked with her own sweat, causing her damp uniform to cling to the curves of her body—an image some dark corner of his mind found appealing. He looked at the milky blue orbs she had for eyes and was enthralled for a moment.

He buried the pain of his memories under his charmer's mask and with a sly smile of his own said, "A proper host might apologize for the rather dismal breakfast this morning, and your utter lack of Vernian coffee."

Her lips twisted into a smirk. "I have been accused of many things, but being a proper host is not one of them." Changing the subject, Taura continued, "I notice you were playing chess on the landing, and throughout most of last night."

"Chess sharpens my mind."

"I don't believe I saw you win a game."

Marco raised an eyebrow and then turned to the forest. "Fine, chess teaches me humility, then." Taura smiled. It was now Marco's turn to change the subject. "Captain, considering the events as they've unfolded over the past day, do you think you could inform me what it is we're here for?"

"No. You'll know when we reach our objective," Taura said.

"So any moment now," Marco replied, irony in his voice.

Before Taura could retort, the two were caught by surprise as a figure seemed to magically materialize out of the woods. Marco's pistol was out in a flash. Taura, on the other hand only acknowledged their unexpected presence with a tilt of her head. The rest of the Kalbarian camp, however, quickly assumed a defensive perimeter. Marco's gun was barely out of its holster before a dozen soldiers leveled menacing weapons at the stranger.

The intruder wore a long green poncho reaching down to his ankle. The man was slight of frame with long auburn hair that flowed to his shoulders. His eyes were clear water blue.

The man strode forward with a hint of arrogance, seemingly unaware of the numerous weapons directed at him. He was short—about the same height as Taura, and his face was noticeable for its finely chiseled features.

"Welcome to Ullrion," the he spoke in accented Seedtongue. "I am Kan Rath, and am sent as an ambassador from our government to your people."

Marco responded first with a loud, brash voice laced with irony. "Well, it was kind of your government to give us the night to assess our situation with the stench of funeral pyres fresh in the air before opening up diplomatic relations."

Kan Rath eyed Marco with ice in his eyes.

Taura quickly stepped in front of Marco. "I am Captain Lucia Taura of the K.S. Novafire. I represent the Kalbarian League."

"Hm, yes, we were informed that you would be arriving," Kan replied. "I would first like to apologize on behalf of my people for the most unfortunate accident that occurred yesterday."

His words were laced with diplomatic pleasantness and Marco's dislike for him was growing. Kan Rath continued, "Certain elements of our population are not comfortable with the arrival of peoples from other worlds. The situation has been assessed, and I assure you, proper disciplinary measures have been taken."

Ignoring the comment, Taura asked, "You said you were informed of our arrival. Who informed you?"

"Emissaries from The Holy Nephretian Empire," Kan Rath replied with a smile. Marco noticed Taura's jaw muscles tighten. "Yes, the Nephretians warned us about you. They have taught us that Kalbarians are—now how did they put it? Oh yes, 'a brutal, manipulative nation of bloodthirsty curs.'" Kan paused for effect, and then continued, "I don't suppose you would describe them in any kinder terms."

"No."

"I suspected as much."

"How long have the Nephretians been here?" Taura inquired.

"For a seedship week."

Taura continued, "Then I imagine you know why we are here."

"Yes. We appear to possess an item that both you and the Nephretians desire. Our government is not interested in simply giving this item away, as you can imagine, and I believe you now suspect we are capable of defending it," he said, his eyes briefly glancing to the remains of the pyre.

"So, is there anything we can offer you in return for this prize?" Taura asked.

A grin spread on Kan's lips. "Well, I believe there is. You see the Seed Project on Ullrion was executed almost perfectly. Unfortunately, Ullrion is a world poor in the resources required for space flight. Certain metals and fuels are very difficult to find. At any rate, the people of Ullrion focused their attention on what they had an abundance of—life," he said, spreading his hands to encompass the surrounding forest. "We are very adept at molding the life around us to fit our needs.

"Take our camouflaging, for example," he said indicating the green poncho he wore. "We call them lorillien cloaks. Within these forests are several species that have the chameleon-like power to change color to whatever substance their outer skin touches. They, of course, did not evolve to be worn by humans, but our sages solved that problem centuries ago. And our weapons—we call them vanesti guns. I understand with regret you've seen their effects first hand.

"Despite our advances in biotechnology, though, we have yet to leave our planet. However, the arrival of space faring peoples presents us with a rather unique opportunity. You see, you can give us ships that will allow us to travel to our moons and other lifeless planets within our solar system. There, we can extract whatever materials we need to take our first, independent steps into space, without marring our own world."

"If it's ships and mining equipment you need, then Kalbarai can easily supply them," Taura said.

"Oh, I suspected as much," Kan Rath replied with a smile. "And so can the Nephretians as well as the Alathians. Yes, we know of the Alathians, too. We have begun to learn a little of the political climate out there, and we hope you can teach us more. We are delighted, you see, that delegations of both the Nephretians and Kalbarians have arrived, for the Nephretians are avid teachers, but a little biased in their views. Also, it is not only the key to space we now seek. We are interested in finding the most politically advantageous choice for our people. Perhaps we should give you some time to discuss with your government exactly what it is that you can offer us."

"If you know what we're after," Taura responded curtly, "then you know time is of the essence. The ship will activate soon, and then you'll have two nations with battle ships in orbit above your planet to contend with."

Marco noted the odd choice of words—the ship will activate soon. It was a hint as to his mission here, but he couldn't fathom its meaning.

"I assure you," Kan responded, "the Nephretians have informed us of the time-sensitive nature of your prize. When the time come, we can deactivate the ship, leaving what you need untouched."

Leaving what untouched, Marco wondered to himself in frustration.

Poorly concealing her irony, Taura replied, "We appreciate your thoroughness"

"Well then," Kan Rath said, "there is no more to discuss today. If we meet again tomorrow morning as we did today, would that give you sufficient time to discuss matters with your superiors?"

"I believe so. By the way," she added, "who is it that represents the Nephretian interests?"

Turning to leave, Kan replied, "I believe his name is Lord Suten Hamu of the Firstborn."

At the name, Marco's attempts to decipher the clues as to the purpose of his mission ceased. Once Kan Rath had left, he exclaimed, "The Fist!" He turned to face the captain. "Did you hear that, Taura? Lord Suten Hamu, the Fist of the High Prelate, second most powerful individual in the Holy Nephretian Empire is here, and he's interested in whatever toy you dropped on this planet! That just smashing!" Marco turned and stalked toward the wrecked landing craft.

Chapter 6

The night did nothing to lessen the heat. The drone of insects was broken occasionally by the growl or scream of an animal. Marco was sleeping fitfully inside a tent located near the landing craft when a hand over his mouth awoke him from his slumber.

Eyebrow cocked inquisitively, Marco opened his eyes. He was staring straight at a barrel of a rather menacing handgun. Behind it was one of the Kalbarian soldiers—Fullo, if Marco recalled his name correctly. He removed his hand from Marco's mouth and placed a finger over his lips in a gesture of silence. Leaning over, Fullo whispered at a barely perceptible pitch into Marco's ear, "Mr. da Riva, how'd you like to see what this mission is about?"

Marco's eyes switched from the barrel of the gun to Fullo. "I'd love to. It doesn't involve shooting me in the face, though, does it?"

"No." A smirk spread across Fullo's face as he holstered his weapon. "It does require a bit of discretion though. You up for it?"

"What's with all the secrecy?"

"I've got my orders from Rear Admiral Canus himself that if the team gets bogged down, I'm to obtain the pay data covertly. The captain's troops stay here to keep the enemy's attention. You're the computer cracker, so I need you. None of them know what we're up to so if we're caught, we're just a couple of wild cards acting on our own."

"I can't say as I'm a fan of leaving the captain and her boys here to the whims of the Ullrionis while we slink away."

"Don't worry. Once we have what we're here for, we'll be able to negotiate their release easily enough. Now, I need your cooperation to get this done. You want to see what this is about or not?"

After a moment's thought, Marco shrugged. "I wasn't getting much sleep any ways. What's your plan for getting us out of here?"

"I've got a distraction planned. Get your gear and start moving."

* * *

Taura was ripped out of her slumber by a massive explosion that sent her tent, with her in it, flying. She landed roughly, but quickly tore through the fabric of the tent with a blade that snicked out of her mechanical arm. Where the crippled landing craft once rested, brilliant violet and green flames emanated illuminating the campsite and surrounding forest in macabre shadows. Taura knew the color of the flames indicated a null-boson reactor leak.

Lieutenant-Commander Victor, with a massive K-96 rifle attached to his arm, was bellowing at the troops as he organized his men into a defensive array. No continuing threat appeared to manifest itself, but the soldiers were a hair's breadth from basking the surrounding countryside in weapon's fire anyway. Taura turned to her lieutenant-commander. "Victor, report."

"No hostiles spotted," he replied. "Fullo's not linked in. No other casualties to report."

"Search the camp to make sure our perimeter's intact," Taura ordered. "Find Fullo. And find out what caused that explosion. I want a full report in an hour."

"Aye, Captain," he replied with a salute before jogging off to comply.

Taura surveyed the camp. Where the Fates was Marco? "Lieutenant Kaeso!"

"Yes Captain," Kaeso responded jogging up to her.

"Mr. da Riva's tent was by the landing craft. See what you can find of him."

When Victor's hour was up, the sun had begun to rise over a horizon obscured by foliage. But its presence could be felt as the stifling humidity of nightfall was augmented with a crushing heat. Victor approached the captain with his report. "The null-boson driver leaked, triggering the explosion. Can't say as we know why the leak wasn't detected before becoming critical, but I'll keep yelling at our men until they figure it out. No sign of Fullo or the smuggler. If they were near the craft, they'd be vapor now."

"Your mother's teat the reactor leaked without setting off an alarm," Taura replied. "Something's up. Figure out what it is."

* * *

Yesterday, Marco would have said that he was uncomfortably hot encamped on Ullrion. Today, he knew he was wrong. As stifling as Ullrion was from the Kalbarian camp, stalking through the forest as quickly as stealth and the dense undergrowth would allow was much worse. Marco wore standard military camouflaged clothing supplied by Fullo that seemed to bend light around him, leaving him nearly invisible. Fullo led the way, resorting to some piece of equipment in his hands wired into a node in his temple. Every once in a while Fullo would halt the duo and take cover. When this happened, Marco would hold his breath as the rustling of unseen bodies whispered past.

They had traveled quickly and steadily without respite for several hours since the brilliant explosion in the Kalbarian camp lit the pre-dawn sky. Shocked by the blast, Marco had said, "That was some distraction you rigged up."

"Kalbarians don't do subtle," Fullo had replied. That had been their only conversation that day.

Now, Fullo hunched down on hands and knees and crawled to the top of a ridge overlooking a valley far below. Marco followed suit. A lens slid down from his helmet over each of Fullo's eyes as he stared down into the valley. "This is it," he whispered.

Marco peered down into the valley. He could see a yellow structure set in the dark green of the forest, but could make out no details. After adjusting a set of dials on the side of his helmet, lenses dropped over Marco's eyes. Immediately whatever he looked at in the distance zoomed into focus. He turned his attention to the structure in the valley. It was a massive sandstone-colored edifice, charred black in several areas, crushing the foliage beneath it. Shaped like a chalice, it was composed of a wide base upon which stood a thin stem that supported a large body at its apex. The base had five angled sides, each surface having an expansive ramp narrowing toward one of five entrances at the foundation of the stem. The stem of the structure also had five surfaces, corresponding to each ramp in the base. Wide at its foundation, the neck narrowed at its peak. Crowned atop the neck was the body of the structure. The underside of the body mirrored the base but rose petal-like to the sky above.

Some corner of Marco's mind noticed the back of his neck appeared to be feeding a population of insects. He waved absently at them as he increased magnification on the binoculars. Along one length of the stem of the structure was inscribed the name E. S. Yggdrasill. Realization of what he was looking at dawned on Marco as his breath caught in his throat. He had seen such a structure before on his home planet. The monolith below was almost an exact duplicate of the Museum of the E. S. Verna—the Earth Ship Verna—the seedship that spawned the civilization on his home planet. Marco, not more than twelve years old at the time, had visited the museum with his mother. The E. S. Verna had been ancient when Marco had seen it; its fine corners weathered to blunted curves and its color dulled to a dusty yellow after centuries of exposure to the elements.

By way of comparison, the E. S. Yggdrasill did not appear to have suffered a day of rain or to have felt the stinging pierce of a speck of wind-blown dirt. The forest around the base of the ship had been recently burnt away.

"That's a seedship!" Marco exclaimed. "A new seedship that's just landed. It hasn't begun colonization yet. What are the odds that a seedship would land on a planet already colonized? By Luca, if it hasn't begun colonization then the navigation computer is probably still intact. That's what this is about, isn't it? That's what the Nephretians are after. With an active navigation computer on a newly landed seedship, a course back to Earth can be plotted. We can find Earth!"

Why humanity's forbearers on Earth undertook the creation of the seedships was more a matter of speculation than fact, for the makers never shared their reasons with their progeny. Nor did they hint at their reasons for hiding the route back home. The navigational computers of the seedships would hold such knowledge as a reasonably skilled computer technician could backtrack the path flown by the ship. However, these computers were thoroughly cannibalized for parts in other equipment essential for the breeding and rearing of a new generation of humanity.

Marco turned, rubbing the growing beard on his chin. His hair, slick with perspiration, hung limply to his jaw, framing his face. He whispered, more to himself then anyone, "Dust and ashes, if the Nephretians get that data their belief that they are the chosen ones will be confirmed. It will galvanize their armies and could well drive people to their banner, which could tip the scales of war in their favor."

Turning to Fullo, Marco continued, "This find will define war—and peace—for generations to come. Aside from all that, can you imagine walking the land that witnessed the birth of humanity, to breathe the air and explore ancient ruins of our forefathers?"

Staring Marco in the eye, Fullo replied, "In order to retain our place of hiding and the element of surprise, it's important, Mr. da Riva, that you shut up."

The Mar N'lan

It has been said that ever since there has been a creature that could be called human walking the land, the city of N'ark has stood. Although that is most likely not true, it is nonetheless a city steeped in antiquity. There are no histories stored in the grand libraries of the mar n'lan—the rulers of the great metropolis—that record a time before the city was raised by its founders. N'ark, so the foolish claim, existed when water still flowed along the surface of the land before the Ravager's first strike. Regardless of what the truth might be, N'ark is ancient and its ghosts have outnumbered the living for millennia.

The spirits of N'ark were restless today, Seir T-pan thought as she watched the dust dance while the wind whipped through the streets. The sun had just breached the horizon, slamming the city with its heat. The wind had started soon thereafter. There was going to be a howler today, Seir T-pan knew. These winds would pick up intensity until sand blackened the sky and the screech of the gale overwhelmed all other sounds.

There were only a couple of hours before the howler shut down the city. Seir T-pan had to work fast. She needed to find some ration chips to buy a day's supply of water, and hopefully some food before the howler struck full force.

Seir T-pan had grown up on the streets of N'ark's Grey Maze—slums where the vast majority of the city's residents lived. Life was brutish in the Grey Maze. It was horrendously overcrowded and violent, with a perpetual churn of gangs fighting for control of blocks of the huddled, dilapidated houses carved of mud and stone. Occasionally a patrol of mar n'lan would sweep through, rounding up slaves for their armies or building projects.

Seir T-pan had no idea how old she was, though she had recently reached an age that some might call her a woman.

Surviving as long as she had was no small feat for someone who was viciously orphaned when she was a small child. Her body was lithe and lean and her skin chocolate colored, as was the skin of all mar p'augh—the lowest caste of the human race. Her face was gaunt, creased by hunger. She was not overly strong, but, oh, was she fast and agile.

She wore rags. Around her waist was a loincloth. Her breasts, which had only recently developed to the point where they might be considered cumbersome, were bound in a band of leather. She wore tattered leather shoes, and a leather strap on her forearm secured a long dagger carved from obsidian with bound rope for a hilt. Her hair was a tangled mess that she kept tied in a wild pony tail with a cord.

Keeping the last watch of the night, she sat on an old stool as she stared out the second story window of a building. Nar and Ketan still slept on the floor. The three of them had managed to scrounge up enough chips to rent the room for a week. They had roamed the Grey Maze together for a little more than a year now and were becoming an accomplished band of cutthroats and thieves.

Nar and Seir T-pan had known each other years ago as children, so it was natural that they would work together now. Ketan, Nar's older brother, suffered Seir T-pan's presence most likely because he wanted to bed her. Seir T-pan had resisted his advances so far, fearing that once she relented he would soon tire of her and force her out of the gang. Or, worse yet, he wouldn't tire of her. His advances were coming more frequently and with greater insistence. She would either need to sleep with him or kill him soon. But that was a decision for another time. Today, they must find enough chips for water and hopefully some food before the howler set in.

It was with this frame of mind that she spotted a figure walking along the street below. It did not belong in the Grey Maze. The figure—likely a male from his bearing—was tall and stocky, which was a rarity in the Grey Maze where food was scarce. His brown cloak, hood pulled over the head to protect the wanderer from the wind, was in too fine a shape to have weathered many nights in these streets. The cloak alone would buy enough water for the three of them. The fool had no guards, either. Perhaps he was a drunken trader, lost on his way home from a bar.

She nudged Nar awake and roused Ke-tan with a not-so-gentle kick. She pointed the figure out to her companions.

"Where? I don't see anything," Ke-tan said.

"There," Seir T-pan said impatiently, pointing to the street, "by the third door from the end of the block."

Ke-tan looked closer, straining his eyes. "Ah, I got him," he finally said. "I'm surprised I missed him."

Within moments, the trio was on the move. Such quarry would not last long in the Grey Maze and if they did not act quickly, they would find themselves having to fight other denizens of the slums for whatever goods the wanderer might possess.

Seir T-pan flitted out the window to the roof of the building with the grace of a cat. She leapt from ruined roof to ruined roof, skipping ahead of the stranger as he made his way.

Nar and Ke-tan glided out to the streets. Ke-tan had a knife, its obsidian blade catching in the sun. Nar had a club fashioned from a ruined chair.

Others were moving about the streets, yet no one seemed to notice the man. The desperation of setting their trap before someone else got their prey drove them to move quickly, not noticing the oddity of his unperturbed passing.

Seir T-pan slipped down the side of a building half a block ahead of the man. Stepping over refuse and human excrement, she turned the corner not more than three meters away from the hooded figure. Nar and Ke-tan were almost on him from behind. Seir T-pan bolted to close the distance, obsidian knife out and driving for his belly.

Before she could strike, her mind was hammered by a savage blow. Powerful emotions, unbidden and uncontrolled shattered her thoughts. The fearsome agony of watching her parents slaughtered in a dark alley as she hid under the body of a dead maze hound surged through her, intermingled with the nervous exhilaration of the first time she bedded a man. She could still feel his hungry hands groping beneath her breeches. The terror of her first kill, fresh as the moment it happened, danced and swirled with the joy she felt when Nar had accepted her as part of his gang.

Her world spun and she stumbled under the weight of the emotional barrage. It was a mind-rage, an incapacitating mental attack meant to stun rather than kill.

As Seir T-pan's faculties began to clear, she found herself on her knees. Her mind screamed at her legs to get up, to move, but her mind was trapped in a body she no longer controlled. The hooded figure stood before her, the wind picking up and tugging at his cloak. Nar and Ke-tan were on their knees behind him with vacant eyes and slack jaws. The crowds of the street moved around them seemingly oblivious to the scene playing out before them.

Blast the sun's rays, Seir T-pan cursed to herself, he was a powerful mindslicer.

He reached out to her with a slender, gaunt hand. His fingers wrapped themselves in the knots of Seir T-pan's wild hair and snapped her head back as he leaned down to her. The pain of the movement stabbed at Seir T-pan scalp, but she did not have enough control of her body to cry out.

Her prey-turned-hunter had gaunt cheeks with several days worth of black and white stubble. He smelt of dust and something more exotic—was it laurandreil spice? His eyes were piercing grey and void of any trace of warmth and his skin possessed a pale iridescence. Seir T'pan's heart sank as the realization dawned on her that she had attacked a mar n'lan—one of the cruel masters of the city.

"You saw me," he said, as his fists tightened in the nest of her hair until she thought her scalp would tear. "Speak!" he commanded in a harsh whisper, "tell me how!"

Her mouth fumbled as Seir T-pan regained control of it. Her voice was driven out of her, forced through some unseen compulsion.

"You were there plain as day. I have eyes to see," she said, blurting the first thing that came to her mind.

The man's eyebrow cocked and a crooked smile cut his face. "Indeed you do."

He threw her back, and her limp body splayed on the ground as he loomed over her. He half turned his head to Nar and Ke-tan behind him. "Interesting company you keep," he said. Seir T-pan knew she still had control of her voice, but chose to say nothing. The man cocked his head as if listening—no doubt using his mindslicer abilities to scan the thoughts of his captives. "They planned to rape you. Did you know that? Not the type of people I'd throw my lot in with."

"I can handle Ke-tan," Seir T-pan said.

"Not just Ke-tan," the man said as he stared at her with hard eyes. "Nar also, though I believe Ke-tan was intended to go first being the elder."

The words rocked her. Not Nar, she thought. They had been friends—or as close to it as one gets in the Grey Maze. Perhaps the mar n'lan was lying—trying to trick her. She had felt as though Nar was family. Yet, in her heart she knew she was not Nar's family. Ke-tan was.

The mar n'lan closed his eyes, as if in deep thought. With a grunt, both Nar and Ke-tan collapsed lifeless behind the man.

He continued briskly, "It matters not, now. They are dead. I haven't much time—you've delayed me for a meeting. You have skills I can use, though. Serve me and I will be your patron. You will find that I am not a kind master, but if you are looking for a way out of the Maze, I'm it. If not, a pack of maze hounds approach and they will find you and your companions quite a feast."

A patron, Seir T-pan thought. There were few pleasant ways out of the Grey Maze for its residents. Sometimes, though, the wealthy would take on a promising thief or murderer to serve as assassins and spies. Under the protection of such a patron, a Maze dweller could make a name for themselves—or so most Maze dwellers thought.

Seir T-pan looked him dead in the eye as she said, "I will serve you."

His eyes narrowed. "Good. I am Nk'ty. Mark the name well for you belong to me. Now get up. I want to finish my business and be out of the Grey Maze before the howler hits."

Nk'ty walked past her with long strides. With a jolt, she regained control of her body. As she was getting up, she looked over at the lifeless corpses of Nar and Ke-tan. No sign of trauma marred their body—they were just dead. Such are the ways of the mindslicer.

People started to notice the two corpses as Nk'ty distanced himself from the spot. A young boy was already pulling at Nar's boots. Seir T-pan turned to follow her new patron as the snarling howls and padded footfalls of a pack of approaching maze hounds echoed from a side street.

Chapter 7

"Fates, Victor, if that weasel Kan Rath wants to talk again, remind me to ram his teeth down his throat," Taura said to her lieutenant-commander.

"Somehow, I don't think you'll need reminding for that, Captain," Victor replied.

Taura had just finished meeting with the Ullrioni ambassador. He had inquired about the explosion, and Taura told him what she knew about the event, which wasn't much—the cause of the explosion was unexplained and two members of her landing party were missing. In turn, he informed Taura that some tracking beast of theirs had picked up the trail of two individuals leaving the camp. Kan Rath found it quite an amazing coincidence, since that was exactly the number of individuals Taura reported dead and unaccountable. So did Taura, truth be told.

The two missing individuals seemed to be heading straight for the seedship, casting more suspicion upon Taura's group in Kan's eyes. Talks between the Kalbarians and Ullrionis had been put on hold until this matter could be resolved in the ambassador's mind. Somehow, the Nephretians were behind this, Taura was sure of it.

Kaeso strode nervously up to her and snapped to attention.

"Yes, Lieutenant."

"I've finished the analysis on the explosion, Captain."

"And?"

"There's a Nephretian detonator signature emanating from the blast area. At present, it doesn't appear that Fullo or Mr. da Riva were caught in the explosion, though if they were in the vessel at the time, they would've been vaporized."

Her suspicions of Nephretian involvement confirmed, Taura asked, "How the Fates did sack-licking Nephretians get into our damned camp?"

"I—I don't know, Captain."

"Damn it, it doesn't matter now. Victor!"

"Aye, Captain."

"This ride's going to get choppy. Get the dogs ready for a rumble."

"About time. The troops are getting fat from all this waiting."

* * *

Marco huddled for cover behind the trunk of a large tree, his heart hammering in his chest as the reverberations of explosions knocked leaves off and sent shards of wood and turf flying. Human shouts and weapon's fire echoed throughout the woods. The vale shook with eruptions as Fullo covered Marco's action with heavy gunfire.

As Marco caught his breath behind his cover, two things struck him as odd. First, Fullo seemed oddly capable of providing a tremendous amount of weapon's fire to bear—more than seemed reasonable for even a Kalbarian soldier. Second, it seemed to Marco that there were other figures cloaked in shadow that fought against the Ullrioni guards stationed in the woods protecting the seedship. However, he was not afforded the opportunity to reflect upon these oddities as weapon's fire splintered the massive tree he was hiding behind.

Marco peered around the giant trunk and aimed his blaster at what appeared to be one of the doors into the E. S. Yggdrasill. A stream of ionization from his blaster tore the portal apart. Two near invisible Ullrionis who were guarding the entrance shimmered into sight as they fell and lay unconscious on the ramp. Marco inhaled and sprinted for the opening he just blasted open. He ran up the ramp past the fallen guards towards the entrance of the seedship. In the adrenaline rush of combat the time it took to sprint up the ramp seemed to yawn into eternity. Marco felt horribly exposed. He could not see clearly into the ship, but he held his blaster out and fired wildly into the entrance area as he ran. He felt something whisk past his head and heard bullets whistling through the air nearby. With a yell, he dove through the door.

He landed solidly on his belly, knocking the wind out of him. Ahead lay a short hallway ending in a pentagonal room. Marco quickly scrambled out of the hall into the area beyond.

Immediately, he felt as though he had been transported to another world. The room was dark, save for the single beam of light from the gapping entrance Marco had just leapt through. The area was dominated by a large circular pillar stretching from the floor until it was lost in the darkness above. At its base was a single door. To the side of the door was a square plate raised slightly off the surface of the surrounding wall of the pillar.

No guards appeared to be present, although if they were wearing lorillien cloaks, they would be nearly invisible. Marco strained his senses, trying to see the visual distortion of any camouflaged guard or hear their movement, all the while expecting to be shot by a concealed assailant. Nothing happened. He looked at the floor to see a fine layer of dust dimly illuminated by the single beam of light. Except for his passing, it was undisturbed.

Inside this hall the sound of combat outside was muted and a deep reverent silence fell upon Marco. He quickly moved to the door at the base of the pillar, running his hands across it. It was dark pewter in color and cool to the touch. Not knowing what else to do, Marco pressed the raised plate to the side of the door. It whispered open and a wash of stale air wafted over him as he inhaled deeply, imagining that he might actually be breathing in the air of Earth, the air the mothers and fathers of every known seed colony had breathed. Beyond was a small area dimly lit in muted yellow light.

Marco stepped into the small room and the doors softly shut behind him. Turning, he saw a panel of thumb-sized discs with glowing symbols inscribed in them at waist height to the right of the door. He squatted down to better observe the inscriptions. They were runes of the ancient Seedtongue. Marco's mother—herself a university professor—diligently taught her child to read and write Seedtongue. The runes were numerical demarcations. He lightly ran his fingers over the rows of discs. With an eager smile spreading across his lips, he randomly pressed a disc in the middle of the panel.

Marco felt a temporary increase in gravity's pull. A display over the door began to flash incandescent runes identifying numbers increasing in sequence. He could feel the room he was in slow to a stop as the display presented the rune matching the disc he pressed. The doors slid open and he was on a new level of the seedship. Beyond the portal, inky blackness reigned except for the dull illumination from the small room in which Marco stood.

Holstering his gun, he struggled through his pack and retrieved a flashlight. Turning it on, a bright beam of light sliced through the darkness revealing a long hallway stretching ahead. Softly, afraid to disturb the silence, Marco stepped out of the elevator. With a whisper, the doors closed behind him and his world was reduced to what he could see in the beam of his light. As Marco moved down the hall, he came to a set of doors, one to his left and another to his right. To the side of the doors were discs engraved with more runes. Marco studied the markings by the door to his left, running his hand over the rune to clear the fine layer of dust. As he did so, the door slid open in near silence, sending Marco stumbling back in surprise.

He shone his flashlight into the room beyond to see a vast array of cribs lining the wall that trailed off into the darkness. A look of concern cast itself over his face as he whispered to himself, "How in the nine heavens am I supposed to find the navigation computers?" He waved his flashlight up and down the length of the room, which extended farther than the beams of his light illuminated. He noticed a panel on the inner wall beside the door containing a screen and a series of tiny ellipses, each of which was marked with small runes.

It was an interface with the ancient computer system of the ship.

His face erupted in a grin. Marco prided himself on being able to crack any computer system developed by humans, and indeed, such abilities were what recommended him for this assignment from the Kalbarian government.

Marco retrieved his own computer from his pack, setting it on the ground. He then began carefully prying back the panel of the ancient computer interface using the blade of a jackknife he pulled out of his pack. Behind the panel rested a series of glowing wires and plugs. He pulled out several coiled data jacks from his bag and began inspecting the plugs to see if any would fit the ports of the seedship's interface. Seedship technology was arcane, so, naturally, none of his jacks could be plugged directly into the interface.

He produced a cutting laser-knife, pliers, and a number of other tools from his pack. He then set about modifying his data jacks and dismantling the data ports by the seedship's computer interface by the light of his flashlight that he held in his mouth. Within moments he had hastily constructed a connection between his computer and the seedship's.

"Sweet Luca," he quietly prayed to his goddess of fortune, "guide my hands today." He attempted to access the seedship network through his own computer.

He received an error message from his computer in reply.

His hands glided over the screen of his computer as he adjusted his program and tried again. Another error message blinked at him on his screen. "Don't feel like talking, eh?" he said to the seedship's computer interface in front of him.

After a few more failed attempts, he succeeded is establishing a connection. "Alright, let's have a look around."

He set his computer to quickly scan the seedship network for navigational data, but there was none. Looking at the list of files streaming across his screen, he seemed to be linked into a facility administration system: lights, power, CO_2 scrubber status and so on in an endless list.

"Boring. Well, let's see if you have any cute friends, then," he said to himself as he set his computer to scan for files containing the layout of the seedship. In moments he was viewing schematics of the complex projected in 3D above his computer. "There's the main computer hub," he said tapping an area of the projected image. The action resulted in a series of directions leading him from his present location to the room he pointed at.

Packing up to leave, a thought struck Marco. After delivering a few commands to the seedship through his computer, the area was basked in a white glow that seemed to emanate from the walls and ceiling themselves. Quite content with himself, he turned off his flashlight and returned it to his pack. Disconnecting his computer, he began to make his way to the computer hub.

* * *

Perched in orbit high atop Ullrion, the K.S. Novafire sat fortress-like as the clouds of the planet drifted past several hundred kilometers below. The ship was scarred and blackened with jagged holes marring its surface. But for all its scars, it emanated pride laced with an unremitting will. Commander Vetus Servius sat on the bridge, mind full of heavy thoughts. His chin rested in his quicksilver hand. His flesh and blood right hand absently rubbed the stubble growing in on his normally shaved scalp. He felt helpless, and that angered him.

The hangar doors could not be repaired in deep space. Without the facilities of a space dock, extensive repairs risked depressurizing vast sections of the ship, further straining the already stressed life support systems. His crew had been working around the clock since their battle with the Nephretians, but they had barely begun to scratch the surface of the damage to the ship. They had a few operational banks of weapons now, and the engines were barely functional. In an emergency, they could slip into the Q-wave slipstream to escape, though the probability of ionizing the entire ship in the process was alarmingly high. Servius could not remember the last time he slept.

The last two days had been a stream of damage and casualty reports, and subsequent repair orders for numerous systems in the ship, cannibalizing this piece of equipment for essential parts for another area. Through near constant communication with Captain Taura and Rear Admiral Canus, he understood the mission on the planet was spiraling out of control and it would be weeks before reinforcements could arrive to help the beleaguered crew of the Novafire.

A warning bell rang across the bridge, rousing Servius from his reverie. The ringing of warning bells had become commonplace over the past days.

The navigation officer informed the bridge of the complication. "Sir, I'm picking up three Nephretian battleships. One of them is the Reclaimer."

"The Reclaimer," Commander Servius commented. "It seems the Fist of the High Prelate has decided to grace us with a visit."

"They're hailing us, Commander," said the communications officer. "They're ordering our surrender."

The Nephretians had long since given up trying to convert the Kalbarians. Since then, it was rare they asked for surrender, preferring to wipe the Kalbarian blight from the universe. They must be trying to impress Ullrioni diplomats with their merciful nature, Servius mused.

Assessing the damage to the Novafire through his neuronal inputs, the commander concluded that attacking the Nephretians would be an almost silly gesture. "Officer Pavo."

"Yes, Commander," the communications officer replied.

"Get me the captain."

Within moments, Servius was on a comm link with Taura, apprising her of their deteriorating situation.

"If The N. S. Reclaimer is there, you can bet Commodore Kahotep is leading the fleet," Taura said. "What's the Novafire's status?"

"Our engines are slagged. We have two weapons banks online. Death and injury has reduced our active crew by more than half."

"Is the ship able to enter the Q-wave slipstream?" the captain asked.

"Probably. Yes. The inertia dampeners were damaged and we haven't had a chance to test the repairs, but we should be able to slide into the stream."

"Commander," Taura ordered, "keep my crew safe. Get out of there. Get to the Claw Cluster."

"We can't leave you, Captain."

"I'm ordering you to retreat to the Claw Cluster, Commander," Taura repeated over the comm link. "Marco and Fullo went missing last night, and there is a battle going on in the distance. We are gearing up to move out and engage. We've lost control of the situation on the surface. You cannot defeat the Nephretians. If the only thing you can do is get my crew out of there safely, then by Fangere's teeth, you will get my crew out of there safely! Is that understood, Commander?"

Servius had served with Taura for many years aboard the Novafire, even before she had been captain. He had formed a bond with her that only those who face death together can share. The longer he served in the military, the more he realized he did not fight for Kalbarai, nor did he fight out of blind obedience. He fought to protect his fellow soldiers. Abandoning Taura on the surface of this planet made him ill. He looked about the bridge of the Novafire and the young faces of the crew. Many of them were doing a poor job of pretending they were not listening to the commander's conversation with the captain. To attack was death. Surrender to the Nephretians was worse.

"We'll return for you or avenge you, Captain," Servius finally replied.

"Fates, are you still there! Go!"

"Helm," Servius ordered, "initiate the slipstream and pray to Sudus Velume we hold together."

* * *

Following the map Marco downloaded, it was a simple matter to find the room he was looking for. Excitement flowed through him as the door to the central computer hub whisked open. Before him in the room, dominating the area, were five massive columns stretching from floor to ceiling surrounding a pentagonal slab. A matrix of lights and discs with inscriptions in the ancient Seedtongue criss crossed each column. The slab possessed a series of darkened panels. The area was lit in bright light though there was no obvious source of illumination. There were five columns built around a central hub shaped like a flat pentagonal slab. Marco studied the inscriptions on the column. Upon examining the third column, Marco's breath caught in his throat. The inscription on the third column read "Navigation."

Reaching out his hand, Marco reverently touched the column, almost as if some part of his mind could not accept its reality and needed tactile confirmation of its existence. Standing here, Marco was the first human to see the navigational computer and to touch it—to feel it beneath his fingers—in eons. Somewhere in the dark recesses of time, some great catastrophe may have destroyed the home of humankind. But, humanity's seed lived on, passing silently and alone through the void of space for the heavens only knew how long. Then, one day after its long sojourn, the first seedship had found fertile soil and humanity once more was a part of the universe.

Alathia, having the distinction of being the oldest seedship civilization discovered to date was over twelve thousand years old.

The youngest, however, had only existed for a mere five centuries. How many other seedships were still lost among the stars, Marco wondered. How many had landed on barren soil where civilization faltered and died? How many had thrived and still remain undiscovered? Marco circled the navigational computer, lost in such thoughts.

Returning to the task at hand, he found a data port and began connecting his computer to the navigational system. Marco was, of course, conscious of time. No one knew where he was, and it would take some time to search the ship, but it would not be long until either Fullo or the Ullrionis came looking for him.

Marco was soon interfaced with the navigational system and downloading the ship's navigational data.

As information was downloading, Marco created an algorithm that began deciphering the information his computer was collecting. A map of star systems flickered in 3D above his computer screen, and the course the seedship had followed was backtracked, thousands of years of space flight compressed into seconds. The path quickly led out of any system Marco was familiar with and continued back and away until finally, the course stopped and a pale blue dot on his screen flashed where the seedship's journey began—home.

Home.

The Nephretians taught that only once humanity had redeemed themselves in the eyes of their creator god, Amahté, would the path home be revealed. Marco stared with wonder at the dot flashing on his computer screen. This information was worth more than the hundred-thousand SpeCred he had been offered by the Kalbarians.

And with that thought, Marco's mind returned to the here and now and he recalled some earlier observations he had found troubling. He remembered seeing shadowy figures fighting the Ullrionis in a coordinated effort with Fullo—shadowy figures who were, in all likelihood, not Kalbarians since the rest of the landing party from the Novafire was left unawares back at the crashed landing craft.

Perhaps, Marco reflected, some insurance was in order. He set about entering commands into his computer. After several minutes, satisfied with the program he just created, Marco disconnected his computer and stored it in his pack. Standing in front of the navigational system of the seedship, he reached out his hand and touched it once more. Whispering to the column, he said, "Forgive me for what I must do, but, as long as you exist, I am expendable." Backing away, he drew his blaster from his holster and sent several quick shots into the navigational computer. Within moments, the most prized possession in human civilization was nothing more than a burning wreck of twisted metal and wires. The data it once contained, however, was safe in Marco's own computer now.

Suddenly, Marco's heart skipped a beat and his stomach twisted into a knot as he heard the percussion of running feet and the call of voices on the other side of the door leading into the room he was standing in. He was fluent in eight languages, including those of Kalbarai, Alathia, Nephreti, Seedtongue, along with others including his mother tongue of Verna. However, he could not identify the language being spoken just beyond the door to the computer room. If he had to guess, though, he would guess it was Ullrioni. Frantically looking about, Marco saw there was another exit on the far side of the room. He grabbed his gear and ran.

Chapter 8

Marco, with a gun in each hand, crept up behind one of the Ullrionis pursuing him. The lorillien cloaks the Ullrioni wore were good camouflage, but did not render the wearer completely invisible—especially if the wearer was moving swiftly.

Marco had laid a trail in the fine layer of dust on the floor that the Ullrioni were now following. Using the map of the seedship he had downloaded earlier, he had double-backed on them. Marco pistol whipped the rear Ullrioni on the back of the head. The man collapsed onto the dusty floor of the ancient seedship.

The two other Ullrionis turned quickly, but Marco had caught them by surprise. Dropping to the floor with the soldier he just knocked out, he fired with both pistols. The echo of gun shots reverberated down the empty corridors of the seedship, and blood, bone and flesh of the remaining two Ullrionis stained the ceiling, walls and floor of the hallway as they crashed to the ground.

When the lorillien cloak died, so did its camouflage abilities. The cloaks on the two soldiers he shot were as dead as they were. The unconscious soldier's cloak, however, was alive and well. He stripped it from him.

In a silent whisper into a comm link Fullo provided, Marco reported, "I have our meal ticket. I'm about to leave the seedship."

Fullo's reply was transmitted to a receiver that fit neatly into Marco's ear. "Good. Can you get to the hill where we first spotted the seedship?"

Looking at his newly acquired lorillien cloak, Marco replied, "Probably faster than you could."

"Good. Meet me there in fifteen minutes. Our escape vessel is descending as we speak."

"An escape vessel! I'm glad you thought of a way out of here."

There was no reply.

Marco donned the cloak. It was refreshingly cool—a perfect temperature, Marco thought. Following the map of the seedship he had downloaded onto his computer, Marco made his way to an elevator. He found the main level was once again empty, although now bodies littered the floor and blood pooled. Some battle had transpired here while he searched through the seedship, but the only casualties appeared to be Ullrioni.

He cautiously made his way to the exit. Outside a war was raging and several fires burned as more explosions rocked the forest. Marco dropped to his belly and slithered from the ship to the ground. His cloak changed from the sand color of the ship to the brownish green of turf. He scrabbled on his belly to nearby foliage where he stood up. The lorillien cloak turned green as it touched the leaves.

Marco carefully made his way through the undergrowth to the hill where he was to meet Fullo. Seeing that he had not yet arrived, Marco opted to remain hidden in a clove of greenery. Explosions rumbled across the woods just as Fullo ran onto the hill. He had obviously been sprinting and was winded.

"Marco," he whispered harshly, "Marco, are you here? We have to hurry."

"Right beside you," Marco replied stepping from the bushes. Once away from the bushes the cloak took on the light green color that seemed to be the natural hue of the creature.

"Good. Will your computer slow you down?" Fullo asked pointing to the briefcase-like computer Marco held in his hand.

"No. Look, can we leave now?"

Fullo's eyebrow cocked. With an upward flick of his hand, a wire flung from his wrist with blinding speed. Before Marco could react, a needle at the end of the wire pierced his chest and an electrical current surged through him. He dropped to the ground completely stunned. His mind reeled in a body out of control. The last thing he saw was the image of Fullo flicker and change to that of another person. Before he could clearly see this new person, his vision blanked as his eyes rolled into the back of his head.

Moments later, Marco shuddered violently as he slowly regained control of his limbs and rose to his knees. He wiped at drool on his thin beard. Fullo—or rather his doppelganger—and

Marco's computer were gone. More pressing, though, were the forms emerging from the surrounding woods. They were Ullrionis, and their weapons were unwaveringly trained on him. Cursing to himself, Marco raised his hands and surrendered. An Ullrioni moved behind him and struck the back of Marco's head. For the second time that day, his vision blanked.

* * *

The tension in the camp was a living, malevolent thing. Taura had just ordered Commander Servius to take the K.S. Novafire and retreat. For the soldiers on the ground, there would be no escape: imprisonment or death seemed the only outcomes.

"Fates," she whispered in prayer, "see that Servius gets my crew to safety."

In the far off distance, the rumblings of a battle whispered through the trees. The captain had the camp on high alert and ready to move out. The soldiers were tense, angry and cornered, for the forest around them was teeming with Ullrioni soldiers, camouflaged with their lorillien cloaks, but vaguely perceptible under infrared vision. The two sides waited, weapons trained on each other in the sweltering heat.

"Captain, a report from the perimeter has come in," Lieutenant-Commander Victor stated as he approached her.

Taura sat with her legs crossed on a felled tree her soldiers had blasted down the day before, her relaxed affect concealing the tension cramping the muscles throughout her body. Her hair, as usual, was in an intricate braid that glistened with perspiration. Her mechanical hand, night black with designs of inlaid molten crimson was clenched in a fist. "Report."

"The Ullrionis look to be massing. It's tough to tell—the denseness of the surrounding woods makes it hard to assess exact numbers."

Taura's eyebrow cocked over her marble blue eyes. "Fates!" she cursed. "Get the soldiers ready for a fight." With a silent thought transmitted electronically to all the soldiers over the neural net, it was done. Taura's ears pricked. "Do you hear that?"

Victor concentrated for a moment. "Landing craft."

After a heartbeat, three aerial troop transports sailed over the tops of trees, whipping the uppermost branches of the forest. Two of them fanned out to flank the Kalbarian camp. All three were red and bore the Nephretian insignia of a black phoenix rising out of flames on a white background with black border. They were bristling with weapons. Time stood still for several moments, the tension nearly unbearable. But nothing happened.

"Bit odd they're not killing us, don't you think, Victor?" Taura commented, rising from her seat.

"Maybe they plan to torture us with a sermon, first," he replied. Although intended as a joke, Taura felt there was far too much of the truth in Victor's quip. She had no intention of allowing her men to die at the hands of Nephretian torturers, or worse, risk being converted. A Kalbarian warrior should die shedding the blood of an enemy, not languishing in a prison or a conversion camp.

She was a hairsbreadth from issuing a command to blanket the land in weapon's fire when a figure materialized from the surrounding foliage. It was Kan Rath. He bore no weapons.

"You wanted me to remind you to pound his teeth in next time you saw him, Captain," Victor said quiet enough that his voice did not carry.

"Thanks, Victor."

"Captain Lucia Salonious Taura," Kan Rath called out, "we have suffered an unwarranted assault and theft at the hands of Kalbarians."

"Oh, you'll be backing that up," Victor said, hoisting a menacing looking assault rifle and leveling it at Kan Rath, "or if only one Ullrioni dies today, I'll make sure it's you for your lies!"

Kan Rath looked coolly at Victor with utter disdain in his eyes. He turned to Taura. "Do you allow such insubordination from your men, Captain?"

Taura replied, "It ain't insubordination if I tell him to do it. Answer him, or you'll die with us today."

Kan Rath scoffed in disgust and continued, "We've captured one of the individual's responsible—a Marco da Riva. He indicated that Fullo, one of your soldiers, was his co-conspirator."

"Fullo was acting on his own then—I gave him no such order," Taura retorted.

"Of course. Nonetheless, firsthand accounts of the battle make it quite clear it was a Kalbarian who escaped after orchestrating the attack."

Taura's mind seized on the word—"escaped." So whoever was masquerading as Fullo was still free. She may not have complete control of the situation, but neither did they. An ember of hope flickered. Fullo—or whoever he was—had needed Marco to access the seedship's navigational computers. Kan Rath accused the Kalbarians of "theft," suggesting that the duo had met with some success towards those ends.

Taura repeated, "None of these actions were authorized by me or the Kalbarian government."

"Perhaps," stated Kan Rath, raising an eyebrow, "you could assure us of the good intentions of your government by surrendering. As it stands now, our government is on the verge of declaring war—with the full backing of the Nephretian Empire. They have taken great interest in our weapons."

The thought sickened Taura. The Ullrioni civilization had advanced enough to produce weapons as sophisticated and deadly as their vanesti guns. She shuddered to think what other ideas their weapon-makers had dreamt of. It did not really matter as the Nephretians had the upper hand. They would have the Ullrioni's soul as well as their weapons soon. But to the Nephretians, the path to Earth would be paramount.

Taura took a gamble. "Fine. You will, of course, want to know where my soldier has taken the downloaded navigational computer data."

"That information will be given as a part of your surrender."

More hope. Although Taura did not, in fact, know where the data from the navigational computers was, the Ullrioni ambassador just confirmed that the Nephretians did not know either.

Meanwhile, Victor stood taunt, weapon unwaveringly aimed at Kan Rath. Taura gently placed a hand on his massive arm. "Victor," she said calmly, "stand down." She knew her lieutenant-commander would rather die in battle than in prison—perhaps to the point of defiance. She chose her next words very carefully and with subtle emphasis, "We came here to download navigational coordinates to Earth from a newly landed seedship. It seems the Nephretians don't have those coordinates. We are still needed to find them."

Victor did not move. The raised ridges forming the shapes of entwined dragons and roses under the skin of his biceps writhed and glowed a menacing red. Taura tried a different tact. "Lieutenant-Commander, don't be a slag head. Today is not a good day to die. Put down your Fates-damned gun."

"Aye, Captain," he replied after moment, lowering his brutish rifle. Then, yelling to the soldiers of the camp, "You heard the captain, it's not a good day to die today. Stand down." Slowly and with great reservation, the other soldiers lowered their weapons.

Turning to Kan Rath, Taura spoke, "To prove the good intentions of the Kalbarian government, I offer our surrender to the Ullrioni authorities until this matter can be resolved."

One of the Nephretian troop transports floated gently to the ground in the clearing where Taura and Kan Rath faced one another while the other two continued to hover menacingly. Once settled, the hatch door opened and Nephretian soldiers streamed out in ordered proficiency, surrounding Taura and her men. Two soldiers dragging a rather beaten Marco da Riva exited the transport and threw him at Taura's feet. Looking up to face her, Marco, brushing blood caked hair from his face, smiled weakly.

"You've been busy, Mr. da Riva," Taura said.

"Never thought I'd say this," Marco rasped in reply, "but I almost prefer Kalbarian hospitality, despite the lack of Vernian coffee."

Beaten but not broken, Taura mused to herself. She pondered for a moment what path had led Marco to the current life he lived, but her attention was soon drawn to the individual exiting the ship. He was moderately tall and stout with grey hair combed back to the nape of his neck. "Commodore Hetshepsu Kahotep," Taura spoke to the man, "they still letting you command after that shaming I gave you at Caldar? I'm surprised you didn't get busted down to trash duty."

The Commodore stared at Taura with eyes of green steel. His face was hard with the menacing smile of a hunter. "Captain Taura, I look forward to teaching you some respect." He moved to stand behind her.

The Nephretian soldiers stood at attention for the final figure leaving the craft. There was no mistaking this man. Slender and with arrogant demeanor, Lord Suten Hamu, the Fist of the High

Prelate stood before them. His eyes searched Marco, and then Taura with wolfish intent. His clothing was black, except for the scarlet phoenix rising from the flames on a white shield dominating his torso.

Kan Rath approached him. "In accordance with the treaty between our nations, Lord Hamu, I present to you these prisoners."

"I thank you, Mr. Rath," The Fist's voice was smooth and strong. His eyebrow rose. "Commodore Kahotep," Lord Hamu continued, "teach these prisoners how to kneel."

Chapter 9

The Ullrionis had a creature they called a naloth. Roughly translated, the word meant "Pain Demon." It appeared to be a mammal of some sort with eight spider-like legs. It could fit neatly in the palm of a hand. What it looked like, however, was of little importance to its function. In nature, the naloth was a bloodsucker. It would first incapacitate its prey by inserting a needle-like projection into the spinal cord and stimulating a rather intense pain response, literally incapacitating the creature. It would then stay and feed on its victim until the unfortunate host was dead. Often, this would take days, perhaps weeks depending on the strength of the prey. A horrifying way to die— but like all animals of creation, the horrors it visited on its food seldom weighed on its mind. The longer the prey survived the less work the naloth underwent to feed.

Darker elements of the Ullrioni military thought this was a wonderful little creature, requiring very little engineering. The only modifications they gave to the naloth was to provide a mechanism to allow a handler control over the insertion and release of the pain-stimulator, whose effectiveness was also much amplified and specified for the human nervous system. Additionally, the naloth no longer fed on its victim, allowing prisoners to be horribly tortured ad naseum without fear of dying.

Marco currently writhed under the ministrations of a naloth in the middle of a clearing while Nephretian soldiers constructed prison barracks. He bore no shackles to stop his escape. Excruciating pain inflicted by the naloth pinned him to the spot as effectively as a guarded cell. He lay on the ground motionless, save for the random convulsions or gasps set off by the naloth repositioning itself for comfort.

Night had fallen and the next day's sun was high in the sky before Marco's prison was constructed. Once completed, soldiers dragged him into his cell and the naloth was mercifully removed. The ecstasy of the release from pain overwhelmed Marco. This ecstasy, however, was short-lived. No sooner had Marco regained his senses than two Nephretian soldiers entered his cell, manhandling him to his knees.

Lord Hamu entered. One of the soldiers roughly grabbed Marco by the hair, forcing him to look up into The Fist's face. His skin was tan red, as was the norm for true blood Nephretians. Intense eyes rested below arched eyebrows. The nictitating membrane—a mutation introduced in the first generation of the seed colony to protect them from the harsh sun of Nephreti—languidly blinked as The Fist appraised Marco.

The Fist spoke in a strong voice, confident of his authority. "I understand you are Marco da Riva, a smuggler hired by the Kalbarians to steal the most sacred knowledge in the galaxy from us."

Still reeling from the naloth, Marco could not voice a reply.

"I also understand," Lord Hamu continued, "that you are responsible for destroying the navigation computers of the E.S Yggdrasill … the most sacred and holiest of artifacts in existence."

Marco regained enough control of his voice to rasp, "I can see how you might see that as a bad thing. But consider this," he continued, struggling for breath, "maybe we're not ready yet to find the path to Earth. Maybe I'm the hand of Amahté, keeping the knowledge hidden until we are ready."

Lord Hamu's eyes narrowed a fraction. He leaned close to the prisoner's face and enunciated every word as he spoke, "Your sins are legion. Not even the High Prelate himself can absolve you of them. You're a smuggler for hire, Marco. You owe no allegiance to the Kalbarians. Do what you can to redeem yourself. Tell me where the coordinates are."

"Can't say as I know," Marco replied.

The only outward expression of Lord Hamu's emotional reaction was a clenching of his fists. He continued in a gentle voice, as if speaking to a child. "Marco, I encourage you not to squander my time. You have something I desperately want, and I will get it, even if I have to tear the truth from the ashes of your soul."

"Ah, Hamu," Marco replied in resignation, "you already have the truth from me."

"We shall see."

* * *

Taura was on splayed knees, arms bound behind her back on the dirt floor of a hastily assembled prison cell. Disheveled hair framed her pale face and her breath came in ragged gasps. A Nephretian wearing the robes of a predicant—one of the lower rank and file of the Nephretian clergy—had overseen the preparation for her conversion with the help of two young acolytes throughout the night. Sleep had been substituted with pain as the trio attempted to break her resolve, to shatter her resistance, to free her and allow the words of Nephretian scripture to enter her soul. Once dawn broke outside, Commodore Kahotep had relieved the trio and had been tending to Taura personally.

He loomed over her, flush with his absolute victory. He remembered the day he first encountered the K.S. Novafire. Hetshepsu had relentlessly clawed his way up the ranks in the Nephretian armada. With no family or associates one might call friend, all he had was his ambition, and it had taken him far from the estate he grew up on near Khenemet, the capital of Nephreti. Possessed of a vicious and merciless intellect, he had won ever-greater successes in the battlefield, rising to the rank of commodore in the Holy Nephretian Armada where he served as the right hand of the Fist of the High Prelate himself.

One of his first campaigns as a commodore was to oversee the capture of Caldar, a mining colony supplying Kalbarai. The Kalbarian ships guarding the system put up stiff resistance. Grossly outnumbered, though, the defiant Kalbarians were being beaten back—victory had been in the commodore's grasp. He sent a force to charge through the lines of Kalbarian ships, fragmenting their defense. That force ran straight into the K.S. Novafire and was fought to a dead standstill. The commodore would not have thought it possible given his numerical superiority had he not seen it himself.

The campaign was lost. A blemish—a gross embarrassment—on what had hitherto been a spectacular career. He had lusted for a chance to meet the K.S. Novafire in combat once more. And now, her captain was on her knees before him, bound and completely at his will. Grabbing her by the hair, he snapped her head back so she looked him in the eyes and then with bared teeth, he drove the tip of a sarsmak rod into the exposed flesh of her chest.

Once coded to a specific individual, the sarsmak rod sends an energy burst through the victim's nervous system into the brain at such a wavelength to shatter all neural patterns, momentarily allowing all thoughts, all emotions to rampage in a burst of stochastic freedom. The Nephretians had long since learnt there is nothing more horrifying, no pain greater than the utter and complete loss of control over one's mind. The Nephretians used the device to shatter the mental defenses of "resistant" converts to their faith. If the individual's psyche was not completely annihilated, they became prodigally susceptible to suggestion.

The attack from the sarsmak rod rocked Taura onto her back. She writhed and choked for several moments as the effects dissipated. Just as she was regaining control of her mind, Hetshepsu once more grabbed her by the hair and dragged her to her knees. He drove the sarsmak rod into her chest, but kept her on her knees through his grip on her, letting the sarsmak rod shatter her mind for moments before he released her, gagging, to fall on her face.

A dark and commanding voice from behind Hetshepsu asked, "Is your questioning proceeding well, Commodore?"

The commodore turned to face Lord Suten Hamu, whose tall and slender frame dominated the door to the room. "Kalbarians," Hetshepsu grunted dismissively. "It takes some effort to ready them for questioning."

"Don't bother," the Fist replied, "she knows nothing."

"You've finished questioning the smuggler?" the commodore asked.

"He was betrayed by his accomplice, Fullo."

"Pity we don't need to put her to the question, then," Hetshepsu said, looking regretfully at the captain as her convulsing subsided.

Seeing the direction of the commodore's gaze to Taura, the Fist stated, "You are acquainted with her, if memory serves me correctly."

"Yes," Commodore Kahotep replied. Then he added dismissively, "She was a competent captain."

"Competent," Lord Hamu mused, "as I recall she was responsible for halting your conquest of Caldar."

The commodore bristled at the embarrassment that his commander would be so familiar with one of his greatest failures. Not quite managing to hide his anger, he simply replied, "Yes, my superior."

The Fist knew men like Commodore Kahotep well and was adept at motivating them. "Commodore, find the missing Kalbarian—Fullo—and she's yours."

Now, with less anger and more hunger, Hetshepsu repeated, "Yes, my superior."

* * *

Victor felt his age weighing down on him. He was tired and he could not remember a time when his body did not ache. He had commissioned the finest artisans in Kalbarai in the design of his enhancements, but not even the finest artisans can beat back the relentless onslaught of time, each year crashing into his body like a wave against a crumbling cliff face.

He was sitting on the floor of a cramped cell that he and the other remaining Kalbarian soldiers had been herded into. They had been fitted with disrupter collars that interfered with their ability to link up into a phalanx. As well, braces and locks had been placed on their various enhancements, preventing the soldiers from accessing the numerous weapons concealed within their bodies.

Reports from behind Nephretian lines, always spotty and full of conjecture, implied Nephretians had given up trying to convert Kalbarian prisoners a number of years ago. Kalbarians were tough to convert and reverted back too easily. Reports from escaped prisoners and captured Nephretians indicated prisoners of war were herded into labor camps where they were worked to death. Some reports suggested many prisoners were simply executed en masse. The Triumvirate War had dragged on long enough that atrocities were becoming commonplace.

Victor did not covet death in a prison any more than he coveted being crushed by old age. Yet, here he was, in a pen. His gaze scanned his men. They were sullen. Anger smoldered in some, fear in others. Victor's attention rested on his lieutenant. Procyon Kaeso was sitting squarely in front of the door, staring at it without emotion. This worried the lieutenant-commander. The situation called for anger, or fear, or something, anything more than a blank stare.

Victor had led men long enough to know that nothing eats at the will more than hopelessness. He moved to sit beside his lieutenant and quietly said, "Hey Kaeso. I've been in tighter spots than this," which was true, "we'll get out of here," which he wasn't entirely sure of.

Kaeso was startled out of his reverie. "I'm sure you have, sir." Then he resumed his vigil of the door.

"Hey, Lieutenant," Victor continued snapping his fingers to get Kaeso's attention, "you can't stare the door down."

Kaeso turned a very serious stare to the lieutenant-commander. "Don't be so sure, sir. The Nephretians neglected to lock my eyes down."

Victor was a bit taken aback by the response. "Explain yourself."

Kaeso tapped his temple, "I've a number of visual enhancements, including radiographic and ultrasonic vision.

"And that means?" Victor asked.

"I'm looking for flaws in the structure of the door and walls."

"You can do that?"

Kaeso replied, "Yes," as he turned his attention back to the door.

Victor was impressed. Kaeso was not a typical Kalbarian and had trouble fitting in with the regular soldiers. He was slight, by Kalbarian standards, as well as shy and quiet. But Victor suspected he had underestimated him. While his soldiers were busy being glum and impotently angry, Kaeso was quietly busying himself finding a means of escape. Victor liked fighters. If they got out of this, he'd have to keep his eyes on Kaeso. "Found anything?" he asked.

Kaeso looked quite thoughtful while answering, "Not a lot. It's a standard security door made from heavy gauge silk steel with a hollow core filled with permacrete. Same with the walls, and the door's bolted pretty deeply into the wall," he said while indicating a point in the wall where the bolts securing the door frame ended. "Electromechanical locks connecting to a latch bolt control the locking mechanism. There's also a keyed cylinder for manual locking and unlocking."

"I don't want to know how to build a Fates-blasted prison. I want to know if we can smash the door down."

"Not without a tank," Kaeso replied. A passionate curse escaped Victor's lips. Masterfully ignoring Victor's outburst, Kaeso continued, moving to a corner of the room where two walls came together. "Your weak spot's here," he said pointing to an area about knee height off the ground."

"What's weak about it?" Victor asked, moving to inspect the area.

"This cell was hastily constructed. The walls are held together by metal braces on the outside. One of the bolts here is stripped, giving the brace a bit of give. The wall is also secured by a metal stud over here," he continued, moving about two meters from the corner. Knocking lightly on the wall where the stud was, he continued, "The stud should be secured in concrete, but they didn't have the time to do that, so it's been secured in the turf. It should have a bit of give to it, too."

Most of the soldiers were paying attention to the conversation now. Kaeso continued, "I believe someone with the weight and strength of you," he said pointing to Victor, "with a complete disregard for their physical well-being should be able to hammer a breech that could be forced open."

"Well," Victor replied with a grizzled smile, "that one more option than we had a minute ago." A little bit of hope to feed the troops. "Dogs," he called out to the other soldiers in the cell, "huddle up. We need to talk."

Chapter 10

Once the Fist had left, Marco's conversion began under the tutelage of a predicant named Ekur. The man was not a native born Nephretian, as denoted by his absence of red skin and second eyelid. This was not strange—the word of Amahté had found many converts across the galaxy. The lessons had started off simple enough.

"There are four paths to Amahté. The Path of Akori—the foundation. The Path of Barit—birth and growth. The Path of Akhom—change and knowledge. The Path of Kepi—destruction and rebirth."

Marco knew this already. One did not become a successful smuggler without knowing the societies one must work with. He observed an insignia on the collar of the predicant's robes. "That label," Marco pointed, "that indicates you're a priest of Akori, does it not?"

The predicant looked impressed and smiled. "Yes, yes it does. I follow the Path of Akori, and will do so until, Amahté willing, I advance to High Elder, at which time I will be blessed to walk the Path of Amahté."

"Akori, god of stone right?"

Again, the predicant was impressed. "Yes. You know much of our religion."

"Just my luck to be brainwashed by the most boring of all the Nephretian cults," Marco said.

His conversion did not proceed well after that. He could not remember the last time he was allowed to sleep. Marco had been fed Nephretian dogma rather than food. Water had been splashed in his face once in the heat of the afternoon. It was not enough to shrink his tongue swollen with thirst. Food, sleep, water—these things were rewards for acceptance of Nephretian beliefs. Marco's compliance had thus far been poor, but it would not be much longer before that changed. Anyone can be broken—it is only a question of time.

Before each session with Ekur, acolytes would place an anx on his head. The anx was a tool of the Nephretian clergy. It rested on the head of a pupil like a cap and sent short bursts of EMR into specific regions of the brain with the aim of re-routing neuronal pathways. Through this mechanism in conjunction with other tools such as the sarsmak rod, the clergy could literally change the thought patterns and belief systems of the pupil, turning deadly enemies into ardent members of the faith in a matter of weeks.

How long the teaching had lasted, Marco did not know. Time was useless to him—less than useless. It was his enemy as the Nephretian acolytes and predicants relentlessly hammered at his resolve and molded his thoughts. He had been granted half-an-hour of sleep for finally repeating the phrase, "Humans are scattered across the cosmos for their sins. To be reunited is to be redeemed," to his teacher. During his brief respite, those words plagued his dreams.

He was jolted awake by searing pain. With him in his room were two acolytes, one with an electric prod that had been used to awaken him. By the door was a female predicant clad in the flowing robes of her caste, emblazoned with the rising phoenix. He hadn't seen any of them before. Neither the predicant's acolytes nor the priestess herself bore the standard Nephretian characteristics of reddened flesh or inner eyelids.

"You will come with me, Mr. da Riva," she said. The two acolytes forced Marco to his feet. All three were tall and slender with plain features. Marco staggered along, allowing himself to be led out of his cell. Outside, two more acolytes, one on either side of the door, joined them. The woman led the way, followed by two of the acolytes, then Marco, then the last two acolytes. They briskly traveled down some short hallways, Marco doing his best to keep up while trying to clear his sluggish mind. They were traveling through a building hastily constructed by the Nephretians, and were approaching a door, when a commanding voice brought them to an abrupt halt.

"Stop where you are," the voice ordered in Nephretian. Marco and his entourage turned to the source of the command.

Behind them, two Nephretian soldiers, weapons drawn were advancing slowly. One said, "This prisoner was not to be removed, by Commodore Kahotep's orders."

Without warning, the chest of each of the soldiers exploded with a wet sound and they were thrown back. No gunshot echoed down the hallway—only the sound of shattering bones and liters of blood slopping on the floor. The adrenaline crystalized Marco's mind, and he saw the nearest two acolytes quickly conceal weapons of some sort. Alathian blasters, if Marco had to guess.

A puzzled frown overcame Marco's features. "Am I being rescued?" he asked.

"Silence, Mr. da Riva," the priestess replied.

"You have no idea how many women tell me that."

"Mr. da Riva, your being conscious is preferable, but not necessary," the predicant said. She turned and continued towards the door, Marco's guards pushing him onwards."

The doors led outside to the Nephretian encampment on Ullrion. It was dusk and few individuals were out. Marco quickly surveyed the compound, noting other prisoner or guard quarters. In the center of camp was a moderately sized building with a large guard tower rising from the roof to survey the surrounding rain forest. It most likely was Commodore Kahotep's residence while overseeing the installation of the Nephretian's first base on Ullrion. That was also, most likely, where Taura was being kept.

"Are you rescuing any of the other prisoners?" he asked.

"No, and if you don't shut up, you'll be staying, too," the predicant replied.

Marco idly turned to a pair of Nephretian soldiers guarding another building, "Hey, over there. I'm being kidnapped by Alathians."

Marco's escorts had their weapons drawn in a flash. Definitely Alathian, Marco noted as he saw their dagger-shaped pistols. The Nephretians tried to bring their weapons to bear, but their torsos were ripped open in silent fury, the only sound was of blood and flesh spattering the wall of the building behind them. Much to the consternation of Marco's escorts, however, one of the guards reflexively pulled the trigger of his weapon, sending several blasts into the ground by his feet. A heartbeat later, an alarm was raised throughout camp.

The predicant turned on Marco, staring incredulously at him. He shrugged sheepishly, and then punched her in the face. She was flung to the ground. Marco ran for the building the two Nephretian sentries were guarding and dove through the door as it was opening from the inside, adrenaline fueling his battered body. He crashed into a group of five Nephretian soldiers who apparently had been drawn by the alarm and were coming to assist. They all crashed to the floor in surprised disarray as Marco flew into them.

Grabbing one of their blasters, Marco began firing into the mass of bodies, shooting the surprised soldiers before they could react. The wall and part of the door frame erupted as blaster fire further down the hall began raining around Marco. Grunting, he turned and ran back out the door to the outside. The gun fire from the Nephretians from within the building tore into the standing acolytes that were with the predicant. Their own weapon's fired wildly as they were thrown to the ground in a bloody heap.

Meanwhile, chaos erupted throughout the base. It seemed the camp was surrounded by an unseen enemy in the dense forest who opened fire the moment the alarm was sounded. The Nephretians were hurriedly assembling their defense.

Marco ran hard for what he believed to be the commodore's residence where he thought Taura might be. He shot wildly at the door, cutting down the stunned guards and blasting the portal inwards. Marco dove through, landing roughly on his belly, surrounded by smoke. The smell of incinerated metal filled his nostrils. He was alone in the entryway, but the cries of many voices, yelling, filled the inner hallways. The sound of running feet echoed. "Dust and ashes," Marco cursed to himself, "why am I always doing stupid things for women?"

* * *

Victor and his soldiers had languished in their prison for over a day. They had been completely ignored by their captors, which would have been good if the neglect hadn't extended to a lack of food or water. The room was poorly ventilated—the only source of fresh air was through narrow slats on the ceiling—and the heat and overwhelming humidity compounded the lack of water. Victor's head throbbed from dehydration.

Through Kaeso's radiographic and ultrasonic vision, they had ascertained they were housed in a standalone building with two guards manning the door. After going over the escape plan with the men, Victor was confident they could breach the building if they had enough time. But time was the issue. In the time it took to force a breach in the hastily constructed cell, the two guards could call down the camp on them. Regardless, if food or water did not come soon, the soldiers would be too weak to mount an effective escape.

It was with these thoughts drifting through his head that Victor was jolted to awareness by the staccato of blaster fire nearby. He rose to his feet. An alarm sounded while more gunfire erupted, and then the camp was engulfed in the blast of a mass of weapon's fire.

"Lieutenant," Victor yelled.

"Yes sir," Kaeso replied.

"What are our guards doing?"

Kaeso flipped through his various visual systems and scanned the walls, "They're gone, but the camp is crawling with soldiers."

"Bah," Victor grunted dismissively as explosions ripped through the camp outside, "It's time to take 'em to school, dogs! Just like we planned it now!" Victor paced like an angry lion to the far side of the room, opposite the weakened corner. "Get the Fates out of the way!" he bellowed, and his soldiers tripped over themselves to clear a path. Screaming, Victor raced across the room, his massively augmented legs propelling him to great speed. With a thud that caused the entire structure to shudder, he crashed into the weakened corner and bounced back, landing on his feet, swaying. The structure held while pain echoed throughout Victor's very bones.

Kaeso looked at the wall with his radiographic vision. "A little to the left."

"Slag!" Victor cursed, stomping off to the far corner. He repeated his charge, ramming his body into the corner with preternatural strength. The building shuddered and a tiny gap appeared between the two walls.

"I said to the left, sir," Kaeso stated.

"I heard you the first time!" Victor snapped, seething as he stalked back to the far corner. The design of intertwined dragons and roses embedded under the skin of his biceps glowed an unearthly light as they writhed and coiled, as if possessed of a life of their own.

Kaeso turned to the men in the room, "Get ready. Another blow like that should tear the bolts."

Victor charged, a blur firing across the room. He hammered into the corner once more. This time, with a loud crack, the two walls separated and left a gap that a small child could crawl through. The force of the blow threw Victor roughly to his back. As one, the soldiers in the prison surged to the gap, pushing and straining, driving the walls apart. Outside, explosions and gunfire rolled through the camp, drowning out the screams of men. The gap widened and soldiers were able to make their escape.

Victor was slow to rise. Kaeso was by his side, helping him to his feet as the last of the remaining soldiers made their way to the compound outside. Victor's world was reeling. Each heartbeat was a hammer in his head and his vision became spotty as he struggled to retain consciousness. Kaeso, concern in his young face, asked, "You alright?"

"Shut up and get outside," Victor replied, regaining his footing.

Outside, Victor and his soldiers huddled by the side of the wrecked prison under cover of the darkness of night. The Nephretians were busy defending the camp from attackers hidden in the forest. Balls of fire belched into the sky in the surrounding forest as well as within the camp and the chatter of weapon's fire was a constant, screaming presence. They had a moment unobserved, but it would not last—and they were unarmed to a man. The locks on their enhancements held fast, preventing the full use of each soldier's body modifications and their disruptor collars prevented the soldiers from linking up to create a phalanx. This was not going to be pretty, Victor thought to himself.

Quickly assessing the battle, Victor mused, "Surrounding woods seems about as safe as the camp." Then, turning to Kaeso, "Thoughts on where the captain is?"

"If they haven't taken her back to The Reclaimer, she'd be in the center of camp," Kaeso replied, pointing, "that way."

Screaming over the surrounding sounds of gunfire, Victor yelled, "Well, let's hope she's in the camp because I don't feel like attacking the Reclaimer today. Just like we planned. Crab formation! Go!"

Even though the Kalbarians were kept from forming the phalanx through their disrupter collars, they fought as a tightly coordinated group nonetheless. The squad split into three teams as they ran across the pathway to the building opposite their prison. Two of the larger groups flanked the building—Kaeso led one team, Victor the other. Three soldiers with augmented bone and musculature ran straight at the building and with superhuman strength, leapt to the roof in a single bound.

Victor's squad encountered Nephretians right away. The fighting was in close quarters. With the Kalbarians driven to terror from their lack of weapons, and the Nephretians driven to terror by confronting a squad of desperate Kalbarians, the resulting fight was uncommonly vicious. The Kalbarians had the element of surprise. Victor, with his prodigal strength, crushed two Nephretians under mighty blows, giving his soldiers two guns. Another Kalbarian also managed to take a gun from a dispatched Nephretian. After that, the moment of surprise was gone and both Nephretians and Kalbarians with their newly acquired weapons opened fire at point blank range. Within a heartbeat blood washed the walls and pooled into the soft loamy earth where it was quickly absorbed. The Kalbarians were left standing once the fight was over, though their numbers were considerably fewer.

Silently, three Nephretian weapons were tossed up to the Kalbarians on the roof and the rest were distributed about. Two additional weapons were again tossed to the soldiers on the roof to pass to the squad on the other side. There were still more Kalbarians without weapons than with.

The three soldiers on the roof laid covering fire, leaping from rooftop to rooftop, clearing a path littered with blood and broken bodies for the soldiers on the ground as they raced for the middle of the camp. The fighting was fast and intense. The Kalbarians were a people who had never known peace, and they fought with the fiery rage of a race bred for war. They moved through the compound like a bristling knot of violence. They fought with anything they could find suitable for a weapon: blasters acquired from defeated enemies, furniture, stones—anything. Victor, with his prodigious strength, wielded the bodies of fallen enemies as lesser men might wield a bat. When no other tools presented themselves, the Kalbarians fought with foot and fist, biting and clawing their way through the enemy. Grossly outnumbered, their ranks dwindled as they progressed, but the Nephretians paid a heavy toll for each Kalbarian they managed to bring down.

In the sky above the camp, aircraft engaged in aerial warfare. Missiles crisscrossed the sky, plowing into the forest, the camp, and other aircraft. The fiery detritus of their conflagration rained down. Several buildings were aflame as was the surrounding forest.

After what seemed like an endless stream of fighting and death, the Kalbarian squad made visual contact with what appeared to be the central complex of the encampment. It was crawling with Nephretians and protected by a guard tower rising from the roof. A relentless barrage of weapon's fire was erupting from the tower into the surrounding woods. Kaeso made his way to Victor. "I count about fifty soldiers in eye shot. Can't see what's in the tower. The guns could be automated."

Victor looked over the remnants of his squad. There were seven Kalbarians left, including Kaeso and Victor. "Slag, this'll be messy."

Chapter 11

Marco had acquired a uniform and two pistols from a Nephretian soldier he had surprised and knocked unconscious. Though he was not a warrior, Marco was fast and smart and possessed a remarkable ability to carry off any lie, honed by years of slipping through blockades smuggling food, supplies, and weapons. Having a mastery over numerous languages and fluent with the intricacies of many cultures, he was armed with a handsome face and charming smile, allowing him to fit seamlessly into most environments.

He moved quickly through the central building in the Nephretian camp. His uniform was that of a private, so he attempted to look like he was purposefully going somewhere, lest a commanding officer tried to give him some orders. With the sounds of battle outside and frantic activity of men in the building, the search for Taura felt like it was dragging on for a dangerously long time.

He was asking himself why he was risking so much for Taura. Perhaps it was survival instinct. He suspected his treatment at the hands of Alathians would be no better than the Nephretians. As long as he kept more than one of the powers in the same room with him they'd be more likely to woo him rather than torture him. On the other hand, she was attractive, and Marco, like so many men before him, was prone to acts of foolishness when faced with a woman of beauty. Bereft of family, friends, and home for so long, his loneliness had long ago wrapped its hollow embrace tight about his heart, driving him to suicidal levels of derring-do in the pursuit of human connection.

The search was taking too long. Desperate, he took a gamble. Two soldiers were running down the hall in the opposite direction. Slipping into his mask of authority, he confidently stood squarely in front of them and ordered in flawless Nephretian, "Halt! Commodore Kahotep has ordered me to take Captain Taura to The Reclaimer. Where's her cell?"

One soldier turned and pointed, "Down the second hall on the left, it's the—"

He was cut off by the second soldier. "Wait, why didn't the commodore tell you where she is?"

Marco knew his facade was weak. He did not bear the physical characteristics of Nephretians. Moreover, he had been tortured for several days without sleep, and try as he might, he could not hide the haggard look in his face. Undaunted and with utter confidence, he replied, "He is seeing to the defense of the camp and did not think to tell me." To add some urgency to his request, he added, "She has knowledge vital to the seedship. It is imperative she does not fall into enemy hands."

The second soldier remained unconvinced. Gripping his weapon, he continued, "Who is your commanding o—" His question was cut off with a blaster shot as Marco, gun in each hand, shot both him and the first soldier. He moved past them before their bodies hit the floor.

He took the second hall to the left—it was mercifully short. Three doors, two on the right, one on the left. With a shrug, he opened the first door on the right. It led to an empty office. The door on the left opened into a cramped room. Suspended from the ceiling by heavy chains about her wrists was Taura. Her hair, usually held in an intricate braid, hung loose, matted with sweat and blood. Her shirt was a tatter of rags, barely concealing her lithe torso that now bore the deep cuts of her torture. Marco could see where her mechanical arm and shoulder joined with her body—the transition was seamless, as if the unnatural appendage grew from her body. He could not help but notice that her figure was beautiful and slender—and in the peak of health as Kalbarian military training demanded. She was surrounded by three Nephretian guards, each with a weapon trained on Marco.

Turning to the lead guard, Marco snapped to attention and dropped his chin to his chest, shouting "My superior," in a perfect Nephretian salute. He stood like this, unmoving, as the guards warily assessed him. Taura's utter shock and surprise was only registered by a cocked eyebrow as she watched this unfold.

The lead guard demanded, speaking in Nephretian, "Report, convert." Convert was the term some Nephretians used to refer to new adherents to the faith. It was a slight, implying ones faith was not absolute, as they had not been born into their religion.

Marco visibly bristled under the insult. With his head still bowed in subservience, he replied, also in Nephretian, "I'm no convert, my superior. I was born into the faith on Draxa." Draxa was a colony held by the Nephretians for over fifty years.

The guard scowled, and continued, "I said report, soldier."

Marco raised his head and said, "Commodore Kahotep wants the prisoner prepped for transport to The Reclaimer."

"Why didn't he radio the order in?" the lead guard asked.

"The Alathians are monitoring our communications," Marco lied without hesitation.

"Alathians," the guard responded. "Is that who's attacking?"

"Yes, my superior."

The lead guard turned to one of his compatriots, "Sebi, check the comm link." At that moment, each guard's attention was on their leader, whose attention was on Sebi. Marco drew a blaster in each hand and shot the lead guard and Sebi. Using the slumping lead guard as a shield, Marco and the third guard exchanged shots. Bullets thudded into the final Nephretian's body as Marco returned fire, hitting his final assailant, first wounding him, and then killing him with a follow up shot.

As the echo of gunfire faded, Marco let his human shield drop and turned his gaze once more to the chained captain.

"Mr. da Riva," Taura said with a smile, looking through the strands of her long hair with her inhuman eyes, "as surprised and glad as I am to see you, if you don't stop leering at me and get me a shirt, I'll rip your eyes from your head."

"Leering!" Marco exclaimed. "I was assessing the extent of your injuries." Marco blasted the chains holding Taura and took off the jacket of his uniform and tossed it to her.

As Taura put on the jacket, she commented, "Your Nephretian's pretty good." Then speaking in her native language, she asked, "How's your Kalbarian?"

"Passable," Marco replied in Kalbarai's mother tongue.

"I'm impressed, Marco," Taura said. "Do you have any other surprises?"

Marco looked thoughtful for a moment before replying, "I'm a pretty good cook."

"That doesn't impress me as much."

"Well, you haven't eaten anything I've made yet." Tossing Taura a blaster from one of the dead guards, Marco said as he moved to the door, "We'd better get out of here. From the sounds of it, this camp won't be standing much longer."

Following Marco to the door, Taura asked, "How'd you escape?"

Marco was about to answer, but as he left the room he found himself staring straight into the barrel of an Alathian pistol pointed at his face. It took a moment before he could pull his attention away from the gun to look at its possessor. It was the female predicant from earlier who had orchestrated his escape from his Nephretian cell. The hallway behind her was filled with a number of soldiers wearing Alathian camouflage fatigues, weapons pointed at Marco and Taura.

"I was rescued actually. By her," he said pointing to the woman holding the blaster at his face.

"She's a charmer," Taura stated as she dropped her gun and raised her hands.

The woman in predicant garb said, "Come along, da Riva, you're coming with us."

"I had to work pretty hard to rescue her," Marco stated indicating Taura, "so I'm not about to leave without her."

"She's irrelevant," answered the predicant as she turned the gun on Taura.

Marco quickly interjected, "I know why you need me. If you want my co-operation, she comes with us."

A smile spread across the predicant's lips as she turned to Marco, "Certainly. And if you give us any more trouble, she dies. Now, we really must leave."

* * *

Kaeso watched Victor duck his head back around the corner of the building he was taking cover behind as blaster fire ripped into the wall. "Sack lickers!" the bulky lieutenant-commander cursed viciously. Victor was holding a Nephretian gun. It looked like a toy in his massive, meaty hands and would have been comical in other circumstances, Kaeso thought. Victor popped around the corner once more and fired.

The Kalbarian soldiers were plotting their attack of the central compound in the camp when a squad of Nephretian soldiers had spotted them. The Kalbarians were now fighting for their lives, and they were losing. After Victor ceased firing, he hid once more behind the building as bullets tore into the surrounding wall and ground. He turned to Kaeso, sitting beside him, "Fates take it! I don't think we'll be getting into that compound today."

Kaeso, still a relatively young soldier, was struggling to keep his composure as the world was being torn apart around him, his ears filled with the sounds of men screaming in agony and anger and the hammering of weapon's fire. Movement caught his peripheral vision down the pathway he and the remaining Kalbarians were taking shelter in. Thinking it was Nephretians attempting to flank their position, he had his weapon up in a flash. A number of other soldiers, seeing his actions, took up defensive positions in the same direction Kaeso was facing.

A bit confused, Kaeso switched through a number of visual fields. "Lieutenant-Commander," he said to Victor, "I don't think we need to get into that compound."

Observing the direction of Kaeso's gaze, Victor, squinting into the night asked, "What do you see, boy? My eyes aren't as good as yours."

Kaeso, pointing, replied, "The captain is there, about a hundred meters that way, heading into the forest. She's accompanied by Marco and what appears to be a Nephretian predicant."

Victor grumbled, "A Nephretian! By Fangere's teeth, what's she gotten herself into? Lead the way, Lieutenant." The remaining Kalbarians slipped into the night following Kaeso. Within minutes, they closed the distance to where he had seen the captain exit the camp. As the battle raged about them, they discretely slipped into the rain forest. The soldiers, each possessing typical Kalbarian visual augmentation, switched their sight to low light vision. They, therefore, were able to make their way in the near darkness of the dense woods without too much difficulty.

Suddenly, Kaeso stopped short.

"What is it, Lieutenant?" asked Victor.

Pointing at the turf in front of him, Kaeso replied, "The ground here has been disturbed. I've switched to infrared vision— slag! It looks like a mine's been buried here—"

Victor grabbed Kaeso and dove into the surrounding foliage while ordering, "Take cover," to the rest of his men. There was a wet thud as a Kalbarian soldier was torn from his feet and collapsed lifeless on the ground, his blood seeping into the verdant soil beneath him.

"Those didn't sound like vanesti guns," Kaeso said.

"Aye, they're not. Those are Alathian blasters," Victor replied. The remaining Kalbarians returned fire as more blood was lost to the soil of the sylvan planet.

* * *

Still clad in her Nephretian robes, Marco's mysterious rescuer led both he and Taura through the rain forest as darkness fell. The Alathian soldiers accompanying them in the camp had melted into the surrounding forest. A war was erupting around them as they ran, the Nephretians tearing apart the foliage with their weapon's fire. Answering this barrage with equally deadly intent were shadowy forms flanking the escaping trio.

After scrambling up a short rise, Marco could see the outline of an aircraft in the dimming light ahead in a small clearing. Marco's anonymous rescuer was urging them towards the craft.

Suddenly, the searchlights of three Nephretian aircraft slowly soaring over the treetops of the clearing obliterated the deepening darkness. Missiles whistled from two of the craft and shook the surrounding woods with tremendous explosions. The third Nephretian ship fired upon the escape craft on the ground, annihilating it with a fiery eruption. The force of the detonations flung Marco, Taura, and their rescuer onto their backs.

From the forest, return fire was directed toward the Nephretian craft. Two of the craft were able to rise out of range suffering minor damage, but the last was torn to shreds in a hail of mini-eruptions. In flames, it crashed on top of the wrecked escape craft.

Observing the scene, Marco yelled over the weapon's fire to their rescuer, "Tell me you have a Plan B!"

"This way," she directed to the forest, "some of my men will draw off the Nephretians." Taura and Marco obeyed.

* * *

Commodore Kahotep knelt patiently, waiting for the Fist's reaction to the news of the escape. He did not have to wait long.

"Alathians," the Fist of the High Prelate whispered, sighing heavily. His room was dimly lit and cloaked in shadows. The Fist stood, staring at a distant sun through a window from his personal chambers aboard The Reclaimer. His black ceremonial clothes were wrapped about him, making it difficult for Kahotep to discern where his body ended and the darkness of the room began. "Inform our newly obtained Ullrioni allies that it is in their best interests to recapture the escaped prisoners forthwith. Send two more legions down to the planet surface to assist.

"As for the Alathians, their ship must be nearby. It is the only route of escape for the prisoners. Find it. Destroy it. Assuming you are up to the task, Commodore," he added.

Commodore Kahotep knelt before the Fist, enraged at the rebuke. To lose both Marco and his prize, Taura, while the Fist watched over him was intolerable. He would die—he would kill—rather than suffer such shame. "I will find the Alathians, my superior, and they will be made to suffer for their interference."

Strand-walker

Nk'ty stood in front of a door deep in the bowels of the Grey Maze. Seir T-pan—the cutthroat who had tried to attack him with her small gang and whom he had just assumed patronage over as he was making his way to this meeting—stood tentatively behind him. The sun hammered down on them as the wind whipped at the sand on the streets. The howler was coming.

Nk'ty hated this place with a seething intensity. He hated the buildings crumbling in the sun. He hated the stench that wafted up from the very stones, stained by the blood, sweat, shit, and piss of generations. And most of all, he hated the pathetic weakness of its inhabitants, crowded, stupid and wretched as they were. If it wasn't for the occasional need of slaves and killers, the Grey Maze would have been burned away centuries ago.

Yet, Kie would speak to no one but Nk'ty, and so he had to suffer the journey into the Maze every couple of years or so. He turned his hard grey eyes on Seir T-pan and studied the length of the chocolate-skinned ruffian's lank body. At least this trip he would get something more useful than Kie's inane ramblings, he mused.

The street in front of the house was empty—an anomaly in the Grey Maze. The milling masses of the slums just never found their way to this part. It was a mindslicer trick, Nk'ty knew, that Kie was employing to keep wanderers away.

"Hide. Kill anyone approaching this door," he said to Seir T-pan. Seir T-pan sped away to carry out her orders.

Nk'ty turned to the door and yelled, "You know I am here Kie! Open the door so you can tell me your latest ranting!"

Kie was a strand-walker—a mindslicer with the ability to walk the strands of causality up and down the continuum of time. This made them extremely valuable as predictors of future events.

*However, walking the intertwined strands of probability confounded
their sense of reality, driving them quite mad, which, given their
powers, made them dangerous. Most strand-walkers had to be put
down before they reached their full strength. Kie, however, was
spared by the masters of the city—a fact that gnawed at Nk'ty.*

*The door opened, and a stench even more overpowering than
the reek of the Grey Maze issued forth, gagging Nk'ty. "Sun take
your eyes, Kie, you wretched, filthy bastard."*

*A gaunt man, completely naked with the pale, iridescent skin
of the mar n'lan showing through a layer of dirt and filth, huddled
by the door. His grey hair was tangled and hung limp past his bony
shoulders. His eyes were wild and blue and darted about, quick as
daggers.*

*"Do I disgust you so?" he said with a strong, clear voice all
at odds with the frail wild appearance of the body.*

*"By the sands, yes! I am here at your summons. Tell me what
you will and be done with it."*

*A grunting laugh escaped Kie's mouth. "What I have to tell
you is not for the street's ears. Come in, dear brother."*

*Nk'ty lunged at the naked man, grabbing him by the strands
of his greasy hair. "Call me 'brother' again, and I'll have your
tongue, strand-walker or no!"*

*Kie's eyes wandered vacantly for a moment, as if he was lost
within himself or watching some other events play themselves out
that none but he could see. Within moments, they snapped back to
Nk'ty looming over him. "Shut the door behind you," he said.*

*Nk'ty released his hold on Kie and slammed the door behind
him as he followed Kie into the hovel. He looked around the dark
room they entered, lit only from whatever rays of sun found their
way through cloth-covered windows. "You've been busy, Kie."*

*The room was completely bare except for piles of feces
littering the floor. The buzzing of flies filled the house. The walls
and ceiling were covered with strange writing and pictures, drawn
in charcoal and chalk. Nk'ty inspected the scrawling script on a
nearby wall. Some passages were written in N'arkian, the
language of the city, others in the script of far-off Se'tal. Many
other passages were unfamiliar to Nk'ty.*

*"You've become quite the linguist, haven't you, Kie? If the
other mar n'lan saw you writing here where the dreks might see,*

though, I'm not sure the protection of the Academy could save you."

Kie's head snapped to look at Nk'ty. *"Dreks! Dreks, yes, odd that you should mention them."*

"Is it?" Nk'ty responded absent-mindedly.

In N'ark, there were those who ruled, there were slaves and there were dreks. Dreks were nothing more than slaves without a master. Since no one owned them and they had no land or money, they had no one to protect or support them. Slaves, at least, were a financial asset in society's view. Dreks were less than property.

"Speaking of dreks," Kie said as he picked up a piece of chalk and continued writing on a bare corner of the wall, "who is the girl you travel with? The one you ordered to guard the door while you're here with me?"

"She is drek no more," Nk'ty replied, turning to Kie. "I own her now. She has the power of Sight. I wonder what other powers she might possess."

"She's a feral slicer," Kie said dismissively. "Every other drek out there has a feral power or two. An interesting strand she walks, though. Odd you should choose her."

"Yes, I'm sure. Now, why have you summoned me?" Nk'ty asked.

Kie dropped his chalk and turned to Nk'ty, eyes unfocused and head cocked, as if listening to something. After a moment of silence, his eyes turned to Nk'ty and he stated with solemn intent, "The Lost Dreks return."

Nk'ty stared, fists clenching for a moment. Then, he lunged at the naked man, grabbed him by the throat and slammed him into the wall. "Who cares about the comings and goings of sand-blasted dreks!" Nk'ty screamed into Kie's face. "Now, why did you summon me?"

Kie, gasping for air, managed a smile. As his face began turning purple under the choking grasp of Nk'ty, he croaked, "Not dreks. The Lost Dreks."

Nk'ty threw Kie hard to the floor. "Sands, do I hate you! Explain yourself, if you even can!"

Kie's laughter stumbled over his gasps for air, "During the Dagomirs' ascension, the mar p'augh fought the mar n'lan. The Dagomir prevailed, but many of the mar p'augh's dreks were lost to the stars when the Ravager first struck. Now, they come. They come home, lost no more." Kie stopped, staring at Nk'ty with an expectant smile on his face.

Nk'ty returned the stare with a look of incredulity. At length he managed to whisper, *"Is there no shred of sanity left in you? Is there any truth to your words, or do you just ramble madly now? Sun's fire, let it be me who gets to put you down."*

"Oh, but you will do well, Nk'ty," Kie said, oblivious to the insults hurled at him. *"You will do our family proud in the coming conflagration,"*

"I have had enough of your idiocy," Nk'ty said as he left the room and bolted out the front door. Out on the street, Nk'ty took what he thought would be a deep, cleansing breath of air. Although less fetid than Kie's house, the air of the streets was still foul and choked him.

Seir T-pan, with the quiet agility of a cat, landed on the ground behind Nk'ty from the low slung roof of a neighboring hovel. The wind was picking up, whipping sand down the crooked streets.

"My business is done here," Nk'ty said as he walked away with long strides. Seir T-pan followed.

Both stopped and turned as Kie, still naked and wretched, ran out onto the streets shouting, *"Tell the Dagomir! The Lost Dreks are more powerful than when they left—but they are wounded! If he strikes quickly, before they regain their strength, he will rule them. Tell him! He must strike quickly!"*

Part II

"There is no greater risk than trust."

—Katholikos Limitanei, 304th First Councilor of the Alathian Alliance

Chapter 12

"By the nine heavens, is it your plan to walk us to death?" Marco asked as he and Taura struggled to keep pace with the Alathians leading them.

The sun was beginning to rise over the forest canopy, and the humidity of the night was slowly being augmented by the heat of the day. The Alathians had kept Marco and Taura moving throughout the night by administering stimulants to keep their fatigued and beaten bodies going. The drone of insects and calls of animals offended by the human intrusion of their territory was ever-present as they trudged on.

"Fine. We'll rest here. You've got ten minutes," the woman leading the group stated. The woman—who was never more than an arms-length away from Marco—had identified herself as Sergeant Major Ariadne Maleina. That notwithstanding, Marco had overheard one of the other soldiers refer to her as Lokanos, which he knew was Alathian for Captain.

Their escorts had not changed from the shadowy Alathian forces flanking them in the woods and the female predicant of the previous night. However, the ceremonial predicant garb Ariadne had worn the night before had been exchanged with camouflaged clothing made of a fabric that played with the light, rendering her almost impossible to see. Marco and Taura had also been given such clothing, but had been offered no weapons to defend themselves, nor had they removed the lock on Taura's machine arm. Marco was certain they had not been rescued, but rather stolen from the Nephretians.

Ariadne was tall and slender, which was not unusual for the Alathian race, and was otherwise, quite nondescript. Her hair was short and brown and her eyes dark and inquisitive. She was pretty, Marco thought, but by no means exceptionally attractive. She would not warrant a second glance in a crowd on most human worlds.

"Marco," Ariadne said once the group was settled, "you probably know why we're interested in you."

Fatigued, yet artificially alert with the Alathian's stimulants, Marco replied, "I have a few theories." Taura feigned disinterest, yet Marco was certain none of this was escaping her attention.

"Why don't we help each other out, then?" Ariadne asked.

"Help? Now, I don't wanna be the guy keeping score here, but if memory serves, it was one of your agents who left me to be captured by the Ullrionis."

"If my memory serves," Ariadne replied with a slight smile, "I freed you from the Nephretians."

"Be that as it may, I still don't feel particularly endeared to your cause," Marco said with a sidelong glance.

"You could be extremely well rewarded for your co-operation," Ariadne tempted.

"Only a fool would trust an Alathian's promise," Taura stated with a sneer.

At this, Ariadne seemed genuinely offended. "Once an Alathian gives their word, it is never broken."

Historically, this was true—sort of—Marco reflected. In a society so steeped in corruption, a peculiar honor in adhering to contracts and agreements had arisen. However, Alathians only make binding agreements in rare circumstances, and their ingenuity at discovering loopholes coupled with a tendency towards malicious obedience to self-serving interpretations of their contracts made for dangerous business partners.

"Of course, if positive reinforcement has no effect on you, Marco, let me tell you about the kartaka flower, indigenous to Alathia," Ariadne continued.

"I'm not really into horticulture."

Ignoring him, Ariadne said, "It is a beautiful flower that blooms once every two years. A chemical in the pollen, dithrace, is a potent toxin. Most non-Alathians are allergic to it. In small quantities, it makes most humans very ill. In large quantities, the allergic reaction kills."

Marco turned to Taura. "Care to guess where this is heading?"

Ariadne smiled, and continued, "Along with the stimulants we have been administering to you is dithrace sequestered from your body in time-release capsules. Presently, these capsules are circulating through your bloodstream being slowly dissolved. Once completely dissolved, the dithrace will be released, and you will die a choking death. You will take your knowledge to the grave Marco, and you'll take Taura with you."

"You, I assume, have an antidote?" Marco asked.

"Of course."

Taura was unable to contain her curiosity any longer. "Why are the Alathians so interested in you, Marco? They already have your computer with the coordinates to Earth, don't they?"

"Well, after I copied the information from the navigational computers from the seedship, I destroyed the memory banks."

"You did what?" Her eyes were wide with surprise.

"I destroyed the memory banks. Then, I put a personal lock on my computer. It was one of my better lock designs. If anyone tampers with it, it'll fry the memory, which would be very frustrating, since I have some personal items there as well."

"And my kudos to you, Marco, your security measures are best of class," Ariadne said, "and we Alathians know something of security measures."

"She's bluffing with the dithrace," Taura said to Marco. "If they kill you, they lose any chance of ever getting to Earth."

"That's exactly what I was hoping," Marco replied, a little jittery from the stimulants.

"All locks can be broken in time," Ariadne stated. "Even without Marco, his computer is still a powerful bargaining tool with the Nephretians, which, in turn, will also make it a powerful bargaining tool with you Kalbarians."

"I hate being dispensable," Marco muttered, mostly to himself.

Suddenly, Ariadne sat straight up in alarm. "Oipho!" she whispered sharply under her breath. Marco knew the word was an Alathian swear, though he had never learned what the precise meaning was. "Something's wrong. Get down!"

Marco was trying to clear the fog from his mind to identify the source of her concern when a whispered thud echoed through the forest and shards of wood splintered from a nearby tree. He knew this sound well—it was a vanesti gun discharging, signaling they were under attack by Ullrionis. One of the Alathian guards flanking them in the undergrowth was flung to the ground, and another's arm was ripped open. He dropped screaming to his knees, and was dead in a moment, a victim to the insidious nature of the vanesti gun.

Ariadne and the remaining Alathians drew their weapons and fired blindly into the woods. Alathian weapons were also silenced, firing without a hint of sound—not even a whisper of wind. Marco and Taura dove for cover behind a tree as shadows darted about.

Marco's heart raced and the familiar fear of battle gripped him as he desperately tried to see who was shooting at them. Are they trying to save me or kill me, Marco wondered. He could see none of the soldiers and only the muted whispers of bullets whisking through the air was heard, punctuated with the screams of wounded and shredding of undergrowth.

"Can you see what's happening here with your ocular implants, Taura?" Marco asked in a loud whisper as the forest around them came alive as Ullrionis and Alathians battled.

Taura was already looking around with her eyes of marbled blue. "I've counted about twenty Alathians in the woods surrounding us. They've been our silent shadow since last night. The Ullrionis, I can't get a strong fix on." Marco could only see shadows move as the firefight raged on in near silence.

Taura moved to the fallen Alathian escorts and took their weapons. They were sleek and small—easily concealable—and shaped like daggers. She tossed one to Marco, "I'm better at detecting the Ullrionis than you, so I'll fire at them. You take out any Alathians you see," Taura ordered.

"Wait, we need the Alathians to clear the dithrace from our system!"

"If we even have any dithrace in our system," Taura retorted. "Just shoot anything that's not me." Taura turned and began firing into the forest. Within moments, however, the battle began to slow and the only people Marco could see were Taura, Ariadne and himself.

A shocked gasp escaped Taura's mouth as a large group of Ullrionis melted out of the dense foliage, weapons bared on the three remaining fugitives. Marco scanned the dozens of guns pointing at them and raised his hands in surrender. Taura and Ariadne followed suit.

Crashing through the bush behind the Ullrionis, a Nephretian officer emerged wearing green fatigues. The outline of the phoenix rising from the flames was stitched over his chest, its color slightly offset from the remainder of the uniform, allowing it to be seen only under close observation. His skin was the tan red of indigenous Nephretians, and his hair cut military short.

The officer smiled, wiping the perspiration from his face with the back of his sleeve. "The Fist will be pleased. I will be rewarded well for your return," he pointed to Marco

"I guess cowering behind a tree while your Ullrioni thugs do your dirty work paid off, then," he replied.

The officer glared at Marco. The nictitating membrane of his eye, common to all natural born Nephretians, flicked closed then open. "However," he continued, "the women are of no consequence." With that, he drew his own weapon and prepared to shoot Taura and Ariadne.

The whispered shot of a vanesti gun cut through the woods, followed by a muffled thud as a gaping wound appeared in the Nephretian's chest. He stood, staring at the expanding circle of red staining his chest in silent amazement, swayed, then collapsed. Before his body hit the ground, a volley of whispered shots cut the air, tearing through the ranks of the Ullrionis surrounding them. Those Ullrionis still standing quickly dissolved into the forest canopy. Once more, the woods came alive with the sound of hushed combat, punctuated by the grunts and screams of the wounded and dying. Marco, Taura, and Ariadne dropped to the ground and picked up their weapons once more.

"What's going on out there, Taura?" Marco asked.

Straining to see into the surrounding foliage, Taura shook her head, "It looks like the Ullrionis are fighting each other."

"This is insane," Marco exclaimed as a stream of vanesti bullets tore into a nearby tree, "there's a war going on that I can't even see!"

The ground trembled as a dull rumble rolled through the rain forest, violently shaking trees and bushes. A cacophony of human screams and moans immediately followed. Within moments, there was a second such explosion, followed by a third. Leaves from the

surrounding forest began to rain down. The sound of vanesti
gunfire increased in intensity. The shadowy distortion of figures
wearing the lorillien cloak came into view. Marco thought he could
see their weapons extending in front of them, firing into the forest
at some unseen enemy. They were gone before he could find his
own weapon and bring it to bear. Now, as Marco was looking into
the forest, it seemed alive with such shadowy visual distortions as
the combatants fought.

After several intense moments, silence fell upon the woods.
A group of five Ullrionis melted out of the surrounding forest,
crouched low to the ground, eyes nervously darting about.
Ariadne, Taura and Marco pointed their weapons tensely upon
the intruders.

"Come with us," hissed one of the Ullrionis in heavily
accented Seedtongue.

"I don't think so," snapped Taura, pointing her weapon
directly at the speaker.

"We are enemies of the Nephretians," the Ullrioni whispered
tensely, "and this is not our land, so if you don't come quickly, we
may not be able to save you."

"Can you cure dithrace poisoning?" Marco interjected.

"Probably," came the reply.

Moving to the five Ullrionis Marco whispered to Taura,
"Good enough for me." Taura and Ariadne followed suit.

The Ullrionis began handing out camouflaged lorillien cloaks
when Taura pointed her weapon to Ariadne's head, "Where do you
think you're going?"

Staring at the barrel of Taura's gun, Ariadne swallowed
deeply, and then replied, "We have the computer, Captain.
Wherever Marco goes, I go." Taura did not waver. The Ullrionis
and Marco stared at the two, the Ullrionis fading into the forest
canopy as they donned the hoods of their lorillien cloaks. "I'm not
the bad guy here, Captain," Ariadne bargained. "I'm the one that
rescued you from the Nephretians."

"Actually, that was me," Marco corrected. Ariadne glared at
him. "Don't give me that look," he protested. "Technically, I did
save Taura." Now Taura also turned to stare at Marco. Looking
from one woman to the other, Marco cleared his throat, then put
his cloak's hood over his head and faded into the background.

Taura turned once more to Ariadne, "Hand over your weapon. Consider yourself my prisoner—or consider yourself dead."

Slowly, Ariadne handed Taura her gun. Taura scanned her prisoner, flipping through the various wavelengths of light that her eyes afforded her, searching for concealed weapons. She found two of them. One was a monofilament blade hidden up Ariadne's sleeve; the other was a standard issue Alathian handgun shaped like a dagger strapped to her abdomen under her shirt. "All of your weapons," Taura commanded.

Ariadne raised an eyebrow in consternation. At that moment, a wounded soldier moaned in pain, distracting the captain. In a flash, Ariadne batted Taura's gun aside. Before Taura could strike back, Ariadne activated the camouflage of her Alathian fatigues and disappeared into the dense undergrowth of the forest. Taura grabbed her gun and shot wildly into the foliage where she last saw Ariadne.

Marco's voice spoke from the forest canopy beside her, "She's gone, Taura. We have other places to be—let the Ullrionis deal with her."

With a grunt of anger, Taura put her hood on, and then she too, disappeared into her surroundings.

* * *

Fatigue crushed both Marco and Taura as their journey continued under the guidance of the Ullrionis. Ariadne had followed the troop discretely for a while, but the Ullrioni escort in an attempt to capture her had scared her away into the forest and she had not been seen for hours.

The last stimulants the Alathian captors had given Marco wore off long ago, and he found himself supported by his hosts frequently as the last vestiges of his strength gave way. Looking over at the captain, she didn't seem to be doing much better.

Despite this, Marco found the sensation of his lorillien cloak cool and refreshing. The garment clung tightly to his body and seemed to slip through the forest's undergrowth, never once snagging on a branch or thorn. More importantly, it was amazing at keeping the insects at bay. He remembered being told that the living cloak actually fed off the insects that were unfortunate enough to land on it. A damp rain had begun, though the trees of the forest filtered out most of the precipitation except for a fine mist.

Marco had difficulty keeping track of the guides. The faint distortion of the lorillien cloaks required a keen eye to see. More than once, one of their Ullrioni guards had to tap him on the shoulder and guide him back to the correct path.

After what seemed like an eternity of trudging through the foliage, they came upon a clearing where a number of people were camped. Their escorts were removing the hood from their heads effectively turning off the camouflaged cloaks they wore.

Their guide's leader turned to them and said, "You're safe here. You may rest."

Taura slumped into a clear patch of ground and immediately passed out. Marco staggered to the base of a tree, and then followed Taura's example.

Chapter 13

Dawn found Lieutenant-Commander Victor and Lieutenant Kaeso alone in the rain forest. They had desperately tried to rescue the captain, but their night had seen extreme violence that left them lost and the remaining Kalbarian soldiers dead. The Nephretian weapons they had stolen from their guards in the prison had long since run out of ammunition. However, Victor had acquired one of the Ullrioni's vanesti guns, and he had it drawn and ready. In addition, he had come by a Nephretian dagger that was currently tucked in his boot. Kaeso had two Alathian pistols. He held one in his hand as he made his way through the woods; the other was tucked into the back of his trousers. On the verge of dehydration, they risked drinking from marshy pools they found as they marched.

The two, surrounded by clouds of buzzing and stinging insects, cautiously followed a trail that appeared to have recently been cut through dense undergrowth. At mid-morning, just as the humidity was becoming unbearable, the sky opened up and rain began to fall. The canopy of trees prevented much of the precipitation from reaching the two soldiers making their way through the forest, though a light mist permeated the air. They came upon an area of the woods that had been forcibly cleared where the rain fell in a downpour. Victor was the first to notice an aircraft nearly invisible under camouflaged netting.

"It's Alathian," Victor stated. "It's standard Alathian practice to have a number of escape vessels around their areas of operations."

Moving to the craft, Kaeso commented, "If I can bypass the locking mechanism on the door, we can get in and get away from here."

Victor grabbed Kaeso by the shoulder. "Give your head a shake, boy. The Alathians have no doubt rigged this thing to blow if we so much as look at it the wrong way. And, if you get past the booby-traps, where you planning that we get away to? The Novafire's gone, leaving only Alathian and Nephretian battle cruisers circling the skies above."

Kaeso, blushing slightly under the rebuke, asked, "What's your plan, sir?"

"I figure the Alathians had something to do with the captain's escape. We'll take up positions in the surrounding woods. Some Alathian is bound to come along for this ship, and when they do, we'll persuade 'em to help us find the captain," Victor said with a smile that Kaeso found quite intimidating.

"What if it's not an Alathian that finds this ship, sir? Nephretians and Ullrionis know there's an Alathian presence here and will be looking for them," Kaeso asked.

"Then we'll improvise, boy. Now quit yer bitchin' and get in the bush, keep your damn mouth shut and your eyes open. And keep looking in the infrared—if anyone shows up in those Fate-blasted lorillien cloaks, we got a better chance of seeing 'em in the IR than in visible wavelengths. If anyone shows up, you stay in the bush and let me do the talking. Y'got that?"

"Yes sir," Kaeso crisply replied,

The two entered the surrounding forest, camouflaged themselves as best they could with the foliage and waited. The humidity soaked their clothes and dripped in their eyes. The day wore on.

Late in the day, as the sun was beginning to set, their patience was rewarded. Kaeso noticed a figure approaching the aircraft. They were wearing sophisticated camouflage clothing rendering them almost invisible in normal light. But their movements could be vaguely observed in the infrared as they stalked through the forest. However, given the ambient temperature it was difficult to get a clear image—if the person had not been moving, it may have been impossible to distinguish their heat signature from background heat sources. Aiming at the person as they moved to the craft, Kaeso tightened his grip on the weapon he was holding and waited.

With a loud grunt, Victor pounced out of the surrounding bushes and tackled the person as they approached the craft. In moments Victor incapacitated the person and deactivated their cloaking device. Kaeso could see that the person was a woman with short brown hair and dark eyes, which stared up defiantly at Victor who happened to have his gun pointed in her face.

"So," Victor growled, "who might you be, lass?"

"I am Colonel Ariadne Maleina. Who are you, Kalbarian?" she replied with a scowl.

Victor, shaking her, snapped, "You're in no position to ask questions, Colonel. Where's Captain Taura?"

"Who?" Ariadne asked.

Kaeso was watching the interrogation unfold from his hiding place when he felt a cold hard object—a gun he assumed—placed at the back of his neck. His heart skipped a beat. He slowly raised his hands and his weapon was taken from him by an unseen captor. Kaeso looked at Victor, who was still questioning his prisoner. Lacking the physical prowess of his compatriots, Kaeso lived in fear of letting his fellow soldiers down and had long ago resolved to do whatever was in his power to ensure he was not the one who caused his brothers and sisters-in-arms to suffer. Squeezing his eyes shut, Kaeso screamed, "Ambush!" He waited a moment, expecting his head to explode from being shot by whoever was holding a gun to him. However, the person guarding him only cursed softly in a language Kaeso was unfamiliar with.

Victor, after Kaeso's warning, had leapt up, dragging Ariadne with him. He was moving so that his back was to the camouflaged Alathian lander and was wielding Ariadne as a shield with his weapon defensively pointing at the surrounding woods. Although Ariadne was somewhat taller than Victor, with his massive strength Victor was able to manhandle her as though she weighed no more than a handful of the leaves carpeting the forest floor.

When nothing immediately happened, Victor called out, "Lieutenant, report."

In reply, over a dozen figures appeared from the surrounding forest. They were Ullrioni, all wearing lorillien cloaks, and all with vanesti guns pointing at Victor. Kaeso, too, was led out into the clearing, a weapon still pressed against the back of his neck.

Victor, eyes darting over the group of Ullrionis surrounding him, finally lowered his weapon and cursed violently, stirring a flock of birds to take flight over the trees of the rain forest.

* * *

Marco awoke more refreshed then he ever remembered feeling. He inhaled, feeling like it was the first time he had breathed in his life. He was staring up at the sky, which was a vibrant blue spotted with wisps of white clouds framed by the dark green of the forests that surrounded him. The trees seemed impossibly tall reaching hundreds of feet above him.

He noticed his left hand was cold and wet. Looking down, he was surprised to see his arm was encapsulated with a reddish brown membrane. Instinctual fear crept up his chest to his throat. However, he was feeling no pain—just the opposite, in fact.

Kneeling beside him was a woman, apparently monitoring the strange membrane enveloping his arm. She was wearing one of the lorillien cloaks with the hood down, which seemed to deactivate the camouflage. When the cloaks were not camouflaged, they were a dark green, almost brown color. Her hair was a striking red and flowed like silk. Her face was smooth and pale, her eyes a startling pewter. She seemed preoccupied with her work.

"Good day," Marco spoke in Seedtongue, interrupting her ministrations.

The woman looked at Marco and smiled. "Good day," she replied in a thick accent unlike any Marco had heard before.

Barely maintaining the look of calm on his face as he looked down on the strange fixture on his arm, Marco asked, "So, uh … what are you doing to me?"

"Right now, I'm removing toxins from your blood stream," she replied as she turned her gaze back to the encapsulating membrane on his arm.

That would be the Alathian's poisonous dithrace, Marco thought. Looking down at his arm he continued, "Right. And how are you going about doing that?"

A thoughtful expression fell upon the woman's brow as she struggled to find the words. Finally she replied in her enchanting accent, "Well, this membrane," she began indicating the substance on Marco's arm, "works like your liver, which, as you may know, detoxifies your blood. This membrane is orders of magnitude more efficient than your liver, and, of course, placing a liver on your arm would do absolutely nothing for you, so there are some obvious differences."

Marco looked at the membrane in puzzlement, "Is this derived from one of the creatures of this planet, like your ponchos and weapons?"

"Well," the woman responded as she cocked her head to the side, "only if you consider humans to be one of the creatures of this planet."

"This is from a human!"

"The base genetic code is," the woman said. "The analogy with the liver was not entirely inadvertent. This was originally engineered from a human liver, but it's been highly modified, as you can see."

Marco looked at the woman, a little more uncomfortable then he had been a moment before. "Is it alive?"

"No. It doesn't reproduce, nor can it sustain itself. It's a tool made of biological counterparts, no more alive than the thigh bones that one of humanity's ancient ancestors fashioned as a club to go hunting with."

"But it's made out of cells. If you don't nourish it, it'll die."

She thought deeply for a moment, and then continued, "Let me ask you this. If you cut yourself and your blood falls on the ground, is your spilt blood alive? Does it have a living force that gives it animation?"

"No, not really," Marco replied.

"I agree with you," the woman said. "Without you, that spilt blood is nothing more than an assortment of biological machines which will mindlessly perform their task to the best of their ability until their energy supply is exhausted, at which point they decay and expire. So, now what happens if I come along, take some of that blood and place it in a nutrient bath in the proper environment such that those cells don't die? Have these cells suddenly obtained a living force simply because I've provided the substrate they need to function?"

"That's a tough one," Marco said.

A smile formed on her lips. "In all honesty, I agree with you. We still have debates about such matters. Personally, I see living things as a collection of a whole. An assortment of fabric and buttons does not make a shirt until they are all properly assembled," she said, tugging at his torn clothes. "In the same way, I believe you are greater than your parts. Your liver isn't you; your blood cells aren't you. You don't become you until enough of those parts are assembled into a functioning system."

"Dust and ashes, you are one of the most interesting people I've met in the past couple of days." He flashed her his charmer's smile as he sat up. "Already then, how about this. If you had my cells in a nutrient bath, they'd divide, reproducing like bacteria, right? And, they respond individually to stimuli, don't they? Aren't those qualities of living things?"

"There are those of Ullrion that hold to that tenet. They are called Grand Synergists. They maintain, as you suggest, that every cell of our body is an individual living entity, and that only through a co-operation—or a synergy—between all these living entities are greater life forms such as humans, or any other creature, created."

"In other words, I'm simply a colony of trillions of self-organizing entities."

"Basically, yes," the woman said. "If you extend that philosophy, then we humans, and perhaps the living systems we exist in, are also part of a greater whole. Me, I'm more of a Gestaltist."

"A Gestaltist?" Marco asked.

"Yes. I believe a living entity is composed of its parts. A critical number of these parts—or biological tools—are required for an entity to be considered alive. Blood, by itself, is not alive. Same with your femur, or your baby finger. Only once enough of the components are together do you have a living thing."

"Speaking of living things, will I be remaining one for the foreseeable future?"

"Yes, your blood's almost completely detoxified, and we've repaired the wear and tear the past couple of days has had on your system," the woman replied as she began to peel the membrane off Marco's arm. It slipped off like a wet glove and snapped into a small ball once fully removed. "Your companion's over there," she added pointing to a group of people on the other side of the clearing. Marco could see Taura amongst them.

"Thanks. I'm Marco, by the way," he said, extending his hand with a confident smile.

After a pause, she shook his hand. "I'm Maralan."

"Smashing," he replied, not breaking their hand shake. "I'd like to learn more about you. Maybe if you're still around later we can pick up our conversation."

Maralan looked at him thoughtfully for a moment before replying, "Maybe." With a smile, she turned and left.

Marco stood up, brushing himself off. He looked about the camp. A large number of Ullrionis were present, each absorbed in the work they were doing. They all wore the lorillien cloaks that constantly amazed Marco, although none of them (that he could see) were camouflaged presently.

The Ullrionis, from what he observed, were a slender and delicate looking people with fair skin. They moved with grace and fluidity. Hair color amongst them ranged from a luxurious black to pure white, even though none of them appeared to be particularly old. All of them grew their hair long—the men to their shoulders, the women, well past their shoulders in braids. Their eyes ranged from blue to green to brown and were strikingly intense. As a community, these people seemed to be very much at home in these forests. They glided through the foliage, barely disturbing it as they passed. They were a part of the land, rather than existing within it.

He made his way to Taura, who was just finishing removing the locks on her augmented arm with the help of an Ullrioni. She greeted him with a smile.

"How are you today, Captain?" Marco asked.

"Very well, and yourself, Mr. da Riva?"

"Surprisingly good, considering I still don't have any Vernian coffee. Have you made any friends, yet?"

"None who will tell me anything of importance."

"You Kalbarians are so practical in the acquaintances you choose," Marco replied

"We'll have to work on that," she said, raising an eyebrow. "It sounds like a special envoy will be arriving soon to greet us. Perhaps he'll be able to help."

"Another politician? Did you tell them we already spoke with Kan Rath?"

"It seems that the Ullrionis don't have a united government. Our rescuers call themselves the Uvonesti. Apparently Kan Rath and the group associated with the Nephretians are called Duraanesti."

"Well, if we don't have a space ship, and they don't have space flight, then we're still in a world of problems," Marco said.

"The Kalbarian government'll be sending in reinforcements soon," Taura replied.

"And until then, I offer you our hospitality," came a third voice. Accompanying the voice was a man who effortlessly drifted out of the surrounding foliage. He was of medium height, slightly taller than the other Ullrionis in the camp, but still noticeably shorter than Marco and only slightly taller than Taura. He held himself with the bearing and grace of nobility with a hint of arrogance in his angular face that seemed to come to a point at his aquiline nose. However, his smile seemed genuinely friendly. His hair was bright blonde grown to his shoulders and his eyes were the deep blue of the ocean and almond shaped. As with every Ullrioni Marco had seen, he appeared to be in his twenties.

The man was accompanied by a creature that reminded Marco of a young dog. He scratched its head and spoke to it in a language Marco didn't understand, after which it ran off and was lost within the bustle of the camp. Turning once again to Taura and Marco, the stranger said, "My apologies, I did not mean to eavesdrop. Please allow me to introduce myself. I am Silmion Qualanthus of the Uvonesti. I have been authorized by the Elder to initiate relations with you and your people."

Turning to meet him, Taura said, "I'm Lucia Salonious Taura, Captain of the Kalbarian Ship Novafire. This is Mr. Marco da Riva."

Silmion continued, "I'm afraid we must cut our introductions short. Although we are within our realm, we are not safe here."

"Before we go, I have soldiers here that were captured by the Duraanesti and their allies, the Nephretians. They might've escaped when the Alathians broke us out of camp. I can't leave them here," Taura said.

"Based on reports from our scouts, I believe your soldiers may have escaped though I don't know their current whereabouts. I assure you, if an opportunity arises, we will attempt to rescue them even though we risk all-out war doing so. For now, we are close to the Duraanesti border and risk recapture. We will fly you and Mr. da Riva to Selfariene."

"Selfariene?" Marco asked.

"Fly?" Taura inquired.

"Yes, Selfariene—it's the capital city of Uvonesti. By flight, we should arrive there tomorrow."

"A city!" Taura exclaimed, "We detected no city on this planet."

At this, Silmion smiled. "Come, you shall see."

Chapter 14

As impressed with Ullrioni technology as Marco was, nothing prepared him for their mode of transportation. The encampment had gathered in a clearing, the center of which was dominated by large winged creatures. Two humans could sit quite comfortable upon their backs and indeed something like a saddle clung to their body just above where the wings met their muscular torso. The creature's feathers were a golden red and seemed to scintillate with a life of their own. While on the ground they walked on four muscular legs. Their faces ended in curved beaks that Marco suspected were capable of cracking a human's leg. Their eyes were golden and struck Marco as being filled with self-assurance and dignity. A mane of dark red or more rarely black feathers ran from their foreheads to shoulder blades and their bodies tapered to a tail of crimson feathers. While on the ground their wings were folded compactly along their flanks. One of the creatures lazily reared back on its hind legs and stretched its wings to their full breadth of nearly four meters.

Silmion saw Marco's gaze as the yawning creature folded its wings along its flank and plopped down to all fours again. "Despite their rather formidable wingspan, they possess great agility," Silmion said. "You see they have joints along their wings. In flight, they can reduce their wingspan almost in half. They can't do much more than glide when they do, but it allows them to maneuver their way with ease through thick foliage. Of course, they usually fly above the forest where they can soar at amazing speeds."

"What are they?" Marco asked.

"We call them dalinroghs," Silmion replied.

"Man, I know some people who'd pay good money to have one of these guys in their stable," Marco said, his trader's sense piqued.

One of the saddles noticeably repositioned itself on its mount, prompting Taura to comment, "Those saddles are alive. What are they?"

"They're saddles," Silmion said with a shrug. "Once you sit in them, they'll encapsulate your body, holding you to the back of the dalinrogh and protecting you from the elements such as wind, rain and so on. There's a swivel joint between the seat and the appendages attaching it to the body of the dalinrogh that allows the rider maximum mobility. You can even turn around and face backwards while remaining firmly attached to the creature in flight."

Marco noticed that as Silmion talked, he became filled with a quiet animation that reminded Marco of his mother when she'd begin lecturing on something of interest to her.

He looked leerily at the thin appendages that held the saddle in place. "Is it safe?" Marco asked.

"Of course it's safe! We've dallied enough here. We ride!" With that, Silmion strode forward to the beasts. He tapped the saddle and an appendage that was clasped around the torso of the dalinrogh unwrapped and lowered to the ground extending a small flat platform upon which Silmion placed his foot. Almost immediately, the saddle engulfed his leg as it lifted him up the dalinrogh's flank. Once his waist was level with the creatures back, he kicked his free leg over, and the saddle enclosed around it, too, wrapping up to shoulders and down his arms. An appendage slithered around the dalinrogh's torso securing the saddle with Silmion in place.

Taura mimicked Silmion with another dalinrogh and was quickly secure in the saddle and testing out her available range of motion. The saddle did not appear to restrict her at all.

Marco said quietly so no one could hear, "This is weird," and moved to a dalinrogh. The giant creature turned its head to him, trilled softly and clacked its beak together several times. "Listen, bird," Marco whispered as he tapped the saddle the way he had seen Silmion do, "I don't need any more attitude today." The saddle encapsulated his leg. It felt soft and warm and possessed a gentle, yet unyielding strength as it lifted him up the side of his dalinrogh that was presently trilling to another dalinrogh beside it who responded by clacking its beak. All the dalinroghs in the clearing trilled softly, some shaking their heads flaring the feathers in their mane.

Marco looked at Silmion and pointed at his dalinrogh. "They better not be making fun of me."

Silmion smiled and the arrogance in his face evaporated. "Your beast is called Windracer, Marco. You'll like him—he's fast."

Marco patted his dalinrogh as the saddle enclosed his other leg and wrapped about his body. "Fast, eh? Maybe we'll get along okay then." Marco leaned closer to the beast's head and whispered, "Just so long as you're faster than that crippled mare Silmion's on."

There were only enough dalinroghs for the three of them plus four Ullrioni escorts. The remainder of the camp would make their own way to their nearest base. Maralan, the Ullrioni medic that had first tended to Marco, settled in on another dalinrogh securing her supplies to the back of her ride and gave him a wink. Marco smiled and waved back, careful not to lose his balance. Taura held both legs out and with a quick movement spun around to face backwards.

"Wrong way. Do they really let you pilot a ship back home?" Marco said with a playful smile. Taura turned her eyes of marbled blue on Marco and stared stoically at him until the smile left his face and he turned to study his saddle intently while muttering something inaudible about Kalbarian's sense of humor.

Once everyone was settled, Silmion addressed the group. "I understand it was Kan Rath of the Duraanesti who brokered your capture thereby solidifying their alliance with the Nephretians. He's an ambitious man, but has been out of favor in the Duraanesti court for some time. I suspect this alliance was to be his political redemption. Your escape will not sit well with him. We must be on our guard. I wish we could spare more dalinrogh riders, but this border has not warranted much guarding for a great while and so our forces are deployed elsewhere. You must accept my apologies, but we will use speed and stealth to protect you."

"Kan Rath is greedy, but you don't think he'd risk bringing his nation to war against the Uvonesti again by striking so deep in our lands, do you?" Maralan asked.

"With a nation from the stars as allies, they shall do more than risk war—they'll court it. And Kan Rath is smart enough to know that the Duraanesti must strike in concert with the Nephretians before we can cement an alliance of our own with emissaries from the stars." Silmion directed this last statement at Taura. "We linger here too long. Fly!"

With a shrill roar the dalinroghs leapt into the air, and in no more than two mighty flaps of their wings, the beasts cleared the top of the forest canopy, a height of dozens of meters, and were streaking their way across the sky.

As they rose, the saddles encapsulated the riders' heads, forming a helmet. A smile cracked Marco's mouth as he stared through the visor of the helmet. He was stunned to note that when he stared at an area intently, the visor would magnify his field of view as a pair of binoculars might.

Silmion's voice sounded in their helmets. "You'll notice we can communicate with one another clearly."

"Wait, Silmion," Taura said, clutching tightly to her dalinrogh, "how do you control these beasts?"

"It's not about control, Captain," Silmion answered, "these are creatures as are you. You are an extension of them, your will an extension of theirs."

"Thanks for being so … precise."

Marco was oblivious to the conversation. His teeth were bared in a grin that stretched across his face as he leaned over Windracer, the two skimming over the treetops, the world flashing by in a green blur below. The uppermost leaves of the trees rustled and the branches swayed in their wake.

* * *

That night the group camped underneath the forest canopy. Although during flight above the trees, the sun was able to beat down on the group with its full fury, the saddles helped maintain a comfortable body temperature. To free oneself from the saddle, a bulbous projection in front of the rider was squeezed and the saddle would release the individual and set them upon the ground in the reverse of the process with which they were seated.

Marco watched the Ullrionis setting up camp. The dalinroghs were contentedly feeding from nearby foliage and drinking from mossy glades. Glowing bulbs were placed around the clearing's perimeter and an opaque awning was being raised above the camp at Silmion's order. Apparently he had received a report of rain from his communicator and the purpose of the awning was to keep the group dry. The communicator was made of biological components—nervous tissue instead of wires. Silmion had told Marco the receiver was modeled after the eardrum, although it was obviously highly modified and more versatile than a set of eardrums and could be tuned to different frequencies. A nerve plexus translated the received signal into sound, transmitted through membranes within the compact device.

Of more interest to Marco was Ullrioni computers. Marco prided himself that there was not a computer system developed by a seedship colony he could not crack. The founding principles of Ullrioni computer technology were those of other seedship civilizations. However, their hardware was one of biological tissues. Based on conversations with Maralan, Marco learned that somehow the Ullrionis had developed enzymatic pathways serving as ion traps controlling the qubits used to achieve quantum computation. Marco did not read Ullrioni, and so was not able to understand the user interface to manipulate the computer. Instead, Maralan showed him how to open the creature so that Marco could observe and try to make sense of the hardware. He was having difficulty determining which strand of tissue or cartilage performed the basic computer functions he was familiar with.

Marco's legs were painfully stiff from an entire day of dalinrogh riding, and he had felt the need to stretch. So, he left the computer alone and took a walk through the camp.

The woods were alive. Nearby, animals called and screamed. The perpetual twilight of the forest floor was darkening to night and the awning over Marco's head was awash in the soft light of the glowing bulbs. Apparently these orbs were similar to fireflies, familiar to many worlds, only modified to be larger, more robust, more efficient and less prone to flying away. The Ullrioni would turn them on with a tap of the hand. Marco also noticed that they seemed to attract the hordes of flying insects away from the inhabitants of the camp, for which he was grateful. Meanwhile, the lorillien cloak he was given to wear protected him from the overwhelming heat and humidity. Ullrioni hospitality made their time in the rain forest almost pleasant.

Thunder rolled in the distance and the sounds of the forest continued unabated. Marco approached Taura and Silmion, who appeared to be arguing. Maralan had joined them and offered Marco a drink as he sat down. The beverage was cool and tasted like citrus fruit. He was immediately warm inside and felt ever so slightly light-headed as some narcotic in the drink worked on his mind. Marco had yet to meet a culture where you could not find something to alter your mental state—an interesting facet of human psychology, he had always thought.

Silmion was saying, "Oh, come now, can't you see that unlike you we don't live at the expense of the world." Marco groaned to himself, but sat down to listen to the two.

"What the Fates do you mean 'unlike us?'" Taura asked. Marco noticed she was speaking quite angrily.

"What I mean to say is, I suspect your people live through the consumption of your world."

"Yeah, how do you figure?" Taura crossed her arms across her chest and stared daggers at Silmion.

"Does your society feed itself through advanced agricultural technologies, Captain?"

"Of course."

"And I suppose that your home world of Kalbarai had conveniently evolved such that land was neatly set out with whatever grains you grow, to the exclusion of all else just for your eating pleasure," Silmion said.

"Of course not. Farmers work the land."

"Right, they till the soil, poison weeds and keep pests at bay. They do everything in their power with the technology your society has at hand to ensure that only one species survives and thrives in their field—the species they want to grow. A monospecies ecosystem is unnatural. Living systems—true living systems—depend on diversity. How many ecosystems have your people utterly annihilated so that farmers have land to till? How many forests cut back? How many species pushed to the brink of extinction? You don't consider destroying the diversity of the land so that you can enslave entire ecosystems to suit your needs to be living at the expense of the planet?"

"Whereas you live by corrupting nature around you. Do you truly believe your way is better? Rather than destroying, you twist. You make that which was natural, unnatural," Taura said, the heat rising in her voice.

"You think it's better to destroy biological systems for your survival than to change it?" Silmion retorted.

"But these are living things you are playing with. Life feeds on life—it is natural to destroy in order to live. As brutal as it sounds, that's nature's way and every creature out in that forest knows it," Taura said pointing to the darkness outside their camp.

"Natural?" Silmion replied. "Hardly! Humanity's crime is we survive too well. We have the base instincts of an animal. To, as you say, feed on life. But our intelligence gives us such an unfair advantage that if left unchecked we unbalance nature. We become what our people call dranaqi—a disrupter of Selestari, or, how do you say in Seedtongue ... the Cycle. The only way we as a species can endure is by bringing ourselves into balance with nature, and we cannot do that by tearing down the life around us."

"Oh, but you can by twisting it?"

Marco cleared his throat. Slowly, all eyes turned to him. "If you ever looked at our physical bodies, you'd have to agree we're poorly adapted to survive anywhere—embarrassingly so. Naked," he turned to Maralan with a wink, "and in our natural form, we can only stand a narrow band of temperatures. There are few things we can outrun, and fewer still we can outfight. Yet here we are," he continued, spreading his arms, "surviving in every climate imaginable. Why? Because our greatest survival advantage is the ability to change the environment to one in which we can thrive.

"From arctic realms to arid deserts, we pick up sticks and rocks and fashion them to the tools we need to survive wherever we are. Tiny microcosms of clothes to keep the cold away—and rain. Who wants to get wet anyway?" Marco said pointing to the awning which was beginning to hammer out a tattoo as the clouds above opened up with a drenching downpour.

Marco leaned forward conspiratorially, looking over his shoulder to the forest before whispering, "That's our secret. There are so few places in this universe we can survive, so we change wherever we are to become a place where we not only survive— we thrive. Your farmers do it, Taura. So, too, do Silmion's biotechnicians. Silmion, your people are arrogant would-be masters of nature. Same with yours, Taura—and mine. Different methods, same goal—let's kill those beasts while they're far away and make sure we have food nearby. If it's not about twenty to thirty degrees Celsius, let's make sure there's someplace close that is. If you can't sleep because of all the chatter," Marco paused to stare at Silmion, then at Taura, "let's drink the juice of fermented fruits and vegetables until the part of our brain that cares is numbed. Maralan," Marco said turning to the red-haired Ullrioni, "pour me some more of that fire water."

Maralan chuckled and refilled Marco's cup from a canister she had at hand. Taking a swig, Marco asked her, "Is there a fun area of the camp you could show me?"

"The dalinrogh riders are always a hoot when they've been drinking. Follow me." With that, Maralan led Marco away into the camp.

* * *

Laughter erupted from the far side of the camp. Taura could hear Marco's voice above the ruckus. The smuggler had an innate ability to make friends, she thought while the rain hammered down on the awning above them.

Silmion and Taura returned to staring at one another.

"You should thank me, Captain," the Ullrioni said.

"Thank you, Silmion; it's been a long time since my culture's been insulted in such a manner."

"There are many of my people that feel the way I do. We have not been off our planet, and we have never interacted with a culture other than our own. You may find us somewhat, dare I say, conceited in our views." Taura suppressed a laugh. Silmion continued, "There are those in the Elder's council who will see your arm and your eyes and will not like what they see—it will offend their beliefs of what should be."

"You twist the forest's creatures into weapons, clothes, and computers and my metal arm offends you?"

"There is a sacredness to living things and the cycles of nature. We believe we live in accordance with Selestari—the great

Cycle. That arm and those eyes aren't living things. It represents a different view of how things should be. It will make negotiations with my people difficult."

"Perhaps the thought of Nephretian battle cruisers burning your planet from above will soften their views," Taura said.

"That is my hope. Otherwise, we are lost," he said. Focusing on Taura, he continued, "With your arrival on our planet, all that I know is changed forever. My culture will never be the same—it may die."

"Only the strong survive, Silmion, and everyone up there knows it," Taura said pointing to the stars above.

Smiling to himself, Silmion softly replied, "Foolish of me to expect sympathy from a woman with eyes of stone. Sleep well, Captain. If fate smiles, you shall stand before the Elder tomorrow."

Chapter 15

The next morning, Taura found Marco leaning against a fallen tree, his face as gray as the clouds above the rain forest, with head hung low and hair wet and limp. On his hand was the strange creature that Maralan had previously used to detoxify his blood. Taura looked at him from across the camp as the Uvonesti prepared for the day's travel. With a smile, she walked over to him.

"Mr. da Riva, I trust you slept well," she beamed at him, patting him roughly on the shoulder. Marco looked wretchedly up at her.

A smile stretched across his haggard face. "I had a wonderful night," he said, his voice a little more than a croak. "I think I made some meaningful cultural inroads."

"I'm sure Maralan agrees," Taura said. Marco tried to look offended, but managed to merely grimace. He hiccupped deeply, his body rocking with the sound. The detoxifying organ on his hand pulsated and shifted.

Taura sat down and commenced to eat her breakfast of rations offered by the Uvonesti.

"Their ale is potent," Marco commented. Taura grunted in reply as she noisily consumed her food. She offered him some, making sure he got a good smell of her rations. He pushed away the food with his free hand.

Silmion approached the two and bade them a good morning with a diplomatic smile. He sat down on the other side of Marco, "I trust you two slept well last night."

Taura replied, "We slept well, Silmion, thank you." Marco smiled weakly. Maralan arrived and began to check on the smuggler, who, in response, tried to sit up a little taller while straightening his hair.

"The Elder looks forward to meeting with you, Captain," Silmion continued, "I trust you are ready for the meeting."

"I am, Silmion. Do you have any advice?" Taura asked.

"The Elder is a good ruler. He cares for his people and takes his duty to protect them seriously. We are facing the greatest threat we have ever known with the alliance between our neighbors, the Duraanesti, and the Nephretians. He will do what he must to save our nation. Remember that when you speak to him."

Finishing her breakfast, Taura replied, "Thank you." Silmion smiled coolly, and then excused himself to see to the preparations of the day's travel.

Somehow, despite Marco's hangover, he had managed to make Maralan laugh. With a smile she gave him a drink from a pouch she was holding. Almost immediately his coloring improved. Maralan removed the detoxifying organ from Marco's hand and placed it in her pouch. She playfully touched the tip of his nose, winked, and left to finish preparing for the day. He smiled as he watched her leave.

Taura, eyebrow arched, turned to stare at Marco, who appeared to be feeling much better. Marco's smile vanished once he noticed Taura's glaring attention. "What?" he asked. Taura snorted, and then left to pack her belongings leaving Marco staring at her back, shaking his head.

* * *

Taura was slowly becoming accustomed to flying her dalinrogh. She was not very comfortable trusting herself to an animal, and the creature she rode seemed to sense it. Above the canopy of trees, the mighty beasts and riders soared. The sky was still heavy with clouds and rained poured down in sheets, though the saddles that enveloped their body protected them from the weather.

She looked over to see Marco flying beside her, noticing with envy that he seemed much more comfortable flying these creatures.

A ripple of trilling calls passed between the dalinroghs and the Ullrionis began signaling to each other. A lot of chatter erupted over the communications network transmitted through the saddle's helmet, but it was in a language Taura was unfamiliar with. With senses honed by years of military training, she felt the tension in the group as the outriders repositioned themselves to assume what the captain immediately recognized as defensive positions above and to the sides of Marco, Taura and Silmion.

Silently from the clouds above, other dalinroghs bearing riders gracefully dropped and attacked. The air was rent with the trilling screech of dalinroghs as battle erupted around Taura. The dalinroghs swirled and rose to attack as their riders fired at one another with larger, rifle-versions of the vanesti guns secured to their saddles. In a heartbeat, several dalinroghs with their riders from both attackers and defenders dropped into the forest in a twisting mass of feathers and bodies. The dalinroghs that Marco, Taura and Silmion rode began a stomach-churning dive to the woods below. The Captain held out her augmented arm and began its weapon transformation.

Her fingers melted together in a shimmering ripple. Then, her hand spiraled open like the bloom of a flower with petals black as night marked with stochastic veins of liquid crimson. Low-explosive quantum bolts fired from her arm. Two of the attacking dalinroghs and riders were torn to shreds and spiraled in a shower of flaming feathers and a haze of blood and gore into the woods below.

The targeting system of her weapon was slaved to her vision—where her eyes focused, the gun unerringly aimed. Three more attackers plummeted to their death from her fire before her dalinrogh dove into the cover of the forest. The dalinrogh's wings folded to half-size and the creature darted with unnerving speed and serpentine agility through the dense branches of the forest.

* * *

Marco's battle was progressing poorly. He had a small hand held vanesti gun he was firing at the enemy. However, it was difficult to aim the unfamiliar weapon, and its range was not optimal for the distances encountered in an aerial battle.

As his mount, Windracer, was diving for the cover of the forest, he felt the muscles of the beast shift underneath him and the trajectory of his flight change. Ahead, he saw an enemy dalinrogh dive at him, claws outstretched and beak open in a horrible roar.

The enemy rider was leaning over the shoulder of his dalinrogh and fired with a long-barreled weapon mounted on his saddle. Marco leaned into Windracer, who was screaming his own battle roar, and returned fire.

The two flying beasts slammed into each other with a force that jarred Marco and sent his weapon flying from his hand. Marco's saddle held him firmly in place as he flailed from the force of the impact. The dalinroghs spiraled uncontrolled, clawing each other and tearing with their beaks. Marco's heart pounded as they began to free-fall. He struggled to force air in his lungs as the tops of the trees of the forest below sped up towards them.

The other rider, more accustomed to such aerial combat maneuvers leaned over the shoulder of his mount and fired into Windracer. The shot tore through the beast's wing—it was only a matter of time before the beast died from the deadly effects of vanesti ammunition. Marco managed to catch his breath and yelled, "Luca damn you, I liked this mount!"

At the last possible moment before plunging into the forest, the dalinroghs separated. Still alive, Windracer dove into the cover of the woods slipping through the branches of the forest canopy. The enemy gave chase. Marco flattened himself along the back of his mount to keep from being hit from the outstretched branches of the trees and desperately clutched the beast's flanks. Windracer wavered, skimming a branch that knocked its balance off. The beast began to tilt as it smashed into another branch.

"Aw, come on, Windracer, hold on a bit longer," Marco said. But, the deadly efficiency of the vanesti gun had taken effect— Windracer was dead. The dalinrogh limply crashed through the branches while Marco clung to its neck.

With a sickening crunch, Windracer crashed into a tree branch as thick as a road. The branch did not give. Instead, it snapped the dalinroghs neck causing it to somersault head over tail through the canopy of trees. Branches thrashed Marco horribly during the crash to the forest floor, though his saddle encapsulating him offered significant protection. After a moment of free-fall that seemed to last impossibly long, the dead dalinrogh hit the ground and bounced. The force of the impact tore the saddle from the beast's back, sending Marco sailing wildly into a thick tangle of vines.

Marco, partially upside down, struggled to gasp air into his lungs. His body ached dully and the world swam before his eyes. However, the thick growth of the forest had slowed the decent of the dead dalinrogh and its rider to non-fatal speeds. Furthermore, the saddle, which now hung dead and bleeding from his body, took the brunt of damage as he fell through the forest canopy. As Marco carefully righted himself, he reflected that things could have gone much worse.

He struggled out of the dead saddle, which proved a difficult task. He stumbled and fell in his attempt. Rolling on the ground, he finally freed himself from its bondage. As he began to get up, he found himself looking at a pair of boots. Slowly, he gazed upward to see the face of Kan Rath staring down at him with an arrogant smile of triumph. He held a vanesti gun at Marco's head.

"Don't let me stop you, Mr. da Riva. Please, on your feet—slowly, keep your hands where I can see them." Marco complied. Once up, Marco stared down at Kan Rath. The Ullrioni's features were exquisitely chiseled and elegant as glass. His ice blue eyes stared up at Marco with satisfaction as he spoke, "Lord Hamu has offered a phenomenal reward for your capture."

Marco did not relish another encounter with the Fist of the High Prelate. However, he smiled a boyish grin and commented, "Naturally, he looks forward to questioning me."

"Yes, it appears you have some very valuable information." Kan Rath continued.

"Oh, so he wants me alive then?" Marco asked.

"Alive, yes; unharmed, optional," the Duraanesti ambassador replied.

Marco looked meaningfully down at Kan Rath's weapon, then up into Kan Rath's eyes. If he was wanted alive, then his captor would be unwilling to use the vanesti gun, Marco reasoned. Kan Rath smiled at Marco as if inviting an attack or attempt to escape. Marco was not an overly large man, but at almost six feet, he stood much taller than Kan Rath and outweighed him by quite a bit. Marco's boyish smile turned into a grimace of determination as he balled his hand into a fist and sent it cracking down into Kan Rath's smug face with all the force and momentum he possessed. An explosion of pain erupted in Marco's fist and shot up his arm.

Kan Rath used the momentum of Marco's blow to spin around and plant a kick solidly in Marco's abdomen. The force of the blow lifted Marco off his feet and sent him sailing through the air. Marco's right side slammed painfully into a tree, sending him spiraling wildly until he hit the ground. Marco's stomach convulsed and he vomited. Blood coated his mouth and lips and pooled on the ground in front of his face mixing with the contents his stomach just expelled. Marco struggled to draw in air, but he choked and sputtered as he collapsed to his side. His abdomen cramped into a ball of pain. Coughing and gasping in gurgling spasms, he shakily turned over to face Kan Rath who stood quite a distance away basking in self-satisfaction.

"You have overstepped your bounds, Kan Rath," a voice from the forest spoke. Kan Rath glared at the origin of the voice. Silmion stepped from the shadows to face the Duraanesti. Both men held their vanesti guns at one another.

"So," Kan Rath said, "The Scourge of Kulan once more shows his face. Need I remind you, Silmion, that it was you Uvonesti who first kidnapped these off-worlders from the protection of the Duraanesti?"

"From what I observed of their health, I'd say we rescued these emissaries from an aggressive nation corrupt with dreams of power," Silmion replied.

"I have more pressing matters to attend to than to listen to a political diatribe from a dranaqi such as you," Kan Rath said. He fired his weapon, but with lightning-quick reflexes, Silmion ducked and spun, using his momentum to kick the arm of Kan Rath bearing his weapon. Though the kick flung the arm wide, Kan Rath held onto his gun. The two were in close quarters and struck at each other with fists, knees and elbows, their movements a blur. In such close proximity to an enemy, the vanesti guns they held seemed to come to life and struck out like snakes snapping and spitting venomous bullets.

Marco watched the two battle. Both fought with grace and agility—there was a rhythm to their struggle and the two seemed engaged in a violent dance with the other. Marco looked around for a weapon. His gun was lost within the depths of the dense forest. He grabbed a branch that had snapped during his crash. He struggled to move closer to where Silmion and Kan Rath circled each other amidst a flurry of blows, their vanesti guns writhing and snapping at each other.

Marco's body was racked with pain and his breath came in short painful sputters. Without the protection of his lorillien cloak, he found himself immediately beset with the annoyance of insects settling upon his face and neck. Despite his pain he crawled and stumbled along.

Silmion and Kan Rath continued their fight without pause— each combatant was engaged in a flurry of leaps, spins, kicks and punches. Silmion saw Marco struggling towards them. He adjusted his attack to keep Kan Rath's back to Marco.

After what seemed a long time, Marco was on his hands and knees behind Kan Rath, struggling to breathe and collecting his strength to strike with the branch he held. Before he could attack, Silmion placed a powerful kick in Kan Rath's chest, causing him to stumble backwards, tripping over Marco and landing on his back.

Without a moment's hesitation, the supine Kan Rath kicked Marco in the flank with both feet, sending Marco flying towards the knees of Silmion. Silmion had anticipated the move and leapt over the flying form of Marco and landed with a knee to Kan Rath's chest and a fist to his face. Kan Rath, however, pounded his fists into either side of Silmion's ribs as he landed. Kan Rath bucked his body throwing Silmion off of him.

Both Silmion and Kan Rath stood up slowly, gasping painfully. Marco moaned on his back behind Silmion. A rustling in the trees caught the attention of both. Some of Silmion's mounted dalinrogh riders were darting through the forest overhead to his aid.

Kan Rath turned to Silmion. "It's a pity we won't be able to finish this now. Bringing Silmion Qualanthus, the Scourge of Kulan, to justice would have benefited my career immeasurably."

Silmion coolly replied, "Instead, you shall leave empty-handed. And you have directly attacked a member of the Uvonesti government on Uvonesti lands. No nation shall ally themselves with you this time."

"It is of no consequence." Kan Rath smiled arrogantly and said, "We have new allies now."

"You mean puppet-masters," Silmion said.

"The Nephretians are easily manipulated," Kan Rath said. "I don't think they have ever dealt with a people like ours." Kan Rath spared a quick glance at the fast approaching dalinrogh riders and said, "We shall meet again, Silmion, and when we do, your cities shall be in flames." With a quick motion he flipped the hood of his lorillien cloak to engage its camouflage ability and vanished into the undergrowth behind him.

* * *

Taura dismounted her dalinrogh and looked for Marco. She found him looking the worse for wear sitting against a massive tree. She walked over to him.

Seeing her approach, Marco smiled, "Hey, Captain. Kan Rath sends his regards." Marco flexed his right fist, which Taura noticed was swollen and bruised.

"I'm sure you gave him my best in my absence," Taura replied sitting down beside Marco.

"Right." Marco chuckled to himself, and then choked on his breath as he winced in pain. Once the pain had subsided, he continued, "Listen, Taura, it seems he and Silmion have made each other's acquaintance before. He accused Silmion of being a war criminal and kept calling him The Scourge of Kulan or some such."

"Sounds like the whining of a sore loser," she said.

"Maybe," Marco replied, "but there's some history here we don't know about. More than that, let me tell you, Kan Rath wasn't the first short little pretty-boy I've punched in the face, but usually after I slug 'em they drop like a wet sack. Look at this, Taura," Marco held up his swollen hand, "Maralan had to mend my bones in this hand. I cracked my knuckles on that runt's jaw! Then, in reply, he kicked me and sent me sailing. Maralan tells me I'll be passing bloody stool for days."

"Charming," Taura replied.

"Any rate, I suspect the Ullrionis have modified more than the world around them with their genetic manipulations. We'll be leaving for their 'city' of Selfariene shortly where you'll be negotiating for our wellbeing and safety. Just remember, these Ullrionis look pretty, but they're dangerous."

Chapter 16

Later that morning, when the sun was beginning to cut through a whimsical mist wrapping itself through the highest boughs of the forest, Marco, Taura, and their surviving Ullrioni escort led by Silmion flew over the outskirts of Selfariene. Marco had never seen anything so elegant and beautiful.

It was immediately apparent why the K.S. Novafire's preliminary scans detected no signs of a city, for Selfariene was grown from the very forest itself. Trees were shaped and fused together to create splendid structures, many the size of single family dwellings, others of immense berth stretching what would be several city blocks on a more mundane world. Numerous living spires and towers reached into the sky, piercing the otherwise even roof of the forest's canopy.

The city existed on many levels with paths winding through the floor of the forest, and wide bridges made from the living structures of the buildings themselves. These catwalks crossed and intertwined at multiple layers throughout the breathing metropolis. The city was awash with activity as countless Ullrionis went about their business. Many were on foot, bustling their way through the pathways and bridges of the city. As they flew overhead, Marco could see several dalinroghs darting through the buildings and between catwalks carrying riders. Other flying creatures of different shapes and sizes carrying passengers could also be observed. Along the ground Marco saw a variety of creatures and structures that roamed about, some at great speeds, each carrying riders or cargo.

Marco noticed some of the bridges seemed to be dedicated to human traffic while others were devoted to creatures that ferried the Ullrionis from one area of the city to another. A score of birds in the distance took off from their perch in the forest's canopy and flew towards the afternoon sun.

Silmion glided his dalinrogh between Marco's and Taura's. His voice sounded through their helmets. "Selfariene has stood for thousands of years. It is home to over a million people and is the capital of the Uvonesti. The Grand Ziggurat, our parliament building, lies ahead over there."

Silmion pointed to a structure in the distance rising out of the rain forest. It was a multi-tiered pyramid created by the joining of thousands of trees and other living forms. It was a mosaic of colors, including light browns, vibrant greens, bright reds and lively yellows. At each of the four corners of this structure stood helical columns stretching higher than the point of the main building. The top of these columns bloomed into large platforms that were a deep violet in color. Railed bridges sloped upwards from the peak of the pyramid to the platform at the top of each of the four columns.

As they approached they could see each tier of the pyramid was lined with people, as were the bridges and walkways surrounding the building.

"Your arrival has caused quite a sensation amongst our citizenry. Many have shown up to see our kindred of the stars," Silmion said.

"You got your we-come-in-peace speech ready?" Marco asked Taura. He was starting to feel excitement at their upcoming meeting. These were a people unlike any he had met before and he was eager to learn more about them.

"Being the only free Kalbarian in several light years has helped me polish it up," Taura replied.

"If you say something that upsets them, make sure they know I'm not with you."

"You kidding? I'm telling them if they want a piece of me, they've got to get through you."

Shortly, Silmion began to lead them down below the treetops and landed in a clearing before the immense parliament building. The great crowd stared silently at the visitors. In another civilization, the silence of such a crowd would have been unnerving. Here, however, the silence seemed bred more out of a respect for the privacy of Marco and Taura—an almost unwillingness of the mob to impose themselves. Marco scanned the faces of the crowd. Many wore expressions of curiosity, although some seemed filled with hope and others with distrust. He was surprised by how young everyone was. There did not appear to be anyone older than thirty in the gathering.

Marco looked at the parliament buildings and was amazed by how much larger it seemed now that he was on the ground looking up at it. He noticed a path lined with white and yellow flowers leading from the clearing where they had landed up to a set of stairs that ascended to an entrance set into the first tier of the building.

A woman appeared in the entrance. She's pretty, Marco thought. Her frame was slight, which was common for Ullrionis. With eyes of startling violet, her hair was a beautiful auburn that seemed to catch and magnify the sun's rays. It was grown long, well past her shoulders, and was kept in a simple braid. She, too, seemed to be in her twenties. She wore a light green dress that flowed to her ankles just above her delicate, sandal-clad feet.

Silmion walked towards her and indicated for Marco and Taura to follow. Once before her, Silmion made introductions, "Allow me to introduce Ashala Kulari, First Minister of the Uvonesti." Turning to the woman, he continued, "May I introduce Captain Lucia Taura of the Kalbarian Ship Novafire, and Mr. Marco da Riva." Marco flashed her a wink and a smile.

"Thank you ambassador," she said to Silmion. Then, turning to Marco and Taura, she added, "May I offer you the greetings of the Uvonesti people. We are honored by your arrival on Ullrion and deeply distressed by the attacks you have suffered while under our protection. Please allow me to lead you to our Elder, the head of the Uvonesti nation."

Despite her gracious words, Marco sensed tension in her voice and body language that suggested she was not entirely at ease. She turned and led them into the parliament.

Once inside, Marco was immediately struck with the immense size of the hallway they were lead through. Giant, dark tree trunks rose from the floor to a vaulted ceiling high above, which was decorated with red, green, and yellow vines intertwined in an elegant arabesque design. The walls were lined with ivy that glowed a soft white light illuminating the entire chamber in its sylvan glow. The floor underneath was solid, but soft to tread on and the air sweet, reminding Marco of over-ripe cherries and grapes.

Ashala led the party past a number of hallways that ran off to either side, bringing them to a large set of double doors grown into the wall at the end of the immense entrance hallway. As the group approached, the doors began to swing inward of their own accord allowing entrance to the area beyond.

Past the doors was a parliamentary chamber. The end of the room opposite the grand double doors was dominated by an elegant chair raised about three meters off the floor, seemingly grown out of the wall behind it. Railed stairs led to the seat, which was occupied by a male Ullrioni who appeared to be in his late thirties. His hair, straight and grown to his shoulders, was dark blond in color and marked by wisps of gray. With eyes the color of pewter he sat with a welcoming smile, intensely observing the party as they entered the room. He wore a dark tan colored suit with a light blue shirt underneath.

To either side of this man, the chamber was dominated by ascending tiers occupied by Ullrionis who sat at desks that seemed to flow from the very floor. Ashala led Taura and Marco to the center of the chamber and then moved to her own desk that was in the center of the first tier to the right of the man seated at the front of the room.

Before taking her seat, she announced in a voice that rang clearly through the chamber, "Elder Karlan Shoalbrau, I present Captain Lucia Taura of the Kalbarian Ship Novafire, and Mr. Marco da Riva."

Nodding, the Elder acknowledged in accented Seedtongue, "Thank you, Ashala." Then, spreading his arms in a gesture of greeting, he continued, "It is with pleasure that I welcome you travelers to Ullrion. My heart was filled with deep regret and shame when I heard about your treatment upon your arrival to our world. Although only a token of recompense considering how you have suffered, allow me to extend the hospitality of the Uvonesti people to you, our honored guests."

"Thanks for your offer. We don't fault you for our hard welcome," Taura said. Speak for yourself, Marco thought silently to himself. Taura continued. "Rather, we think another group of spacefarers, the Nephretians, to be the source of our troubles."

"Well spoken, Captain," the Elder replied. "If you are willing, I would like to discuss the Nephretians later. Now, however, what can you tell me of your people? Your appearance is quite unusual, although not in an unpleasant way, and I suspect your history to be an interesting one." Tones of real curiosity colored his voice as he spoke.

"I'm a Kalbarian," Taura began. "We're explorers by choice and warriors by necessity. Marcus Terentius Regulus, First of the Kalbarai, rules us. As for my appearance," she said raising her false arm of black obsidian marked by molten red inlay, "my people pride themselves on their mastery of technological forms and their artistry in blending the strengths of the living and the mechanical to create a new whole."

"They are ubarmein," Ashala said from her seat, seemingly unable to contain her distaste. Marco did not know the word "ubarmein," but the tone of the First Minister made it obvious it was insulting. Looking around, Marco could see by the faces of those present that Taura's explanation was not well received. The Elder's expression, however, was completely unreadable. Only a pleasant, welcoming smile was present upon his mien.

"Now, First Minister," the Elder chided Ashala, "I believe Captain Taura had the floor. Please, continue Captain."

Taura continued, though Marco could now sense a hint of nervous caution in her voice, as it was apparent not everyone in the audience was friendly. "To those as advanced in the tinkering of living systems as you are, I'm not surprised that there are those among you who would take offence to the merging of a human life with a lifeless machine. I can't change the morals of your culture, nor will I try."

"But yours is a warrior culture—'warriors by necessity,' so you say. Will you not simply attack our culture and destroy it as conquistadors of old?" the Elder said, leaning forward.

"We are warriors, yes," Taura replied. "We conquer our enemies, but we seek alliances with those who don't mean us harm."

"Alliances whose nature undoubtedly favors Kalbarai," Ashala said from her chair. Marco was starting to worry that this First Minister would sabotage any hope of help they might find on this planet.

Taura raised an eyebrow as she turned to the First Minister. "Of course. Why, do the Uvonesti make a habit of entering alliances where they suffer?"

"We certainly do not," Ashala replied.

"There are enough dangers that we don't feel the need to attract new ones. If a people prove themselves worthy of friendship, we'll fight to defend you. Otherwise, if you don't bother us, we won't bother you. In the face of greater threats such as the Holy Nephretian Empire and the Alathian Alliance, perpetual conquest is a drain on resources that only weakens us," Taura said.

"So," Ashala said, "if not for the Alathian Alliance and the Nephretian Empire, Kalbarai would engage freely in conquest."

"If the Alathians and the Nephretians didn't exist, then the politics of the universe we find ourselves in would be unrecognizably different. The reality is we are not here as conquers. The Nephretians are. The Kalbarian League would be willing to intervene militarily to protect the Uvonesti and any other Ullrioni state against aggression if you demonstrated you were willing to assist us in fighting them."

"Pleasant talk, Captain Taura, but I wonder how pleasantly your words would be if you had a fleet of your battleships hovering above our planet?" Ashala asked as she settled back in her chair.

Marco prided himself on being a fast-talker, and he was about to enter the debate, but Taura beat him to a reply. "I understand why you don't trust me. In your entire existence, you have never had contact with another human culture. Yet here you are, exposed to two—and ones who possess technologies you do not. One has already allied with your enemies, the other offers you their friendship, but you know nothing of them."

Taura turned to address the greater assembly in the room. "You're the leaders of the Uvonesti, and your decisions regarding who to trust will not only affect the safety and security of your people, but will also affect every nation on Ullrion. This isn't an enviable task since you don't have all the info you'll need to make an informed decision. Yet a decision you must make, and soon, as the Nephretian fleet could burn your cities from above at any moment."

That was a good speech, Marco had to concede.

At this point, Silmion stepped forward. "If I may address the assembly?"

"Of course," the Elder replied. "We are always interested to hear what the Hero of Kulan has to say." Marco's ears perked up at the epithet. Hadn't Kan Rath called Silmion the Scourge of Kulan?

Clearing his throat, Silmion began, his voice and manner one of unwavering confidence as he spoke in front of the most powerful people of his nation. "I believe Captain Taura is correct regarding the Nephretian threat. The Duraanesti have allied with the Nephretian Empire, and I don't think I need to convince this council of their desire for revenge and conquest. In my encounter with Kan Rath, he spoke openly of war against us with the aid of their Nephretian allies. Indeed, they brazenly invite war with their most recent attacks so deep in our lands, and they believe they will have the full military support of the Nephretians."

The Elder nodded and asked, "What is it the Nephretians want, Captain Taura?"

"They're religious slag-heads who believe humanity has been fragmented across the galaxy for our sins. They see it as their sacred mission to unite humankind and their divine right to rule over us. They are single-minded in the pursuit of their goal." Marco half expected her to spit at the end of her statement.

"No, Captain Taura, what is it the Nephretians want with you and your associate?"

Taura tensed imperceptibly. "We have information they require to find Earth."

At this comment a slight murmur wafted over the assembly hall. The Elder raised a hand and there was silence. He spoke with a whimsical smile. "They seek a path to the Garden of Eden, do they? We had heard reports that such was the case, but it is still shocking to have this verified by firsthand accounts. It is also our understanding, Captain Taura, that you acquired this information from a seedship that had recently landed in Duraanesti territory."

"We didn't know it was Duraanesti territory. Our instruments were not able to detect the unique nature of your civilization, so we thought the planet was uninhabited."

"Regardless," Ashala chimed in, "the Duraanesti will still claim you stole it, which could certainly undermine our position in forming a counter-alliance against the Duraanesti retaliation that is soon to come."

Marco decided it was time to enter the discussion. He cleared his throat and said, "If I may, I am the one who obtained this information. At the time, I was not operating under the direction of Captain Taura, or any other Kalbarian for that matter. It was actually the captain's intention to negotiate with the appropriate governments for the seedship data."

"And what inspired you to perform such an audacious act?" Ashala asked.

"Well, at the time I was actually being manipulated by an Alathian agent."

"Oh," replied Ashala in barely disguised mock belief, "an Alathian made you do it."

"Yeah, that's kind of how they operate."

"Would you be so kind as to show us this map to Earth?" Ashala asked.

Marco shrugged as he replied. "It's not as simple as that. The data was transferred to my computer, which was stolen by the Alathians. However, I was able to place a biometric lock on my files so that if anyone but me attempts to open them, they'll be destroyed."

"Is this data no longer available on the seedship computer?" the Elder asked.

Marco laughed nervously. "Funny thing about those seedship computers —"

"No need to elaborate," the Elder interrupted. With a cool smile, he continued speaking to the entire assembly hall. "We have treated our guests poorly. They are surely tired from their journey and wish to clean themselves and rest. We shall show you to your quarters where you may freshen up. Tonight, we'll have a banquet in your honor and, I trust, continue our discussions in a less formal setting."

A silence Marco found unnerving followed them as they were led from the chamber.

Chapter 17

Marco looked around the spacious hall, his eyes gazing over the tangled masses of politicians and people of note who mingled together. The floor was made of dark wood grown in place. The walls were lighter and lined with a fine interlacing of filaments that glowed softly, basking the room in a strange light. These luminescent filaments merged into the ceiling that consisted of a thick tangle of dark green leaves interspersed with vibrant brown and red patches. Evenly spaced glowing orbs floated high above the crowd, adding their light to the vast space. There were wide patio windows spread across one side of the hall opening onto balconies overlooking the lights of the living city in the forest below. The patio doors were open, allowing a gentle breeze to animate the soft, silky curtains hanging to either side of the entrances. The air was comfortably cool and carried the faint scent of crushed leaves. Melodious music heavy with passion and energy coursed through the hall. A floor filled with couples that danced with grace and joy to the music dominated the center of the room.

Marco held a glass of the same strange ale he had drunk the night before in the forest. He sipped at his drink parsimoniously, remembering the potency of the liqueur. He swirled it in his glass and enjoyed his moment of solitude in the crowd. There had been no shortage of people wishing to speak with him. Indeed, he had quite enjoyed his conversation with an attractive and engaging young woman who punctuated most of her sentences with a quick touch on his arm or chest. It did not take long, however, for her husband—a very serious and aloof young man—to introduce himself before whisking her away to meet some 'important people.' Thus, the ebb and flow of mingling had left Marco a moment without company.

Although able to casually fit into any social situation, he never felt more alone than he did in a group of people. Years of drifting without a home had left him with a trail of broken relationship and stunted friendships. He did not yearn for solitude, but felt at home nowhere.

Taking a deep sip from his drink, he noted Taura had just arrived and was presently by an entrance to a balcony a short distance away. She wore a red dress whose shade reminded him of autumn leaves. The gown flowed down the curves of her body and was cut at an angle such that one side of the dress reached down to her ankle whereas the other side rested slightly above the knee barely concealing the muscles of her leg. Marco's gaze lingered on her obsidian arm marked with scarlet details in arabesque patterns as he marveled at how naturally it moved and conformed to her body.

A small crowd of Ullrioni statesmen surrounded her. They were awkward, some trying too hard not to stare at her arm, others unable to look away, none able to make contact with her eyes of marbled blue and white. Taura carried herself with poise, though her smile seemed forced.

Marco began to navigate his way through the sea of people to her with a rakish grin. He had cut his beard quite short and trimmed it such that it framed his strong jaw. He wore loose fitting brown pants with a shirt of the same color that hung past his knees. Marco towered over most of the men and women in the room and carried himself with a casual confidence. Taura, smiling warmly, maintained eye contact with him as he approached.

Marco excused his way past the group of politicians that fluttered about Taura. He softly placed his hand in the small of her back while saying by way of introduction, "Taura, you don't look very captain-ish this evening."

"You, however, look every bit the rogue," she quickly retorted.

"A rogue!" Marco exclaimed. "I'll have you know that I spent a lot of time getting ready this evening."

"It's your girlishly-long hair," Taura replied, indicating his dark hair combed past his collar. "There's a good barber back on the Novafire who'd have you looking respectable in no time."

Marco withdrew his hand from Taura's back and smiled. "Respectable isn't the look I'm going for."

Before Taura could reply, the crowd parted as The Elder, Karlan Shoalbrau, approached. He was wearing a black suit in the same style as Marco's. Following closely was Silmion dressed in pure white. He said, "The two of you look refreshed. Did you find everything you needed?"

"A shot of coffee'd hit the spot," Marco replied.

"Your hospitality has been most gracious," Taura said before anyone could reply to Marco.

The Elder smiled, and then said, "I have pressing news. We have received word that Nephretian envoys shall arrive tomorrow to demand that we hand you and Mr. da Riva over to them."

Marco felt ill.

"I have been giving your position a lot of thought," the Elder continued. "As ruler of the Uvonesti, I would like to state plainly that we are far more interested in pursuing relations with the Kalbarian League than the Nephretians. However, we cannot protect you from an attack by the Nephretians—indeed there is no place on this planet where you will be safe. Although I am confident we could repel a ground-based assault, we simply haven't the technology to defend against an orbital offensive. Your presence on our lands invites a Nephretian attack, and I doubt they'll accommodate our desire to wait until your fleet has arrived, Captain. Therefore, as Elder of my people, it behooves me to get you off our land as soon as possible."

Marco wanted nothing more than to fade into anonymity, as he had so many times before after a big job. But, he was now the key to the next phase of a power struggle between empires intent on each other's destruction, and he knew each member of the Triumvirate would hound him to the end of known space. Yet, not a trace of distress touched his face as he casually sipped his drink. Years as a smuggler had taught him to hide his emotions well.

The Elder continued, "However, a situation has presented itself, which, even though you may not find it ideal, is our best hope at satisfying all concerned parties. I have at my disposal the means to get you off our planet, thereby redirecting the animosity of the Holy Nephretian Empire away from us long enough, hopefully, for your fleet to arrive."

"How exactly are you planning on getting us off the planet?" Marco asked.

"Just you be leaving that to ol' Vic," came a voice from behind Marco and Taura. The two turned to see Lieutenant-Commander Quintilus Victor, a grin cracking his grizzled old face. Although immense in size, Victor was quite a bit shorter than Marco and it was obvious the Ullrioni hosts had difficulty finding clothes that fit him. His pants were dark, his shirt light blue, and both strained against his bulk. Marco was sure one flex of Victor's Herculean muscles would tear the garments.

Beside Victor stood Lieutenant Procyon Kaeso, who was somber and austere in appearance. His clothes were dark and his manner reserved, although he did permit himself a welcoming smile as he was reunited with his captain.

As for Taura, she could not suppress the smile that spread across her face. Marco had to take a second look at her, for she looked beautiful as happiness lit up her features. Taura composed herself, and then addressed her troops. "Lieutenant-Commander Victor, Lieutenant Kaeso, I should have expected it would take more than the might of the Nephretians and Duraanesti to keep you two at bay. And do I hear correctly that you have a ship?"

"Aye, Captain," Victor replied, "just a little something we picked up on the way."

Taura asked, "What of my other troops?"

Both Victor and Kaeso's expression turned grave at the question. It was Victor that replied, "Sadly, Captain, 'tis only the lieutenant and I that made it to stand before you now."

The captain's smile faded and her eyes, mechanical orbs that they were, were ladened with sadness. "I see."

"If it's any solace, Captain, they all died on their feet giving the bloody Nephretians cause for regret—they took more than they gave," Victor said.

Taura's smile returned somewhat, although it was overshadowed with hurt. "Well, I'm glad you two made it."

Marco cleared his throat and, addressing the Elder, spoke into the ensuing silence. "Elder, you said we wouldn't find your plan 'ideal.' What's the hitch?"

A woman Marco had not noticed standing beside him replied, "I'm afraid I'm the 'hitch.'" Marco turned to look at the woman. She was slender with short brown hair and dark eyes. Wearing a simple black gown, she was, all in all, rather plain looking. He recognized her immediately as the Alathian who had orchestrated their escape from the Nephretian camp.

"Marco," the Elder continued, "I understand that you have already made the acquaintance of Colonel Ariadne Maleina."

Marco was the first to recover from his shock at seeing Ariadne there before them. "Colonel?" he asked. "During our rescue, I thought you said you were a Sergeant Major. That's quite a promotion."

"You must have misheard me," Ariadne demurred.

"Of course." Marco was quite certain he hadn't misheard her.

Ariadne smiled and turned to the rest of the group. "My ship is nearby, and her engines are warm and ready to leave at a moment's notice."

"That's clever, Elder," Marco said, "you win a reprieve from the Nephretians and cozy up to both the Alathians and Kalbarians without really picking any sides."

Clearing his throat, the Elder continued, "It is not our intention to abandon you to your enemy, Captain. I am sending one of our most esteemed countrymen to journey with you. Silmion shall be by your side every step of the way, and I am charging him with your safety until this mess with the seedship can be sorted out."

Ignoring Ariadne, Taura turned to Silmion. "I am glad to have you as a traveling companion."

Silmion stepped forward and bowed his head to Marco and Taura, "It is my honor to journey with you. As they say in my tongue, dal lai Selestari klasien os. It translates roughly as 'until the Cycle breaks us,' and is a statement of fealty."

"Thanks, Silmion. You, however, are another matter." Taura turned on Ariadne. "Despite what you may claim, you tried to kidnap us and then poisoned us to get what you want. I am not stupid enough to trust my troops to your 'hospitality.'"

Ariadne smiled in a conciliatory manner while replying, "You're right, Captain. I haven't supplied you with reason to trust me. Nevertheless, the Elder is correct. Your presence here endangers this planet. No government here will want to protect you, and most would turn you over to the Nephretians in a heartbeat. There is no Kalbarian fleet hovering over the planet to save you, and the Alathian presence here is not strong enough to repel the Nephretians. Once you've left Ullrion, the Uvonesti can tell the Nephretians that you escaped with the aid of Alathian spies, redirecting their animosity until a more formidable defense against the Nephretians has been established. No one here shall grant you sanctuary. No one, that is, except me."

"I have no intention of becoming a 'refugee' seeking asylum with the Alathians and Fates take me if I let you get the directions to earth," Taura replied.

"We already possess the directions, Captain. It is the key to unlock them we are in need of," Ariadne said, looking meaningfully at Marco. "Think of our assistance as a sign of good will—a prelude to fruitful negotiations between the Kalbarian and Alathian people."

"Only the desperate negotiate with Alathians."

Marco exclaimed, "I'm feeling a hint of desperation! This job has been a whole lot more than I bargained for. I'm not Alathian, Kalbarian, or Nephretian and as far as I'm concerned, you're all as bad as the other. You've all bashed one another to the point of ruin, and taken many a good world with you." Marco had to pause to keep the rage in his heart under control with his last comment, the flames of his family home flickering through his mind. "If you wish to fight and bicker about who did what when as an excuse to resume your stupid war, have at it. I, for one, am leaving on the first ship out of here. And frankly, Taura, you need to work with the Alathians—they have my computer with the coordinates on it."

Taura leveled a hard stare at Marco for several moments. After some thought, she turned to Victor. "Lieutenant-Commander, could I have a few words with you in private?"

"Aye, Captain," Victor replied, and the two stepped away. Marco exchanged his empty glass with a fresh drink from a waiter carrying a tray of glasses filled with a sparkling, crimson liquid.

Ariadne broke the silence with what appeared to Marco as schoolgirl shyness. "You're looking well, Marco."

"Well," he said with a shrug, "I've been getting a lot of fresh air lately."

Ariadne laughed softly. "By the way, Marco, I must compliment you on the locking mechanism you have on your computer. It's ingenious. Our technicians are petrified of tampering with it for fear of destroying it. It's completely novel. Where did you obtain such a device?"

Marco looked doubtfully at Ariadne. "You don't really expect me to tell you, do you?"

Once more, Ariadne laughed softly. "I would have some serious explaining to do to my superiors if I didn't try."

At that moment, Taura returned with Victor. She asked, "Marco, I assume you can fly an Alathian lander?"

"Of course, don't be insulting," Marco replied distractedly. He just noticed Maralan in the room, her striking red hair a perfect complement to her violet dress. She was walking about, looking for a conversation to enter. After a moment, she noticed him and their eyes held for a number of heartbeats. A smile spread on Marco's lips.

"Good. Marco, you'll be flying us out," Taura continued. "Lieutenant-Commander."

"Aye, Captain."

"I am placing Ariadne in your custody. Make sure she stays out of trouble."

"Aye-aye," Victor replied.

The captain turned to Ariadne. "Once we're safe, we'll commence negotiations between Kalbarai and Alathia regarding the information obtained in the seedship."

Smiling politely, Ariadne replied, "You wish to take me prisoner in my own ship. Your hand isn't that strong, Captain."

The sound of rending fabric caught their attention as the sleeves on Victor's tunic tore while his muscles bulged and the designs under his skin writhed to life, glowing a dark red. He said, "I'd not be so sure of that."

Taura placed a calming hand on his monstrous shoulder. "We're not taking you prisoner, Colonel. We each have something the other needs. I'm just making sure we have an even playing field for the negotiations."

Ariadne thought about it a moment, then replied pleasantly, "Certainly, Captain."

"Good," Taura continued, "we must hurry. We'll meet outside this hall in an hour and leave from there. Will that give everyone enough time to prepare?"

Marco thought about it for a moment. Maralan had begun conversing with a small knot of people, but her gaze continued to drift to Marco. He replied, "It'll do." Another future broken relationship, Marco mused darkly though his smile never wavered. "Now, if you'll please excuse me, I think we all have a lot of work to do and a very short time to do it." With that, Marco put on his charmer's mask and began navigating his way through the crowded room to Maralan.

Chapter 18

Ariadne sat impatiently in a hallway outside the ballroom where the festivities in honor of the Kalbarians and Marco were still ongoing. Victor stood like a statue across from her with arms crossed, never taking his eyes off of her. Kaeso sat by him on a nearby bench, quiet and introspective. Taura had left to prepare for the journey and Marco had disappeared with Maralan.

That Marco was out of her sight irked her considerably. If she lost him it would only be a matter of time before she found a knife in her back. The last number of years had been dangerous for her. She had risen quickly through the military with the help of her powerful father's patronage. However, his standing in Alathia's political assembly dropped considerably about six years ago and her mother found herself in prison under mysterious circumstances. With her family wounded, Ariadne had to fight the many enemies her rapid rise had created alone.

She had been stationed on Deurgal, managing standard counter-insurgency operations when she first learnt of Marco. He had escaped her then, but Ariadne had painstakingly tracked him down. Strange the paths Sor T'van's Lies wander, for Marco's trail had allowed her to steal the path to Earth—perhaps the most significant discovery since Alathia first reached out into space and made contact with other seedship colonies. That Alathia teetered on the brink of ruin made the finding all the more critical. And now Marco, the key to unlocking the path, was no doubt bedding some floozy.

He was an exceptional smuggler, having slipped through the Alathian blockade on Deurgal—both to get onto the planet, and once again when fleeing. That he was out of eyeshot drove Ariadne to distraction with anxiety.

Acting as though the thought just occurred to her, she asked Victor, "Do you think it wise to let Marco out of our sights? He is rather important."

"Where's he gonna go? Nothing but trees out there," Victor replied.

Foolish brute, Ariadne thought. Victor was a ball of muscle, incapable of understanding the resourcefulness of someone like Marco. Rather than convince him Marco might successfully flee, she tried a different tact. "I'm not so much worried about him escaping as someone doing something to him."

"The only one doing anything to him is that woman, and I don't think Marco'll mind too much." The smile on his face suggested Victor was pleased with his crass humor.

Ariadne pandered to his ego by chuckling at his bawdy quip, but persisted. "The Ullrionis don't speak with one voice. Anyone afraid the Nephretians will attack regardless of whether or not Marco is here might find him an appealing peace offering. Perhaps we should find him."

Victor was obviously troubled by her logic, but his soldier's instincts took over—as they do for all brutes faced with complex choices. He said, "You're staying right there, and I'm staying right here. Now keep quiet before I decide to gag you."

Ariadne kept quiet, certain the troubling seed of doubt she had planted in the soldier's mind would start to sprout.

More time passed, and finally Taura returned. The first words out of Victor's mouth were, "Marco not with you?"

"No, why?" Taura asked.

"Any Ullrionis wanting to make friends with the Nephretians might figure Marco's the way to do it," Victor replied gruffly. "Maybe we ought to track him down."

Ariadne smiled inwardly to herself. Brutes were so easy to manipulate.

Taura looked thoughtful. "Good point. Kaeso, go find Marco."

Kaeso snapped to attention and saluted before leaving.

* * *

Dust and ashes, Marco cursed to himself. How was he to know Maralan had an over-protective father? And her father had come looking for her at a most inopportune time, Marco mused as he quickly walked down a hallway, shirt and shoes in hand. And he had been quite angry to the point of violence. Marco's hand still throbbed from his fight with Kan Rath, so he didn't covet a fight with another Ullrioni, so he had fled. Maralan had delayed her father long enough for Marco to make a hurried getaway.

He quickly ducked around a corner and put on his shirt. He was hopping on one foot putting on his shoes when he spotted Kaeso. Marco hissed and waved to get his attention.

"Mr. da Riva," Kaeso greeted, "there you are."

"Enough small talk," Marco replied, looking up and down the corridor, "we need to get out of here before the Nephretians arrive. Is everyone ready?"

"Yes," Kaeso said as Marco brushed past him. He turned and tried to keep up with Marco, who was walking at a near jog.

Before long, they came across the rest of the group who had been joined by Silmion. "Maralan sad to see you go?" Victor asked with a knowing smile.

"Yes, she was quite distraught," Marco replied.

Before he could continue, Taura interrupted, "You're wearing that?"

Marco looked down. He was still wearing the fine evening wear he had worn at the ball. "Yes, well, my old clothes smell like Nephretian." Turning to Ariadne, he continued, "Say, I heard you had a ship. Should we go? You know—before the Nephretians get here." Looking over his shoulder he moved on past the group, not waiting for a reply.

Victor chuckled, grabbed Ariadne by the arm and followed him. The rest fell in behind.

* * *

As he piloted Ariadne's ship through the upper atmosphere of Ullrion, Marco found himself trying to decide if he liked Silmion. The Ullrioni was cordial enough, though haughty. He seemed intelligent, though he enjoyed showing his intelligence off to others more frequently than Marco liked. To his people, he was the Hero of Kulan, yet his enemies called him a war criminal. And what was the word Kan Rath had used to insult Silmion—dranaqi? Hadn't Silmion himself said that was someone who unbalanced nature?

He looked over to Silmion sitting in the co-pilot's seat. Marco didn't need any help flying the craft, and since this was Silmion's first trip into space, Taura offered the co-pilot's seat to him. Silmion stared out the observation window intently with his almond-shaped eyes as the blue of the atmosphere started to give way to the blackness of space. He took in the scene with a composed, stoic nature. His eyes widened and a quiet gasp escaped his lips, though, as Marco rotated the craft upside down so that they could view the vibrant green and blue orb from space. Clouds drifted lazily hundreds of kilometers below.

"Few things more beautiful than seeing one's home from afar," Marco commented.

Silmion, regaining his composure, sat back and replied, "Indeed."

A prolonged silence fell over the two. It was Silmion who broke it. "Marco, perhaps you could help me understand these cultures my people have found themselves entangled with."

"Sure. What can I tell you?"

"Well, I think I've got a pretty good sense on the Nephretians. They seem to worship a number of gods, the main one being Amahté, right."

"Yep. They figure Amahté kicked us out of house and home for misbehaving. Only once we redeem ourselves will we be shown the way back."

"Right. What about the Kalbarians?"

"The Kalbarians figure that whatever god created the universe doesn't care anymore and left the ruling of things to his servants, the Fates. It was a particularly nasty Fate called Fangere that stumbled on Earth and destroyed it. Because we were too weak, we couldn't defend it, and the last remnants of humanity created the seedships to escape extinction. If I remember my Kalbarian lore correctly, I seem to think they believe another Fate whose name escapes me helped humankind escape, and won't let us find the way back until we're strong enough to defend ourselves from Fangere."

"That explains why in every other sentence the Kalbarians are asking the Fates to damn something," Silmion commented. "And the Alathians?"

"Ah, the Alathians believe creation is guided by spirits. Some spirits—I think they call them torpiliko—seek the destruction of all things and others, the dimiourgos, are all about the law and order of things. It was a torpiliko they call Sor T'van the Liar who swindled humanity out of Earth."

"And what do you believe, Marco?"

"Me? I don't think we have a gods damned clue why the creators of the seedships did what they did or what makes the universe tick, but we humans need to feel we're part of some grand narrative, so we make stuff up so we feel important and answer any questions that aren't spelled out for us."

A light flashed on the console in front of Marco. "Good," he muttered, before Silmion could follow up on his questioning, "that should do it."

Marco called to the back of the ship, "Taura, I've got us in orbit around Ullrion. Near as I can tell, we've managed to avoid detection from the Nephretians."

"You'll address me as Captain," Taura replied, moving forward to the bridge.

"You ain't my captain," Marco muttered.

The Kalbarians with Ariadne had been sitting in a cramped mess hall behind the bridge during the flight up. Ariadne sat demurely in a chair. Opposite her, Victor sat with his hulking arms crossed. Kaeso was studiously exploring the Alathian ship's computer systems.

Ignoring Marco's remark, Taura asked, "Do the Alathians know we're about?"

"I don't think so. I've disabled their transponder and have set up a block of any outgoing messages from this ship, but who knows with Alathians."

Taura grunted in reply.

"So where to?" Marco asked.

"Can this ship make it to Kalbarian space?" Taura asked in reply.

"You'll risk detection running the Nephretian blockade," Ariadne interjected. "Our cruiser is closer and better able to evade detection."

"Victor, take the prisoner to the cargo hold," Taura ordered.

"Aye, Captain."

"We have Marco's computer, Captain," Ariadne said as Victor dragged her from the mess hall as if she were no heavier than a doll. "It's only a matter of time before we hack into it."

"Not bloody likely," Marco replied.

Any further remonstrations by Ariadne faded out of earshot as Victor hauled her away.

"You know, she has a point," Marco opined once Ariadne had left.

"About what?" Taura asked.

"The Alathians have my computer," Marco replied. Silmion and Taura stared at him. "I'd like it back. A quick little smash and grab and we'd be off with it."

Taura stared at him incredulously. "You want us to sneak onto an Alathian cruiser and 'smash and grab' your computer away from them? Do you know how many troops an Alathian cruiser carries?"

"What are you worried about, we have two Kalbarians."

"Three Kalbarians," Kaeso corrected from the mess hall.

"Three Kalbarians," Marco continued, "and Silmion here is pretty good in a fight, aren't you Silmion?"

"I am excellent in a fight," Silmion responded, "but I am not authorized to initiate hostilities against Alathia."

Marco leaned in conspiratorially to Taura. "Drop him in the middle of an Alathian cruiser, he'll fight."

Taura was becoming agitated at Marco's badgering. She asked, "Have you thought about how we'd find your computer? Cruisers are big ships."

"Taura," Marco replied, feigning insult, "of course I've thought about that. I have a plan." Marco cast a suspicious gaze on Silmion, "Perhaps we should talk in private so as not to upset Silmion's fence sitting."

* * *

Once more, Ariadne found herself staring at the massive bulk of Victor. Patience, she thought to herself. She had Marco. All she had to do now was wait and an opportunity would present itself to get him onto the nearby Alathian cruiser. Then, they would have all they needed to rule the Nephretians and bring Kalbarai to its knees.

Her thoughts were interrupted by an argument brewing in the fore of the ship.

"Are you insane or just stupid!" Taura yelled.

Marco replied in a cool, level voice. "I think if you considered my plan rationally for a moment you'd see the merits of—"

"Merits?" Taura interrupted. "Merits? Forget it, Marco. This is what we're going to do. Victor!"

"Aye, Captain," the lieutenant-commander replied.

"Get that Alathian over here."

"Aye-aye." Victor got up and grabbed Ariadne's arm with one of his meaty hands. She was helpless against his strength, and so she did not resist. Within moments, Victor manhandled Ariadne into the mess area where Taura and Marco stood. Kaeso and Silmion entered as well.

"Ariadne," the captain stated.

Rubbing her arm where Victor had grabbed her, Ariadne replied, "Yes, Captain."

"Marco is going to pilot us to a safe location on Ullrion," Taura said, glaring at Marco as he began to interrupt. He thought better of it and kept quiet. Taura continued, "You, me, and Silmion will get off. Marco will pilot the lander away with the rest of my men, at which point you'll call your cruiser to pick us up. Then, Silmion will broker negotiations between us as we discuss what to do about the computer you have and Marco, who we have. That is, if you're willing to act as mediator, Silmion."

"I would be pleased to do so, if you feel this is wise," he replied.

Marco interjected, "So I'm a piece of meat to be bartered over then, am I?"

"Hold your tongue, boy, unless you want ol' Vic to hold it for you," Victor said.

Marco threw his hands up in exasperation, but remained quiet.

Ariadne was filled with suspicion—a familiar emotion to her. Her plain brown eyes narrowed slightly as she stated, "I am surprised you're willing to negotiate with Alathia, Captain. Kalbarians aren't known for their trust. Wasn't it you who said only the desperate negotiate with Alathians?"

"You dare talk to me of trust," Taura said. The blue in her marbled eyes was blazing. "If Alathians had any honor, you would find us far more willing to talk with you."

"Our word is our bond, Captain," Ariadne replied.

"Your word is dust."

Silmion spoke with a calm, yet forceful voice. "In the spirit of negotiation, I think it best if we all keep our opinions to ourselves and focus on the issue at hand."

Still smoldering, Taura forcibly calmed herself. "Fine. Marco, take us down to the surface. Silmion, help him find a safe, uninhabited place to land."

Marco was about to argue, but he bit back his words when he saw Victor, massive arms crossed across his barrel chest, glowering up at him. "Fine," he managed to bite out before turning to leave for the bridge. Silmion followed.

Ariadne took this all in, looking for the deception. She could find none in Marco, and only saw anger in Taura. The captain's plan did not neatly fit Ariadne's needs, but it was a step in the right direction. Once she had Taura aboard the Alathian cruiser, it would only be a matter of time before Ariadne could reel in Marco.

"Kaeso," Taura ordered.

"Yes, Captain."

"Take Ariadne to the aft of the ship and make sure she doesn't get into trouble. I have some instructions to give Victor before we land."

"Yes, Captain," Kaeso said with a salute.

As she was being escorted out, Ariadne overheard the captain say, "Lieutenant-Commander."

"Aye," Victor replied.

"This is what I want you to do …"

Chapter 19

The A.S. Semissalis was an Alathian cruiser, shaped like a dagger, slicing through the darkness. It was as black as the dark void of space and reflected no light—a ghost unseen until you were in its grasp.

Ariadne led Taura and Silmion down the corridor of the shadowy cruiser. The ship was a maze of walkways, designed to confound would-be invaders with their byzantine meanderings. The halls were empty, giving the appearance that the ship was abandoned save for Taura, Silmion, and Ariadne herself.

This, of course, was illusion. Their every step was monitored, and they were shadowed by squads of soldiers in adjoining halls, as well as ahead and behind them.

Ariadne's thoughts were troubled, although her plain face betrayed none of her concerns. She did not trust Taura's intentions, yet could not see the trap. Ariadne's position in the military hierarchy was tenuous, and much of her time now was spent fending off her enemies. Stealing the seedship's coordinates to Earth out from under the nose of both Nephreti and Kalbarai would have attracted the attention, and protection, of very powerful patrons. Losing those coordinates now would destroy her. The game was in play and she was, quite literally, fighting for her life.

Ariadne led Taura and Silmion into a meeting room. The room was empty except for a table, three chairs, and Marco's portable computer.

"There it is," Ariadne said, pointing to the computer. "This is what it's all about."

Of course that was not true. The computer was a replica. Marco's actual computer was in another section of the ship where technicians worked at this moment to undermine his security system.

"I don't know what you hope to accomplish with negotiations, Captain," Ariadne said after she had taken her seat. "It is only a matter of time before we crack Marco's locking mechanism."

"I think we both know what'll happen to you if one of your monkeys triggers Marco's self-destruct program," Taura replied with a smile that failed to touch her eyes. "Cut the slag and stop pretending I have nothing to offer having Marco guarded by two of my men, and start negotiating."

With a smile that also failed to touch her eyes, Ariadne replied, "As you wish."

* * *

"So, what is it that we're doing here?" Kaeso asked.

"Skulking about like thieves is what," Victor replied. Victor was a man of action whose temperament was not well suited for stealthy ventures.

"The Alathians stole my computer," Marco interjected. "We're just getting it back is all."

The three stood alone in a dimly lit storage room on the same Alathian cruiser where Taura and Ariadne had begun negotiations. Two unconscious Alathian soldiers lay in a crumpled heap on the floor by their feet. Marco was working at a computer interface imbedded in the wall by the entryway. Kaeso and Victor stood guard, armed with Alathian weapons they had acquired from Ariadne's ship.

"Be that as it may, this seems overly risky," Kaeso said.

"It ain't for you to question the captain's plan, lieutenant," Victor admonished.

Straightening, Kaeso snapped back, "Aye-aye, sir."

"It was my plan, point of fact," Marco said as he concentrated on attaching wires from a data pad device he had inserted into the computer terminal on which he was working.

Victor slowly looked at Marco, grizzled eyebrow raised. "Slag, is that true?"

"Indeed it is," Marco replied as he continued to work on the hastily constructed interface with the Alathian computer he was working on.

The hulking lieutenant-commander commented, "I don't know. Seemed to me she wasn't impressed with whatever your plan was."

"That was for show," Marco said. "I've found the best way to get what you want from an Alathian is to deceive them."

"I've found the best way is to take whatever you want from their corpse," Victor rebutted. Marco ignored the retort as he continued his work. Victor was not sure how, but somehow Marco had been able to navigate their lander to the Alathian cruiser without detection. He never would have thought it possible. Then, to his amazement, Marco softly docked the lander on the underside of the massive cruiser by a worker's hatch. They had been able to enter and make it to this room unmolested except for the two soldiers, and Victor had been able to deal with them easily enough.

"I can't believe we've got so far undetected. How is it you're able to do all this, Marco?" Victor asked.

Marco seemed genuinely surprised that someone would pose such a question. He replied, "This is what I do."

"He's a thief and a smuggler," Kaeso said.

Marco's anger began rising as he said, "Your stupid war has destroyed any honorable commerce. The only thing that's been traded for a decade now is weapons and munitions. And such cargo requires a certain amount of … deftness to deliver sometimes."

"Shut up, the both of you," Victor ordered. "Are you almost done there, Marco?"

"Just about. I need to log into their system now, and they have a biometric scan. Help me get one of these guys up so I can scan his retina," he said indicating the two unconscious soldiers at their feet.

With one hand, Victor grabbed the back of the head of the closer unconscious guard, and lifted him off his feet. With his other hand, he pried open one eye and placed the face near the scanner. A green light flashed on the console.

"Thanks," Marco said as he began entering information into his data pad that was now connected to the terminal. Victor let the body he was holding drop.

"There we go," Marco stated as a hologram of the Alathian ship appeared above his data pad. "We are here," he said pointing at a yellow dot of light near the bottom of the ship. "The captain and Silmion are here," he pointed to a point of blue light in another section of the ship. "And my computer is here," he finished, pointing to a green point of light elsewhere in the ship.

There was a lot of distance between each light.

"Once we have Marco's computer, how do we get the captain out? How do we get ourselves out?" Kaeso asked.

A smile cracked Victor's worn face. "Oh, I got a couple ideas. You just leave that to ol' Vic."

* * *

Taura was exasperated with the 'negotiations.' There had been a lot of talk, and Silmion was annoyingly good at keeping things civil. She was more convinced now than ever that the Alathians had no intention of dealing with her fairly. They were only stalling for time to find Marco, at which point she would be taken prisoner.

Marco is closer than you think, fools, she thought bitterly. *What better place to hide than in the viper's den.* Taura hoped they would signal her soon so she could end this charade.

Without warning the ship lurched violently, sending Taura, Silmion, and Ariadne violently to the floor. A claxon began wailing, and the ship shook once and then twice more. In the distance, Taura heard explosions.

That was some distraction Victor and the boys had cooked up.

* * *

"Dust and ashes, what was that?" Marco asked as he struggled back to his feet. All three of them had been knocked to the deck. Explosions rumbled nearby and an alarm wailed overhead.

"The ship's being attacked," Victor replied.

"Damn the Fates," Kaeso cursed, "what do we do now?"

According to the ship's schematic Marco had downloaded to his data pad, the trio was a little over two corridors away from his computer. Unfortunately, at least one squad of soldiers, possibly more, blocked the way. Their shouts of confusion echoed down the hall.

"Quit yer bitchin', Kaeso," Victor said. "You take rear guard and link in. Follow my advance. Keep Marco alive—at least long enough to unlock his Fates damned computer."

At that moment, time seemed to halt. A squad of about ten Alathian soldiers just rounded the corner of the far end of the corridor. Obviously surprised to find intruders within the halls of their vessel, they stood just as frozen as Marco, Victor, and Kaeso.

"Aw, slag!" Victor cursed.

Before either side could make a move, though, the ship was viciously rocked yet again, sending everyone sprawling along the ground. Victor was the first to regain his feet, and he tossed the Alathian weapon he was carrying to Marco and flexed his empty hands into fists. Marco looked at the sleek weapon Victor had passed him, then back to the lieutenant-commander. "Evening the odds by going at them bare-handed, are we?"

A vicious smile cracked Victor's aged face. "Not quite."

Victor stepped out into the middle of the hallway facing the Alathian soldiers who were scrambling to their feet.

In one fluid motion, braces slid out of concealed slots on Victor's calves and hammered into the floor of the hall, stabilizing him. At the same time, compartments in his thick forearms opened and the barrel of a pulse rifle slid out from each one.

The weapons began firing in fully automatic mode sending streams of low-explosive quantum bolts down the hall. The recoil from each blast rocked Victor's body, but the braces that just shot out of his calves prevented the massive pulses from pushing him back. A grin from ear to ear split the lieutenant-commander's face. Down the hall, the quantum bolts from his weapons tore into the soldiers, each shot hitting home. Blood sprayed the walls and ceiling and pooled on the floor.

Marco watched in shock as the subdermal etchings crisscrossing Victor's biceps began to glow an unnatural red as he fired and black smoke began to rise from them. The lieutenant-commander stood like one of Kalbarai's mythical Fates, raining terror and fire upon his enemies. A few fortunate Alathians at the far end of the hall managed to escape around a corner. Victor ceased firing and began advancing down the hall with heavy, clomping steps.

In shock, and some horror, Marco turned to Kaeso. "Nice culture you have there."

Alathian soldiers appeared at the end of the hall behind them. Kaeso let loose with the Alathian weapon he carried. True to form, Alathian weapon's fired soundlessly. The only noise was rending metal as the bullets tore through walls, wet thuds when they hit people and the screams of the wounded and dying.

"Go! Go!" Kaeso yelled. "Stay with Victor!"

Marco scrambled down the hall after Victor with Kaeso close behind him. The hall was littered with the ruined bodies of Alathian soldiers and ricocheting bullets. Marco and Kaeso fired madly behind them with the silent Alathian guns while Victor decimated the hall ahead with his pulse weapons.

Another explosion hammered the ship, sending both Marco and Kaeso stumbling. Victor, with his foot braces, retained his balance and continued advancing.

An announcement in Alathian blared over the PA system. Marco cocked his head as he listened.

"Do you understand Alathian?" Kaeso asked, yelling over the sound of the alarm and explosions, accompanied now by Victor's gunfire.

"Of course," Marco replied. "Sounds like they've been boarded."

"Shut up, you old ladies and fight," Victor yelled as he turned a corner. He began opening fire again as Alathian soldiers taking cover at the far end of this hall began to return fire. Victor's volley of explosive energy pulses tore them apart. Kaeso was laying covering fire against the soldiers coming up behind them. Linked together into the Kalbarian phalanx, the two advanced in lock-step, Kaeso able to seamlessly walk backwards as he fired, the neural net he shared with Victor giving him the topography of the ground, littered with bodies, as they pushed ahead.

"Marco," Victor said.

"What?"

"Where is it, where's your computer?"

Referring to his schematic, Marco replied, "It's at the end of this hall. Second door from the end on the right," he said, pointing.

With surprising speed, Victor advanced to the portal and with a mighty blast of his pulse rifle, smashed the door open. He fired a handful of shots into the room.

He turned back to Marco. "Area's clear. Time to earn your pay."

Cautiously, Marco peered into the room. Two bodies were splayed on the floor, and a third flung over a desk. On a nearby bench he saw his computer.

He turned, smiling at Victor, and said, "Jackpot.'

"Just shut up and get your computer," Victor replied.

* * *

Taura was pulling herself off the deck. Silmion was on his feet— his sense of balance was unnatural, and he retained his footing as though he were standing on solid ground and not a ship being torn apart by enemy fire. Taura's eyes immediately hunted for Marco's computer. She quickly found it lying on the floor in shattered pieces revealing that it was nothing more than plastic casing.

She eyed Ariadne, regaining her feet, and said, "It's not even a real computer."

Unable to deny it, Ariadne shrugged. "No, it isn't. So, is it your—"

Before Ariadne could complete her question, Taura, with blinding speed, spun around and kicked her in the head. Ariadne crashed into the wall behind her and collapsed unconscious to the floor.

Silmion raised a condescending eyebrow and said, "Captain, that was highly uncalled for."

Taura's machine arm blossomed into her pulse blaster. "Find a weapon, Silmion, and try to keep up." With that, Taura fired into the door, tearing it to shreds, and left the room.

Silmion looked around the spartan chamber, then at his empty hands. With a shrug, he followed the captain out of the room.

The labyrinthine halls quickly confounded their sense of direction, and it was not long before a squad of Alathian soldiers had them trapped in a small store room. Silmion had managed to acquire an Alathian blaster from a soldier they had overcome on the way and was firing at them from the doorway.

"Victor, report," Taura spoke over the neural net with her soldiers.

"Aye, Captain," Victor replied. "We got Marco's computer, but we're pinned down between Alathian and Nephretian positions."

"Nephretians!" the captain exclaimed.

"Aye, it's them that attacked the ship."

"What's your location?"

"Two floors up from you and to the starboard."

Silmion jumped back as a volley of weapon's fire tore shreds out of the door frame. "Damn, your weapons are crude and stupid," he cursed as he resumed his position and returned fire.

Ignoring Silmion, Taura asked Victor, "Where's your ship?"

"On the cruiser's underbelly at the aft. Marco downloaded the ship's schematics and uploaded them to the neural net. I'm transmitting it to you now. That'll make your job of getting around easier."

"Excellent, Victor," Taura replied. She immediately called up a map of their current floor onto her optic center. "Received. Lieutenant-Commander, rendezvous with us on this floor. From here, we'll make our way to our escape craft. Understood?"

"Aye-aye. We'll meet you there soon."

* * *

Two floors up and to the starboard, Victor, Kaeso and Marco huddled in a shattered room. Although weapons' fire rocketed by outside in the hall, it was being exchanged between Nephretian invaders and Alathian defenders, neither of which realized the trio was hiding in the room. Victor, Kaeso, and Marco were each covered in sweat and dark soot.

"So, what'd she say," Marco asked while he frenetically worked away on his computer.

"She wants us to meet up with her, then we'll make our way to our ship," Victor replied.

An explosion raged through the hall outside, shaking the walls of the room.

"Any thoughts on how we'll get there?" Marco asked.

"I'm working on it."

"What are you doing, Marco?" Kaeso asked.

From out in the hall, men screamed as a fresh round of weapon's fire and explosions commenced.

"I'm backing up Earth's coordinates on my data pad. I don't want to go through the hassle of getting this again, if—"

Marco was interrupted as a squad of tattered Nephretian soldiers burst into the room. Some of them carried wounded compatriots as others took up defensive positions at the door. So intent were they on attacking their Alathian adversaries on the other end of the corridor that they did not notice the three men huddled in the back of the room.

Immediately the room was filled with gun fire, shouting and the moaning of wounded. And then one Nephretian's gaze settled across Victor, Kaeso, and Marco, whose hands were frozen over the input board of his portable computer. For a single heartbeat they stared at each other.

Victor said, "I got an idea how to get out of here now," as he came to his feet.

The soldier screamed an alarm to his comrades.

"Aw, dust and ashes," Marco swore viciously under his breath moments before Victor opened fire.

Chapter 20

Commodore Hetshepsu Kahotep stood with his back to the wall as a squad of soldiers fought their way ahead of him. The Fist had ordered him personally to oversee the boarding of the Alathian cruiser to recapture the computer that held the coordinates to Earth. Command of such a mission was an honor, Hetshepsu knew, though only if successful—death was the price of failure on a quest such as this.

There was a lull in the fighting and he and his squad advanced up a corridor. He ignored the beseeching wails of the injured and stepped over the bodies of his soldiers who had fallen in battle. The souls of the dead were already in the Void, he thought, awaiting resurrection in the continuous cycle of life and death humans were chained to until Amahté called his children home.

Then, at the far end of the corridor, an explosion knocked a door out and a group of people tumbled into the hallway. Both groups froze, weapons pointing at one another.

A smile touched Hetshepsu's thin lips. Amahté favored him today, it seemed. Across from his soldiers he faced none other than Captain Lucia Taura along with the smuggler Marco, a couple of her soldiers plus an Ullrioni of some sort. The commodore's eyes were fixed on Marco and the computer he held in his hands. The group looked horrible, covered in burns and blood.

"Captain Taura," the commodore said, "you have done me a great favor today by bringing Marco and his computer to me."

"Fates take you, you slag-headed preacher-bait," Taura replied as she brought the weapon that was her mechanical arm to bear.

Before any shots were fired, an explosion tore the hallway open behind Taura's group. The shock wave sent them flailing down the corridor. Time seemed to slow as Hetshepsu watched the computer fly from Marco's hands, sail through the air, then land and skittle across the floor until it was no more than two steps away from the commodore.

It was Amahté's hand, leading him to victory, he thought. What else could explain such serendipity?

With a glorious yell, filled with self-righteousness, the commodore screamed, "Fire at them!" Chaos consumed the hall. With a quick leap, Hetshepsu grabbed the computer off the floor and went running back down the hallway.

The Nephretian soldiers stood their ground, firing at Taura and her companions. Standing up in the cloud of smoke, Victor roared and let loose with his pulse rifles in either forearm. Nephretian bullets tore into his chest, but bounced off his dermal armor that was fused into his flesh. His fire, on the other hand, ripped through the Nephretians.

Behind the Kalbarians a team of Alathians entered the hallway through the hole they just blasted through a wall. Taura and Kaeso turned to fire on them. Silmion and Marco took cover between the Kalbarians, firing the weapons they had managed to acquire during their flight.

Hetshepsu was beyond caring. He ran back down the hallway, clutching the computer to his chest. Amahté had blessed him today, he thought to himself proudly.

Leaping aboard his boarding craft that had punched a hole in the Alathian ship's hull, he yelled, "Disengage!" to the pilot. He hammered the communications button, broadcasting to the entire assault force. "I have it! I have it! All ships, rally to me!"

* * *

When the commodore's boarding craft disengaged from the ship, the depressurization tore Marco and his companions off their feet, dragging them towards the breach in the hull. Their headlong tumble only stopped once DECOMP doors slammed shut, sealing off the breach. Their momentum sent the group sliding along the floor into the now closed pressure doors.

Regaining his feet, Victor screamed and slammed his mighty hands against the DECOMP door. The resounding thud echoed back down the hull.

"Marco," Taura called, pulling him to his feet, "tell me the lock on your computer is still intact."

"No, I took it off while I was backing up the coordinates," Marco replied, gasping as he regained his breath.

Taura screamed and punched her metal fist through the wall of the corridor. Turning on Marco, she yelled, "Why didn't you reset your lock, Fates take you!"

"Because I was busy getting shot at!" he yelled back.

"Wait," Taura said, quickly regaining her composure. "What were you doing with your computer when you unlocked it?"

"Backing it up on this," Marco replied, holding up his hand-sized portable computer.

Shocked, Taura asked, "You have the coordinates on that?"

"Yeah," Marco replied with a lopsided smile growing on his face.

"Then we're not sunk yet," the captain stated, "we've got to get back to our ship."

"Obviously," Marco replied.

"We might have a bit of trouble with that," Silmion coolly interjected, pointing to the squad of Alathians behind them who were advancing on them, weapons drawn.

Victor, fuming with rage, pushed passed him, nearly knocking Silmion down, and, without a word, opened fire on the Alathians, tearing them apart with the pulse rifles in his arms.

Glaring back at the group, Victor said, "Problem solved. Let's go, dogs."

* * *

A glorious fire lit the ice-blue eyes of Lord Suten Hamu as he stared down on the grey head of Commodore Kahotep kneeling before him. In the commodore's hands upraised was the computer that held the path to Earth.

Reverently, the Fist took the computer from the commodore and passed it to an awaiting technician. "Officer Mkhai," The Fist spoke with a deep, resonant voice, "connect this to our helm and plot a course for Earth."

The technician took the computer from the Fist, bowed wordlessly and left to his task.

"I must confess I had begun to doubt you after the fiasco on Ullrion," The Fist said turning his attention to the kneeling figure before him. "But, you have done well, Commodore Kahotep. You are redeemed. Amahté blessed you today and made you a hero of our people."

A smile spread across the commodore's lips and a malevolent shine glinted in his soulless green eyes. "I am born to serve Amahté's glory, my lord."

"You are commodore no more. Arise, Admiral Kahotep," the Fist commanded.

Hetshepsu tried to contain his joy at his promotion as he rose to face The Fist. Admiral … he relished the rank.

"We shall give you lands and a title once we return to Nephreti," The Fist promised. "After we return from Earth, that is."

"I am humbled by your praise," the new admiral replied, although he felt anything but humility at this moment.

"Kan Rath," the Fist called out.

The Ullrioni ambassador of the Duraanesti nation stepped from the shadows behind him. "Yes, Lord Hamu."

"Although your people allowed the Alathians to capture the computer, Amahté smiles on us today," the Fist spoke. Kan Rath visibly bristled under the criticism, but kept his thoughts to himself.

The Fist continued, "Despite your mistakes, your people have offered us much in the way of assistance and new technology. To repay you, I will give you the honor of travelling with us to Earth."

Forcing a smile, Kan Rath replied, "I would be pleased to do so."

"Before we agree to bestow this honor on him, I'd like him to explain why in my encounter with Captain Taura she was in the company of one of his fellow Ullrionis," Kahotep interrupted.

Kan Rath's eyes narrowed. "As you are well aware, my people are not united under a common planetary government. Could you describe this Ullrioni that accompanies your enemies, Admiral?"

"He had golden-blond hair grown to his shoulders and a sharp, angular face."

Some dark emotion seemed to ripple behind Kan Rath's eyes, but his voice was composed as he spoke. "As I've mentioned, your prisoners were freed by the Uvonesti. If I had to guess, I'd say the Ullrioni you saw was Silmion Qualanthus. He is quite popular amongst his people, and he has close ties to his nation's rulers."

"Their ruler," the Fist interjected, "Elder Karlan Shoalbrau, told us Alathians kidnapped our prisoners." Shadowy nictitating membranes slowly closed and opened over The Fist's eyes as he studied Kan Rath with an appraising gaze. Finally, he broke the silence. "It would seem they were too much for the Alathians to hold on to. It matters not, now, though. Admiral Kahotep, see to the destruction of the Alathian ship, then set course for Earth. Inform me when we are underway."

"Yes, my superior," Hetshepsu replied to the Fist, who had already turned and was exiting the bridge. With a dangerous glint to his eye, the admiral turned to face the bridge. "Bring the forward cannon array on line."

* * *

Taura and her companions had made it back to the hatch on the besieged Alathian cruiser where their ship was docked when they stumbled into a boarding squad of Nephretians. The fighting was in close quarters and was mostly hand-to-hand.

Taura, Victor, and Kaeso were fighting in the Kalbarian phalanx—their actions coordinated through their shared neural net. Their enemies were not fighting three individuals, but rather one entity with multiple arms, legs and points of view. As one mass they fought. Few enemies could withstand the onslaught of the Kalbarian phalanx, despite the fact Kalbarians chronically found themselves outnumbered. To an observer, the attack of a phalanx seemed intrinsically choreographed. Taura ducked as Kaeso fired a short burst over her head point blank into an oncoming assailant, then Kaeso knocked a Nephretian's gun away while a blade snicked out of Victor's elbow and hammered home into the Nephretian's head. In this manner the trio made a relentless, brutal progress through the mob of Nephretians. Kaeso took a kick to the knee, and the phalanx automatically adjusted to accommodate his now limping gait.

Meanwhile, Silmion was cutting through the Nephretians like a scythe. He was fast, graceful, and possessed a strength that belied his slender frame. He flitted through the battle like a lethal dancer.

Somehow Marco had made his way to the ladder unmolested, Taura noticed and was climbing to the hatch that led to their ship.

The Nephretians, however, were concentrating on the Kalbarian phalanx. The trio was pushing themselves to their limits, Victor's augmented muscles and Taura's mechanical arm tossing bloody Nephretians into the bulkhead at blinding speeds. However, members of the phalanx were sustaining injuries that continued to hamper them. First Kaeso's knee, then Taura took a crack to the head from an elbow that sent her reeling.

Victor's tactics shifted from offensive to defensive. Blades snicked in and out of his fists, elbows and knees as he cut through any Nephretian in reach. If the Nephretians were foolish enough to give him space, he brought the pulse rifles in his arms to bear. Kaeso, and then Taura once she reclaimed her senses, protected Victor's back and flanks.

A group of Nephretians tackled Taura—the phalanx was being overwhelmed. Fire from Taura's blaster arm tore two of her attackers apart before the third pinned her arm to the wall. He was no match for the mechanical strength of her appendage, and she hammered him into the ground with it. But two more were on her.

One of them drove his knee into her ribs. Her breath left her as she doubled over. The other smashed the butt of his rifle on the back of her head, sending her to the floor.

She rolled over, dazed and shaking unconsciousness away. One Nephretian pinned her mechanical arm to the ground with his foot, pressing down with all his weight. He jammed the barrel of his rifle into her face.

Then his chest exploded, spraying blood onto Taura as he collapsed. The gore blinded her momentarily, but she hefted the body off and wiped the blood from her eyes.

"Fates curse you, what are you doing here?" Taura asked when she saw who had saved her. Ariadne was kneeling beside her with an Alathian rifle. She fired soundlessly into the Nephretians attacking the rest of her phalanx. Although Taura would never allow herself to admit it openly, she knew that action had saved Kaeso and Victor, who were on the verge of being overwhelmed.

Sparing a glance at Taura, Ariadne replied, "The Nephretians have the map to Earth. As long as that is true, we are not enemies."

Ariadne fired a couple of soundless shots into advancing Nephretians, and then dragged Taura to the ladder leading to their ship. Marco had already opened the hatch and was firing up the ship's engines.

They were all knocked off their feet as explosions rocked the Alathian cruiser. Metal screeched as the connection between the cruiser and the landing craft was strained with the rocking of the ships.

Silmion, who had never lost his footing, leapt to the ladder and scurried up. Kaeso was helping Victor finish off the last of his assailants, and then he too was up the ladder.

The ship rocked again under more explosions as Victor approached Taura. Struggling to maintain their footing, Victor glared at Ariadne.

"What's she doing here?" he asked.

Taura could not conceal her distaste, but she and her men were alive due to Ariadne's actions, and that was a debt she could not ignore. "She's coming with us," she finally said.

"Your mother's teat she is," Victor replied.

"I said she's coming with us, soldier, now get her and yourself in the ship."

Grumbling, Victor complied.

Taura followed, closing the hatch behind her.

On board the landing craft everyone was cursing as explosions rocked everyone except Silmion to the floor or into bulkheads. Taura stumbled her way to the bridge where Marco was seated preparing for takeoff.

"Status report," Taura demanded.

"Glad to see you too," Marco replied. "We have three Nephretian battleships tearing the Alathian ship to pieces."

"Are you able to sneak by them like you did the Alathians?" she asked.

"Of course. Try not to be insulting. Watch this." Turning to the back of the landing craft, he yelled so everyone could hear him, "Brace yourselves!"

With that, Marco tapped a few commands into the craft's console. They disengaged from the Alathian cruiser, which was spiraling uncontrollably from the Nephretian barrage now hitting it. Momentum flung the lander off into space, spinning wildly.

Curses filled the landing craft as everyone struggled to keep themselves from being tossed around the cabin. Marco cut the power to the ship's computers and most of the lights.

"That's your plan?" Taura asked.

Marco smiled. Damn, he had a good looking smile, Taura cursed to herself. "Yeah," Marco replied. "The Nephretians are blowing up that Alathian cruiser. They'd expect to see debris. We," he pointed to the ship for effect, "are debris. My guess is once the Nephretians are done, they'll high tail it to Earth."

Taura grunted, and then said, "That's not how I would have done it."

"Yeah, well, I didn't feel like ramming one of those battleships with our tiny landing craft."

In the distance, the Alathian ship disintegrated under the Nephretian barrage. Moments later, the Nephretian ships slipped into the Q-wave slipstream and were gone. Marco powered up the ship and took it out of its uncontrolled spin.

There were more curses as everyone regained their footing. Kaeso joked, "He flies worse than you, Victor." The lieutenant-commander glared at Kaeso until he muttered an apology.

"So," Ariadne said, righting herself, "what now?"

"We won't be able to follow them for long in this small landing craft," Taura commented. "We'll need to rendezvous with the Novafire to give chase."

"Bit of a problem with following them," Marco commented as he hooked his data pad up to the ship's computer system. A three-dimensional star map appeared above the console. "Based on these calculations, the fastest route to Earth passes through Nephretian space. I could slip a small Alathian craft like this through it, but a Kalbarian battle ship'd be tough. Especially since they'll be expecting Kalbarai to follow. But a craft this small couldn't handle the interstellar distance we need to cover. "

"It'd be easier with an Alathian cruiser," Ariadne said.

Taura cut her off. "Yeah, I don't think so."

"Captain, the Nephretians threaten us both now. The game's changed," Ariadne persisted.

Taura turned on Ariadne. "The only Alathian cruiser I saw around here is now space debris. You got another one nearby?" she asked. Ariadne glared back, but did not reply. Taura continued, "I'll take that as a no. The clock's ticking. If the Nephretians claim Earth as their own, then this war will get an awful lot harder to win. As far as I know, the Novafire's the closest ship capable of deep space flight. And even it is days away! I don't intend to give them any more of a lead then they already have."

"I know you realize you can't just sail a Kalbarian battleship through Nephretian space." Ariadne said. "We need stealth, and that's something an Alathian cruiser can offer."

She was good, Taura thought. Out of the corner of her eye, Taura saw Marco turn to the landing craft's computer console.

"Kalbarian ships were built to be seen, Captain. You of all people know you've no chance of passing through undetected. And as powerful as the Novafire is, you can't expect to pound through Nephretian lines alone," Ariadne said.

"Nice!" Marco exclaimed, disrupting the flow of the argument.

Taura turned to see Marco working on the computer console of the ship. The star map emitted by his data pad subtly changed. "What've you done now?" she asked.

Obviously pleased with himself, Marco replied, "As I suspected, the Alathian navigational computers have a bit of intel on the placement of Nephretian military installations. I've updated my map to incorporate that."

"That's not real-time information," Ariadne said, obviously a little distressed at Marco's prodding into Alathian intelligence. "Deployment of the Nephretian defenses will change now that they're trying to block the route for us through their space to give chase."

"Yes, yes," Marco said with a dismissive wave of his hand. "It'll change, and it'll change somewhat predictably, since we've a good idea of their objective. Something a military adversary might exploit." He let the suggestion hang in the air. Once Taura and

Ariadne had a chance to digest his comment, he continued, "I've got an idea, though Kalbarai and Alathia will need to work together."

Marco and his plans, Taura thought ruefully to herself. A moment passed before Taura finally said, "Let's hear it."

The Librarian

The Librarian of N'ark floated naked in her ornate vat of biofluid, which served as the focal point for the lowest chamber of the library complex in the palace district of N'ark. Soft golden lights shined on the stone walls casting a warm glow throughout the vast, vaulted chamber.

Her bloated, corpulent form pressed against the clear walls of her opulent vessel as she stared contemptuously down on Nk'ty. The Librarian's body, utterly dependent on the fluids and gasses immersing her, was forever trapped in the cistern that held her. Her mind, however, knew a freedom unattainable in the outside world. As the Librarian of N'ark, she was the hub of the vast network of the Dagomir. Thousands of years of history lived by the mar n'lan of N'ark coursed through the network of the collective, and she was free to dance amongst the strands of knowledge.

Yet she was bound to serve the mar n'lan of the surface world, and through them, the Dagomir. She resented their incursions on her explorations, though, and exacted a heavy toll for her assistance. Consequently, she was disturbed only by the most serious—or desperate—searchers of information.

With his impatience getting the better of him, Nk'ty said, "Librarian, I have done as you asked. It is time for you to hold up your end of the bargain."

The Librarian did not like being told what to do. "Nk'ty is it?" she asked, her disembodied voice reverberating from the tank that encompassed the totality of her physical existence. "I remember the first time you stood before me. You were nothing more than a boy as your father introduced you and your brother, Kie, to me. You failed to impress me. Was that so long ago? You stand before me a man now, and a greying one at that. Has it been so long?"

Nk'ty scowled, The Librarian noticed with satisfaction. He repeated, "I have done as you asked. I'm sure we both have better things to do than reminisce."

"Indeed," the Librarian said. "Let's get on with it then. Show me his head."

Nk'ty snapped his fingers and a young woman the Librarian hadn't noticed stepped forward. The Librarian looked at the woman in stunned surprise. This was her realm and she hadn't thought it possible that someone could enter it without her notice. "Who is she?" the Librarian asked, shock gripping her voice.

Nk'ty's eye's narrowed as he noted the Librarian's change in tone. "She is Seir T'pan—my slave."

Still flustered, the Librarian admonished, "You bring a mar p'augh in my presence! Her dull skin is an offense!"

Nk'ty's tone changed to one of condescension as he said, "She is my slave, Librarian. Her presence shouldn't vex you more than would a chair. Are you quite alright?" he asked without a trace of concern in his voice. "You seem agitated."

Ignoring his question, the Librarian composed herself and repeated, "Show me his head."

Nk'ty stared at the Librarian thoughtfully, and then nodded to Seir T'pan. She opened a sack she was holding and withdrew a head, the dead flesh still retaining the pale iridescence of a mar n'lan, with a ragged bloody stump for a neck and a grimace of shock frozen on the face. Seir T'pan tossed the bloody head on the floor before the Librarian's vat. It landed with a hollow thud that echoed through the cavernous chamber.

It was the head of Har Kal. He was—had been—a powerful mar n'lan whose ambitions had started to grow beyond the interests of N'ark. The Dagomir would be pleased this had been dealt with.

The Librarian looked once more at Nk'ty appraisingly. A mar n'lan as powerful as Har Kal would not have been an easy kill. Perhaps Nk'ty's activities bore closer scrutiny if he was becoming this powerful, the Librarian thought to herself.

"Well done, Nk'ty," the Librarian said at length. "Tell me the information you seek."

"I wish to learn about the Lost Dreks," Nk'ty replied.

The Librarian closed her eyes and allowed her mind to travel back through millennia of past memories of the mar n'lan that had ascended to the vast collective of the Dagomir. Further and further still she travelled. It had been a long time since she had to delve this far back into the memory of the Dagomir. Finally, she found it.

She opened her eyes and spoke. "Odd that you would even know to ask about the Lost Dreks. This is not for the ears of a mar p'augh. Send your slave away."

With a flick of his wrist, Nk'ty dismissed Seir T'pan. Once the Librarian was sure the slave had left the chamber she continued her story. "The phrase 'Lost Drek' is a crude translation of a term used only briefly near the start of the Ravager's Darkness."

Nk'ty cocked his head in thought before saying, "The Ravager first struck more than 50,000 years ago."

"52,139 years ago, to be precise," the Librarian said.

"Please," Nk'ty prompted with unusual politeness, "do continue."

"Before the Ravager's Darkness, humanity's writ extended far beyond our land into the heavens. The Dagomir Wars raged in heaven and earth as the mar p'augh fought their rightful masters. But, when the Ravager first struck and then struck again and again without end, combined with the devastation of the Dagomirs' ascension, humanity was pushed to the edge of oblivion. It was rumored that a tribe of mar p'augh, fearing their demise, constructed arks to carry their unborn spawn to the stars where they might seed themselves to start anew. Given the chaos of the time, this was never confirmed. These are the Lost Dreks of which you speak."

Nk'ty stared at the Librarian for a moment, and then asked incredulously, "Mar p'augh tribes in the heavens?"

"Yes," the Librarian replied. "We have fallen far. The Ravager took much from us."

"Are there ..." Nk'ty hesitated, afraid to ask, "Are there still mar p'augh tribes in the heavens?"

"Don't be a fool. The mar p'augh are in their rightful place— beneath the mar n'lan."

"And these Lost Dreks?"

"Rumors, nothing more."

Nk'ty stood deep in thought with a calculating look in his eyes.

"Where did you learn of the Lost Dreks, Nk'ty?" the Librarian asked. "Was it your brother, Kie, the strand-walker?"

Nk'ty looked at the Librarian with a wolfish gleam in his eyes. "You've laid no head at my feet to loosen my lips." With that, Nk'ty turned and strode out of the chamber.

Part III

"If the Ravager has taught us anything, it is this: We must fear that which we cannot control. And then we must either master it, or destroy it."

—Dagomir Bar Lin, commencement speech of the 35th millennial celebration of the Dagomir's Ascension

Chapter 21

In many ways, the Pounding Stone Pub was similar to ale houses throughout human civilization, Ariadne mused. Groups of people sat clustered around tables and bars, each group lost in its own conversation. The establishment was alive with a cacophony of noises: voices of varying volume, banging and yelling from the kitchen, hoots and curses, music throbbing overhead. The room was busy, but not overcrowded as servers wound their way through the maze of tables to relay orders and deliver food and drink. Like the rest of the town it was in, the pub had seen better days. Paint peeled from the walls, the wooden tables were scratched and many of the chairs wobbled.

Ariadne liked the Pounding Stone because it was located near the space docks of Narite on the small planet of Alburna deep in Nephretian territory. The nearby Nephretian base was originally intended to protect the mining operations, though as the war progressed and other bases were destroyed or moved the Narite base had grown in strategic importance.

Scanning the room, Ariadne noticed that although the conversations seemed peaceful enough, the tone of the place lacked any sense of joviality. The majority of clientele were gaunt and starved. The menu was sparse. Food options were limited to various combinations of bread, potatoes, and soups—and exorbitantly priced at that. Alcohol flowed freely, though. If you can't feed your people, drug them.

Marco had chosen the bar well, Ariadne thought as she scanned the inhabitants of the room once more. The bulk of the clientele were roughnecks working in the nearby mines or drilling rigs, interspersed with several Nephretian soldiers from the base located just out of town, dock workers from the nearby spacedocks, and the crew of supply ships that flew in and out of town every day. It was a perfect place for outsiders like Marco and Ariadne to fade into the background.

Marco had been speaking with the man behind the bar, leaving Ariadne alone for a while now. She noticed one of the soldiers stand up and make his way to the restrooms at the back of the pub. She impatiently looked back to find Marco finally wind his way through the busy tables to their booth.

"It's done," was all he said as he sat down across from her.

"Oipho!" she cursed in Alathian, "Took you long enough. By Sor T'van's Lies, do you have to make friends with everyone you talk to?"

"You never know when not being a bitch will work out to your advantage," he replied. Then, changing the subject, "So, how're our boys doing?"

"One's gone to the back already, and," she hesitated as she spotted a second soldier make his way to the restrooms, "there goes the second."

"Already?" Marco asked, "I didn't see you spike their drinks."

"Marco, the day you spot me slipping something into someone's drink is the day I need to retire from service. Now come on." Ariadne got up to make her way to the back of the pub, Marco following behind.

They were only part way there when the music stopped and a holo-image appeared in the end of the room. It was an image of High Prelate Ialu Ibenré, the supreme ruler of the Holy Nephretian Empire. Ariadne rolled her eyes—they had been replaying this clip constantly for days now. Nonetheless, the conversations came to a dead stop in the pub as a room full of hardened, hungry eyes turned to the image.

"People of the Holy Nephretian Empire, I bring you the most blessed of news," the message boomed.

Although everyone in the bar had heard this message at least once by now, each person sat on the edge of their seats with a gleam of desperate hope in their lean faces.

"I know you have suffered these long, long years as we battle evil and ignorance. I know you are tired and hungry and wonder if we can ever know victory against the sea of darkness that beats upon our shores in wave after wave. I know you have faced struggles that would shake a weaker people's faith to its foundation."

Both Marco and Ariadne had been forced to take seats—continuing to move through the crowd as this message played would draw too much attention. But the delay gnawed at Ariadne's gut, and she couldn't help but cast a furtive glance to the hall down which the restrooms were located.

"And I stand here before you today," the image of the High Prelate said, rising in volume, "to tell you that Amahté bears witness to your struggle …"

"Praise be to Amahté!" someone in the bar exclaimed to muttered approval.

"… and has decided to reward us for our faith."

"May Amahté smile upon us," someone else yelled. The excitement in the room was mounting. Marco, hands raised in the air, called out in perfect Nephretian, "Amahté, show us the way!" to shouts of approval.

"Today, we have found a new seedship! A seedship that has not yet started colonization, and through that seedship, we have found our way back to Earth!"

The bar broke out in frenzied excitement, as it had done the multiple times the message had been played out before. As one, both Marco and Ariadne used the pandemonium to cover their continued movement to the restrooms.

The image continued on over the sound of the din. "I have sent my most trusted warrior, Lord Suten Hamu, The Fist of the High Prelate, with a fleet of ships to claim Earth for the Holy Nephretian Empire." This was greeted with more screams of hysteria. "In the meantime, we must gather our strength and become the hammer of Amahté. The forces of evil will see this as their last chance to strike us down. Already, the bloodthirsty Kalbarians and blasphemous Alathians have joined forces to launch a combined attack."

When she had first heard of it, Ariadne was shocked at how fast a truce had been agreed to between the Alathians and Kalbarians. A testament to the desperation both empires felt.

The rest of the High Prelate's message was drowned out by the yells of the crowd. Unnoticed, Marco and Ariadne slipped down the hallway to the restrooms. Ariadne stood in the hall as

Marco entered the men's washroom. In a moment, he popped back out. "They're down. Game on."

"Good," Ariadne replied, "let's get 'em out, just like we planned it."

Marco slipped back into the restroom. After a moment, a knock on the door came from the inside of the men's washroom. That was the signal Ariadne was waiting for. No one in the common room was looking down the hallway. She pushed the men's door open and Marco came out. He dragged one of the soldiers, unconscious now with arm draped over his neck, down the hall to the emergency exit into the alley beyond. Marco came back and the process was repeated with the second soldier.

In the alley, both Ariadne and Marco dragged the unconscious soldiers behind a nearby dumpster. There, they proceeded to take the soldiers' uniforms off as well as undressing themselves before putting on the soldiers' clothes. Ariadne made sure Marco saw her in her underwear before bashfully putting on clothes of the soldier lying at her feet. By such subtle tricks did men become women's servants.

"Do I look like a good Nephretian?" Marco asked as he straightened the jacket of his uniform.

"You look fine. Help me drop them in the dumpster." After several moments of exertion, both soldiers, clad only in their briefs, had been manhandled into the dumpster.

"Ok," Marco said looking at his data pad, "let's go, we don't have much time."

As Marco was turning to go, Ariadne drew her Alathian blaster and with two quick twitches, shot both soldiers. Although the gunshots were silent, the sound of the bullet entering the body made a wet, visceral noise that echoed in the confines of the dumpster. Marco spun back quickly to see Ariadne holstering her weapon.

"Dust and ashes," Marco swore, the color draining from his face as he rushed to the dumpster to see the two corpses now in it. "Why in the nine heavens did you do that?"

"They were enemy soldiers," Ariadne stated.

"They were unconscious,"

"And if they came to in the middle of our operation, you, me, and everyone on the bloody K.S. Novafire would be dead,"

"You're an Alathian spy," Marco said. "Don't tell me you don't have some concoction that could knock them out for days."

He's sentimental, Ariadne thought to herself. Let's play to that sentimentality. She allowed her voice to waver slightly as she spoke, as though she were struggling to hold back tears. "My supplies have been limited since my ship was destroyed and its entire crew killed by Nephretians."

"This isn't about revenge," he replied, though Ariadne could see her show of emotion had taken him off guard.

"I'm not doing this for revenge," she said. "We must succeed at all costs. If we fail, a lot of people are going to die."

Marco looked once more into the dumpster, his face haggard and ill. He closed the lid. "You know as well as I that either way, a lot of people are going to die."

Ariadne marveled at Marco. He seemed so tired, so sick of it all. After all these years living as a smuggler, profiting off the proceeds of warlords, could the death of an enemy truly affect him so, she wondered. Or was he playing her?

After a long moment, she said, "Come on. We've got to go."

* * *

"This is a dangerous plan," Victor said again. "You know the objective, and you know we may need to be flexible to achieve it."

"Yes sir." There was no one he would rather have by his side in a battle than Victor, Kaeso thought to himself. But he could sense in his superior's words that he was uncertain of Kaeso's abilities. I don't blame him, Kaeso thought to himself. I've had little combat experience and I'm not exactly the warrior type. He kept his uncertainties to himself as he said, "I understand the risks."

"Risks," Victor said. "You mean like trusting our lives to that smuggler and Alathian harlot? Yeah, there're risks, all right."

The two were in the back of a ground transport parked by the intersection of Main Street and Third Avenue, several blocks away from the Pounding Stone Pub as well as two blocks away from the main road leading out of town to the Nephretian base. They were surrounded by crates of explosives and weapons. Marco had arranged for their supply, though Kaeso hadn't the foggiest notion how.

"I still can't believe Kalbarai signed a treaty with Alathia. We're allies with them now," Kaeso said. He imagined the news of the armistice and agreement to join forces against the Nephretians had rocked most of Kalbarai and Alathia alike.

"No we're not. It takes more than a treaty to make allies. The second you think they're on your side is the second you'll find a dagger in your back. Follow your orders, but keep that Alathian in front of you, where you can see her."

"Marco seems dependable, at least. After all, he broke the captain out of the Nephretian camp, didn't he?"

"Maybe. I don't know about him. He saved our captain, and for that we owe him a debt. But, I don't know if he saved her out of a sense of honor, or because he figured if more than one of the Triumvirate was in the room with him they'd be more likely to negotiate rather than torture him."

A light on a band strapped to Victor's wrist flashed. "That's the signal," the lieutenant-commander said. "Alright, stick to the plan, Lieutenant. We play it by the numbers." Both Kaeso and Victor picked up a case of explosives.

Victor turned to the door of the vehicle, weapon in one hand, explosives in the other, then looked back at Kaeso, "Ya ready, kid?"

"Yes sir." Kaeso tightened his grip on his rifle.

"Pray to the Fates that Alathian snake hasn't stabbed Marco in the back and left us all for dead. On three. One ... two ... three."

On three, Victor slammed the door open with his boot and ran out onto the street. Kaeso followed, crossing over to the far side of the lane. Time seemed to slow as adrenaline brought Kaeso's perceptions to hyper-alertness. He noticed that the sky was overcast and a light rain was falling on the dirty and cracked streets of Narite. He could see the faces of people walking along the sidewalks, and he heard their screams as they saw the two Kalbarians run to either side of the road, weapons drawn, about to throw the cases they were carrying through the window of nearby buildings.

At that moment, a roar filled the air as an attack craft breasted overtop a building to hover menacingly over the center of the street. Dozens of Nephretian soldiers poured out of buildings and side streets, weapons drawn, all of them screaming at the two Kalbarians. The pandemonium and chaos made it difficult to hear individual voices, but the words, "Drop your weapons!" and "Get down on the ground, now!" were repeating themes.

Both Victor and Kaeso looked around stunned as the soldiers circled them, a twitch away from burying them in weapons' fire. The two Kalbarians closed ranks until they were back to back. "Slag!" Victor cursed, "I think they got the whole Fates-damned base out here for us. I should toss my box of explosives back in the ground transport—there's enough munitions there to clear out this block, take every soldier here with it." Although Kaeso couldn't see Victor's face, he knew he said the last with a smile.

"Although true, I'd rather you didn't, sir," Kaeso said.

After a moment, Victor cursed viciously. "Slag! Put down your weapon, boy." Both Victor and Kaeso slowly laid their weapons down. No sooner were their weapons gone then a mob of soldiers were on them. In moments, they were lying belly down on the ground, bruised, bloodied, and shackled, with specialized locks on Victor's body augmentations preventing him from bringing the weapons concealed in his body to bear.

Kicks to the ribs rolled them onto their backs. A Nephretian walked into their field of vision—a true Nephretian with red skin and double eyelids. He was a captain, Kaeso could see from his insignia. "Stupid Kalbarians," he smiled smugly as he spoke, "your own agents in Narite tipped us off to your presence —"

The captain's words were abruptly cut off as Victor screamed, "That bitch!" so loudly Kaeso thought he might tear a vocal cord.

* * *

"Luca save me," Marco prayed to his home-world's goddess of fortune under his breath. "What in the nine heavens am I doing here?" He had lived a life of risk as a smuggler, but none larger than the one he was presently undertaking.

Marco sat in the bustling command room of the Nephretian base in Narite. The base was commanded by Colonel Meti, who was now no more than the length of two men away from Marco.

Meti was busy coordinating the capture of the Kalbarians in the town of Narite.

Marco and Ariadne had spent weeks in town, learning about the base and key personnel in it. Ariadne had managed to acquire passable forgeries of identification cards and biometric mimics. With these and the uniforms he and Ariadne had obtained from the now dead Nephretian soldiers at the Pounding Stone Pub, Marco had managed to enter the base earlier this day with the intention of achieving a single goal—to find a link into the base's central computer system. With such a link, he could program the base's surveillance system to ignore the K.S. Novafire as it passed through Nephretian space on its way to Earth.

To Marco's dismay, he could not find a remote link. He had then made the decision to do the most foolish thing he had ever done. In the full light of day, he walked into the busy command center, which was certain to have access to the central computer system, and walked over to a nearby vacant computer port.

Perhaps it was desperation that clouded his judgment. With more time, he could have found a more isolated remote link. But the plan was in motion, and if he failed his companions would die—or face Nephretian conversion. By now the Novafire had entered Nephretian space, and if Marco did not complete what he set out to do, it would certainly be detected and destroyed, killing everyone on board, stranding him, the man who ruined the original seedship map to Earth, in Nephretian space, and giving The Fist free run to humanity's birthplace. So, here he was, working on a computer port in the heart of Nephretian operations in Narite, praying that everyone would assume he was part of the bustle of the complex.

He was currently downloading a program into the Nephretian computer system that twelve hours from now would send a signal that the system would interpret as brief glimpse of a squad of Kalbarian battle cruisers positioning themselves to attack a nearby off-world mining operation. The purpose of this was twofold. The first was to distract the Nephretians. The second was to pin the nearby Nephretian fleet in place to prevent any pursuit of the Novafire should it be discovered that it had passed through in pursuit of The Fist.

"Come again, Captain," Colonel Meti spoke into a communication link, "you say you've only captured two Kalbarians. Our reports suggest there should be more of them. Put them to the question to find out where the rest of them are."

Dust and ashes, Marco swore to himself, the Nephretians were supposed to bring Victor and Kaeso to the base, not interrogate them in the streets. He still had nightmares of his own recent questioning at the hands of The Fist. He quickly turned to the computer port and began entering another program that would distract the Nephretian ground forces.

Chapter 22

Victor's mind reeled as chaotic emotions and memories rampaged through his brain under the assault of the sarsmak rod wielded by one of his Nephretian captors. His body went into a convulsive seizure, and when his thoughts finally cleared he found himself lying on his side, retching. The light rain drizzled down on him. Kaeso was less than a meter away, convulsing under his own treatment with the sarsmak rod. Victor prayed to the Fates that Kaeso was strong enough to take it. Fates, was I ever that young, he thought to himself as he looked on Kaeso's youthful face, racked in spasms. The Nephretian torturing Kaeso wasn't much older.

The Nephretian captain used his boot to roll Victor onto his back, and then kneeled down, placing his knee on Victor's neck. "We know you're not operating alone," the captain said. Victor's face was beginning to turn red as the captain's knee continued to crush his thick neck. "The sarsmak rod breaks everyone. It is inevitable that you will tell us. Save you and your fellow soldier some pain and tell us where the next attack is planned." He took his knee off Victor's throat, who gasped for air and coughed uncontrollably for a moment.

Victor managed a grin as he replied, "I don't need to resist your sarsmak rod forever. Just long enough to let the others do their business."

"By Kepi's fire," the captain said, "you Kalbarians are insufferable in your obstinance!"

"Aw, quit yer bitchin'."

The captain leaned in close until Victor could feel his warm breath on his face. After a moment's assessment, the captain spoke. "You'll be tough to break. But him," he turned to Kaeso, "him I'm not so sure of." Kaeso stared at the sky indignantly. The captain stood and walked over to Kaeso. "How about you, boy? How long can you withstand the sarsmak rod?"

Kaeso, wet from rain and sweat, looked defiantly at the captain. "You are welcome to find out."

Good boy, Victor thought to himself.

The captain smiled. "Such spirit, such bravado!" He turned to Victor. "Even your children are filled with arrogance." Placing a foot on either side of Kaeso, the captain leaned in close, grabbing Kaeso by the neck, choking him, and said, "For all your brave words, boy, you've the face of one who's never been tested. Well, now you're going to be." Kaeso struggled for air under the captain's hold.

The captain let him go and stood to his full height. "Just a moment, boy, I'm getting a transmission." He placed his comm link by his ear for a moment while he listened to the voice on the other end. Once done, he said to his soldiers, "We've a report of Kalbarians by the space docks. Get ready to move out!"

He looked down at Kaeso and with a smile said, "Looks like I'll get to break you later. It's better that way 'cause I'll get to do it slowly." He turned to a squad of guards standing by a prisoner transport. "You—get them to the base and lock them down."

The guards snapped to action and in moments rough hands lifted the two Kalbarians and tossed them unceremoniously in the back of the transport. A troop of guards accompanied the Kalbarians in the back of the vehicle. The door was slammed shut and the transport began moving.

Victor sat up on the floor. He was surrounded by armed Nephretian guards. They were wearing light armor with their faces partially obscured by visors extending down from their helmets. With his arms firmly bound and locks on his body augments, there was very little he could do.

After several moments of bouncing in the back of the transport, one of the guards finally broke the silence. Speaking to another of the guards, he asked, "What regiment are you with soldier? I don't recognize you." The guard being spoken to was slight of frame with a pale and angular face visible under his visor. Victor noticed his helmet seemed too big for his head, and he held his weapon clumsily—as though he didn't quite know what to do with it.

"Obviously," the accused guard replied, "since we've just met." No one in the transport quite knew how to reply to that response. The accused guard saved them from trying. He twitched his hand and something flashed. Immediately the back of the transport was filled with a fine mist suspended in the air. Victor felt a cool tingling sensation on his exposed flesh, and then he blacked out.

When he opened his eyes again, he found himself still bouncing in the back of the transport staring into the face of Silmion. "Good afternoon, Lieutenant-Commander," the Ullrioni greeted. Silmion, disguised as a Nephretian guard, was withdrawing some strange, sponge-like item from Victor's neck.

"Silmion, good to see you," Victor said. He sat up and looked around. The armed guards lay collapsed and unconscious throughout the back of the transport.

Silmion moved to Kaeso's inert form and pressed the sponge-like substance to his neck. With a quick inhalation, Kaeso regained consciousness. "Lieutenant," Silmion greeted.

Moving back to Victor, Silmion took another item from his pocket—this one a long and slender dagger-like instrument—and placed it on the shackles binding the lieutenant-commander. The instrument oozed a fluid that immediately began to dissolve the metal of the lock.

"Status report," Victor demanded. After a moment the metal of his shackles became brittle from whatever fluid Silmion had placed on it, and with a quick flexing of his arms, Victor broke free. Silmion moved onto the locks binding Victor's other body augmentations.

"Ariadne's up front," Silmion replied indicating the cab of the transport where the driver sat separated from the back holding cell by a thick sheet of metal.

"I'm surprised she didn't betray us," Victor said.

Silmion shrugged in reply, and then continued. "There's another guard up there with her that we'll have to take care of if she hasn't already. Marco, far as we know, infiltrated the base earlier this afternoon. Haven't heard a word from him since, so, here's hoping."

* * *

Marco had just finished uploading his program to the Nephretian base computer system, as well as some other programs that would keep the base's soldiers busy throughout the town of Narite chasing illusory Kalbarians for the afternoon. With a confidence that belied the fear tearing his stomach apart, Marco gathered his gear, stood, and walked for the exit.

A voice behind him called out in Nephretian, "Corporal!" Marco stopped while he inconspicuously checked the insignia on his arm. He was wearing a corporal's uniform.

So close, he thought to himself.

He turned to see a lieutenant who had been assisting the base commander approach him. Marco snapped to attention, dropping his chin to his chest. "My superior," he replied in flawless Nephretian.

The lieutenant's eyes narrowed as he approached Marco. "I don't recognize you, Corporal. What's your regiment?"

Marco had his answer ready, though he hadn't had a chance to test its plausibility. "I'm Corporal Seth of the N.S. Tempest. I'm overseeing a supply run before we leave to patrol the off-world mining colonies. Captain Sadji has me updating our star charts while I'm here." Marco had picked up his backstory in bits and pieces over the past weeks as he frequented the bars surrounding the space docks. He and Ariadne had clashed more than once over what she perceived as his partying and drinking, but the information he gained through his drunken revelries had proven invaluable many times over already. Marco was hoping it would prove useful once more.

As Marco completed his response to the lieutenant, Colonel Meti turned to look at him, "Captain Sadji did you say? I know him well."

Inside, Marco was cursing violently. Outwardly, he turned smoothly to the base commander. "My superior, do you have any message you'd like me to convey?"

"Yes. Tell him little Shamisé just completed First Cycle of the Rites."

"Congratulations, my superior," Marco replied, but the colonel had already turned his attention back to his work.

The lieutenant turned to Marco. "Corporal, I think we're going to be here a while today. Do you know where the canteen is?"

"Yes, my superior," Marco replied. He had passed by it several times throughout the day as he was searching the base for a computer access point.

"Good. Be a good lad and get the colonel and myself a coffee, would you?"

"Of course, my superior."

* * *

Silmion was sitting in the back of the prisoner transport with Victor, Kaeso, and half a dozen unconscious guards. The vehicle had just come to a stop. There were no windows, so the trio could not see where they were or what was going on. The sound of doors closing reverberated through the transport.

"Remember," Silmion said, "there's a Nephretian guard with Ariadne that we'll need to deal with."

"Gotcha," Victor replied as his inhuman muscles rippled along his arms, twisting the subdermal dragon motif on his biceps.

"Subtly," Silmion said with a hand on Victor's huge shoulder.

Victor turned to look at Silmion as blades snicked out of his knuckles. "I can do subtle." Silmion doubted that.

The latch on the lock turned and the door swung open. On the other side of the door was a Nephretian soldier, a look of surprise lighting up his face. Behind him stood Ariadne dressed in the garb of a Nephretian sergeant.

In a flash Ariadne made a quick movement behind the Nephretian, and his body lurched forward. At the same time, Victor pounded his knuckle blades through the Nephretian's light armor and into his chest. Grabbing the collapsing soldier Victor lifted him effortlessly and tossed him in the truck. Ariadne quickly stepped in behind him.

"Where's Marco?" Victor asked.

"Don't know," Ariadne replied. "He's supposed to be here."

"There he is," said Kaeso pointing. Marco was just exiting the building through a nearby door. In one hand, steam rose from a cup that he was blowing on to cool. In his other hand, he held a tray with four more steaming cups.

"A bit cocky isn't he?" Silmion said as they watched him stroll to the transport.

"Not the word I'd choose," Victor replied.

"You're late," Ariadne said as Marco arrived.

"You're early!" Placing the tray of cups on the floor of the transport, he said, "I got you all coffee." Marco dug into a pocket of his uniform and pulled out his data pad. Tossing it to Kaeso, he said, "Here you go. Just type in the transponder codes for the Novafire and hit enter. I've set the Nephretian surveillance system to ignore any ship with that code."

A smile broke Victor's face as he reached for a cup. "Fates damn you, Marco."

Ariadne grabbed a cup as she exited the transport. "I'll meet you at the rendezvous point."

"See you then," Marco said with a wave. Ariadne quickly left the vehicle and crossed the compound.

"You," Marco said pointing to Silmion. "You're with me in the front. Victor, Kaeso, you sit tight back here."

"Here you go," Kaeso said, tossing Marco's data pad back. "The code's entered. Our ship should be able to slip past the Nephretians now."

"Good. Time to get us back to the Novafire to continue our pursuit of The Fist," Marco said as he caught the data pad.

"You just planning on driving out of here?" Victor asked Marco.

"Well, that's plan A," Marco replied.

"You got a plan B?" Victor asked.

Marco smiled and slapped Victor on his massive arms. "You're my plan B, big guy." Victor grunted in reply. Marco grabbed a second cup of coffee as Silmion closed the door of the transport, imprisoning Victor and Kaeso once more with the bodies of their former guards.

Both Marco and Silmion climbed into the cab of the transport, "Hey Silmion, you guys have coffee on Ullrion?" Marco asked, handing one of his cups to Silmion.

"I doubt it," Silmion replied.

"Try it," Marco said as he started up the vehicle.

Silmion took a tentative sip of the hot liquid and a scowl immediately wrinkled his face. "Bah, it tastes like ... burnt dirt!"

Marco chuckled as he drove the truck forward. "Yeah, the Nephretians have pretty low standards for the stuff. You know who's got the best coffee?"

"No," Silmion answered distractedly as he searched for a place to set his cup.

"Verna. Once you've tasted Vernian coffee, all other coffees will be ruined," Marco said. Silmion noticed a smile touched Marco's lips as he spoke about Verna.

"Hmm, I can't wait," Silmion said as he found a holder for his cup and turned to look out the window.

The transport pulled up to the checkpoint of the base. "Ok," Marco stated as he pressed a button to open his window, "we need to hide your face, so get your helmet on and try to act natural."

"I am acting natural," Silmion said as he donned his helmet.

"Really?"

Before Silmion could reply, Marco had pulled up to a guard waving them down at the checkpoint. He and the guard conversed in Nephretian, a language completely unknown to Silmion. Marco handed the guard a card, which he scanned into a data pad. The guard laughed at something Marco said. Silmion laughed also, feigning understanding.

After another brief exchange, the guard returned Marco's card and waved them onwards.

Marco moved the transport forward and turned to Silmion as he was closing the window. "Man, remind to take a spare set of underwear the next time I sneak into a Nephretian base. That was nerve-wracking!"

"You have poor taste in humor and drink," Silmion said. He was beginning to wonder how long the bitter aftertaste of coffee in his mouth would last. "But I must concede, you have a penchant for getting into and out of places most people would consider impossible."

"Thanks, Silmion. I think you have poor taste in humor and drink, too." They looked at each other a moment, and then Marco broke out laughing. Silmion could not suppress a smile.

After they were several kilometers away from the base, but well before the town limits of Narite, Marco stopped the transport. Wordlessly, the two exited, walked to the back and let Victor and Kaeso out. Victor carried a limp guard in each hand to the cab and positioned them in the chairs as driver and passenger. Then the entire group walked off the side of the road a ways and turned back to the transport.

Marco turned to Victor, "So, think you can make it look like a squad of Kalbarians attacked the transport?"

Before Victor could answer, a rumbling explosion cut through the air. Back in the direction of the base a giant fireball was soaring to the sky.

"Dust and ashes," Marco swore. "Ariadne's early again." A Kalbarian landing craft was streaking along the ground towards the group.

Victor turned to the transport. Bolts drove out of his calves and pounded into the ground, stabilizing him. Compartments on his forearms opened and massive rifles slipped out. The weapons opened fire with a roar, tearing into the prisoner transport, causing it to erupt in a ball of fire.

By now, the Kalbarian craft was landing beside them, door hatch opening. Ariadne was visible in the cockpit.

"Huh. I honestly expected she'd leave us here," Victor said.

Marco smiled and slapped Victor on the back. "You, my good sir, are underestimating just how much she has grown to like me over the past couple of weeks."

"You're not that good looking, Marco," Silmion said. "The Novafire's her only way to Earth, and we all know just what Taura would do to her if she returned to the ship without us." He pushed passed them and climbed aboard the craft.

Chapter 23

Admiral Hetshepsu stared angrily with hard green eyes at the 3D map generated by their long range sensors. The image of the map floated before him, dominating the room. His attention was focused on a red light blinking behind the location of the Reclaimer and its fleet in the Q-wave slipstream. The K.S. Novafire, battered and several weeks behind, was nonetheless in hot pursuit, and on her, Captain Lucia Taura. The Admiral couldn't begin to guess how, but it seemed the Kalbarian ship had slipped through Nephretian space to give chase.

The Nephretians had six battleships including the Reclaimer. Although loath to admit it, the Kalbarian vessel outmatched Nephretian ships one-on-one, and possibly even two-on-one. But Hetshepsu's numerical advantage tilted the odds in his favor. Still, Taura had defied the odds before.

Lord Hamu, resplendent as ever in the regalia of Fist of the High Prelate, stepped up behind Hetshepsu. "For weeks now, you stand here in our navigation room staring at this map."

"Yes, my superior," Hetshepsu replied.

Hamu moved to the area of the map where the indicator beacon of the Novafire flashed. "And it is this, an insignificant dot that vexes you so."

"Yes, Lord Hamu," Hetshepsu replied, finally turning his full attention to the Fist. "The Novafire nips at our heels. One of Kalbarai's best class of warships, led by an accomplished captain."

"Captain Taura, if I'm not mistaken," Hamu said as he turned to his admiral. "How many times has she escaped your grasp now? Is it three?"

White hot rage welled in Hetshepsu's breast—he'd have the heart of any other man who spoke to him so, but could do nothing but take the insult from the Fist. He couldn't stop himself from narrowing his eyes in anger, but that was the only outward trace of emotion he showed before mastering himself. "Twice, my superior."

"My mistake," Hamu replied. Purposefully, the Fist walked to the other end of the map that was dominated by a star with a number of orbiting planets. "We'll arrive in the Earth system in the hour. I trust you have made good use of your time staring at this map, Hetshepsu. You've no doubt a plan to deal with the Novafire?"

Hetshepsu's anger from a moment earlier was forgotten and a smile touched the admiral's lips. "Indeed I have."

* * *

"We'll be slipping out of the Q-wave slipstream and entering the outer rim of the Earth solar system momentarily, Captain," Commander Servius said. He absent-mindedly rubbed the arabesque circuitry along the side of his head with his flesh hand.

"Thanks, Servius," Taura replied.

The bridge of the Novafire was alive with activity—indeed the whole ship was. The ship was badly damaged and hadn't had nearly enough time in the docks to fully repair it. Taura had crews performing repairs around the clock while they were waiting for their team on Narite to smooth the path for them to pass through Nephretian space undetected. Now that they were in the Q-wave slipstream in pursuit of the Nephretians bound for Earth, their ability to finish the repairs on the blast shield and other external systems were limited.

Damage notwithstanding, the Novafire was still a study in intimidation, its body marked by jagged scars and burn trails. Many of the statues adorning its outer shell were shattered, their broken forms adding a haunting beauty to the elegant menace of the ship.

"You excited about reaching the Earth system?" the commander asked.

"Shut up and prepare yourself for an ambush," the captain replied as she eyed the preparations on the bridge through her marbled blue eyes. The Nephretians had a head start of several weeks. Without doubt, their sensors would have told them the Novafire was behind them in the slipstream. Hetshepsu had plenty of time to set a trap.

Servius chuckled. "You seem pretty certain they're gonna hit us. Scanners don't show anything at the drop point."

"That's what'll make it an ambush," Taura said. "There's a limited amount of space we can exit the slipstream given our trajectory. They have a pretty good idea where we'll be. If they give us time to find them, then we'll be bringing the attack to them and fighting on our terms. Hetshepsu won't allow for that. No, they'll hit us as we exit the stream."

"Well, we'll find out soon enough," Servius said as he turned to look at the rest of the bridge.

An audible countdown began, measuring the final seconds until they arrived. A wave of silence swept through the entire ship. With a subtle bump, the Novafire exited the stream and entered normal space. The front monitor showed empty blackness marred by a bright star—the central sun of the system in the far distance.

"We've entered the outer rim of the Earth system, Captain," one of the bridge crew said.

A taunt stillness gripped the crew of the Novafire. Nothing happened.

Servius turned a knowing look at the captain. "Don't get cocky yet," Taura said.

The silence was shattered by the hammering of an alarm. Ensign Nerva, manning the scanners, yelled, "Enemy ships coming out of the slipstream!" That was all he managed to say before three Nephretian battle ships, each of them shaped like the mythical phoenix, snapped into existence and descended, hammerhead missiles preceding them.

"Batteries, launch flak firewall!" Taura ordered. A stream of glittering lights poured forth from the Novafire and started forming a barrier kilometers away. The firewall screened out most of the incoming hammerhead missiles, but two slipped through. The Kalbarian's null-bosonic field disabled one of them, but the remaining one rocked the Novafire as it slammed into its blast shield.

"Ahead three-quarter speed, bearing five degrees to port, inclination twenty degrees. Firing sequence J-1," Taura ordered. The bridge became a flurry of activity.

210 Hammer of Amahté

The fortress that was the Novafire, dwarfing the Nephretian ships, soared between two of its adversaries. It was a daring move, bringing the Novafire close enough that the flak firewalls were actually able to engage one another. The tiny orbs of flak from the Kalbarian and Nephretian ships darted and spun amongst one another, flashing in bright explosions as they made contact. Having thinned out the enemy's flak firewall, the Novafire launched a barrage of RAC missiles at near point blank range into the hulls of the Nephretians. The Nephretians paid back the Novafire in kind.

In moments, the Novafire reversed its course and once again smashed through the trio of Nephretian ships, which soared and swooped about the Kalbarian behemoth, raining fire down upon it. The Novafire hammered back at its adversaries as the four ships danced through space, tearing at each other.

The bridge of the Novafire was alive with the shouts of orders, the dull thuds of explosions keeping time in the background. "Ariadne!" Taura shouted.

The Alathian turned her attention from the computer console she was sharing with Marco. "What?" she asked.

"Status report. Have you hacked into one of their ships yet?" Taura asked.

"It's not as easy as you might think, Captain," Ariadne replied. "We'll need more time."

"Don't listen to her, Captain," Marco said. "It's easy. She's just not very good at it." He flashed Ariadne a wink and a smile.

"Just get it done," the captain replied.

* * *

Kan Rath, Ullrioni ambassador to Nephreti representing the Duraanesti nation, easily maintained his footing as the Nephretian ship heaved under a Kalbarian barrage that sent the Nephretian soldiers sprawling. Since Ullrion had never achieved space flight, he was unaware of the intricacies of space combat. That said, it was readily apparent the Kalbarian ship outclassed the Nephretians. Even though they outnumbered the Novafire three to one, the Nephretians were hard pressed to beat the Kalbarian craft down. As the vessel rocked again, it began to feel more like a tomb than a space craft.

What would happen to his essence, he wondered, if he were to die in the void of space? How would his body replenish the life of his homeland? These thoughts troubled his mind as the Kalbarians pressed their attack.

During his journey to the Earth system, he had grown to dislike Nephretians deeply. They were arrogant and unyielding in their foolish beliefs and insisted that some low-level clergymen prattled on to him about the "Paths to Amahté" every single day. He detested that he had been made to stay on one of the attack ships while Lord Hamu and Hetshepsu continued the journey to the origins of the seedships. He took solace in the fact that the war criminal Silmion was likely aboard the Kalbarian craft. There would be some comfort in bearing witness to his death.

"Ambassador," Nsu, the captain of the ship called, "we are about to launch the dreighnar. Are you sure they will work?"

Kan Rath had come to accept that this condescending doubt was typical of the Nephretians. Arms crossed, he looked at Nsu just as the captain's nictitating membranes were closing and opening over his eyes. "Of course they'll work," Kan Rath bit back. Overseeing the dreighnar, one of many Ullrioni weapons, was the reason for his presence here.

"Good," the captain replied, "it's time to give the Kalbarians a little surprise. Firing sequence dreighnar one!"

* * *

Victor struggled to regain his footing as the Novafire was rocked by another explosion. A defense drone kept pace, hovering beside him.

Something had happened with the latest barrage. Several of the missiles were not, in fact, explosive. Rather, they transported something that had boarded and infested a growing area of the Novafire. First-hand reports from the crew were panicky and abruptly cut off. His link through the neural net with the ship was showing something advancing, tearing through his soldiers and defense drones, but what it was he did not know.

But he had a hunch who might.

He slammed open a door in the crew corridor. A squad of sixteen soldiers were struggling to retain their balance as the ship rolled. In the midst of them was Silmion, standing steady as though the ship was not rocking beneath his feet.

"Come with me," Victor ordered. "All of you." He turned and marched away, his feet hammering into the ground like a tank.

"What's going on?" Silmion asked, racing to catch up to Victor.

"The Nephretians ambushed us as soon as we entered the outer reaches of the Earth system. We've just been boarded by ... something." The lieutenant-commander called back to his soldiers. "Link up, dogs!" Silently, they linked into Victor's neural net, forming the phalanx.

"I'm honored you think I can help," Silmion said, tying his shoulder-length golden blonde hair into a tight pony tail to keep it out of his eyes.

"The thing is, Silmion, I've no idea what's boarded us. It ain't drones, and it ain't soldiers. I got a feeling it's a gift from the Ullrionis to Nephreti."

Victor entered a freight elevator and the phalanx followed. He entered a code by a keyboard on the wall while the doors whispered shut and they descended into the depths of the ship.

Pulling his vanesti gun from under his cloak, Silmion asked, "Do you have any description of what's attacking?"

The elevator bell rang out rhythmically as it dropped down floor after floor.

"Nope," Victor said. Then, he said over his shoulder to the soldiers following him, "We're going into a hot zone, and our defensive drones in the area have been destroyed, so we're going in blind. If it's not a Kalbarian, shoot it. If you don't know what it is, shoot it."

The ringing of the elevator slowed. Victor readjusted his massive K-96 heavy RAC rifle attached to his arm. Muscles rippled along his body and the subdermal patterns of dragons on his biceps began to writhe. "Nothing gets past us, you hear me, dogs? Next stop's ours."

With one final ring, the elevator came to a stop and a taut silence fell over the troop. The doors whispered open. The defense drone that had been following Victor silently hovered ahead of the troop, relaying tactical information to the neural net of the phalanx.

The hallway was cast in shadows—many of the lights were wrecked. Blood drenched the walls, floor and ceiling, and the debris of destroyed drones were scattered across the floor, but the hall was otherwise empty. Each soldier struggled to stay upright as the ship was violently rocked by a series of explosions, though Victor noted that Silmion easily maintained his footing.

Over the neural net, the lieutenant-commander highlighted four of his soldiers and ordered them forward as the defense drone led the way. The four slid and tripped as the ship rumbled and heaved under the attack of the three Nephretian cruisers. Victor sent another group of four after them, then the remaining eight plus Victor and Silmion took up the rear. There was a pause in the rumbling explosions wracking the ship, and then with a jolt it was tossed about once more as weapon's fire pounded into it.

The advance guard of four came to a T-intersection, one hall continuing on ahead, another turning to the right. Maintaining cover behind the wall, the defense drone advanced and relayed what it observed back to the phalanx. It was a short connecting hallway ending in another T-intersection that ran left and right. Littering the floor were corpses of three Kalbarian soldiers.

"Fore guard, set up a defensive position at the far end of this hall," Victor silently ordered over the neural net. The four soldiers in the front quickly made their way, ignoring the corpses of their fallen brethren, and set up a defensive position at the far end of the short hall with the defense drone. Victor ordered the body of the phalanx into the hall, with a rear guard of four set at the hall's entrance.

Silmion approached one of the corpses in the corridor, vanesti gun at the ready. The body was lying face down, arms and legs at twisted angles. A pool of blood surrounded the corpse and the stench of meat and death hung thick in the air.

"Any ideas what did this, Silmion?" Victor asked.

Silmion, pointing his vanesti gun at the corpse as if it might rise and attack, hesitated a moment, then with a quick fluid motion, grabbed the corpse and turned it on its back. His face wrinkled in disgust and curses escaped the lips of a number of nearby soldiers.

Another explosion rocked the ship and everyone struggled to maintain their footing. The corpse went sliding along the hallway.

The face of the corpse was frozen in a death-rictus of fear and agony. A gaping hole dominated its entire torso, which was hollow with the exception of fragments of flesh and tissue.

"Dreighnar," Silmion whispered.

"What?" Victor asked.

"Can you quarantine this section of the ship?" Silmion asked as he rose to his feet.

"What?" Victor demanded again.

"This section of the ship," Silmion replied, "can you quarantine it? Seal it, like if the hull was breached?"

"Yeah, why?" the lieutenant-commander asked. "You're freaking me out here, Silmion."

"Do it," the Ullrioni ordered.

Victor struggled to contain his anger. "You better tell me what's going on first."

Their conversation ended as a sound began to echo through the hallway. It sounded as though hundreds of metal ball bearings were rolling along the floor. The defense drone was reporting that is was sensing a moving mass approaching.

"Just do it," Silmion said.

Before Victor could reply, the air was rent by the roar of gunfire. The advance guard along with the defense drone at the front end of the hallway had started shooting.

Chaos gripped the hall for a moment while the ship rocked as more Nephretian missiles crashed into the Novafire in the ongoing space battle. The Kalbarians were tossed to the floor while only Silmion retained his footing.

"What the Fates is that!" someone yelled. Curses and screams accompanied the staccato of gunfire.

Victor scrambled to regain his feet and turned to the advance guard to see their position overwhelmed by a large number of spheres the size of a grown man's fist. They appeared to be scaled and dark green or black in color. Along the floor, walls and ceiling they rolled. One of them leapt and landed on the torso of one of the guards. The sphere spun and whirled in the soldier's abdomen, tearing through armor and clothing and into soft flesh. The soldier screamed as blood erupted from his torso and he dropped to his knees. With a violent convulsion, the soldier was thrown onto his back where his body writhed and flopped as the thing tore through his insides. The soldier was dead, even though his body continued shuddering.

"Slag, it tore through his armor!" someone yelled.

Victor hefted his blaster rifle and screamed, "Quit yer bitchin' and shoot 'em!"

Gun fire erupted from the squad. Optic links slaved the soldiers' guns to their eyes. Whatever they looked at, their gun unerringly fired upon. The RAC projectiles shot from the weapons further modified their course and armament to adjust for the enemy's changing tactics at a picosecond time scale. The neural net of the phalanx connected each soldier to the whole allowing for instantaneous coordination of attack and defense. But waves of the creatures tore into them in an unrelenting tide. The advance guard was in the thick of it, but desperately held their ground while the remaining phalanx tried to come to their aid. Another soldier went down screaming as his insides were torn to shreds and the defense drone was torn to ribbons and clattered onto the floor.

Silmion, quick as the wind, was in the fray, vanesti gun firing rapidly. When one of the attacking creatures came too close, the vanesti gun, a living creature itself, snapped out and locked the attacking sphere in vicious jaws, whipped the creature about, and then tossed it away before resuming firing.

A succession of explosions rocked the ship tossing soldiers to the ground. From their backs and bellies they fired desperately.

Silmion seemed to be trying to make his way to the bodies of the recently fallen soldiers, but was forced to halt his advance to defend himself. He turned to Victor and shouted over the gunfire, "You have to shoot your fallen soldiers!"

"Slag that!" Victor yelled back.

"No," Silmion shouted, pointing at his torso, "you have to shoot your fallen men!"

Behind Silmion, the first soldier to fall to the attack finally stopped convulsing. Silmion turned to look at the body. "Aw, blight take it!" he said.

The soldier's chest and abdomen exploded outwards as three of the creatures Silmion called dreighnar sprung from him. Caught by surprise, two soldiers fell back as their abdomens were torn open. The third creature leapt towards Silmion, but the vanesti gun snapped it out of the air, thrashed it, and then spat it out.

"Oh, you are kidding me!" Victor yelled over the sound of gunfire. The ship rocked again, but most soldiers managed to keep their footing.

"The body of a human is large enough to produce three of them once infected," Silmion said. "If you don't shoot them while they're gestating, we're going to be here all day!"

The advance guard was completely destroyed, but the bulk of the phalanx was holding their ground in the hallway. In a move that Victor would characterize as foolishly bold, Silmion leapt to the front of the hallway where the advance guard had fallen.

The creatures swirled and spun at him, but with the grace of a dancer and a speed that defied belief, Silmion dodged out of their way. His vanesti gun fired, at turns hitting the creatures attacking him, at turns ripping into the torsos of the fallen soldiers who stopped convulsing once the creatures growing inside them were destroyed. Victor had never seen anyone fight the way Silmion did. It was as though every move was choreographed, every attack from the enemy anticipated, every death blow scripted. And the vanesti gun—was it hissing, Victor thought, or just whipping through the air? Either way, the whirling susurration of the vanesti gun created a haunting melody as Silmion fought.

Once he had hit each of the fallen soldiers, he took two steps towards the remainder of the phalanx and leapt into the air. He sailed above the heads of the lead soldiers and landed in a dive roll behind them.

The creatures surged after Silmion, spinning down floor, walls, ceiling and soaring through the air towards the bellies of the soldiers, but their advance was halted by a wall of RAC projectiles as the full fire power of the Kalbarian phalanx was unleashed upon them.

Silmion, recovering from his roll, was now behind the phalanx in the T-intersection, one hallway leading to the elevator they had entered from, one away, and the third to where the phalanx was positioned. He turned to look at the elevator. The hall was clear. He turned to look down the hall leading away from the elevator. A surge of the dreighnar was rapidly rolling down the hall to strike the phalanx from behind. "They're behind us!" he yelled as he opened rapid fire with his vanesti gun.

As one, the phalanx backed up down their corridor until a rear detachment of four guards joined Silmion. Fluidly, the phalanx melted around the corner to the hall leading towards the elevator. The two waves of the dreighnar merged, creating a single front for the phalanx to focus its fire on.

Victor used his neural net to lock into the ships computer, "This is Lieutenant-Commander Quintilus Victor, vocal access authorization," he yelled out, "initiate hull-breach lock down of aft section P2 through P4, security clearance alpha-four." At his command, the ship began sealing off their section of the ship so that not even a molecule of air could pass. It was a safeguard typically used to seal hull breaches while the ship's self-repair mechanisms sealed the rupture. With a metallic clang that rang out over the gunfire, the seals set in place.

"You hear that, dogs," Victor shouted to his soldiers, "we're sealed in here good and tight. You want out, kill 'em all!"

Chapter 24

Fates, I don't think the Novafire's ever taken a beating like this, Taura thought to herself. She had sent everything the Novafire had against the three Nephretian ships, but their numerical advantage was taking its toll.

"Focus all fire on target beta," she ordered. The ship the Novafire's neural net labeled 'beta' was heavily damaged, and Taura was hoping to knock it out of the battle, leveling the odds. But, the other two Nephretian ships swooped in to screen its retreat to the rear, their flak firewalls screening out most of the RACs the Novafire had just fired. They opened fire on Taura's ship, overwhelming her flak firewall and slamming into her ship's blast shield.

"Engineering, what's the status of the aft engines? Why are they still down?" she asked over the ship's neural net.

"Captain, we can't get to the aft engines. The entire section has been sealed by Lieutenant-Commander Victor."

She hailed the lieutenant-commander over the neural net of the ship, "Victor, what the Fates is going on? You've sealed the entire aft portside of the ship."

A hail of gunfire dominated the communication channel. In her mind's eye, the neural net showed Victor with a phalanx fighting some advancing mass. Victor replied, "Do not lift the seals, Captain. We've been breached by some Ullrioni weapon called dreighnar. It's —" he was interrupted and for a moment there was only gunfire and cursing. He came back on, "It's massacred the crew in this section."

"Damn it, Victor! Our aft engines are down and we can't get anyone to them. We're losing the fight up here. You have got to get to the engines and get them online again or we're dead."

"Uh, sure Captain," Victor replied, "but I can't say as we have any engineers here. Just me and a bunch of dog soldiers."

"Captain, I can get the engines back up," a nearby voice said. Taura turned to the owner of the voice. It was Kaeso, who was currently manning the communications station. "I served half a year in engineering before getting moved to communications," he added. "I can do it."

"Don't be daft, lad, the section's sealed. There's no getting to them. The DECOMP doors are sealed and the entire section is encapsulated in a silksteel blast wall," Taura said

"I could pilot a lander through one of the hull breeches in the section, seal the breech, pressurize the area and meet up with the phalanx."

"While we're in combat?" Taura asked.

"The hell you could pilot a lander through a breech in the middle of combat," Commander Servius said. "What'd you have? Two weeks of lander training in the academy and a crash landing on Ullrion?" He turned to the captain, "I could do it, though."

The captain looked to her second in command, "You? You're needed on the bridge."

"I was a hell of a pilot in my day, you know that. The kid's smart," the commander said, nodding at Kaeso, "and we're getting torn to slag. If we can't get those engines back online, it won't matter where I am. We've got nothing to lose."

"Do it," Taura ordered. Without looking to see them leave, she began speaking to Victor, "Lieutenant-Commander, Servius is going to transport Kaeso through a missile breech in your section. Kaeso will direct your team to get the engines online. Link up with them and arrange to pick 'em up."

There was a pause. Taura could imagine the look on Victor's face as he digested the order. Finally, he replied, "Uh, yes, Captain."

Taura now turned her attention to Marco and Ariadne. "You two! If you're going to make a miracle happen, now's the time."

* * *

"Dust and ashes, their combat security system almost seems Alathian," Marco said to Ariadne

"It is. Whenever they capture and 'convert' our agents, they get a whole host of our tech," she replied.

"Damn it, Ariadne, you're Alathian. Cracking it should be a breeze for you."

"Alathian combat security systems are actually pretty damn good!"

Marco turned to Ariadne as he snapped his fingers. "I've got an idea. If it works, it'll give you a window of about a nanosecond before they shut it down. Will that be enough time to push an attack virus through?"

"Yeah," she replied, "if I slave my virus to your attack protocol, but they'll identify the virus and disable it immediately."

"Aw, don't you worry your pretty brown eyes over that," Marco said. Then, turning to Taura, "Captain, on my mark, I'm going to need you to boost the power to the sensor array by about twenty percent, okay?"

"If you need it, you've got it," Taura said. "Just get it done. Fast."

"Right. Now give me a moment to cobble this together."

* * *

"What did she say?" Silmion asked Victor, yelling to be heard over the gunfire.

Victor was still unsure how to feel about Taura's plan. "The engines in this section are down. If we don't get them up, we're dead. She's sending Kaeso on a lander through a missile blast in the side of the ship to fix them."

"That seems … rash given the circumstances," Silmion commented as he continued to fire at the dreighnar approaching the phalanx. Two more men had fallen since they were backed into the hall leading to the elevator. That said, the remaining ten of the phalanx were holding their ground.

"Fangere's teeth it's rash!" Victor replied.

The behavior of the dreighnar was changing. Their advance had stopped. A mass of them retreated down the corridors from which they had come. Others, though, spun, and with the squealing sound of rending metal, they burrowed their way into the walls, floor and ceiling.

"Slag, they can bore through metal!" someone said.

"They can tear through your armor, so what did you expect?" Silmion said. More than one soldier angered by the condescension in his voice turned a dark eye on him.

"Fates, will they be able to make their way through our DECOMP seals?" Victor asked.

Pointing at the holes left by the vacating dreighnar, Silmion replied, "If they're made of the same material as your walls and floors, then I'd say yes."

Victor grunted, "No, the DECOMP seals are made of the same stuff as blast shields. It'd take a day to cut through with a cutting torch. Let's hope they hold. I also notice they don't show up on infrared vision. I tried to follow them once they ducked into the walls."

"They're cold-blooded," Silmion responded, "so they take on the ambient temperature of their surroundings. You can see them in the normal visual range. You can also see them if you can detect movement or vibrations. Their scales make a pretty loud noise on most surfaces, so you can usually hear them coming. They like waiting by those holes, though, and ambushing you when you get close."

Turning once more to Silmion, Victor asked, "What's controlling them? Do they have a handler, or are they intelligent on their own?"

"No," Silmion said, "they don't have a handler. They're just nasty little beasts that know how to hunt."

Victor cursed as he surveyed the remainder of his phalanx. "We're gonna need more dogs for this fight," he said.

"I'd appreciate it if you stopped referring to me as a dog," Silmion said. Victor was ignoring him, though, as he scanned the neural net for any other soldiers in this section of the ship. He found a number of small and scattered phalanxes barricaded in various areas and across a number of floors. Over fifty soldiers all together. Not a bad force, if they could be brought together and coordinated.

Using his access as a high-ranking officer, Victor linked his phalanx into each of the other ones he had identified creating a much larger phalanx. Immediately, information regarding the enemy's location and abilities as well as successful—and unsuccessful—tactics were shared across the newly formed unit.

"Listen up, dogs," the lieutenant-commander said over the neural net to his soldiers as well as audibly for Silmion, "the aft engines are down, and the Novafire is taking a beating. They're sending someone to fix 'em, but he's coming by lander flown by our very own Commander Servius through one of the holes in the Fates-blasted hull. We need to position a strike force to rendezvous with them, as well as clear a path to the engines. The commander'll be there, so try to pretend you know how to fight. And if they blow the landing and get themselves killed, then we gotta make it to the engines ourselves and pray to Sudus Velume one of us is smart enough to figure the damn things out."

* * *

Streaking across the outside of the K.S. Novafire in a landing craft, Kaeso, though he could never admit it to his fellow Kalbarians, was terrified. Missiles and energy blasts rained down upon the Novafire, who itself sent its own barrage into the heavens. The flak firewall glittered in the distance as it sought to destroy as many of the incoming Nephretian hammerhead missiles as it could. Amidst this fog of destruction, Commander Servius deftly maneuvered the landing craft. They had linked null-graviton fields, effectively slaving the landing craft to the movement of the battleship as it rocked from the impact of missiles.

Doubt and fear gnawed at Kaeso. What am I doing here—I'm no soldier, he silently asked himself, panic clutching at him. Hundreds of taunts and recriminations cast over him throughout his childhood from classmates and teachers alike weighed down on him as the landing craft rocked and wheeled around. He should have been an artisan as his parents had implored him.

But, there was no escape now. Outwardly, he tried to maintain a look of calm, though he wasn't sure how successful he was at it. It didn't matter, though, as the commander's attention was focused on the task of flying. Sweat had long ago formed on Servius' brow as he struggled to control the craft.

Victor's voice came over the communication system. "I'm downloading landing coordinates for you. There's a breech on section P3. It oughta be big enough to fly through, with a little room for error. The engine room's only a few minutes jog away."

"Got it," Servius said. After a few tense moments, the commander positioned the craft so a large, blackened hole in the Novafire's hull dominated their monitor. "Ok, to close the distance, we're going to have to separate the null-graviton fields. That means if the Novafire moves unexpectedly while we're landing, well, let's just say it'll get bumpy." The aperture bounced around in front of them stochastically as the Novafire took a number of hits. "Brace yourself, lad," Servius advised as he powered their craft forward.

Kaeso could see the interior of the ship. A floor had been blown out, and there was no flat area to land. As the landing craft was moving through the opening, the Novafire jerked violently, sending the ceiling of the landing area crashing into them. Their ship smashed and skidded into the floor violently before coming to a cock-eyed stop. Alarms rang in the landing craft and the power fluttered on and off.

"Fates take it!" Servius cursed. "The null-boson array on our craft was smashed off. If we can't get a temporary shield over the breech, we can't pressurize this area, and this whole thing's done."

Kaeso looked at the displays flashing before him. Damn it, think, his inner voice silently screamed at him, that's the only thing you're good for! Think!

"Uh," Kaeso hesitantly grunted out loud.

"You got something, Lieutenant?" Servius asked. "Out with it! What?"

"Uh, we should be able to reroute the sensor to the hull of the landing craft—use our ship as the null-boson array," Kaeso said. "It'll erase most of our flight controls, but this was a one-way trip, anyway."

"Do it," Servius ordered.

"I'll need you to open the access panel and reroute the array's wiring to the ship's ground," Kaeso said. "I'll need to redirect the power to account for the larger surface area of the hull."

"Whatever," the commander replied as he moved to the back of the craft to open the access panel. "I'm on the wiring"

After several hurried moments and crashing about, the two had the re-routed null-boson array set up. "Ready on your orders,"

Kaeso said. Then he added, "If this doesn't work, it'll probably blow out the power supply to the ship. We'll be in a dead landing craft exposed to space with maybe an hour of air."

The commander looked seriously at Kaeso. "The Novafire ain't going to last an hour, kid. Do it."

After a deep breath, Kaeso entered a code into the console of the landing craft. The lights dimmed, flickered, and then shut off, leaving them in a deep darkness.

"Are the Fates pissing on us, Lieutenant? Did we blow our power?" Commander Servius asked.

Kaeso waited a moment. In the background, he could hear the faint hum of power coursing through the craft. He looked at the readouts of his console, and replied, "No, it's working. The null-boson field's up—the breech in the hull is covered."

"Outstanding, boy!" Servius said, slapping Kaeso roughly on the back. Then, the commander linked into the ship's neural net, "Commander Vetus Servius vocal access authorization. Initiate re-pressurization of aft section P3, quadrant 9, security clearance alpha-two." Outside the landing craft could be heard the rush of wind as the atmosphere was pumped back into the area.

Servius turned to Kaeso and tossed him an assault rifle with his mechanical quicksilver arm and ordered, "Gear up, kid. Now the fun begins." With that, he moved to the hatch of the lander and opened it.

The two of them stepped out into the ruined landscape of the ship. Tangled metal, peeled back and charred, surrounded them. Kaeso looked back to the gaping blast hole through which they had flown. He watched the self-repair mechanisms of the ship hard at work repairing the breech. Small arachnoid-like robots he could see scuttled up and down the walls of the ship like ants fixing their smashed colony while the sparks of robotic welders' guns flared. Kaeso also knew that invisible to his eye, swarms of nanorobots were converting scrap material into a refurbished hull.

Looking past this, he was struck for a moment by the beauty of the unending thick blackness of space. Thousands of the universe's creatures would die here today in this battle. Some would die for a cause they believed in. Others would die in pursuit of vengeance, or in defense of their brothers and sisters in arms. Others still would die for the memory of their family, the names of their loved ones a prayer on their lips as their light was forever extinguished.

And the universe would not care. The hardships the universe's creations set upon themselves were their own concern. The vast expanse of existence would carry on in its way unknowing of the desperate struggles of these small tribes of humanity as they engaged in a battle that, for the participants, seemed to dominate all that mattered.

"Come on," Servius said. "Mind your step. The exposed metal's sharp." A tough order to follow, given how the Novafire was rocked about in its ongoing battle. The two made their way with difficulty through this ruined and unearthly landscape, clambering over and around mounds of debris until finally they made their way to a hallway that was reasonably intact, and ultimately to an access hatch.

Servius accessed the ship's neural net and forced the door open. On the other side, they were greeted by a troop of Kalbarian soldiers facing the opposite way down the hall, weapons at the ready. Dominating the hall, rifle cradled in his massive arms, was Victor and behind him, the lithe form of Silmion.

As the hatch opened, Victor turned and flashed a grizzled smile. "Commander—I'm not surprised to see you here. I didn't figure you'd be able to sit back while we were having all the fun."

Servius laughed and slapped Victor roughly on the arm. "You old dog! I thought I'd bring this young pup here to teach you a new trick or two," he said, pointing a thumb at Kaeso.

At that, Victor chuckled. As laugh-lines creased Victor's face, Kaeso was surprised at just how old he looked. Victor said to Kaeso, "Good to see you, Lieutenant. Mind your step—the dreighnar have riddled these halls with ambush sites. Now, let's see what you have to teach ol' Vic."

Chapter 25

The phalanx poured like a fluid through the corridors—perfectly timed, perfectly coordinated. Victor had stationed troops at strategic locations along the path to the engine rooms. As they approached, some teams fell in behind, other's moved ahead as a fore guard while still others poured down parallel corridors flanking the main group.

"How secure's this area?" Servius asked the lieutenant-commander.

"Not very," Victor replied. "The beasts can burrow into floors, walls, and ceiling. If they can't overwhelm you, they try to ambush you."

"Reminds me of our advance on Kaldron," the commander said.

Victor smiled at the memory. "Yeah, that was a day now wasn't it? You lost your hand there, didn't you?"

Servius flexed the fingers on his mechanical quicksilver arm. "Lost a hand but gained a lover."

Victor laughed. He was about to reply, but came to an abrupt halt. Instantaneously, the entire phalanx stopped too, leaving only Silmion to take an extra step before coming to a stop himself. A sound echoed down the hall—the sound of a mass of ball bearings rolling along a metal floor, but muffled as though coming from a distance.

"That them?" the commander asked. Victor didn't reply as the sound came closer until it surrounded them.

"They're all around us! Ambush! Switch to ultrasonic vision! Covering fire!" Victor shouted. The hall erupted in a blaze of gun fire. Through the optic sensors in his weapon, Victor switched to ultrasonic vision. Through this, he could detect the motion of thousands of dreighnar moving through the floor, walls and ceiling. Although the Kalbarian weapons were in rapid-fire mode, every shot was precisely aimed and struck one of the small beasts.

Regardless, many dreighnar slipped through the holes in the floors, walls & ceilings created by the Kalbarian's weapon fire, or they dug their own holes and rained onto the phalanx. The battle was pitched. Soldiers screamed as dreighnar bore into them. But the unit's discipline was tight as remaining soldiers fired methodically into the mass of attackers as well as into the torsos of their fallen comrades before more dreighnar could spawn.

Victor's attention was distracted for a moment as he heard a scream beside him. Time slowed as he looked to see a dreighnar tearing into Kaeso as he screamed in panic and pain. "Slag, no!" Victor yelled as he swung the butt of his rifle like a bat, smacking at the fist-sized dreighnar. The force knocked the dreighnar, but its sharp scales had a hold of Kaeso's flesh and all the blow did was tear Kaeso's abdomen up further. The young lieutenant fell to his knees under the onslaught.

Then, out of Victor's peripheral vision, Silmion's vanesti gun snapped forward and clamped the dreighnar in its maw. With a sound of crushing metal, the dreighnar let Kaeso loose. The vanesti gun whipped the dreighnar about before dashing it on the floor, dead. Kaeso looked at Victor, shock plain on his face as he slumped to the ground.

With a vicious string of profanity, Victor was by Kaeso's side. He peeled back the clothing and armor to look at Kaeso's injury. His torso was torn to shreds and blood poured from his gaping wounds. Over the years, Victor had held so many dying soldiers in his arms, and it filled him with impotent rage that he was doing so once more. He looked at Kaeso's young face as the color left it. "Easy lad," he said, though it scarred him inside, as it always did, to bring calmness to his voice. "Easy now."

The ship rocked with an explosion, sending them sliding along the floor, a smear of blood trailing Kaeso. The rest of the phalanx kept up their desperate defense. Silmion crawled to Kaeso's side and pulled a pink, gelatinous blob from a pocket on his pant leg. Without a word, he dropped it in Kaeso's wound.

With one arm still cradling Kaeso, Victor roughly grabbed Silmion in his other meaty hand. "What did you just do?"

Silmion was nothing more than a rag in Victor's iron grip, but he still managed a tone of defiance in his voice as he replied, "I'm helping him."

The dreighnar were retreating into their holes and down the hall again and a quiet fell on the phalanx. Victor looked down at Kaeso's wound. The pink ball was expanding, encompassing the wounded flesh of the lieutenant. Relief spread on Kaeso's face as he exclaimed in a hushed whisper, "The pain, it's gone." Victor released his grip on Silmion and looked in confusion at the Ullrioni.

Straightening his shirt, Silmion said, "Not all of our technologies kill. Very few do, in fact. Most of our innovations strengthen life—make it better. This," he said pointing at the pink mass that had now completely enveloped Kaeso's wound, "will substitute for all of his damaged tissue. Over time it will be replaced by his own flesh as his body heals. Give him a minute and he'll be on his feet."

"How many of those things do you have?" Victor asked.

"Not many," Silmion replied. "You have to be careful using them. If the damage to the body is too great, it exceeds their capacity to heal and it's wasted."

Silmion looked ruefully at the other fallen soldiers with a pained look in his eyes. "We venerate nature. Yes, life feeds on life—that is nature's way. But we are so much more than our weapons. All you've seen is how we can kill. I imagine you've gotten the wrong impression of us."

A smile cracked Victor's old face. "Aye, I had." Then, looking down at Kaeso, "How're you doing, Lieutenant?"

Kaeso struggled himself to a sitting position. "Surprisingly well, sir."

"Good. Get up. You still have an engine to restart," Victor said.

Still quite shaken from his experience, Kaeso rose to his feet, his shirt and armor hanging in bloody rags from his shoulders.

The phalanx continued its advance down the corridor. In moments, they were pouring through the doors of the engine room. As Victor stepped across the threshold he had to hold down the urge to gasp in shock. The area was a charnel house. Corpses littered the bloody floor, each one of them with their torsos gutted.

The stench was staggering. Out of the corner of his eye, Victor noted Kaeso struggling to maintain his composure. The lieutenant was ashen grey and he couldn't keep the shocked horror from his eyes as he stumbled forward, stunned at the carnage.

Kaeso was young and had suffered more today than a young man has right to, Victor thought. But still, more was needed from him. Military training had conditioned soldiers to blindly follow orders during combat. That ability to turn off one's mind and let another lead the way was the only thing that got new recruits through their first few battles. "Lieutenant!" Victor ordered.

"Yes sir," Kaeso replied. His eyes were dazed.

"Lieutenant!" Victor ordered, even harsher this time.

Kaeso's eye's snapped to the Lieutenant-Commander as he stood to attention and yelled, "Yes sir!"

"Get to the display panel and figure out what's wrong with the engines."

"Yes sir." Kaeso saluted and then ran off to comply with the order.

"What are you looking at, dogs!" Victor yelled at the surrounding troops. "Secure the room! I want a squad up there," he yelled pointing at an overhead walkway, "and there," pointing at another. "Defensive perimeter—keep an eye in the ultrasonic. Shoot anything that moves and isn't human!" The soldiers moved to comply, squad leaders taking charge of smaller teams and moving out.

Commander Servius walked up to Victor, eying Kaeso. "You think he'll keep it together long enough?"

Victor looked at the young lieutenant who was scanning the panel displaying the readouts for the engines. He was just standing there, staring as he swayed slightly. The ship rumbled as it took a hit in the space battle going on outside. "The boy oughta be dead. Cut him some space. He'll pull through," Victor said as he brushed past Servius and stomped over to Kaeso.

As he closed in on the young lieutenant, Victor slowed and calmed himself. He placed an encouraging hand on the young man's shoulder. "What is it?" he asked.

Kaeso stared at the console with a wretched look on his face. "I—I don't know what to do—where to start—" his voice drifted off.

"Kaeso," Victor said, "we run you through hundreds of drills so when the time comes and your mind can't keep up, your body just knows what to do and acts. Your hands know what to do. Press a button."

Kaeso shook his head and stammered, "I don't—"

Victor didn't let him finish. He squeezed Kaeso's shoulder, tight, causing the young man to wince. "Press a button."

The lieutenant raised a shaky hand, hesitated, and then tapped the console. A display opened up before them in the air and an incomprehensible schematic with a drop down list appeared. Victor looked at Kaeso with a smile. The young man closed his eyes and took a deep, shuddering breath. Victor could see Kaeso struggle to master himself, and he could see a change take over him. The emotion left his face, replaced by a cool analytical demeanor. Kaeso opened his eyes and methodically scrolled through the display.

Finally, Kaeso found what he was looking for. "There it is," he said pointing at an item on the schematic. "The coolant line was damaged, and with no one left to repair it, the power core overheated, fusing the power couplings and blowing the Calvina-cell circuitry."

"Can you fix it?" Victor asked.

Kaeso responded, "Yes, though I'll need at least five of your soldiers to help."

"You got it," Victor replied with a smile that creased his aged face. "Captain," he called over his communications link.

"What is it, Lieutenant-Commander?" Taura's voice replied.

"The engine room's secured. Repairs underway."

"Good," Taura answered. "Tell me when the engine's online again."

"Aye-aye, Captain."

Victor scowled as warnings came on over his neural net from the perimeter of the phalanx in the engine room. Softly, but quickly building in intensity, was the sound of a mass of ball bearings rolling along a metal floor.

* * *

"Listen, Marco, this isn't going to work," Ariadne said.

With attention focused on his console, Marco replied, "You don't even know what I'm trying to do."

"Even if your program breeches their security—" she was interrupted as the Novafire heaved under a barrage of missile fire. "Even if it breeches their security, their defense will dismantle my attack program the instant it enters their system."

"Dust and ashes," Marco said. He flashed her his charmer's smile accompanied by a quick wink. "You're a bit of a pessimist, aren't you? Anyone ever tell you that?" Not waiting for an answer, Marco turned to the bridge. "Captain, I need that boost of power to the sensor array now."

"Nerva," Taura called out to a soldier manning a nearby station, "transfer power from life support to the sensor array. Boost power to the array twenty percent."

"Yes, captain," Nerva replied. Marco watched an indicator on his console rise as power was transferred. "To Nephreti with love," he said and pressed a button.

Ariadne was also watching her console. After a moment, she turned on Marco. "There, I told you so. My attack program's been disabled."

Marco stared at his console, tapped a few buttons, and then spun his chair around until he was facing the bridge. Never taking his eyes of Ariadne, he said, "I'm in."

"What do you mean you're in?" Taura asked.

Looking at the captain, Marco said, "I've gained access to the entire computer system of that ship there." He pointed to one of the Nephretian vessels darting like a bird of prey visible through the front bridge monitor. "I believe you've named it 'target gamma.'"

"Outstanding, Marco," Taura replied.

Ariadne looked back at her console. "Sor T'van's Lies, Marco, how'd you do that?"

"I'd tell you, but I'd rather see if you're smart enough to figure it out yourself. Only way you'll grow, you know."

"How much control do you have over their systems?" the captain asked.

"Complete control," Marco replied. "Though, as soon as I start doing something they don't want, they'll send their defenses after me. I'd suggest something quick, but effective. Maybe firing off one of their engines to send the ship crashing into one of the others."

Their conversation was interrupted as Commander Servius' voice came over the communication link. "Captain, we have the engines online. Our position is under heavy attack, but we'll keep the engines up and running." In the background was the sound of heavy gunfire and screaming.

"Fates smile on you, Servius," the captain said.

"And if they don't, then slag 'em," the commander replied.

Taura turned to Marco and ordered, "Do it."

Marco spun his chair around until he faced his console once more and tapped in a quick command. On the monitor, the back end of one of the Nephretian ships jolted violently sideways, sending the battleship spinning into its nearest neighbor. The hulls visibly crumpled before several large depressurizations could be seen venting into space on both ships. The momentum of the collision sent both ships spinning away from one another.

"Nice," Ariadne said. "By the way, you used Nephretian access codes that I assume you stole from the base back in Narite to create an authorized identity. Once you pounded a hole in their defense wall, you piggy-backed on my attack program, using it as a decoy to occupy their defenses while you imbedded your identity in their system. That's how you got in."

"Ariadne, a gentleman never tells of his trysts."

"Helm," Taura ordered, "bearing starboard, five degrees, inclination two degrees. Ramming speed. Brace for impact."

Both Ariadne and Marco stared at each other in disbelief. "Ramming speed?" Marco said.

"This is why I hate Kalbarians," Ariadne replied.

Chapter 26

Kan Rath watched the space battle from the bridge of the Nephretian cruiser. He had witnessed the Novafire take an absolute beating at the hands of the three Nephretian ships, and still it managed to strike back. Captain Nsu looked over at him, "The reports are coming in. Your dreighnar have inflicted horrendous losses on the Novafire's crew."

"I am pleased you find Ullrioni technology useful, Captain," the ambassador replied.

"You will soon witness a momentous event, blessed by Amahté himself," the young captain said. "We'll destroy the Novafire shortly, leaving our rightful claim on the birthplace of humanity uncontested."

Kan Rath found arrogance in others deeply distasteful. Burying the more insulting replies that immediately sprung to his mind, Kan Rath merely said, "The Kalbarians seem to be … persistent foes."

"Bah, they are obstinate and thick-headed brutes forever closed to the truth."

Kan Rath smiled inwardly. That is precisely how he thought of the Nephretians. He was about to reply when events shown on the front view monitor left him speechless. Inexplicably, one of the Nephretian ships in front of them spun wildly, crashing into the ship beside it. They bounced apart, depressurizations rippling along their hulls.

Captain Nsu stared in shock at the events unfolding on the monitor. "What happened? Report!" No one had an answer.

But it was what happened next that gripped Kan Rath in fear. The fortress that was the K.S. Novafire bolted ahead, slicing through space, and smashing through the growing gap between the two Nephretian ships. The gap wasn't nearly large enough, and so the Novafire was grinding into both Nephretian vessels. But, given the Novafire's superior size and armor, the collision was devastating the two other ships, causing them to hurtle out of the way in a mass of disintegrating wreckage.

It was immediately apparent, though, that the two wounded ships were not the main focus of the Novafire. Like an enraged beast, the Kalbarian ship smashed through their flak firewall and sprang upon the third and final Nephretian vessel in which Kan Rath stood. The front monitor was dominated by a haze of missiles preceding the Novafire's charge.

"Evasive maneuvers!" Captain Nsu shrieked as the first wave of missiles ploughed into the sole remaining Nephretian ship. "Evasive maneuvers! Reverse course, full speed, mark 10 degrees to port ..." but the rest of his commands were drowned out as the ship rocked viciously as the massive Novafire crashed into it. For the next few moments, Kan Rath's world was one of fire, screams and weightlessness as he was thrown from his feet and flung about the bridge.

* * *

Marco clung desperately to the console for support as the Novafire leapt ahead, streaking straight towards the gap opening up between the two Nephretian cruisers that had just collided.

"Oipho!" Ariadne said in Alathian, "are we going to fit through the gap?"

"Not a chance," Marco replied. At that moment, the Novafire slammed into the narrow space between the two phoenix-like Nephretian ships, hammering into both of the wounded vessels. The sound of rending metal screeched through the air and the ship shook violently. For what seemed like endless moments, the Novafire shook and screamed as it ground through the two ships. Even though Marco was belted into his seat, he half expected the seat itself to be torn from its brace in the floor from the violence of the reverberations rippling through the vessel.

After many heartbeats, the Novafire was through. Marco caught a quick look at the front monitor only to see that they were diving head on for the sole remaining Nephretian vessel.

"Luca save me," Marco prayed to his goddess of fortune.

Out of the sudden silence, Taura bellowed, "Fire all forward weapons!"

Marco felt the cold terror of death's shadow falling over him as he watched the Novafire bear down on the final Nephretian ship, a wall of RAC missiles streaking ahead. Marco was well acquainted with this terror, having faced death in the form of starvation and disease ripping through the refugee colonies he had called home for so many years, compounded by countless encounters with the violence that only humans can inflict on themselves. And in that moment, he did the only thing he knew how to do when terrorized so.

Donning his charmer's smile, he grabbed Ariadne by the shoulder and turned her to face him. "I think this is it. Last chance to admit your true feelings for me."

Ariadne's gaze turned from fear to anger. "If this is our last moment, I want you to know I think you're an ass."

The conversation ended as the Novafire drove itself into the side of the final Nephretian vessel.

* * *

Dreighnar were raining down from the ceiling onto Victor's soldiers. Screams of his troops, flailing as they succumbed to a dreighnar, and the fire of weapons filled the engine room as the phalanx desperately defended itself.

"You've got to protect the cooling lines! We don't have a backup in place! If they go down, the engines will stall!" Kaeso yelled to Victor.

Silently over the neural net Victor sent orders to re-position his troops to protect the area Kaeso was pointing to.

Silmion had leapt onto a catwalk and was a whirling blur of death. He and his vanesti gun operating as a single, fluid force, shattering the dreighnar as they came. Commander Servius was by Victor's side, his gun hammering into the dense onslaught of dreighnar. Alarm claxons rang and emergency lights flashed as the assault continued.

Then, the Novafire shook with a violence that Victor in all his long years of experience had never felt. The squealing sound of tearing metal rose over that of gunfire and the floor shook so violently every soldier, including Silmion, was thrown from their feet and dashed onto the ground. Dreighnar were shaken and bounced about the chamber. Chaos ensued as soldier and dreighnar were mixed together while the ship heaved and rocked. Equipment toppled over and machines sparked and erupted in flames.

For long moments the only sound was of grinding metal and curses as the combat fell into quarters too close for assault rifles. Blades snicked out of scabbards as soldiers tried to stab at their attackers as best they could while the world shook them about.

Victor was thrown to the floor. For a moment, he had no idea where Kaeso or the commander were. All around him were flailing arms and legs and dreighnar bouncing and darting off of the floor and nearby equipment. A dreighnar landed beside him. The K-96 rifle attached to his arm, useless in such close quarters, automatically disengaged as blades flicked out of the back of his fist and he smashed them into the creature, pinning it to the floor. The rocking of the ship sent him tumbling further, crashing into fellow troops. Dreighnar cut and sliced his skin, but as the Fates would have it, none landed on his torso to strike a killing blow.

The shaking stopped. Screaming in rage, Victor rose to his feet, cutting viciously at the dreighnar darting at him with blades sliding in and out of his wrists and elbows. The moment he was given enough space, he whipped out a pistol in each hand and started firing. The heat from flames blasted over him as smoke filled the room.

"Tether up!" Victor ordered over the phalanx's neural net. He drew a cord from his uniform and, with a flick of his wrist, linked a sturdy clasp over the grab bars of a nearby bank of pipes. Although the tether limited his mobility, it would keep him in place should the ship shake as it just had. Other soldiers complied, but others were still too busy engaged in their close-quarters battle with the dreighnar to find the opportunity to tether themselves.

Before Victor could issue another command, the Novafire jolted violently. The force picked Victor off his feet and drove the breath from him as he was flung against the harness that chained him to the spot. Those soldiers who had not tethered themselves in as well as the dreighnar and the many corpses littering the area were lifted up by the force of the blow and sailed wildly along the length of the engine room until they crashed into a wall or piece of equipment.

After the force of the initial impact, Victor noticed he was not falling back to the floor. Looking about he saw soldiers, dreighnar, corpses and debris floating in the room. The fires scattered throughout had turned from yellow, tear-shaped flames to diffuse balls of blue.

The blow had knocked out the graviton drivers in the area. A smile creased Victor's old face as he watched a dreighnar writhe helplessly in the air. "Prep for zero-g combat," he ordered his men. Those who hadn't tethered themselves and were still conscious did so now. Tethered soldiers tossed lines out to other soldiers floating too far from a solid surface to propel themselves. The dreighnar writhed about, but without a solid surface to propel themselves, they floated helplessly.

The soldiers braced themselves so the momentum from firing their weapons would not send them hurtling uncontrolled in the zero-g environment, and commenced shooting the dreighnar floating about. The soldiers started to laugh and cheer as they slaughtered the last of the creatures with ruthless efficiency.

After several moments, somewhere in the bowels of the ship, the graviton drivers came online once more. The soldiers dropped to the floor amidst curses, but the battle was over as all the dreighnar in the area were destroyed.

Victor rose to his feet, his body aching and crisscrossed in cuts. That notwithstanding, he managed to chuckle as he said, "I think we just found a tactic for dealing with these little bastards. Now, if we could get the captain to fly the ship straight for half a minute, this might even be fun."

* * *

Kan Rath struggled to maintain his footing. The bridge of the sole remaining Nephretian cruiser was a scene of pure entropy. The ship was spinning wildly under the Novafire's assault. His respect for Kalbarians as warriors was rising—and for Nephretians falling. The odds were three to one at the battle's start, and now the crew of the remaining Nephretian vessel flailed about in panicked disarray.

In several careful steps, Kan Rath moved to stand beside the captain who was clutching at his chair to keep his balance. "This is your fault," Captain Nsu said when he noticed Kan's presence beside him. "Your dreighnar were supposed to wipe out their crew."

"Don't be an idiot," Kan Rath replied. "I think a tactical retreat is in order."

"Coward," Captain Nsu said, though his own young face was a portrait of panic.

"Please, let's not be insulting," Kan replied. "This battle is lost. You'll do nothing but weaken your own forces if you allow your ship to be destroyed."

"Kepi's fire, I don't want to die here," the captain said, his panic taking control. "Helm!"

"Yes, Captain."

"Bring the Q-wave engines online. Get us out of here!"

Kan Rath smiled inwardly. In moments, they entered the Q-wave slipstream, escaping the battle.

* * *

Taura watched the front monitor while the last Nephretian ship slipped out of existence as it entered the Q-wave slipstream.

Every fragment of her being yearned to press the attack, but she forced calm on herself. "Where are they heading?" she asked.

Nerva, manning the helm, replied, "Looks like it's the fifth planet—a gas giant. I'm detecting the signature of other Nephretian vessels there."

The Novafire was in no condition to battle fresh ships, Taura knew. "We need to get out of here before they send in reinforcements. What's nearby, Nerva?"

"Not much," Nerva said staring at his monitors. "There's a small planetoid in this sector. It's mineral rich, so we could access raw materials for our repairs if needed."

"Great. Bring us into orbit around it, then shut down the engines and all discretionary systems. I don't want our energy signatures giving our position away."

The Dagomir

Nk'ty paced nervously in the antechamber of the Dagomir's Great Audience Hall. Throughout the chamber were staggering displays of wealth. Support beams of precious adamite steel covered in gold with silver inlay winding through in arabesque design stretched up a dozen meters to support a domed ceiling. The walls were covered in beautiful paintings created and maintained by the most masterful artists N'ark had to offer depicting scenes of the city state's past, both mythical and historical. Statues, carved from the purest marble, perfect in every detail with flowing lines and the illusion of soft curves, stood sentinel throughout the chamber.

The opulence of the room was designed specifically to convey the power of Dagomir N'ark to all those who awaited an audience with him. Within this one room was enough wealth to found a new city out of the sands. Yet Nk'ty paid no attention to it. He was accustomed to lavish displays of power. No, it was his upcoming audience with the dagomir that consumed his attention. There were few people more powerful than Nk'ty, and of those who were, all were mar n'lan. As a mar n'lan himself, he could out think, out compete other mar n'lan, even if their rank did outstrip his.

But the dagomir—even the strongest of mar n'lan was but dust before the dagomir's might. Moreover, the dagomir was ancient, and a mind so venerable it had seen the passage of millennia was unfathomable to a man whose sole experience was contained in one lifetime. And what was the value of the life of one man to an entity that had seen thousands of generations rise and pass? Powerful. Unknowable. Impassive. It was a dangerous combination that a wise man should fear. And Nk'ty did fear it.

It was the fact he was always summoned before the dagomir to report on the prophesies of his brother, Kie, the strand-walker, never knowing where the truth ended and his mad babbling began, that fueled his hatred for his only surviving kin. It was this dread that set him to nervous pacing, oblivious to the ostentatious display of power around him.

He had been waiting for hours. The dagomir made all who would meet with him wait. Nk'ty was never sure if it was to lord his power over others, or because what meaning could time have to a being whose age was measured in epochs.

The grand doors, covered in gold, framed in silver and platinum with panels of graven images, silently swung open. Two Sentinels drifted out of the Great Audience Hall into the antechamber. The Sentinels were aged and frail looking mar n'lan, their pale, iridescent skin pulled thinly over delicate bones. They were, however, the most powerful mindslicers the mar n'lan had to offer, and were thus given the honor of forming the dagomir's personal guard.

Their voice was a whisper, thought but not spoken, drifting over Nk'ty's mind, "Dagomir N'ark will speak with you about Kie's recent prophecy of the Lost Dreks." Wordlessly, they turned and drifted back into the hall, with the whispered command, "Follow," floating through Nk'ty's thoughts.

So the dagomir knew of Kie's vision of the Lost Dreks, Nk'ty thought to himself as he followed the Sentinels. He was not surprised, given his recent investigations with the Librarian. Nothing could be researched in the Library without the dagomir's knowledge. And since all knowledge was contained in the library, no one could learn a thing without the dagomir's awareness.

Nk'ty followed behind the Sentinels as they moved down the vast, empty Great Audience Hall. The floor was well-worn marble with inlays of multi-colored stone creating intricate geometrical designs. Elegant beams of adamite steel stretched a hundred meters into the air supporting a vast dome. Orbs of soft golden light floated half way up the expanse, illuminating the entire chamber in a soft warm glow. The inside of the dome was covered in a vast mosaic of precious stones and metals forming images depicting the ascension of Dagomir N'ark over fifty millennia ago. The scent of spices hung faintly in the air.

At the far end of the hall was a raised dais of metal that seemed to gleam of its own accord. Atop the dais was a massive bench covered in wine-colored velvet. On this sat Dagomir N'ark.

He was a giant of a man, twice as tall as the average person. His skin was alabaster white and seemed to emanate a light of its own. His head was crowned with long golden hair that reached the nape of his neck. Where his eyes should be were dark, hollow pits, and a faint inky-black mist rose lazily from them before dissipating into the air. He was dressed in a simple golden tunic and sandals.

This was, of course, not the actual dagomir, but rather his simulacrum. The dagomir himself was an amalgam of the most powerful mar n'lan during the time of the wars between mar n'lan and mar p'augh. The dagomir's ascension began when these powerful mar n'lan learned the secrets of combining their consciousness to create an even greater whole—and gaining a form of immortality in the process. Over the ages, powerful or highly skilled mar n'lan would be absorbed into the dagomir, adding to his power. The simulacrum was a vessel through which the dagomir could interact with the physical world, and he had several, each for different occasions and in different locations, which he could transfer himself to at will.

At a point before the dais, the Sentinels stopped. Nk'ty lowered himself to his knees, and then down to his belly until he lay prostrate before his lord and master.

The dagomir's voice reverberated like a hammer blow, his words entering Nk'ty's mind a fraction of a moment before the voice reached his ears. "Tell me Kie's prophesies of the Lost Dreks." As the demand was made, the memory of the meeting was forcibly dragged into Nk'ty's thoughts.

Nerves twisted his guts as the answer was torn out of him. "The Lost Dreks return."

"Of this, I am aware," the dagomir said, voice tinted with rebuke.

The memories of his last meeting with Kie tumbled forth in Nk'ty's mind with a life of their own to the last words Kie said to him, which were now dragged from Nk'ty's mouth. "Kie says the Lost Dreks are more powerful than when they left—but they are wounded. If you strike quickly, before they regain their strength, you will rule them. You must strike quickly."

Dagomir N'ark sat quietly and mused over Nk'ty's answer. At length, he asked, "Is Kie mad?"

"Absolutely," Nk'ty replied, unable to hide his true thoughts had he wanted from the dagomir. "But the Librarian confirmed that the Lost Dreks were once rumored to exist during the time of your glorious ascension. However, their existence was never confirmed, and neither the mar n'lan nor mar p'augh resides in the heavens anymore."

"Oh, but they do," the dagomir said. "Two tribes of mar p'augh have just done battle in the heavens above us."

Nk'ty was rocked by the words, though he tried desperately not to let his shock show. That mar p'augh—dreks no less—should reside in the heavens was anathema to Nk'ty's understanding of the natural order. He had not allowed himself to contemplate the veracity of the concept when the Librarian had first mentioned humanity's past dominance of the heavens. But to hear the dagomir himself confirm it with no more gravity than had he been discussing the season's crops from the arid fields surrounding the city—it seemed the concept could not be denied. Once the incredulity passed, anger took its place as Nk'ty seethed at the thought of wretched dreks ascendant in the heavens while the mar n'lan toiled under an angry sun, living in dread of the Ravager's next blow.

Completely indifferent to the seething emotions of the man lying prostrate before him, the dagomir pressed his original question. "Does the strand-walker speak true, or are his the babblings of madness?"

Nk'ty stammered, unsure of himself now and more than a little surprised at the conclusions he was arriving at, "I ... he speaks true. The Lost Dreks ... their return. He speaks true."

"Then, I must strike quickly," the dagomir concluded. Musing more to himself, he said, "I will need to construct a new simulacrum." After a thoughtful pause, the dagomir turned his attention once more to the man lying prostrate on the floor before him, "Nk'ty, tell the mar n'lan to prepare for war."

Chapter 27

The Reclaimer drifted in orbit high above the fifth planet in the Earth system with the remaining Nephretian fleet—four ships in all, though one was a near wreck. The planet was a massive gas giant composed of a rocky core buried in a sea of liquid metallic hydrogen. Dominating the space below them, bands of reddish brown, chocolate and white drifted by on the vast planet.

Hetshepsu sat on the bridge of the Reclaimer, smoldering in anger. One Nephretian ship had returned from the battle with the Novafire. One! And it was more a ruin than a ship. Worse, the Novafire survived and had slipped away to parts unknown. That he would have to suffer the rebuke of the Fist once more for his failure to destroy Captain Lucia Taura filled him with inconsolable rage. He had reviewed the reports received from their long range scanners as well as those Captain Nsu had sent on ahead. The battle had been going so well. And in mere moments, victory was stolen—two ships destroyed, and the third fleeing in wild panic.

"Captain Nsu's landing craft just docked, Admiral" a voice said.

"Good, have a detachment of guards escort him to the bridge immediately."

The admiral quietly marinated in his rage while he waited for the young captain to arrive. At long last the captain entered the bridge along with Kan Rath, the Ullrioni ambassador. The captain, fidgeting nervously, was flanked by four guards, rifles at the ready. "My superior!" The captain's head bowed until his chin met his chest in the Nephretian salute.

"Explain why the Novafire still exists," the admiral said.

"She's a beast of a ship, my superior—"

"And you had three!" the admiral shouted, letting his rage pour out of him. "Three! And now you come to me, one ship in ruins, the other two destroyed and the Novafire still out there! How did this happen? How!" A rational area of his mind looked at Captain Nsu and marveled at his youth. He looked shy of his thirtieth year. He had failed because he was hopelessly out of his league, attrition in the ranks propelling him up the chain of command far beyond his youthful limitations. Alas, this was the best Nephreti had left to offer after decades of war. But with the Fist on board this very ship someone had to pay, and Hetshepsu was determined he would not bear the brunt of Lord Hamu's wrath. And so, he allowed his rage to dominate his reason as he lashed out at the young captain before him.

"I—The Ullrioni," Nsu said, pointing an accusing finger at Kan Rath. "His dreighnar were to weaken the Novafire, destroy their crew—"

The admiral cut him off. "The Ullrioni? And how many ships did he have at his command? How many!"

"None," the captain replied. Anyone who did not need to be on the bridge of the Reclaimer had left. Those required to remain were studiously working at their stations, doing their best pretending not to notice the dressing down happening before them.

"A pathetic deflection of blame, captain," the admiral said.

"I have failed you, my superior," the captain stated.

"No. You have failed Amahté." The captain's head snapped up, eyes wide, pleading. But Hetshepsu pressed on remorselessly. "Allowing you to live is an affront to all that's holy." In a single motion, he stood, withdrew a pistol and shot Captain Nsu in the head. The young man dropped straight as a board to the floor, the light of another mother's son forever extinguished from the universe.

Holstering his weapon, Hetshepsu said to the guards, "Dispose of his body and clean up the mess." The guards jumped to comply.

The admiral then turned his attention to Kan Rath. The Ullrioni stood calmly—any emotion he had after witnessing what had just transpired was not shown on his face. Although physically Kan Rath looked little older than the late captain, he bore himself with a more austere gravity. This was no politician, Hetshepsu thought to himself as he watched Kan Rath ignore the guards dragging Nsu's carcass away. No, he'd seen death in his time.

"I read the reports of the dreighnar's impact in the battle," the admiral said.

"Indeed?"

Hetshepsu smiled inwardly—whatever battle Kan Rath may have seen, he was certainly a politician also. Who else could speak, yet say nothing?

"Impressive," the admiral said. "As far as we can tell, they inflicted casualties of up to a fifth of the Novafire's crew in less than twenty minutes."

"And, they leave infrastructure intact ... more or less," Kan Rath replied.

There's the warrior again, Hetshepsu mused. Reclaiming his seat on the bridge, the admiral said, "I look forward to seeing how your other technologies perform in the battlefield."

Kan Rath raised an eyebrow. "We have technologies far in excess of those that simply kill."

"Oh, I'm sure you do," the admiral replied. "Once we've brought the Kalbarians and Alathians to heel, I'm certain we'll be very interested in reviewing those as well."

Kan Rath's jaw clenched and he turned to look out the front viewport. At long last, he said, "I see you still circle this gas giant. Have you found what you sought?"

"Oh yes. We have found the bases that launched the seedships, preserved so well in the vacuum of space over countless thousands of years."

"You know as well as I that this giant ball of gas is not the birthplace of humanity, regardless of whether or not the bases that launched the seedships hail from here," the Ullrioni said. "If this is the home system of humanity, then the third planet from the main star is the most likely place of origin. Certainly your technicians confirm that."

Hetshepsu leaned back in his chair, smiling slightly. "Indeed they do."

"Then what's the value of examining these abandoned relics when a much greater find beckons?"

"What's the value? We have learned so much from our brief study here. Did you know that our technicians, after pouring over the records preserved in the remnants of the Progenitor's computer system have determined that no fewer than 8,492 seedships were launched from here?"

"No, the late Captain Nsu failed to pass that along to me," Kan Rath replied.

"So? Don't you grasp the significance of that?"

"Not really," the ambassador said.

"To date, we only know of about 160 seedship colonies—and eighteen of those are barely more than tribal, and only three have any real power. There are potentially so many worlds out there to bring back to the fold. Our technicians have been working constantly since we've arrived to determine their locations."

"It seems Nephreti will be busy for quite some time, then," Kan Rath said. "A question, though. As your predicants have so assiduously preached at me during our travels together, my understanding of your religion was Amahté wouldn't show you the way to Earth until humanity had been reunited. Odd that you should be brought here when humanity is even more divided then you had originally surmised." As an afterthought, perhaps realizing his arrogance may have led him to verbalize some offense, he hastily said, "Excuse my ignorance—I did not intend to offend."

"It is not for us to question the ways of Amahté," Hetshepsu replied, though in truth he did not believe in the validity of his own response. Although he believed in the teachings of the High Prelate, he was not particularly devout. Growing up in the halls of power, Hetshepsu had learned that religion was a tool of control, and internal consistency was not required for it to work effectively on a people. Faith was ever a means to an end. For the downtrodden, it was a means of justifying their lot to themselves. For the admiral, it was a means to sate his own ambition and thirst for power. The Ullrioni studied the admiral with a knowing smirk, but said nothing.

"Perhaps the predicants need to speak with you at more length," the admiral said. "It matters not. Our work here is nearly done. We'll be heading to the third planet in less than a day. Before the week is out, we will touch the soil of our true home— and worlds will flock to our banner."

* * *

With hard eyes, Victor supervised the cleanup of the engine room. It was foul, grisly work. The squad of soldiers dispatched to help were obviously raw recruits. The sound of retching that signaled their arrival and the stunned horror that haunted their eyes as they hauled and man-handled the ruined bodies of the fallen gave away their novelty to the battlefield. Victor's gaze fell upon Silmion, who stood on a catwalk cooling observing the soldiers at work.

He made his way to the Ullrioni. "It's their eyes I can't stand," Victor said.

"Pardon? Their eyes?" Silmion asked.

Victor tipped his head toward a group of three recruits struggling to mop up tattered shreds of flesh. "Their eyes—new recruits. Slag, I've seen so many battles, Silmion. Bodies just become … meat. They were people, now they're not. Meat that needs to be cleaned before it rots and stinks up the place. But them," he said pointing at the crew going about their business, "that look … that look like something inside of them, something of who they are, is wounded by what they see. When I see that horror in their eyes, well, I guess it reminds me that what we're doing ain't natural."

Silmion looked at Victor appraisingly for a moment, and then turned to look at the soldiers silently going about their business below. At length he said, "When I was actively serving in the military, I used to hate working with new recruits. Not because they didn't know what they were doing, and not because I didn't know whether they'd run or fight until the bullets started to fly, though those were concerns. No, I hated seeing the ones that made it become more and more like me day after day. I hated seeing that horror in their eyes fade. We should be horrified by what we see, don't you think? I always wondered whether I'd lost something of myself—something important—that I couldn't feel their horror anymore."

"So why'd you join the service?" Victor asked.

"Why'd I join?"

"Yeah."

Silmion shrugged. "Many reasons, I suppose. Originally, because my nation needed me. We were under attack—not just our nation, but our ideals—what we held to be sacred truths. Or so I was told. Later … later, my reasons changed. And you?"

"Bah, I been fightin' for so long, it's all I know. And I'm good at it. As long as my skill can keep my soldiers alive and my enemies on their heels, in the fight's where I need to be."

Silmion turned to Victor with a wry smile. "There'll always be a soldier at risk. You plan on fighting forever?"

"Near enough."

* * *

Gods, I'm still alive, Marco thought to himself. He looked about him. The bridge was in tatters. The wounded and dead were being carted away. Ruins of technology were splayed everywhere he looked. Still alive, he thought more ruefully.

So much waste.

We are so alone in this vast universe, he had always thought, and we have such gifts—self-awareness, intelligence to struggle with the understanding of nature, tools that allow us to touch the heavens. We've only each other as companions during our sojourn across voids of time, and yet we bark and snap at one another like dogs over a piece of meat.

Marco felt ill—and an overwhelming tiredness. He had lived his life surrounded by such waste and squandered gifts.

The massive Kalbarian battleship felt terribly small. Claustrophobic. Everywhere he looked he saw ruin. Ruin and mindless fools who were arrogant in their belief that they had some monopoly on truth, easily led by powers that smashed lives to forward some intractable cause. Marco wanted to scream. Was he the only one who saw the folly of nations? He buried his rage deep in himself where it cooled into a lingering sadness, drifting through him like smoke after a fire.

His attention was distracted by an animated conversation nearby.

"By the Fates, there's a structure down there!"

"Let's see." There was a pause, followed by, "Damn, looks like a mine."

Marco casually walked over to surreptitiously observe what the soldiers were commenting on. The Novafire had made orbit around a remarkably small planet in the outer reaches of what the crew were calling the Earth system. Marco had overheard that the planetoid was composed mostly of rock and water ice with traces of nitrogen ice and other organic compounds. The Novafire was in desperate need of raw materials if its self-repair mechanisms were to patch up the ship, and the Kalbarian technicians seemed to think this dwarf planet should have ample resources to suffice.

Apparently, the crew of the Novafire were not the first to think so.

"Not like any mine I've ever seen," one of the soldiers said. "Seems abandoned. Covered by a pretty thick layer of ice, too."

"Fates, do you think this was a mine dug by the creators of the seedships?"

"It'd be thousands of years old, then. Would a structure that old still be standing?"

"Not much in the way of atmosphere. With minimal weather beating it down, maybe."

Taura interrupted their conversation. "Vibius! Publius! What are you two chattering about over there? You're supposed to be finding raw materials for the Novafire."

"Captain, I think there's an abandoned mine down there," Vibius said.

"Your mother's teat, really?" Taura looked at their monitors over their shoulders.

Marco sidled up to Taura. "You going to check it out?"

"There's a rich ore vein there," Publius said.

Taura thought a moment before replying. "We're short-handed, and we don't have time. This is a military mission, not an archeological dig. We'll mine the vein, but won't be exploring any ruins."

Marco was desperate to get off the ship, even for a short while. "Send me down with one of your mining runs. If I can crack seedship computers, I ought to be able to crack the computers of their makers. If the structure's still standing, chances are good I can get my hands on some of their hardware."

"We're not here to satisfy your curiosity, Marco," Taura said as she began to move away.

Marco put on his charmers smile. "Look, you're outgunned, and you're not going to be beating the Nephretians to Earth. If the computer hardware down there is still in one piece, or close to one piece, I can probably pull some info off it. Tactical information about this system, or what happened here."

Taura looked thoughtfully at Marco for a moment, and then shrugged. "Fine, but I'm sending Kaeso with you. He's pretty good with a computer himself."

"Good. Maybe I can teach him a thing or two."

"Fates, I hope not."

Chapter 28

Marco shivered from the cold as he walked across the ghostly landscape. He was not cold, he knew—the thermoregulators of his enviro-suit made sure he never strayed too far from body temperature. But the cold of the haunted landscape still seemed to seep through his suit to tickle his skin with a chill touch.

The enviro-suit was of Kalbarian design and had to be modified to fit Marco, who was much more slender and taller than most individuals of that race. Despite these modifications, the suit still did not fit Marco well—nor did the menace of the design, which was typical of all things Kalbarian. Filigreed patterns entwined on the breast of the suit fluoresced a soft vermillion. The shoulders spiked out at sharp angles and vicious spikes laced with delicate engravings protruded from every joint—elbows, knees, wrists. Their heads were encased in a helmet, beautifully crafted with sharp angles and luminous orbs whose light did nothing to brighten the darkened landscape behind which their eyes surveyed the path before them. Like silent demons he and Kaeso made their way across the frozen land.

The sun of the system, little more than a bright star in the heavens at this distance, cast only the faintest wisps of light that danced in the frozen crystals of nitrogen crunching underfoot. The landscape was highly irregular with sudden outcroppings jutting from the ground at drunken angles and entombed in the bluish white of ice giving them the appearance of ghosts, cursed to forever trudge across this barren world.

The air was thick with white crystals. Marco held out his hand to catch them as they fell. Fall wasn't the right word. With negligible gravity, they seemed to just hover in front of Marco, imperceptibly making their way to the surface. With little in the way of wind on the dwarf planet's surface, there was nothing to disturb the pattern of frosty flakes as he collected a handful in the palm of his glove. "It's snowing," he said.

Kaeso came up behind him, carrying a case of equipment. "Not quite," he said, handing the case over to Marco. It was light, given the weak gravity of the planet. "The atmosphere's freezing out. This planet has a bit of an odd orbit, and it's currently moving away from the sun. As it cools, the atmosphere freezes and falls to the surface."

"Well, any way, it's nice to look at."

Kaeso stopped to survey the landscape. "I suppose so. Shall we move on?"

The only noise to accompany the two was the soft crunching of snow with each footfall, muted by the near absence of atmosphere. Their passage was marked by swirling eddies of floating ice crystals. The two demons advanced past ghostly sentinels on a world far from the warmth of its star.

They approached a structure rising out of the frozen landscape. Like the rest of the world, it, too, was encased in a tomb of ice. But unlike its wraithlike companions scattered around them, it was large and regular in shape. A building. A sign that here, once, some life strove to carve order out of the void.

"This looks like the main offices of the mine. A lot of the structure seems to be buried. Radiographic inspection shows there's several breaches in the exterior of the structure, though they're covered by the ice," Kaeso said.

"Any large enough for us to fit through?" Marco asked.

After looking down the length of the structure, Kaeso replied, "Yes. Up this way." Kaeso began moving down the length of the frozen building and Marco followed.

"Can you tell how old it is, Kaeso?"

"We'd need to take a sample for a detailed analysis. That said, it could be quite old. It's suffered some structural damage. But, with little in the way of atmosphere, it wouldn't be exposed to the erosive forces you'd find on most habitable worlds. That suggests most of the structural damage is probably caused by the expansion & contraction of the metal due to fluctuations in surface temperature. I don't know how big of a stress that would be, though. As far as we can tell from our measurements, the temperature should only fluctuate in a relatively narrow band close to absolute zero. And the material of the building seems to be similar to the nano-reinforced metal of our blast shields. So, given the damage to the structure I can see under the ice coating, I'd guess it could be many thousands of years old." Marco whistled in reply.

After several moments walking, Kaeso stopped and turned to the wall. "Here we are." Clenching a fist, a short, intense burst of blue flame flicked from the top of his wrist—a torch used to cut through metal and stone. The heat from the torch caused the hovering snow in an orb surrounding the two to vanish. He moved the torch close to the wall. The flame didn't have to touch the structure—the proximity of the heat caused the wall of frozen nitrogen to sublimate into the atmosphere in a gassy haze. In moments, Kaeso had cleared a large opening exposing the metal structure of the building underneath. The wall was rent by a large cut, as though a massive claw had torn through it.

"Here we go," Kaeso said, shutting off his torch. Within moments, frozen crystals appeared hovering all around them once more.

"Well, let's see what we can find." With that, Marco slipped through the crack in the wall and into the building.

The footing was tenuous inside, exacerbated by the low gravity. The crack in the wall also rent the floor, and piled snow sloped towards the chasm. Kaeso carefully entered behind Marco. Frozen crystals hovered in the air inside the building as the frigid temperatures caused the atmosphere to freeze in here as well. The darkness thickened around them, though the low-light sensors in the suit allowed Marco to see. Ahead of Marco, a dark doorway yawned with inky blackness.

"What are we looking for?" Kaeso asked.

Marco looked down at the Kalbarian with a mischievous smile hidden behind the suit's mask. "Something neat. Let's go." Marco started towards the door.

"Define 'neat.'"

"Something that looks like a computer would be nice," Marco replied. "Or a coffee mug."

With a boyish excitement, Marco led Kaeso up and down several halls, popping in and out of rooms. The ruined metal frames of furniture, half buried in the snow and coated with frozen nitrogen, was all that remained.

Breaking the silence after a long while, Kaeso asked, "Do you really think you can get anything off of one of their computers, assuming we can find one?"

"Of course. The same factors that have kept this building from eroding away—namely the minimal atmosphere—should preserve the hardware of any computer system of worth. As long as there's enough pieces of the hardware to assemble together and it's close enough to the seedship design for me to figure out, I should be able to patch it up to get some information off of it."

"I suppose. Even if you were able to pull some info out of it, this was a mining operation. You'll likely just find a mining register—orders in, tonnage out."

"Ah, Kaeso, the banalities of our day-to-day life are imbedded in a matrix of the reality of our times. Who's placing the orders? Where're the shipments going? These things can tell us something."

"Fair enough."

"And here we go," Marco said, stopping short in the room they just entered. Blocks and counters, caked in ice, dominated the floor and walls of the room. "I'll bet you a month's wages some of these are computer terminals."

"I'm not one for gambling."

"Of that, I have no doubt. Let's start here, see if we can find a network hub."

* * *

It had been days since the battle with the Nephretians. Since then, Taura had only captured fleeting moments of sleep. Her ship was a wreck. A third of her crew—over six-hundred soldiers—dead, and half the remaining were walking wounded. When she had first reviewed the casualty reports she was physically ill—as she always was whenever such reports made their way to her. When she assumed command a little over two years ago after her predecessor, Captain Lanatus, was killed in the assault on Praxix V, she had made it her mission to protect her people, to be a shield from those who would do Kalbarai harm. Every day since, she felt nothing but failure. The war ground on with no victor, and a constant stream of casualty reports naming the dead and broken passed before her—each name a symbol of her inability to halt the crashing waves of history upon which she strove to keep her ship aright.

She had been driving her remaining crew to their limits repairing the ship—a near impossible task in deep space. Their need to minimize or shut off the Novafire's non-core systems to retain their position of hiding only added to the difficulties of repair. She hated hiding. But, if the Novafire were to have a chance of stopping the Nephretians, they needed to regain their strength.

Servius, Taura's second in command, walked up to her. He was pale and haggard, but anger still smoldered in his eyes. He was rubbing the intricate weaving of quicksilver circuitry on his scalp with his flesh hand.

"Good, you're here. How's the repair on the blast shields going, Servius?"

"Slag! It'll be a week before they're capable of providing even minimal shielding—and out here in deep space, that's about as good as we'll be able to make 'em. They were mostly torn to shreds," the commander replied.

"Why the Fates is it taking so damn long?" Taura asked. Her nerves were frayed and fatigue was clouding her judgment. She felt guilt almost immediately for lashing out at her commander. She knew the answer.

"We don't have the manpower and a lot of our drones and equipment is wrecked," Servius said.

Taura rubbed her eyes with her obsidian black hand. "I know, Commander. It's a miracle we're not debris. What is it you wanted?"

"Come with me. We've a report on the Nephretian fleet." Taura was beginning to feel ill again as she followed Servius over to the long range scanners. The soldiers there made way for both commanding officers.

Servius called up a small three-dimensional map of the Earth system. "The Nephretians had been stationed by this gas giant here," he said pointing to the fifth planet in the system. "We lost them as their orbit took them behind the planet. We've just picked up their signal again here." He pointed at the third planet from the main star. "This planet is in the green zone—the distance from their sun that can sustain human life. If there's an Earth in this system, this is it."

It was just confirmed what Taura had known in her gut since their first encounter with the Nephretians in this system. They had lost.

"Any signs of life there?" she asked.

"The scanners aren't picking up anything. If they're technologically advanced, they're not using any signals we can pick up on. Our optic arrays were destroyed in the battle, so we can't get a good look on the surface from here."

"How long will it take us to get there?" Taura asked.

"Repairs on the engines are still ongoing—they won't make the distance. Even if they did, there's four ships there, one of which is the Reclaimer. We wouldn't even scratch their blast shields before they pound us to scrap."

"We're not just going to let them have this."

Before Servius could reply, a voice chimed in from behind Taura. "You need to buy time to get your ship repaired." It was Ariadne. Fates, how long had she been on the bridge, Taura cursed to herself. The Alathian continued, "Send in a small strike force to scout them out, disrupt their activities, and slow 'em down. That'll buy enough time to get the Novafire battle-ready."

"We're short staffed as it is. We can't spare the troops," Servius said.

Ariadne shrugged, apparently conceding the point. "Well, if you think you'll be more successful charging them, you're the commanding officer, Captain. You know what your ship is capable of better than I."

Taura had spent her adult life fighting Alathians as well as Nephretians in the Triumvirate War. She had lost friends— brothers and sisters in arms—at the hands of Alathians, and a treaty hastily constructed to jointly attack the Nephretians could not erase the animosity she felt for the woman standing before her.

"Don't play your stupid games with me, Alathian!" It felt good to yell at the Alathian, Taura noted. "You know I'm not about to charge the Novafire into them in this state! A strike force attacking with guerilla tactics to hamper the Nephretians is a good idea."

Servius continued glowering at Ariadne.

"It'll need to be a pretty small group," Taura said. "Small enough to fit on a lander, big enough to pack a punch."

"Victor's a heavy hitter—you'll get a lot of firepower with him," Servius said.

"And Kaeso's a pretty quick thinker," the captain added. "And, I hate to say it, but Marco has the annoying quality of being the best expert at cracking any computer system I've seen."

"How about Silmion?" Servius asked.

"No. If the Nephretians have any more weapons designed by the Ullrionis like the dreighnar, I want him here."

"I should go, too, Captain," Ariadne said.

"Not bloody likely," Taura replied.

"Your team needs to use guerilla tactics. No one's better at guerilla warfare than Alathia," Ariadne said.

"And no one's better at betrayal." Around the bridge, several soldiers noticeably tensed and the odd hand drifted towards holstered weapons. Taura could sense the seething enmity of her troops towards the Alathian, just held under restraint. With a gesture, Taura could have the Alathian killed.

"We've been enemies for a long time—I get it," Ariadne said. If she was aware of the tension around her, she didn't show it. "Peace doesn't come easily. But, we are allies now. We have to fight united if we wish to stop the Nephretians. If our alliance fractures, Nephreti will steal both of our colonies from us and wipe us from the map. Under the terms of our treaty, I am the Alathian ambassador on this joint mission to Earth. I don't have to tell you that the Alathian Council will not take it lightly if you prevent me from fulfilling my obligation under this treaty. Your own orders were to treat me as an equal."

Taura seethed because she knew Ariadne was right. The Alathian's take on the situation was sound, and Taura's orders were, indeed, to give Ariadne the respect of an equal. But she had fought and killed Alathians for so long—so many of her countrymen had been killed by their traitorous hands. A litany of Alathian crimes and betrayals played their way across Taura's mind: breaking of the Rorna ceasefire, the Titan IX ambush, the fall of the Seneslav ruling family on Musatei, the list went on. Damn my tiredness, the captain cursed to herself, I can't think straight anymore.

Don't think. Follow orders. This was the soldier's credo, she reminded herself.

"I don't need you to remind me of my orders," the captain said. "If you go, you go under the command of Lieutenant-Commander Quintilus Victor. He gives an order, you obey it. You don't, I'm giving him orders to kill you, no questions asked. If any of the strike force gets it in their head that you're betraying them, I'm giving them orders to kill you, no questions asked. If you want to go, those are the terms. You don't like it, you go cry about it to your Fates damned council!"

Ariadne appeared to think deeply about the captain's conditions, probably weighing whether or not to negotiate. "Your terms are reasonable. I accept them."

"Fine," Taura said. "Servius!"

"Yes, Captain."

"Recall Kaeso and Marco from the planet surface. Find Victor and get him up here. I want the strike force on their way to Earth in an hour."

Chapter 29

An unrelenting sun bathed the arid land in a torrid blanket of sweaty heat. Transparent vapors that tricked the eye writhed upwards as though the air, singed by the very ground, sought escape. Completely incongruous with the sweltering heat, the sound of babbling water chimed in the air from two creeks bordering either side of the broad, cobblestone road that led to massive iron doors set in the towering walls surrounding N'ark. Large green leaves with tiny orange flowers bursting from the stem lazily floated by on eddies and currents of the streams in blithe defiance of the desert that stretched to the horizon.

This was the Dagomir's Road, and only the most powerful of visitors travelled it. Through the massive gates, the weary traveler would enter the splendor of the mar n'lan district and eventually make their way to the Shield of N'ark—the dagomir's palace that stretched impossibly high into the sky. The water was a gluttonous extravagance that, in a more altruistic setting, could sustain an entire district of the sprawling city. It was, of course, illegal to imbibe these waters, and they were laced with poison so that any who dared disobey would pay the ultimate price for their treason. It was a regular duty of the guards who stood sentinel at these gates to clear out the corpses that littered the nearby fields, frozen in the twisted form their wracking pain left them in when they finally succumbed to the poison.

Without cloud to lessen the sun's fierce intensity, or tree to take succor from its assault on the land, the people assembled on the Dagomir's Road could do nothing but submit to its overwhelming heat. Nk'ty stood, back to the assembled power-brokers of the ancient city, watching the orange blossoms twirl and pass on down the creek. He was told that a mar p'augh tribe of the heavens—the thought of which still filled him with disgust and, if he was honest with himself, envy—was soon to arrive. The most talented mindslicers of the mar n'lan had found this tribe's minds in the heavens and sent them visions and dreams, convincing them that on the surface of this planet they would find their god.

They sounded like fools, lacking even the most rudimentary of ability to block a mindslicer's probe strained and weakened by the immense distance the mental attacks had to be projected. Yet the dagomir was adamant about making contact with this specific tribe—they called themselves "Nephretians"—believing their childish beliefs would make them the most suitable tool to implement his plan.

The assembled mar n'lan had been waiting under the smothering heat for an intolerably long time, but still they waited. Despite the heat, Nk'ty was pleased to be a part of this assembly. The mar n'lan milling about on the Dagomir's Road would serve as the Nephretian god's "heavenly" host. No doubt they would be in the vanguard of the dagomir's assault on the mar p'augh tribes of the sky. The thought of bringing these errant mar p'augh to heel and claiming the mar n'lan's rightful dominance of the heavens filled him with an eager excitement he had not experienced previously in his life.

"They come." The voice of the dagomir's Sentinel was a whisper, more in the mind than a sound carried through the air, yet impossible to ignore. "Assemble." The command, hushed, barely audible, tugged at Nk'ty, pulling him to his designated place on the Dagomir's Road. The Sentinels seemed to float out in front, the mar n'lan fanned out behind them leaving a path in the middle down which the dagomir would arrive. Nk'ty looked at his brethren around him. These were the most powerful mindslicers of the mar n'lan. Their presence here meant one thing—N'ark was going to war. Nk'ty struggled to conceal a wolfish grin.

"There." The sentinel's voice softly susurrated over the host, drawing their attention to the sky. Impossibly high, barely perceptible, there was a glare that looked to Nk'ty like a distant oasis reflecting the sun. Nk'ty had known for many weeks now there were mar p'augh in the sky. To see evidence of it, though, struck him like a hammer. His breath tripped and caught in his throat while his heart raced. The moment of wonder was brief and quickly replaced with a seething rage to see proof of mar p'augh ascendant in the heavens while he stood sweating under an angry sun. He cursed the Ravager for creating such an inversion of order.

The bright dot of light quickly grew in size and was soon accompanied by a sound that reminded Nk'ty of winds coursing over the tops of sand dunes. The light grew into a shape—a raptor of gigantic proportions slicing through the atmosphere. The sound of the beast rose in crescendo as it approached and the wind came to life as it began to settle on the ground in the center of the Dagomir's Road ahead, whipping the sand into violent vortices.

Nk'ty could already feel the minds of its passengers. Weak minds, eager to be led, eager to wage war for a myth, minds filled with an almost infantile excitement, so ready to play their part in the deception the dagomir had orchestrated. Nk'ty looked at the blasted landscape surrounding the city. Bleak sand as far as human vision could penetrate. But with the mindslicers clouding their minds, the stupid mar p'augh would see only a verdant paradise garden. And even though the heat would kill the strongest of humans left exposed for too long, they would perceive only gentle, soothing warmth.

These mar p'augh may reside in the heavens and have mastery over machines that can cross the skies, but their minds were weak—even the dreks in the Gray Maze could put up a better defense.

Control your mind, or control nothing. These were the first words taught at the mar n'lan academy where the ruling class learned to gain mastery over their nascent mindslicer abilities and merge it with the power of the dagomir. These mar p'augh tribes of the heavens would learn the truth of this lesson.

The master of the Nephretian vessel was preparing to exit the craft. Nk'ty could sense the excitement welling up within the mar p'augh as he approached the portal of his vessel. With a metallic click followed by a gentle hissing, the belly of their flying beast opened and a ramp extended to rest on the ground. Eyes wide with wonder, a tall, regal looking man slowly stepped forth. He was well into his adulthood, though old age hadn't touched him yet. His blonde hair was straight and combed back, reaching his shoulders. His clothing looked expensive and finely made to Nk'ty's eyes. He wore loose fitting black pants and a buttonless black jacket with a white crest in the shape of a shield. On that shield was a blood red emblem of a bird of some sort rising from what looked like flames.

Despite the child-like wonder in his eyes, he had the bearing of a man accustomed to power. N'ark's mindslicers responsible for probing these mar p'augh minds had indicated this man was the second most powerful individual in his nation. Good, Nk'ty thought, control the rulers, control the empire. The mindslicers had reported this man's name was Suten Hamu, or some such foolishness as that.

The man—Suten Hamu, Fist of the High Prelate—looked around with wonder. Nk'ty was working in tandem with the other mindslicers present to befuddle his mind, filling his head with visions of a garden paradise and awe. Lord Hamu's eyes settled on the assembly before him. It took a considerable amount of control to subdue his shock—through simple mindslicer tricks, the assembly appeared to him as Kepi, Akori, Barit, Akhom, and other figures and creatures from Nephretian mythology. He fell to his knees, his strength failing him.

A crack hammered through the air, echoing off the walls of the city behind them. Yet another layer of awe transfixed itself on the man's face. Although Nk'ty couldn't see him, he knew the dagomir had just appeared behind the assembly.

"Lord Suten Hamu," a deep, resonant voice boomed. The words were a language Nk'ty had absolutely no understanding of, but using a simple mindslicer ability allowed him to gather the meaning from the thoughts of the man kneeling before him.

Lord Hamu struggled to find his voice. "A—Amahté. My Lord."

"Welcome. Welcome home."

Lord Hamu fell prostrate on the ground. The dagomir calmly strode forward through the assembly of mindslicers. Nk'ty got a look at him as he passed. He had not yet seen the new simulacrum the dagomir was currently inhabiting—constructed specifically for this encounter—and was somewhat taken aback by its odd appearance. It stood twice as tall as an average man, which was typical for Dagomir N'ark. But its skin was brownish red, matching the tone of Lord Hamu's flesh. His eyes, rather than the usual dark voids, were orbs shining the color of the dawn's sun. Wisps of red, smoky vapors rose lazily from these eyes before dissipating. Although he couldn't see it, he knew a mindslicer trick caused Lord Hamu to see a fiery orb over the simulacrum's head, like a miniature sun. The preliminary probes had discovered that this was the traditional image of their dominant god, this "Amahté."

"You may kneel and look upon me, Suten," the dagomir's Amahté illusion said.

The man rose from his belly to his knees and gazed upon his god, stupefied.

"Your people honor me with the resoluteness of their faith. You have grown in wisdom and strength. And so, I have led you back to me," the vision of Amahté said.

"Thank you—thank you, my Lord Amahté," said Suten Hamu, bowing.

"But I have done so to test you. Humanity is still divided and scattered amongst the stars."

"Yes. The Kalbarians, Alathians, and those worlds in thrall to them."

"This displeases me," the Amahté simulacrum stated. "You must shatter their walls. Conquer them. Bring them to the faith, or destroy them if they refuse."

A hint of a vicious smile touched Lord Hamu's lips. "Yes, my Lord Amahté."

"Take comfort in the knowledge you will not fight alone. I and my host will journey with you," the dagomir spread his hands to indicate the assembly behind him. "Be it known, though, that this is a fight of man. Although we could smite your enemies with only a thought, it is for your people to prove themselves worthy of the gift we have bestowed upon you. Are you ready to charge forth and put an end to the enemies of humanity—the enemies of Amahté?"

"Absolutely."

"Good. Now, arise and take me to your ship to meet your warriors."

As Lord Hamu stood to lead the dagomir to his craft, one of the Sentinels communicated silently over waves of thought to his fellow mindslicers, "Dagomir N'ark, my master, I sense another group from a separate tribe are approaching."

"Yes", the dagomir responded silently to the minds of the gathered mar n'lan. "A small force of the Kalbarian and Alathian tribes approach. Their tribes are not suitable for my purpose. Nk'ty—track them. If they land, ensure they never leave Earth."

"As you command, my Dagomir," Nk'ty silently communicated back.

* * *

"What is it, Servius?" Taura asked her Commander. She had been meeting with Silmion, who was busy working with the medics to treat the wounded. Indeed, while repairs to the ships were ongoing she found any excuse she could to visit her soldiers in the medical bay.

Although Silmion claimed he was no doctor, his knowledge of living systems was deep and he had been of good service to the overwhelmed medical facilities. Getting a firsthand report of the day's casualties had put her in a foul mood, though, and she was annoyed at Servius for calling her back to the bridge.

Servius' smile was broad, completely ignoring his captain's distemper. "Reinforcements have arrived."

"What?"

"We were hailed a few minutes ago. Five of our ships just came out of the Q-wave slipstream."

Relief welled up in Taura. This was the best news she had heard in days. Five ships! That should be more than enough to demolish the remaining Nephretian fleet, regardless of whether the Reclaimer was amongst them. "Get them on the comm link."

"Already done," Servius replied. He turned to a nearby console, pressed a button, and an image of a man appeared on the front monitor.

"Captain Lucia Taura! Looks like you've had a rough go."

She recognized him immediately. "By the Fates, Captain Dentatus, it's good to see another friendly face out here."

"I'll bet. Sorry we're late. We had to bypass Nephretian space. My reports say you're alone against six Nephretian cruisers, including the Reclaimer itself."

"Four Nephretian cruisers now, and one of them's limping pretty badly. The Reclaimer was too cowardly to show itself, so she's still in top fighting condition."

The image of Captain Dentatus chuckled. "You sassy bitch. Took out two of 'em all by yourself, did you? Well, I'm glad you left some for us to clean up. Bit of a waste dragging five ships all the way out here if there was nothing left to fight."

"We can join you shortly," Taura said. "We expect our engines to be back on line in a day —"

"Captain," Dentatus interrupted, "your ship is barely holding together. No, you've done your bit. We're just going to drop off some supplies if you need 'em, then haul off and take our share of Nephretian blood. We'll be done and back by the time your engines are online."

"Damn, I was hoping to take another chunk out of them."

"You'll get your chance back home. Nephretians have stalled the combined Kalbarian and Alathian advance and are starting to push back. Still plenty of fighting ahead of us," Dentatus said.

"That'll have to do. We have a small strike force en route to the Nephretian position. They were going to try and disrupt Nephretian activities on Earth. We'll get them to scout out their activities instead. I'll send you their comm link so you can get their report when you're planning your attack."

"Much obliged. Fates smile on you, then," Captain Dentatus said.

"And if they don't, then slag 'em." The image of Captain Dentatus flicked off.

"Commander!"

"I've got the strike force on the comm link. Victor's standing by," Servius replied.

"Good man." She moved to the communications monitor. "Lieutenant-Commander."

"Aye, Captain," Victor replied as his grizzled image came up on the small communications monitor.

"What's your status?"

"We'll be landing in a few hours."

"Good. Have Kaeso and Marco had any luck with that computer they pulled off the mining planetoid?"

Victor scratched the back of his head. "Well, actually, yeah."

"Really!" Taura exclaimed. "They haven't had much time with it."

"Yeah, well, Marco's got some clever tricks up his sleeve. And … I don't know how he does it 'cause the language ain't any we've seen before, but he's doing a pretty good job piecing it together and making sense of it."

"Could he just be making it up?" Taura asked.

"Kaeso's had a look at everything he's done, and he vouches for it. Once Marco explains it, Kaeso can figure it out, which is one step better than me. Good thing you didn't hire me for my brains, eh?"

"Have they learnt anything interesting?"

"They've pieced together some bits. Seems the base was getting regular supplies from Earth—food and repair parts mostly. Then one day, they stopped coming. Marco hasn't found out why, yet. The colony wasn't self-sufficient, so when their supplies stopped, they abandoned the base."

"Well, I'm sure some archeologist somewhere will find that interesting. How's the Alathian?"

"Her?" Victor shrugged. "Oh, minding her own business. Watching everything, but acting like she's not."

"I know I don't need to tell you to keep your eyes on her. She does anything that doesn't sit right with you, kill her. I'll back you up if any higher ups get their nose out of joint over it. Anyway, that's not why I contacted you. Reinforcements have arrived. Rather than disrupt Nephretian activities, I want you to scout out what they're doing on the surface so you can guide our strike force in. Give your report to our ships when they arrive at Earth. They're led by Captain Dentatus."

"Dentatus. He's a tough old dog," Victor said.

"Yeah. Pity we won't get to watch the Reclaimer burn."

"No worries. The Reclaimer will probably turn tail and run."

Taura chuckled. "Right. Maybe we'll get a shot at it on the way out. Hope the Fates are smiling on you today."

"Yeah, me too," Victor replied as Taura signed off.

Chapter 30

"Time to put your toys away, boys," Victor said as he entered the aft of the small landing craft. Marco had been working with Kaeso almost non-stop on the mining station's computer. Pieces of hardware littered the cramped table they were working on. Wires connected bits of hardware to other bits of hardware, and Kaeso was busy entering some information onto Marco's small hand held computer.

Marco cursed silently to himself. He had just started to get a handle on this ancient computer language, and was hoping, perhaps optimistically, that he might discover why the shipments from Earth mysteriously stopped, forcing the colony's inhabitants to leave.

Ariadne sat by herself in the back corner of the craft napping, apparently, and she groggily opened her eyes at Victor's entrance. "We're arriving?" she asked.

"We'll be on the ground in twenty minutes," Victor replied. Marco noted that acknowledging and replying to the Alathian left a look of visible distaste on the old warrior's face. Kalbarai and Alathia had been at war for a long time. Marco half expected the stout Kalbarian to kill the Alathian out of hand. He also expected the Alathian to spring a trap of her own at any moment. Marco had found the trip in confined quarters to be very tense, and was glad for the distraction of examining the ancient computer they picked up from the mining colony.

"Also, we won't be doing any guerilla attacks," Victor said. He was unable to suppress a smile. "Seems a Kalbarian fleet has arrived, so we'll just be scouting out Nephretian activity."

"Do the scanners pick up any signs of civilization on the planet?" Kaeso asked.

"Yep."

"Really, what kind?" Marco asked.

"Scattered pockets of population living in iron-age level cities," Victor answered as Marco and Kaeso started to clean up their equipment. "The land's pretty arid and desolate. I've been able to locate where the Nephretians landed. It's by one of those cities. We're landing out of eye shot and hiking over to see what they're about. It'll be hot, and we'll be travelling fast. I don't want to hear any bitchin' from any of you about the Fates blasted heat."

The group prepared in silence. Victor checked his weapons though he never seemed to take his eyes off Ariadne, who herself simply sat quietly. Marco put his gear away while Kaeso took the helm of the craft as they approached. From Marco's seat, he could see the vast brown landscape looming in the front monitor as they began their descent. The landing craft bounced gently as it hit the planet's atmosphere and the front monitors showed the air glowing the red of a setting sun.

Marco knew he should be feeling wonder as they approached. They were coursing through the atmosphere of humanity's home, and were soon to step foot on her soil. But looking at the blasted landscape they were approaching, he knew this wasn't the home humanity left countless eons ago. Perhaps it was the same planet, but this wasn't the way the world was when humanity first walked under the sun and came of age. He felt only regret at what must have been lost, and curiosity at what could have done this.

They streaked across the cloudless sky, crossing kilometers of unending sand. The landing craft slowed and gently lowered to the ground, sand billowing into the air. Out of the corner of his eye Marco noticed Ariadne looking at the clouds of sand in consternation. No doubt her Alathian instincts bristled at the visual sign of their arrival.

Victor handed out a pack to each of them that included a canister of water, binoculars, and an assortment of Kalbarian survival gear. The two Kalbarians were armed with K-96 assault rifles and Marco with his hand blaster. Ariadne did not have any apparent source of weaponry, nor did Victor offer her any.

"Alright, we're about a kilometer away," Victor said. "I've given you each a locator wristband with the Nephretian landing spot indicated." He pointed at Ariadne. "You're leading the way."

"Me?" she asked.

"Ain't no way I'm having you behind me," Victor replied. "And you're better at sneaking up on people any way."

"All right," Ariadne said, "open the door and let me show you how to do your job."

Victor started to round on her, but Marco quickly interceded. "Save it for the Nephretians, guys. You can kill each other later, but let's deal with the Nephretians first."

Smoldering, Victor opened the exit hatch, glaring at Ariadne who returned a hard stare of her own. A wave of dry heat rolled into the craft and slammed into them.

"By Luca, that's hot," Marco gasped.

Victor turned on Marco, a thick, meaty finger in his face. "I said no bitchin'. Move out!"

Moments later they were out on the sand under the full intensity of a fiery sun. At that moment, though, Marco did not notice the heat that weighed down on him. Nor did he notice the dry sand that his feet slipped in as he walked. Rather, his attention was dominated by two humans—a man and woman—standing not more than twenty paces away, a giant sand dune as their backdrop.

The man stood roughly as tall as Marco. In all his travels, Marco had never seen a skin color similar to this stranger's, for his flesh was an iridescent alabaster. His cheeks were gaunt with white and black stubble, the same color as his short hair. His eyes were grey and filled with seething hatred and a cruel smile curved his thin lips. The woman's skin was the color of chocolate. Her body was that of a teenager, but her face belied years of hard living. Her brown hair was wild, barely tamed by the pony tail it was bound in.

Why didn't the ship's scanners pick up their presence as they landed, Marco wondered. He noticed he was on his knees, the sand burning him through his pants.

That's odd, he thought.

The rest of his companions were also on their knees. The two strangers casually walked up to the group and Marco tossed his gun at the man's feet.

Why'd I do that?

The Kalbarian assault rifles and assortment of daggers and hand weapons were similarly discarded.

He tried to assert control over his body, stopping his hands from tossing the survival pack Victor had just given him moments ago. But, he was an observer now; his body belonged to another. There wasn't even a struggle—the connection between his mind and limbs had ceased to exist. He struggled to keep his mind from panicking as his survival pack landed at the strangers' feet with the packs his companions were also discarding.

Marco's mind was rocked as images and knowledge were ripped to the surface of his thoughts. Who he was. Where he was from. His experience of the Triumvirate War. His knowledge of the K.S. Novafire. Everything. Torn to the surface, his whole life hammered through his thoughts in a seething blast.

It ended. He gasped as drool dangled off his lips, swaying on his knees.

Victor stood up. The blades hidden in his fists snicked out and he stalked over to Kaeso, who tilted his own head down. Victor cut lightly into Kaeso's head just behind his ear, pulled out a small device out of the exposed wound and crushed it between his fingers. It was a transmitter, Marco realized, relaying their position to the K.S. Novafire. Victor then stalked over to Ariadne who bent over lifting her shirt to expose her back. Victor delicately cut into her back flesh and removed a similar transmitter. Kaeso had stood to retrieve a knife previously tossed at the strange man's feet, moved to Victor and proceeded to cut his transmitter out. As Kaeso completed his job, the blasters in Victor's arms slipped out. Ariadne stood and began pulling at wires within Victor's arms, disabling his weapons. After a moment, the now harmless blasters slid back into the slots on Victor's muscular forearms. Once completed, they returned to their knees, their blood absorbing into the dry sand, cut off from any contact to the universe beyond this planet.

The strange man with iridescent skin barked some words that Marco did not understand. The woman jumped and replied.

Perhaps he said her name, Marco thought What were his words ... Seir T-pan?

The man spoke a sentence. His entire life, Marco had possessed a natural talent for languages, almost able to understand what people meant before he gained an understanding of the words. He sensed the man had asked the woman a question— perhaps offering her the honor of choosing what to do with their captives. Inside his mind, he knew—just knew—that how the woman chose to answer was so very, very important.

Marco began to move his mouth, fumbling for control. "S-Seir ... Seir T-pan."

The duo looked at him, the man with what might have been grudging respect, the woman—Seir T'pan—with curiosity.

After a moment's reflection, the woman replied to the man in their harsh language. He seemed surprised, but impressed at her answer nonetheless. He turned a ravenous gaze on the group.

The world went black as Marco passed out.

Chapter 31

"What the Fates do you mean one of them just blew up?" Taura asked. She had been meeting with Silmion on the bridge when Servius came up and told her the news.

"Just that. One of the ships in Dentatus' attack force was just destroyed."

"Did the Nephretians ambush them?" Silmion asked.

"No. The Nephretian fleet is there plain to see—no sneak attacks. Our ships were closing to attack their fleet in orbit around Earth, then one of them was just ... destroyed. Not one shot's been fired. Damn—another ship just blew! What's going on? No shots are being exchanged. The Kalbarian attack pattern is all jumbled and they don't even have their flak firewall up."

Taura pushed Servius out of the way and linked into the long range scanners for herself. A 3D holo-map shimmered into view above the console. The remaining Kalbarian ships were scattered and adrift while the Nephretian ships sat there. No shots were being fired, but Dentatus' fleet was being slaughtered. "Slag," she cursed. Taura turned and shouted, "Helmsmen, plot a course to Earth, max speed."

"Captain, the only thing we'll be is target practice in our current shape," Servius said.

"Fates damn it, Commander, I am not going to sit here while Kalbarians die."

"Captain," the helmsman said, "our main thrusters are down. Repairs will take another day."

"Damn the repairs! Get us there now."

"Captain," Servius said, "we're in the outer reaches of the solar system. Without our main thrusters it'll take months to close the distance. Give engineering the time to finish their repairs and we'll be there in a day."

Taura digested the information and confirmed it over her neural net. With an explosive burst, she smashed her obsidian-colored hand into the railing of her bridge. Kalbarian designers, knowing the abilities and temperament of their brethren, use materials designed to survive such outbursts. That notwithstanding, the railing bent under her blow. Both Servius and Silmion stood back, cautiously watching Taura.

She had worked so hard to defeat the Nephretians here and claim Earth for Kalbarai because she believed this was the key to forcing Nephreti to surrender, drawing the war to its conclusion—the key to finally stopping her soldiers from dying. Instead, all they had found was defeat and death.

After a long pause, she said, "Commander, get my thrusters back online. I'll be watching the rest of the battle in my office."

By the time she got to her office, the battle was over. The Kalbarian fleet was debris floating through space high above Earth and the Nephretian fleet had slipped into the Q-wave slipstream.

* * *

Marco's eyes fluttered open. He was staring at a clear sky. His first sensation was one of heat beating down on him. His mouth was dry and his tongue felt overly large.

He propped himself on his elbows as he had a look around. He and the rest of his companions, who were slowly regaining consciousness around him, were lying in a street—a hard packed dirt road to be more precise. Marco had spent enough time in refugee colonies growing up to know they been deposited in the slums of some city. The stone buildings were ramshackle and dilapidated—little more than ruins, really. The stench of human waste and rot—scents of his adolescence and early adulthood—filled his nostrils with each breath. And the people—the streets were packed with people, all of whom stood and stared at Marco and his companions in silence. And every one of them looked wretched. They each possessed chocolate colored skin like the woman, Seir T-pan, who had accompanied the man who had captured them. Whereas those two wore sturdy clothing, these people wore little more than rags.

Victor was the first on his feet, and he looked warily around at the crowd, flexing his thick fists. "Alright, I need to punch something right about now. Which of you Fates-cursed bastards is up for the job?"

Marco joined Kaeso and Ariadne as they gathered cautiously around Victor.

"You Kalbarians take me to all the worst places. And I've been to some pretty bad places, so that's saying something," Marco said.

"Quit yer bitchin'," Victor replied.

The crowd parted before Victor and a giant of a man strode forward. He was a good head taller than Marco, who himself was quite a bit taller than Victor. The man was thick with muscle, and his neck was marred by a jagged scar. Behind him trailed a gang of about ten other rough looking men and women with the eyes of scavengers. They fanned out, encircling Marco and his companions.

"Here we go," Victor said. Marco noted he seemed relieved at finally being able to fight something.

The giant man spoke in an unintelligible language. Although the words were unclear, the tone was distinctly unfriendly. From a leather band on each arm, he pulled out a dagger. The blade of one appeared to be of ivory or bone. The other, obsidian with a cord of rope bound about one end to serve as a grip.

"I suppose those blasters in your arm aren't working any more after our encounter with that man and woman in the desert," Marco said.

"No, thanks to Ariadne" Victor answered, "but these are." Blades slid out of his wrists. In a silent rush, the streets cleared of people, though they reappeared in windows and rooftops in short order to watch the scene unfold.

The giant man seemed to calm himself and closed his eyes. A shimmering bubble belched forth from his body, surrounding him.

"What do you suppose that is?" Kaeso asked.

"Stop asking questions you know I don't know the answer to and link up to me," Victor said. "If we can make a suitably vicious display of this big guy, we got a chance to back down the others." His massive muscles began to bulge and the ridges of dragons began to writhe and glow a soft red. Faint wisps of smoke began to rise from them. With a grunt, Victor leapt at the giant of a man, blades shining in the desert sun.

Marco watched the Kalbarian hammer his blades into the giant with tremendous force. A finger's length from the giant's body, Victor's blow came to a dead stop and he stumbled back. A small distortion in the field surrounding the giant appeared where Victor's blades had struck. Before Marco could blink, that distortion shifted around the giant's body, up his chest, down his arm and surrounded the obsidian blade he was holding.

"He's got some kind of shield," Kaeso said. "It seems to have absorbed the force of your blow and transferred the captured energy to his blade. Don't let him touch you with it."

"I wasn't planning on letting him touch me with either of his blades."

The giant looked at his obsidian blade, then back at Victor, and flashed a gap-toothed smile. With a roar, he charged in, and the rest of his gang followed.

The melee was rough and nasty. Marco noted that Victor and Kaeso were fighting linked over their neural net, their combat perfectly choreographed. The giant was attacking Victor, who was trying to keep his counterattacks to trips and holds while the giant's shield was up. Kaeso was desperately trying to protect Victor's back from a small mob. Marco lacked formal military training, but he'd learnt the art of battle growing up in refugee colonies where fighting was dirty and desperate. The gang fighting him fought in much the same style. Looking around, Marco noticed with dismay that Ariadne was nowhere to be seen. She had fled.

Alathians.

Most of their assailants were focused on the powerful team of Victor and Kaeso, leaving only three who were attacking Marco. Each of the three had roughly hewn daggers of stone or bone. Marco had nothing. With a quick movement, Marco grabbed a handful of pebbles and whipped them at the face of a nearby assailant while he dove under the attack of another. The third leapt at Marco blade first. He managed to block the blow, the obsidian blade a hand-width from his face. The two were locked together for a moment before Marco bit his attacker's hand and drove a knee into his groin.

Marco broke free and drove his elbow into the nose of one of the women gang members who was angling to stab him in his ribs. She cursed in a language unfamiliar to Marco, and spun away from him, kicking her leg out at the end of her turn, tripping Marco who landed roughly on his back. Out of nowhere, Ariadne appeared, running up behind the woman and hammering her elbow into the base of the attacker's skull. The woman collapsed insensate on Marco.

"Behind you," Marco yelled as one of their attackers was charging Ariadne. The Alathian leapt over Marco in a dive roll. Marco, still on his back, managed to kick his foot into the belly of the attacker and scrambled to his feet. Ariadne was gone again. Marco yelled out as he faced the third attacker. "Dust and ashes, Ariadne, you better have my back!"

The mob had managed to separate Kaeso from Victor. Kaeso was struggling under the assault of three attackers and was bleeding from a number of wounds. Unarmed, he was visibly flagging and the three were taking turns tiring him out and inflicting cuts and punches to wear him down. If no one helped him soon, he would lose his fight.

Victor was also struggling with three assailants, one of whom was the giant surrounded in his shimmering shield. Marco saw the giant yell and slam his bone knife into the Kalbarian's chest. The blade splintered on Victor's dermal plating—a Kalbarian modification where synthsteel is woven into the flesh itself providing a flexible layer of armor to protect vital organs. The blow cut Victor viciously, but did not kill him. Victor looked down at the wound, and then back at the giant. "Looks like I got some tricks of my own," he said with a smile. He grabbed the giant and flipped him over his leg, sending the big man roughly on his back. A second gang member attacked, but a blade snicked out of Victor's elbow and drove through the man's face. The third attacker dove a blade into Victor's thigh, dropping the mighty Kalbarian to a knee with a roar. The giant clambered back to his feet, daggers held high overhead for a killing blow.

That was the last thing Marco saw when a strike to the back of his head knocked him unconscious for the second time today.

* * *

Debris, floating through the void of space, glittered in the light of the sun as the K.S. Novafire drifted through the ruins of Dentatus's fleet orbiting high above the parched Earth. There was no life here amidst the wreckage, just the cold vacuum of space and twisted metal spiraling slowly into the planet's upper atmosphere. Silmion stood on the bridge of the Novafire along with Taura and her commander, Servius, standing vigil over the sea of wreckage they flew through.

"What could have done this?" Silmion asked.

"I have no idea, Silmion. Our sensors indicate no shots were fired. Our ships were just … destroyed," the captain replied.

Servius took a report from a bridge officer and then approached Taura. "Captain," he said, head shaking, "there's still no sign of our strike force. Their landing craft is gone. They're gone. No bodies—they've just disappeared. We've tried every trick we know, but we just can't find them."

"Curse the Fates for bringing us back here," Taura said. On the front monitor, a chunk of debris bumped into the Novafire's blast shields and bounced off spinning into deep space. "Curse the Fates."

Nerva, one of Taura's young bridge officers, approached the group and saluted to Taura. "Captain."

She looked at the young man. Man—that was a joke, Silmion thought to himself. He looked like he was still a teen. Almost everyone on the K.S. Novafire was so young.

"What is it, Nerva?" the captain asked.

"A message from Rear Admiral Canus has arrived through the Q-wave slipstream."

"I'll take it at the communications station." Taura left, leaving Silmion and Servius alone.

Throughout their journey across the stars, Silmion had been struggling with questions he found deeply troubling. Taking this moment alone with the commander, he asked, "What happens to your fallen soldiers out here in space?"

"What happens?" the commander asked. "We ask the Fates for their blessings, though we don't expect we get 'em, and then we blast their bodies into space."

The answer horrified Silmion, though he maintained his composure. "But there is no life out here. Their bodies are …

alone, forever separated from Selestari—The Cycle. They should be laid to rest in their homeland, where their bodies can feed the life of the living systems that will sustain their families forevermore."

"Is that what you do on Ullrion?"

Silmion was taken aback by the question. He had assumed that was what all societies would do. Throughout their whole history, Ullrionis had been isolated on their planet. And with that one question—is that what you do on Ullrion—questioning the most fundamental belief of his people, Silmion realized the profound gulf separating their cultures.

"Yes. That is what we do on Ullrion."

"I'm sorry your people got wrapped up in this," the commander said.

Silmion looked at Servius. He had witnessed the capabilities of these space faring cultures and knew in his heart, with sadness, that his world would never be the same now that they had found each other. And, looking at the ruins of the Kalbarian fleet high above the atmosphere of Earth, Silmion was certain Ullrion would not be changed for the better. Still, he was surprised at the concern in the Kalbarian commander's sentiment.

"Thank you, Commander. But my people know the world is harsh and cares nothing for our wants. If we're strong enough to survive, we will. If not, we won't."

Servius nodded. "Aye, I know what you mean. Reminds me of a saying we have: 'The Fates dance while mothers cry.' I wonder, though, whether we don't make the going harder for ourselves than it needs be, sometimes." They stood in silence for a few moments before Taura returned.

"We got new orders?" Servius asked.

"Yes. We are to return to Kalbarian space immediately."

"What about Victor, and the others?" the commander asked, passion rising in his voice.

Taura turned to her second in command and placed her flesh hand on his shoulder. "I don't want to leave them either, Vetus," she said, using the commander's personal name. "But the combined Kalbarian and Alathian advance has been stopped and the Nephretians are pushing us back. We've just lost five ships here and thousands of soldiers that we couldn't afford to lose. The

Nephretians have control of Ullrion and whatever new weapons they possess, and I don't know what Lord Hamu discovered down there on Earth, but looking at the wreckage here, it's a game-changer. This battle's lost. We've got to go back and try to win the war."

Servius turned to the bridge. A host of young faces were staring at them, listening to the conversation. "What are you staring at!" he yelled. "Quit your moping and get to work! Helm. Set coordinates for the fastest route to Kalbarian space."

Epilogue

Before he was aware of the heat, before he was aware of his throbbing head, and before he opened his eyes, Marco was aware of the stench. An absolutely rancid odor of rotten food, excrement, and stale sweat filled his nostrils. With a grimace, he opened his eyes.

Directly above him, so close he could feel warm breath on his cheeks, was the face of a naked old man. It was he who was the source of the foul odor. His skin was iridescent—the same color as their original captor in the desert—and filthy. Beyond that, the facial structure of this creature also mimicked that of their captor, as though they were closely related. But whereas the man who captured them in the desert emanated self-confidence and strength, this man emanated madness. His dirty grey hair was a tangled mass that hung limply. His body was emaciated, pale skin pulled impossibly taunt over thin bones. His piercing blue eyes darted wildly about, but eventually focused on Marco.

"You," the old man said in thickly accented Seedtongue, "you are Marco da Riva."

"Yes I am," he replied. He struggled to sit up, which only made his aching head worse.

The eyes of the wild old man drifted off Marco and focused on something in the distance. Marco tried to see what the old man was staring at, but could not discern what might have captured the stranger's attention so. Looking around the street, he saw each of the attacking gang members including the giant dead on the ground. Some had died from violence, evidenced by deep gashes and wounds, but most of them seemed relatively free of mortal wounds. They were just dead. The rest of the crowd that had been watching the fight were gone.

Panting, Victor was on a knee, a trail of blood winding its way down one of his legs from a ragged wound. Kaeso was also on his knees and struggling to stand. He was winded and bled from numerous cuts that covered his body. The two Kalbarians were warily eyeing the exchange between Marco and the old man, not certain if this new interlocutor was a danger. Ariadne, of course, was nowhere to be seen.

"Careful, Marco," Victor said. "That old man showed up and these brutes just collapsed dead."

Turning back to the old man, Marco asked, "What's your name?"

The old man jumped in surprise, his eyes darting back to Marco. "Why would you want to know that?"

"So … so that I know what to call you when I need to get your attention."

"Well, if that time ever comes, you may call me Kie. I am a strand-walker." The designation meant nothing to Marco.

"We met another man with skin like yours in the desert. It was he who captured us," Marco said.

"Yes. That's my brother, Nk'ty. He is favored by the dagomir. You are Marco. You speak many languages."

"Right, I speak eight languages fluently. How did you know—"

"I told you, I'm a strand-walker," Kie interrupted. "Of course I know! And now you must learn one more language before your journey begins. Come, come with me." He started tugging on Marco's shirt.

"Wait, what? Why?"

The old man straightened and a wave of lucidity washed over him as he fixed Marco with a chilling stare and spoke in a precisely measured tone. "Well, you don't really have a choice now, do you? Your people face enslavement or destruction at the hands of an ancient weapon left here on Earth, and you personally face death here in the Grey Maze. I am your only hope of saving your people and yourselves." The moment of sanity passed and his eyes began to dart wildly about. "Come," he motioned, shuffling to the end of the street. "You must come. Bring your friends, yes. They have their role to play too. Yes, including the woman on the roof over there."

Marco looked to the roof where Kie pointed. "Ariadne, you up there?"

The Alathian's head popped over the ledge. A moment later, she lithely climbed her way to the ground.

"Good to see you're unharmed," Victor said, his voice laced with irony as he struggled to his feet.

"Enough," Marco interjected, staving off the rebuttal forming on Ariadne's lips. Kie, the strange old man, was shambling on and nearing the end of the street, heedless of whether or not anyone was following him. "Come on, guys. Looks like I made a friend."

CPSIA information can be obtained at www.ICGtesting.com
Printed in the USA
LVOW13s2353260214

375281LV00001B/276/P